Nina D'Aleo wrote her first book at age seven (a fantasy adventure about a girl named Tina and her flying horse). Due to most of the book being written with a feather dipped in water, no one else has ever read "Tina and White Beauty." Many more dream worlds and illegible books followed. Nina blames early exposure to Middle-earth and Narnia for her general inability to stick to reality. She also blames her parents. And her brother.

Nina has completed degrees in creative writing and psychology. She currently lives in Brisbane, Australia, with her husband, George, their two sons, Josef and Daniel, and two cats Mr. Foofy and Gypsy. She spends most of her days playing with toys, saying things like "share," "play gentle," and "let's eat our veggies" and hearing things like "no," "no way" and "NEVER!". She is also working on more books – including the next book in the Demon War Chronicles series.

Also by Nina D'Aleo

The Last City: The Demon War Chronicles 1

The White List

The Forgotten City

The Demon War Chronicles Book 2

Nina D'Aleo

First published by Momentum in 2013
This edition published in 2013 by Momentum
Pan Macmillan Australia Pty Ltd
1 Market Street, Sydney 2000

A CIP record for this book is available at the National Library of Australia

The Forgotten City

EPUB format: 9781760080433
Mobi format: 9781760080440
Print on Demand format: 9781760081232

Cover design by Matt O'Keefe
Copyedited by Sarah Fletcher
Proofread by Chrysoula Aiello

Macmillan Digital Australia: www.macmillandigital.com.au

To report a typographical error, please visit momentumbooks.com.au/contact/

Visit www.momentumbooks.com.au to read more about all our books and to buy books online. You will also find features, author interviews and news of any author events.

For my boys
George, Josef and Daniel

All men dream: but not equally. Those who dream by night in the dusty recesses of their minds wake in the day to find that it was vanity: but the dreamers of the day are dangerous men, for they may act their dream with open eyes, to make it possible.

— TE Lawrence, *Seven Pillars of Wisdom*

PART 1

PART 1

Chapter 1

Croy

KULLRA FORNAX

NÝR-CORUM (SAINT SMITHY BOROUGH)

It was one of those moments John L had warned her about –
when a person looks around, takes stock of life and realizes
there is something seriously wrong with me. He'd called it an
illumination moment – a flash of insight. Croy felt as though a
fire-bomb had exploded in her face.

Her eyes traveled up from the vial of love potion she
clutched in one hand, to the thick, red, grinning lips of the
alleged witch standing before her, to the unidentifiable green
gunk between the witch's stained teeth, to a timeglass on the
wall above her head. Croy's focus zeroed in on the sands
trickling through the glass, grain by grain. Curls of smoke
drifted across her sight, trailing up from the incense crumbling to ash on the witch's table. The musty smell itched
her nose. It reminded her of dark places and dead faces –
of everything she had forgotten on purpose. Croy's vision

blurred and she heard a whisper inside her head – *when did things go from bad to crazy?*

"Mix it with a heavy cider and make sure he drinks it. Three dayturns after, that man of yours will leave her and come right back to you, mark me," the witch said.

Right after I met him ... right after I met Roth.

Croy struggled against herself, despair against reason, and with an effort hidden behind emotionless eyes, she placed the vial of liquid back on the witch's desk.

The charlatan sensed the deal collapsing and her forced smile dropped into a flabby-jowled frown. She tried to cover it, aiming for a sweet tone, but tension clipped the edges of her words.

"Is there something wrong?"

"I've changed my mind," Croy told her. "I don't want it."

"You don't want your man to come back?"

"Correct," Croy lied.

"Well then ... you don't have to take it, but the fee remains," the witch said. "I mixed this extra-special elixir just for you." She tapped her desk with one sharpened yellow fingernail.

"You mean this extra-special sewerage juice and spittle?" Croy baited her.

The woman regarded her through thinly narrowed eyes. She spoke, her voice now glacial.

"Some people say crossing a sorceress is very bad luck."

"I've heard that," Croy said, "but I've also heard that selling contraband to a Controller is fatal." She pushed one hand into her jacket pocket, exposing the badge and Firestorm strapped to her belt.

The witch's slit eyes stretched wide. She took an involuntary step back and, with a gulp, swallowed her words.

"Let's call it even," Croy said. "Agreed?"

The woman bobbed her head and retreated further. Croy gave the scammer and her junk-stew room a final look-over.

She remembered John L saying that sometimes hitting rock bottom was the only thing that precipitated healing and change. She'd asked him how a person was supposed to know when they had reached this lowest low. He'd replied, "You'll know it when you hit it." He was right. He always had been – except for once. And then he was dead.

Croy turned away and walked to the entrance of the tent, the bandage straps around her scarred knee loosening then constricting with each step. She pulled her hood over her head and pushed out into the Strip, most notorious of the Seven Black Markets of Saint Smithy Borough, the arse-end of Nÿr-Corum, in more ways than one.

Sounds crashed over her – voices laughing, murmuring, talking, yelling, calling out deals – all to the bass-thud and twang-jangle of a Smithy Borough band playing somewhere in the background. Croy touched the I-Sect embedded inside her ear and muted all the noise except for the dull static fuzz of the signal pending between herself and the Tower. She scanned the overcrowded marketplace, a constantly changing mass of shapes and forms, flowing in and out and all around the stalls lining either side of the stretch. Here and there, a face, a feature, shot into focus as she recognized minor thugs and smugglers she'd busted at one time or another. They stood around the cider bars and eateries, striking deals over bubbling brew and spitting stew. Warm smells of baking bandy-bandy and overflat bread overwhelmed the more subtle and sinister scents she knew were drifting around the market.

Croy pushed a path into the crowd, her steel-tipped boots clunking on the grid walkway, one louder than the other as she limped forward. The knee had never fully recovered from a childhood injury. Everyone, except John L., had said it would leave her bedridden for life.

Shoulders pressed against her on all sides. Some barged her by accident, others on purpose. Croy shoved back and those she struck stumbled away. She glanced at the stalls as she passed. Legitimate objects lay on display, while the actual wares for sale were kept well out of sight, but not out of mind. Everyone knew why the Strip existed – for wheeling and dealing, peddling and pushing, everything and anything – shonky love potions included. Croy released a heavy sigh, self-loathing mingling unpleasantly with the sadness inside her. It felt as if her broken heart was stuck in her throat.

She passed a group of people huddled around a darkened stall that stank heavily of incense and piss-cheap perfume. One of the figures glanced up at her with the painted eyes and pierced nose of a swaygirl. She was too young. Most of them were. Croy looked away. She'd learned on the first few dayturns as a Controller that stopping criminals was not a simple matter of closing one operation and making arrests. There were always consequences, repercussions, sometimes worse than what was happening in the first place ... and it was always the weak and innocent that suffered the most.

Croy reached the parking point packed full of draggers, drifters and roller-boards. She caught sight of a thug loitering around the entrance turn-circle. His body language was anticipatory – suspicious. She approached with caution, and as she neared, he stepped into her path. Croy raised her eyes along the length of his body. He was tall, musclebound and strapped with something mean enough to bulge the side of his jacket in a significant way – hard-core – all the way up to his hair – a pink tuft, which completely sabotaged his menacing presence. Croy stifled a smile.

"Do I know you?" she asked.

"Five water tokens to release your dragger," he said. He had a sweaty, red face, and missing front teeth.

"It's a free parking point," Croy said.

"Not anymore," he replied and held out an expectant hand. Burned deeply into the center of the palm was the skull-and-flame brand of the Smithy Borough smuggler mob. Footsteps clattered behind them and Croy glanced over her shoulder. Two women stood blocking the way back to the market. One had shaggy white hair, short, much like her own; the other wore a spiked-do, high and purple. The sight of the purple stirred Croy's nerves – any smuggler crazy enough to wear the upper-class color in public was too much crazy for her liking. Both women wore studded collars and were marked with the same smuggler mob brand as their big friend. The white-haired girl sneered and unfurled a clanking length of chain from one hand; the other opened her jacket and flashed a hybrid flamethrower.

Croy moved fast. She spun back around and grabbed the thug by his outstretched wrist. She gave a vicious tug backward and wrenched him off his feet. He yelled a curse as she flung him headlong into the two women. He knocked them sprawling onto the grid, but then he was back on his feet and charging Croy.

A bullet struck the ground between them, bringing him to a sudden halt. He gaped up in the direction of the shot. Croy's partner, Darius DeCavisi, sat leaning forward on his hovering dragger, aiming his Predator 6 Klylock at the smuggler's head.

Purple-spikes drew her flamethrower and screamed, "Drop it or I'll blast her!"

"The Predator spits six rounds in a grain flat. By the time you squeeze the trigger, you and yours will be well and truly bloody, I promise you that," Darius said, his voice uncompromising steel, his aim locked.

The white-haired girl caught on first and started to retreat. "He's Control! So is she!"

"Don't you dare run!" Purple-spikes screamed at her. "We can take them!"

"Are you crazy?" White-hair yelled back.

As she turned to flee, her mob-mate opened fire on her back, engulfing her clothes and skin in flames. She started shrieking, a terrible raw sound. The big thug gasped. He ran toward the burning woman, but instead of trying to put her out, he attacked Purple-spikes – ramming her so brutally that they both crashed into the guardrail and toppled over. Their screams traveled downward fast, cut off by a splatter-thud as they struck the grid below.

Darius fired a bullet into the burning girl's head, silencing her suffering, while Croy moved to the side and stared over. The other two smugglers lay twisted on the walkway below. A group of onlookers had already gathered. Darius flew in and set his dragger down beside Croy. They exchanged a look; neither of them knew what the hell had just happened. They'd never witnessed a group of mob-mates turn on each other like that before. Smugglers were a bunch of treacherous, back-stabbing criminals, but they always banded together when they faced the Corps – even the rival Boroughs would fight side-by-side against Controllers. Croy spotted a group of other Smithy Borough smugglers pushing through the crowd to get a look at the fallen. The smuggler in the lead recognized his dead mob-mates and shouted in dismay. The others rushed forward to see. Darius tapped his Predator on the guardrail to draw their attention and said, "There's another one up here if you want what's left of her."

"Put out your names! Now!" the most senior of the smugglers yelled out in challenge.

"Controllers DeCavisi and Croy," Darius obliged.

The crowd dispersed in an instant, everyone taking off as fast as they could move, with murmurs of *the Saint* left hanging in their wake. The smugglers' bodies vanished with them.

Croy glanced back at the smoking remains of White-hair. Sudden movement flashed in the corner of Croy's sight, and she spun toward it. A shadow darted from the top of the rail beside them, straight up to the walkway above, and vanished. A strange feeling buzzed in Croy's temples, and Darius grabbed at his head.

"You felt that too?" she asked him.

"Not felt – *heard* – a whisper."

Croy moved swiftly to her partner's dragger and swung on behind him. She clutched his waist, feeling hard muscle and the outlines of the weapons he had strapped to his body. His jacket held the mingled scents of leather and tigaro smoke, and even though she didn't smoke, and was repelled by the idea of skinning animals for clothing, it was the most comforting smell in the world.

"Take us up – over there." Croy pointed to where the shadow had disappeared.

Darius revved the engine and the dragger shot toward the walkway above, where they scanned the crowd shuffling to and from Market Six. Everyone looked suspicious, but not out of the ordinary considering where they were.

"What was it?" Darius asked her.

"I don't know," Croy said, "Didn't get a good look. Just saw a shadow."

Darius swore, then said, "We have to go. We have a job."

"I'll call a Search then. Take me down to my dragger." She tapped the I-Sect in her ear, and heard the rustle-zing of the Tower picking up her signal.

"Call connected," an operator answered.

Darius dropped them face-down toward the parking point and Croy's body jolted hard against his back.

"This is Croy. There's been an incident," she said. "Send a squad to extract the remains of two smugglers from the mob known as the Skullfires, and a Search to go through the markets. Tell them to look for a person with a device that emits a buzz or a whisper." As she spoke the words she knew they were strange.

The operator did her best not to sound confused. "Recorded, Controller Croy."

Croy tapped out her I-Sect as Darius pulled up above the parking point. Patting his shoulder, she slid off and dropped the short distance to her own dragger. It was significantly less flashy and worked-over than her partner's vehicle, but it was faithful to its job of keeping her airborne. It lifted upward and she steered it parallel to Darius' dragger. He had taken off his leather jacket and replaced it with his black uniform cloak. Croy followed his lead, identifying them as Controllers to anyone who glanced their way. She noticed her partner was giving her a look and said, "What?"

"What were you doing at the Strip?"

"I needed some medicine."

"For what?"

"Women's concerns," she replied. It wasn't exactly a lie.

Darius held up his hands in surrender. "No longer interested."

He pulled back his dragger and took off, speeding straight upward. Croy watched him fly. John L had once described her partner as a bullet – fast and mean, with one hell of a kick. It was an accurate enough description. He did tend to come across as a hothead, difficult to read, and, at times, difficult to like – but what she saw when she looked at him was not just a partner, or a friend, but family. Despite their best efforts to reject each other when they were first assigned together, they'd bonded. Now they'd been a team for so long that Darius had developed an uncanny way of knowing exactly where she was at any given time. It made keeping secrets difficult – but not impossible.

Croy leaned low over her ride and it jetted forward. As she caught up with Darius, he increased his speed, weaving and winding through the maze of criss-crossing grid platforms and walkways of Nÿr-Corum. They reached the breach tunnel, which joined Saint Smithy with Saint Emmanuel Borough, one of the industry-only zones in the city. The fierce steam of the atmosphere here hit Croy like a wall and broke an instant sweat over her face. She blinked and slowed the dragger, her hands slipping on the handlebars. It was so hot, this close to the Mother Fire, that it was hard to catch a breath. Croy wiped her face and slowed again.

Darius sped ahead, weaving around the masses of towering chimneys billowing black smoke. Both his father and mother had been Grays. Emmanuel Borough was home to him. It was also the oldest part of the city, where history said Nÿr-Corum had first begun, when the Saints broke down from Hell into Kullra Fornax, a frozen mazeland of tunnels and never-ending darkness. The constantly expanding city still only took up a minute fraction of the potential space of the home-cavern the Saints had claimed for their own all those years past, yet it had felt to Croy, lately, as though the population was growing more rapidly than the structures that sustained it. Everywhere was overcrowded. People sat and stood shoulder to shoulder, face to face, inhaling each other's exhaled air, sharing sweat and body odor, cramped and pressed and imprisoned by others all around them. Nÿr-Corum bulged to maximum capacity, uncomfortably over-pregnant, always only moments from bursting. Even though there was plenty of space for expansion, the iron-ore mines were all but depleted, and there was nowhere else in Kullra Fornax that humans could live. Anyone who left the city gates, known as the Saints' Door, faced two impossible enemies – the freezing windstorms and the Dray, the shadow demons that had been haunting humans from the very beginning.

Croy glanced down as she flew. Houses and factories lined the walls of Nÿr-Corum's cavern, making up the Seven Boroughs of the city – Saint Smithy, Saint Emmanuel, Saint Agnes, Saint Boniface, Saint Mariread, Saint Lawless and

Saint Arabel. Walkways and gridlines intertwined and over-crossed as far as she could see into the hazy distance below. Gigantic cogs and conveyor belts shunted through the factories of Emmanuel Borough. The three largest worksites here were occupied by the Mining Coalition, the Steel Works and the Oil Drill. Without these, the Fleetships that tracked and transported the essentials of food and water from the outer tunnels of Kullra Fornax into the city would not fly. Nothing had grown or been born in the city, save for humans, for longer than anyone alive could remember. These worksites, and all others, were owned by Purple Wings and manned by Grays.

At the very base of Nÿr-Corum, effectively marking the end of the city, burned the Mother Fire, the only thing that kept them from freezing to death. There had been several attempts at estimating exactly how long they'd last if the Mother died out. The results were varying, but all pointed to the same answer – not long.

Croy spotted Darius swooping downward and altered the course of her dragger. She followed him past all the upper factory floors. Workers paused to watch them fly – Grays with gray clothes, gray faces and gray hair from fire soot and industrial dust. Their lips were cracked and parched, flecked with white, and their bodies moved in a drudging way. They worked long and hard. The machines never stopped and neither did the shifts – as one ended the next immediately began. Both Darius' parents had been miners killed in a Dray attack. He never spoke of it and Croy knew better than to ask.

Her partner was hovering above the Filter, the city's primary water silo. She swooped in beside him, looking down, past the guards posted all around the topmost edges. The huge structure was eroded and stained where the water level had once reached. It used to stand almost full. Now conditions were critical. Rations were the lowest they had ever been, since the last major expedition into the outer tunnels had failed. The Drays had destroyed the city's largest Fleetship, the *Chimera*, slaughtering all the Fleetsmen, both male and female, and looting everything on board. Now all hopes rode on the second-largest ship, the *Teriscoria*, which had been sent out shortly after. The latest reports said it was heavily laden with supplies and en route to the city. Normal life continued, no one yet saying aloud what everyone was thinking – if the *Teriscoria* didn't make it back, people would start dying. The Conference had released a message claiming it had a backup plan. Even though she was a Controller of the Martial Corps and thus an employee of the Conference, Croy was highly doubtful such a plan existed.

The Conference was made up of the highest of the Purple Wings, who were far too rich and too soft to comprehend what starvation and thirst meant.

"They found a stinker in the silo," Darius called out to her.

"Great – like we have water to spare," Croy replied.

Darius grunted and plunged his dragger straight downward into the darkness of the storage tower. Croy followed him, their engines roaring in the enclosed space. The humidity closed in on them. It had an earthy, sediment scent to it. Croy saw light ahead and then smelled a riper, heavier stink. She felt an immediate reaction – her stomach and throat tightened, her eyes watered – as her body warned her to stay away.

Torch firelights grew larger and brighter and blurred forms took shape as Darius and Croy descended over a floating pier and jetty stretching out into the center of a large body of water. Groups of people were scattered along the jetty. Darius and Croy leveled out and brought their draggers down on the pier. The largest group of people was huddled around something at the end of the structure. Croy glanced at her partner and saw they were both feeling the same thing – here a life had been taken.

Chapter 2

Eli

AQUAIS

SCORPIA (THE GRAVEYARD)

"Now repeat after me – *I am in control. I am strong. I am a worthwhile person with valid and important ideas and beliefs.*" The hologram face of the self-esteem attendant, glowing in the darkness, paused to smile at Eli, and the absolute serenity of her conviction made it completely impossible for him to continue believing that she was a real person who could actually see him – unless she happened to be an attractive, perceptive woman who was also visually impaired or mildly to acutely insane. That way it was possibly conceivable that she could mistake the person she saw before her – the pale, shaking imp-breed with sweat damp spreading across his shirt – with someone to whom the words *in control* and *strong* were applicable.

Even to Eli, it didn't seem likely. "Sorry," Eli whispered to the hologram. "It's not you, it's … well, actually, it is you. I'm very sorry."

15

He reached out and triggered the shut-down sequence, and the attendant's certainty slipped into a wistful kind of disappointment before her image faltered and vanished. That look was all too familiar to Eli. Usually it followed failing someone's expectations and came before an unavoidably bumpy guilt trip. And while disappointing a computer program might have been an all-time personal low, he really didn't have time to dwell on it. Getting underground with all his body parts attached and intact needed to be his all-consuming thought at present. A tech-neutralizing ebomb, set off by gangsters still hunting Androt rebels, had paralysed the external security of his bunker workshop, so he'd brought along the esteem-machine to use its neural circuits in rebooting the system. At first he'd been all about focus and speed, but then the attendant's voluptuous encouragements had distracted him.

"*Stupid,*" Eli whispered, prising up the esteem-machine's hard cover. "*Focus. Focus.*"

Behind him, the twisted pitch-black silence of the transflyer graveyard exploded into a metallic crash and reverberating screech. Eli fumbled the machine and dropped it with a thud. He spun around, his night-vision glasses picking up heat shadows moving through the darkness. The specs framed and reframed the figures, feeding back their stats into Eli's new front-core implant. Gangsters. Members of the Crook'd Town Pride – in a hunting formation and closing in fast.

Eli fell to his knees and dug frantically into the dirt with both hands, unearthing his security's access box. He fused the esteem-machine's CPU with the disarm function and waited for the connection. His breath steamed out in front of him, coming fast and ragged. At first nothing happened, then a distant mechanical whir started up beneath his boots. He jumped back as the dirt caved in to reveal a hidden spiral stairwell. Shielding his eyes, he ran through the rising dust cloud, heavy with the scents of must and old metal. He crashed down the stairs, triggering the re-close when he was halfway down, only just rolling clear of the vaulted doors as they slammed shut with a shuddering boom to seal the entrance.

Eli sat in the dark gulping back his gasps, listening for intruders, but the only sounds, apart from his breathing, were the re-settling metal and the usual laboratory beep-clattery. The relief left him lightheaded and he silently counted back to stop the faint. When the feeling passed, he clutched the wall and stood.

"Lights up," he whispered.

From above, the glow of high-power fluoros flickered then flared, shunting on all the way down the length of an enormous bunker warehouse. It had been a transflyer crusher bay and recommissioning workshop in its former life, but Eli had converted it into his secret laboratory, and had been busy filling it with experiments and inventions. The tracker team had transferred most of its equipment and possessions here from its room in Moris-Isles, though they really hadn't had that much. He, Silho and Jude had lost virtually everything in the bomb raids, Copernicus had managed to recover some of his weapons collection and Diega had brought in just one small square box, with strict instructions – *never ever open this – ever*. Eli's love for his friend kept him to his word – but it was torturous. Saying something like that to an imp-breed would usually be followed by an instantaneous frenzy of box opening, but Eli liked to think of himself as a walking stereotype annihilation. He also liked to think of himself with three blonde pixie-breed sisters, but that was another story entirely. And another distraction.

Eli brushed the dirt off his hands, adjusted his new weapon belt and walked out into the hangar.

"Disable shields," he said, shutting down the more experimental and advanced internal security that had protected everything inside the hangar from the ebomb blast. He stood surveying the scene before him and a smile crept across his dirt-smeared face.

Underneath a spotlight's glow, two transflyers stood side by side – two of the most incredible craft ever made. Eli flinched at his own rampant immodesty, but really it was a fact undeniable. These flyers were the genesis of a new era of craft-tech. Before the Monarchy, the Standard and the United Regiment had fallen at the beginning of the war, almost a year-cycle ago, sky legislation had dictated the lawful specifications of airborne vehicles, but these laws, along with all others, had now disintegrated into wartime anarchy. Which meant, in the case of aeronautics, designers could create without restraint, except that of their imagination and intellect – a small and precious freedom in a time of so much horror.

On the right stood the almost completed *Ory-5*. Beautiful she was not, but the newest Tracker team craft certainly fit the commander's brief – *make it fast, make it strong and do it now*. Built with parts Eli had pilfered from a thousand different wrecks, the newest *Ory* was a masterpiece of speed, a force to rival even the fastest fighterflyer. Its specially treated alloy shell was reinforced with a forceshield boasting a nuclear withstanding strength. Basically, inside this craft the team were untouchable – at least against all modern weaponry. Magics were another matter entirely, but Eli was working on that. Parked beside the *Ory-5* was Eli's new personal flyer, to replace the much loved *Summer Holiday*. While the *Ory-5* had been a product of necessity, this craft was a labor of love. It was only partially constructed, but already it had a name – the *Gypsy Rose*.

"What do you think, girl?" Eli spoke to his pet otter, who had so far snored through the entire ordeal of breaking in. When Nelly didn't stir, he peeked inside his pocket. She lifted her head and gave him a look of absolute indifference and unadulterated boredom, then immediately fell back asleep. Eli took it as a compliment. Then he realized that he was standing there grinning to himself while time raced him to the deadline. He had to finish the *Ory-5* before the fight-in, which was – he checked his chronograph – only four hours away. It might as well have been four seconds, considering the amount of work still left to do.

"Penman!" Eli called, his voice echoing into the vastness of the hangar as he ran to his tooling desk. "I need you!"

A chirring beep sounded in response and two blue orbs appeared in one darkly shadowed corner. A machine-breed that looked like a mechanical flying squid zipped out to greet him, getting in his face and patting him enthusiastically all over the head with its long, dangling tendrils. Compared to Androts, the most advanced of the machine-breed race, a PenmanRamada0318 was an extremely basic robotic model. By the now defunct Laws, they had not even been classified "living". But when Eli had found Penman hiding in the hangar, in fear of the Gangsters that were crushing every machine-breed they could find, he had looked into the little robot's eyes and seen life. He'd seen fear, he'd seen confusion, hope, hunger – not just for food but company too – a desperate desire *to be*. He'd seen a being with a unique mind, looking back at him and reaching out, and he'd reached back. Penman's former owners had kept him down here to disassemble transflyers and Eli had never met anyone who could build an engine so rapidly. Penman provided him with invaluable support while constructing the transflyers, and he also laughed at all of Eli's terribly overused jokes. He'd become a friend.

"We've run out of time," he told the robot. "The team needs the *Ory* in four hours."

Penman gave a series of quizzical beeps, and even though Eli spoke only basic machine code, he understood the gist.

He was asking about the meeting they'd just attended in Lancaster Square.

"Caesar wasn't actually there," Eli said.

Penman tooted shrilly and Eli replied, "I know – we were all surprised too. Everyone expected him to be there in person, but it was just a pre-recorded message. I copied it for you. Here." Eli grabbed the recording bug out of his pocket and threw it into the air. It unfolded and initiated playback.

Eli buzzed his wings and flew to the top of the scaffolding beside the *Ory-5*'s open engine bay as a life-sized hologram of Caesar K-Ruz flashed into light and started to speak.

"People of Scorpia. The war is over. The Ar Antarian king is dead without an heir. The machine-breeds have fallen, and I stand here before you – not as your king – but as a herald to a new era of time. I, and all of you, now live by gangster law. No boundaries are unchangeable. No places eternally off-limits. Each of you now has the right to protect your land, your people, your families. Each of you now has the right to better yourselves and change your circumstance. This is your awakening – your chance not just to make a living but to actually live, to determine your own life-path. Before, you were stuck where society had placed you. Now we all stand even. But do not be complacent. This new city is not a playing field, it is a battlefield. You can all gain land and wealth but you can equally lose it. Everyone is free – which means no one is untouchable ..."

Eli ran a series of engine tests as the speech continued to play – basically Caesar had thrown out a challenge to anyone who considered themselves to be gangster boss material. They were to come to the highest level of Scorpia, Sirenseron, where they would compete in a traditional fight-in, a one-on-one rink fighting tournament, a negotiation where words were replaced by fists and contracts were drawn up in blood. There were no rules, as such, except that competitors could use all their innate skill, but not magics of any kind. It would be a bloodbath, but worse than that, even though the war was done and Caesar was touting freedom for all, the machine-breeds, always the most repressed racial group, were still being hunted down, including women and children who'd had nothing to do with the fighting. Those the gangsters didn't kill outright they were locking into prison camps.

Just after the speech, the commander had received intel that the gangsters intended to mass-exterminate all the machine-breeds in the camps as well. Now that they'd won, they no longer needed the prisoners for bargaining and manipulation, and refused to free them – even the children and babies. Gangster law was merciless. When they'd heard this, Jude, one of Eli's tracker teammates who was half-Androt, half-Ar Antarian, had fallen to his knees, devastated. Commander Kane had immediately decided that he himself would go into the rink against Caesar K-Ruz and win the machine-breeds' freedom before the extermination could begin ...

A feeling hit Eli so suddenly that his first thought was that the canned flint-beans he'd eaten that morning were repeating on him. He stumbled back from the *Ory-5* and leaped off the scaffolding. He landed unsteadily, one hand pressed over his mouth. Then tears stung his eyes and a sob started deep in his chest and exploded out. He staggered to his workbench, hemorrhaging emotions with every step. By the time he hit it, he was crying hysterically.

"Get it together ..." he sobbed into his arm. "Everything is fine ... I am not in control. I mean, I am in control. I am not strong ... I mean ... I'm ..." He was finding it difficult to think straight and impossible in his distress to hold back his compulsive lying and stealing, issues he'd struggled with all his life thanks to the illegal mix of his bloodline.

As his hands uncontrollably shoved random objects into his pockets, Eli realized he must be having some kind of breakdown and pinched his arm viciously. It was something he used to do when he was a kid, trying to force himself to act normal, even though it just wasn't possible. The bruises had blended in with the blue stripes and purples dots of his Glee and Greer bloodline marks.

"What's wrong with you?" he gulped angrily at himself, struggling to regain composure.

He'd been under the belief that defeating a legion of demonic witches and saving the world would have boosted his confidence and resilience, and in ways it really had, but at times – times like this – he felt like a piece of ash – small, fragile and transient – as well as dangerously close to cracking up with inappropriate raucous laughter, either that or passing out cold – or, just as likely, pocketing everything in sight. He restrained himself on all accounts. Rationally, he suspected he was suffering delayed post-traumatic stress, triggered by the thought of the commander having to fight Caesar. For some reason the Pride King had become a kind of catastrophically handsome embodiment of all the horror and pain he'd experienced during the Skreaf uprising, and in the war that had followed. Just the thought of being close to Caesar again ... A shudder ran through Eli. From the long dark of the wars they'd emerged blinking into this new era of possibilities and uncertainties. And, evidently, mental instabilities. It had only been a year-cycle since they'd defeated the Skreaf and the gangsters and machine-breeds had started fighting, but it felt as though it had been going on forever – the horror of it slowing time. Eli sniffled and Nelly crawled out of his pocket and wound herself around his neck like a fluffy constricting python, snuffling consolingly in his ear. He pressed his face against her warm fur and cried until the front-core implant in his forehead beeped and an incoming message signal popped up in front of his eyes. The commander spoke directly into his thoughts.

"Eli."

Eli snapped up straight and answered, his voice thick, "Yes, Boss?"

"I've been trying to get through to tell you. My menu function froze again and I can hear you."

"Oh ..." Eli blinked three times, engaging his implant's hologram menu. He found that the com channel between himself and the commander had opened automatically. It had already done this several times, but Eli had thought he'd fixed the glitch. Clearly not. It was a system far more complex than any of his other com systems, thanks again to the lack of restrictive laws, but it was still a work in progress and full of faults. He was trialing it between himself and the commander before unleashing it on the rest of the tracker team.

"How long have we been connected?" he asked the commander.

Copernicus answered with silence and Eli flinched a little.

"So you heard me talking to the self-esteem program?"

"Yes."

"And the crying?"

"That too."

"Well, that's not embarrassing." Eli felt hot, red splotches of shame break out all over his face and neck.

Faint amusement edged the commander's words. "Of all the things I've caught you doing, Eli, making nice with a hologram and crying into your otter seems like the least embarrassing."

"Thanks, but that really doesn't make me feel any better," Eli gave a laugh, but it became a sob and he slapped a hand over his mouth.

After a pause Copernicus said, with his restrained concern, "What's getting you, Eli?"

"It's nothing, I mean everything ... And I don't know ... This fight-in has just thrown me ..."

Copernicus processed his words for a moment, then said, "I'm uploading a picture to you – can you see it?"

Eli accessed the menu again and saw the waiting file.

An image flickered up in front of his face. It was a kid – a very homely-looking kid – skinny and sitting awkwardly, all nose and teeth and wildly overgrown mane of shaggy dark hair.

Eli stared at the picture, unsure of what to make of it. "Is this one of those moments where we make ourselves feel better by laughing at others?" he asked.

Copernicus snorted. "Who do you think this is?"

Eli studied the hologram again, but couldn't see a resemblance to anyone and he was usually very good with faces. "Who?"

"Caesar K-Ruz."

Eli burst out laughing. "No, really, who is this?"

The commander altered the image and the hologram morphed into another picture of the Pride King as he was today. His face had grown into the nose and mouth and his hair had been shaved short, but it was definitely him. Eli smiled. For some reason he felt a whole lot better knowing that Caesar had once been a gangly kid with the worst haircut he'd ever seen – extremely tough competition considering Eli himself was among the contenders. (His gran'ma used to give him a bowl cut – an actual one, with a bowl on his head.) It wasn't surprising that the commander knew how to make him feel better. He'd always known.

"I think I'm okay now," Eli said.

"Good. What's your progress with the *Ory*?" Copernicus turned to business.

"So far I've almost fainted, stood admiring my work, and then had a mental breakdown – so not much yet."

"You know what to do, then," the commander said.

"Yes, Boss, I'm on it," Eli promised. He disengaged their connection, then double-checked it was off.

Nelly jumped off his shoulder and onto the workbench. She scampered along it to her bowl of pinkfin fish, which Eli had placed just inside her new enclosure. She bit down on the bowl and deliberately dragged it out of the enclosure and onto the bench, pausing to scold Eli in her squeaky chattering voice, before starting to gobble down the fish.

After she'd escaped from his pocket and gotten lost during the Skreaf uprising, and then almost been shot on one of the team's reconnaissance missions into the war zones, Eli had started to have major anxiety about taking her everywhere with him. Before the wars they were never parted – the otter always riding in his pocket or on his shoulder – but they'd entered dangerous times and nearly losing her twice had shaken him badly. Just the slightest thought of anything happening to Nelly made him break down. So he'd constructed a brand new enclosure for her, with so much play equipment, so many feeding chutes, water pools and fountains that Nelly hadn't known where to turn first. She'd loved it – but then he'd closed the door and the love affair between her and the enclosure had abruptly ended, because when she went inside there, it meant he was leaving her. He'd designed it with many mechanisms of alert and escape that would be triggered in the event he didn't return to let her out, and he'd tested them all half-a-billion times or more just to be absolutely sure she would never be trapped. The trouble was, now that she understood what it meant, getting her in there was next to impossible. Nelly cast him a cranky look with fish hanging out the sides of her mouth. She just wanted to stay with him. He understood that. And he just wanted her to stay alive. Unfortunately she didn't understand that. It was an ongoing saga.

Eli sighed and turned back to the *Ory*, the dart-vials stored in the back of the *Gypsy Rose* catching the light and his attention. The vials were full of his latest Ravien antidote. Ev'r Keets, legendary treasure hunter, infamous criminal and now one of his best friends, had transformed into a Ravien after one of the monstrous creatures had bitten her, and Eli had been working ever since to find a cure. After several formula failures, he believed this was finally it, the formula to change Ev'r back ... He just had to get the chance to use it.

Penman zoomed in beside him, staring with bright, inquisitive eyes. The robot made a series of soft beeps of concern.

"I'm alright," Eli said. "But we really have to get to work now. We've only got four hours – make that three and a half – to get the *Ory* airborne. Would you mind grabbing me a star-nose driver and the size 8 infused pliers, please?"

Penman squeaked and zoomed off to get the tools, while Eli grabbed a wrench off his tooling bench and knelt beneath the *Ory* to examine the landing gear. He felt the *whoosh* of the little 0318's fast return. Without turning back, he reached out for the pliers. His fingertips brushed against something smooth and cold – it twitched. Eli gasped and leaped away, rolling and flipping into a crouch, holding the wrench out in front of him like a weapon. Luther loomed over him, his face shifting with disturbing fluidity between the strikingly sharp features of his human-breed side and the monstrous appearance of a Midnight Man. Moses, Luther's big white wolf, lunged at Eli, knocking him onto his back and licking his face with a rough tongue. Luther reached in with shadowy hands that felt like frozen steel and tried to help Eli up, but ended up just pushing him down, crushing him further into the ground. Eli found himself laughing hysterically while in significant pain.

"Luther," he gasped, trying to catch his breath. "Luther, enough, that's okay – just – stop, stop, STOP!"

The Midnight Man backed away and stood staring at him, apprehension in his yellow-green python-blood eyes.

"Sorry, sorry." Eli struggled to his feet. It was the first time Luther had appeared to any of them for more than a few seconds since they'd defeated the Skreaf, and Eli didn't want to discourage him. "I didn't mean to yell at you. Only – that was the worst massage I've ever had, including the time I accidentally walked into a gargantuan-breed grindhouse thinking it was the post office."

Eli meant it as a joke, but Luther's expression saddened.

"No. I'm just – I'm totally kidding," Eli tried to explain.

Luther considered the words, then signed into the air, "*I am not so good with people.*"

"Of course you are!" Eli said. "Trust me. I've had social therapy – a ton of social therapy. Every race has their own social expectations and norms, but as far as Urigin standard behaviors go, you're doing very well, all things considered."

Luther suddenly darted forward. He sniffed at the wrench Eli was holding, then he bared enormous, sharp teeth in his hugely elongated jaw and chomped the tool in half. He chewed several times, then spat it back out onto the concrete with a ding.

Eli tried to hide his shock, but some must have surfaced, because Luther's expression turned to embarrassment. He hung his head.

"Ah ..." Eli searched for words. "Maybe I can give you a few tips ..." He brightened. "How about *Ten Tips to Not Terrify People*? Does that sound okay?"

They heard a mechanical tweet as Penman zipped back in with the requested tools. Luther whipped around and snarled at the little robot. Penman squeaked, dropped the pliers, and shot straight upward, hiding in the rafters of the ceiling.

"Tip One," Eli decided to jump straight in. "No baring teeth – *unless* you're smiling – See? Like this." He demonstrated a grin for Luther. "Try it."

Luther leaned in inches from Eli's face, opening his mouth into a twitching snarl. Even for an imp-breed with no sense of personal space, this was way too close. Eli could feel the heat of Luther's breath on his face and neck.

"Not bad." Eli let the lie happen naturally as he fought the urge to back away. "But just try – a bit further back – so that people can see your whole face."

Luther straightened up and stepped back a few paces, but he was still just as – if not even more – horribly frightening.

"Maybe try smiling without showing your teeth," Eli suggested. Luther immediately closed his mouth, again ashamed.

"There's nothing *wrong* with your teeth," Eli hurried to clarify. "But some people – not me in any way– may feel nervous at their razor sharpness and dagger length ... just a thought."

Luther's unblinking eyes bore into Eli, the snake pupils spreading and retracting as though he were weighing him up for the kill.

"Which brings me to Tip Two," Eli said. "Usually I try to limit my staring. If it's a passing stranger, then a glance is fine – like this ..." He glanced at Luther then away. "If you're talking to a stranger then make sure to look away and back again as you speak. If it's a friend then more sustained eye contact is acceptable, but still with some breaks."

Luther came in closer again and sniffed at Eli's wing. His forked tongue flickered out and tasted it.

"Tip Three," Eli rushed, his voice somewhat squeakier. "No sniffing and no tasting. A subtle inhalation is fine if someone is, say, wearing a perfume you like. But most definitely no inhaling as though you're about to, you know, bite the person's wing off." He gave a nervous laugh, which came out more as a shriek and Luther shied back in horror.

"Sorry, sorry – don't be frightened – that's just me laughing. Tip Four, laughter is okay – as long as it's not random or insane. So I tell you a joke – you laugh, so it's attached to the joke. Generally, try not to burst into spontaneous laughter if you're alone, even if you think funny things, but if you can't help yourself then limit the sound. That's one I struggle with all the time. Would you like to try it: I'll tell you a joke and you laugh?"

Luther gave a hesitant nod and Eli repeated the first joke that came to mind – something about a Fen, an Ar Antarian and a scullion entering a bar. At the punch line, Luther made a shivering movement that signaled his laughter.

"That's great!" Eli said. "Perfect! Only I wonder if there's something we can do to animate your vocal chords. I'll have to run some tests." He reached out to Luther's neck.

The Midnight Man reared up into a massive howling shadow. Eli stared in terror at the surging darkness. Cos magics shook the underground hangar, threatening to bring the dirt crushing in on it.

"Not bad tests," Eli managed to stutter out. "Good tests – I swear. I wouldn't hurt you, Luther – you know that, don't you?"

The shadow tore to pieces with the sound of a thousand frenzied wings and the pieces vanished into the walls.

Eli's legs gave way and he plonked down onto the ground. Nelly jumped out from her hiding place on the bench and ran to him, burrowing back into his pocket. He could feel her little heart beating fast. He remembered then something Ev'r had said – that Luther was most likely the byproduct of experimentation. Who knew what had already happened to him? The thought sat heavy and prickly inside Eli as Penman reappeared above the *Ory-5* and gave a cautious beep, reminding him that they only had three hours remaining. Forcing his ill-ease aside, Eli shook himself off and resumed work at double speed.

Chapter 3
Silho

AQUAIS

SCORPIA (ISHTAMAR)

Silho moved with the night shadows, just a glimmer in the rain, a suggestion of form – there but gone and never was. With her heavy body armor pressing on her shoulders, she stepped carefully on the slippery cobblestones. Ishtamar was one of the oldest levels of Scorpia, the streets winding and narrow, completely unmarked like most of the underside – outsiders not welcome, even before the war. But for her it wasn't a destination, just a through road to where she was going – to where she had to go, even though the thought of it tightened her throat to strangulation. Defeating the Skreaf, and surviving the recovery, hadn't taken away all her fears, but it had given her new strength to overcome them, to walk through them without doubting herself and turning back. Although it hadn't been just the surviving, it had been who she'd survived with – the tracker team. Eli. Diega. Jude. Copernicus …

Guilt stabbed at her. The commander's orders had been to keep to their hideout until they were called to rendezvous, but she'd felt compelled to leave. She knew it was a breach of orders, but with Copernicus distinct boundaries had been blurred – it was what happened when soldiers started kissing their commanding officer. Kissing only, because they hadn't had more than minutes alone since the beginning of the war. The desire for more than a kiss was there – not just there, but utterly overwhelming to the point where the thought of having sex in front of everyone had actually started to seem not so inappropriate. For just on a year-cycle, she and Copernicus had eaten together, slept together, even showered in close vicinity – but they couldn't touch. One of the team was always there and watching, and the frustration was excruciating. Maybe if they'd been together for a while before the war, the limited privacy wouldn't have prevented them from taking things further, but they hadn't, the relationship was new and everything was an uncertain first, made more uncertain by the fact that Diega and Jude's feelings were also tangled up with theirs. Silho could see now that she'd been handling things with Jude all wrong, but if there was a right way, she still didn't know what that was …

Stunted Emotional Intelligence … It was an ugly phrase, one that had stuck with Silho ever since her first-year military training report … "*Recruit demonstrates exceptionally high aptitude in every field except that of Emotionality, where assessment indicates stunted Emotional Intelligence* …"

When she'd read the report, it had felt like her blood had turned to fire and rushed through her body in an inferno of emotion – anger, disappointment, anxiety, shame. Stunted? She'd wanted to go to the Assessor's office and explain, she wasn't really stunted – she'd just been raised in hiding by a hardened ex-soldier in the middle of the Matadori Desert, with little outside contact, except with violent criminals, cannibalistic desert-mutants and scullion tribes ... She wasn't really stunted – just on powerful drugs to keep her secret skills in check. The chemicals had blunted her feelings, so she'd struggled to respond quickly enough to the emotion tests – but she'd known the answers. If she'd actually gone and con-fessed either of these things, it would have put not only her training, but also her life in jeopardy, so she'd had to ac-cept it – *stunted Emotional Intelligence.* Even five years on, in certain moods, the words still replayed and flared her anger. Now more than ever, because she'd started to suspect that this assessment had actually been accurate – and maybe still was.

A memory took form in Silho's mind: her carer, Hammersmith, drawing a line in the sand, then turning to her, his eyes bloodshot glazed, his beard wild and voice a growl, "On one side of this line is love, and on the other is happi-ness. You can't have both. Stick to happiness. Forget love."

At the time she'd just thought he was having one of his episodes, where he spent hours looking at faded holograms and singing old songs to the empty sky, when he'd give his slurred and bitter life advice. She'd let his words blow away in the Matadori wind. Love wasn't a line drawn in the sand. In her mind love had been a boy with dark eyes who would appear on the horizon and come to take her away from the desert. Love was the look between Ismail and Ev'r – Zingara at the time – the way they'd held hands and kissed. She'd longed for that love, dreamed about it, created whole fantasy worlds where it existed – where 'He' existed. She'd thought once she reached the city, love would be there.

As a recruit there'd been hundreds of men around her. One had particularly caught her interest, but if she'd had to explain why, she would have stammered – there was just something about him. It was as complicated and simple as that, and it had caused all kinds of desperate angst when he hadn't been the slightest bit interested in her, yet had still treated her with the same friendliness with which he'd treated everyone else. In a way it had been even worse, or at least more confusing, than if he'd completely ignored her. She hadn't understood how to deal with the feelings, or the rejection, and at one point had thought maybe starting something else with someone else would be the way. She'd gotten lost in a moment, and had almost let her secret out, almost exposed her skill and put in jeopardy all that had been sacrificed for her, just to feel like a normal girl for a second in time. It had terrified her how easily everything could be thrown away, how love, or lust or whatever it was, could take control. How it could lie so believably. She'd said *never again* – but had found attraction and desire couldn't be easily switched off. So she'd diverted it, rechanneled it – put everything into her training, into her study, into her work, and pushed dreams of love aside as far as they would go.

It had worked – until Copernicus Kane. When it came to him, there was no choice. The feelings could not be ignored or put on hold. She couldn't keep her eyes away from him and the fact that he was looking back at her with the same interest still took her by surprise – when fantasies came true it always felt like there should be a catch … And then there was Jude – she'd thought that once he saw that she and Copernicus were together, he'd understand she didn't have feelings for him, but he hadn't. If anything, the more time passed, the more he pressed closer to her. Uncomfortably close. And she couldn't help but blame herself. She hadn't wanted to hurt him, so she'd been trying to compensate on a friendship level, but perhaps it had come off as giving him hope … and perhaps part of her had actually meant to keep him interested for her own self-gratification … perhaps because part of her believed that Copernicus would eventually leave her and she was trying to hang on to what she had with Jude … She didn't know for sure what she'd been thinking. *Stunted Emotional Intelligence.* She hated that phrase.

An air-shaking explosion sent Silho diving to the ground. She scrambled up, readjusting her face mask as a fierce heat roared down the alleyway beside her. She peered around the corner and saw figures, black silhouettes against the backdrop of flames, moving around at the other end of the alley. Someone screamed and Silho jumped to her feet. Keeping close to the wall, she ran along the alley until she had a view of the square beyond. She crouched down in the shadows and watched through the greenish hue of her night-vision mask as three Androts dragged themselves out of their burning transflyer, with gangsters closing in on them from both sides. Their modified electrifiers were aimed and primed. Silho counted the gangsters – five – and through the shadows caught reflective flashes of red and yellow, the colors of Kelly's Crew – the second most powerful gang now that the Galleys had been all but wiped out by the Skreaf. By their panicked scrambling and lack of weapons, Silho knew these Androts weren't rebel fighters, just civilians like so many of the machine-breeds caught up in war. Three young guys probably trying to flee the city under the cover of night. Unfortunately they'd flown right into a gangster net, and were now trapped in a no man's land between the ghost buildings of the Empty Quarter and the gateway to Ishtamar's Grand Markets, an underground maze of stalls and sellers.

Silho squinted and saw the Androts preparing to run for it. They wouldn't make three steps before the gangsters dropped them. A fiery boom exploded from the crashed transflyer and the Androts lunged out from their cover. One immediately tripped over and fell. The others didn't see him through the smoke and ash. The gangsters aimed to fire and Silho blinked into light-form vision. She saw their bodies as a mass of glowing lights, dullest at their weakest points. She lifted a hand

and drew a blast of power from their body-lights into herself, enhancing her own strength. The gangsters dropped instantly, incapacitated, but alive.

With the gangsters down, Silho dashed across the square and used her temporarily heightened strength to drag up the heavy, fallen Androt. She helped him run across to where the other two were hiding behind the ruins of a stall. She threw their friend in beside them and the machine-breeds stared up at her, eyes wide with terror, black barcodes standing out bold on their pale necks. One lunged up trying to strike her with a piece of metal pole. Silho wrenched the pole out of his grasp, hurling it aside. She shifted back to normal sight, then pulled up her mask so they could see her face, but they weren't looking at her, just at her weapon belt and her electrifier.

"I'm not going to hurt you," she told them. "Follow me. I'll take you to cover."

"Get away from us!" one of them yelled, and they took off through the gateway and down toward the Grand Markets. Silho watched them run. The Markets had only one entrance and exit – the gangsters, experts in urban warfare, would easily flush them out.

She stepped to go after them, but a zap of fire aimed her way made her dive down behind the wrecked stall. Voices and running bootsteps headed toward her. Silho dragged her night-vision mask back down over her face and leaped up, racing for the shadows of the nearest alleyway. She ran through, pursued, until she hit a dead end. Fire glanced off her body armor and she whipped around to face her attackers – four more Kelly's Crew gangsters, with electrifiers all pointed at her chest, their fingers tense on the triggers. Their dogs growled behind them, snapping overgrown, trap-like jaws. One barked and the gangsters opened fire. Silho dropped to a crouch, blinking back to light-form. She gestured, drawing from the gangster's body-lights until they slumped to the ground, their dogs beside them. Silho paused, watching their chests rising and falling. She listened to hear if more gangsters were coming. The only sounds were the roar and crackle of the burning transflyer, but she knew that wouldn't last long. Soon more gangsters would be swarming the place and she couldn't risk going back now to find the Androts.

Feeling heavy with ill-ease, Silho approached the stunned men. She could have easily drained the rest of their body-lights, taken their lives with a flick of her hand, and breathed their life force out of her mouth in a blast of fire – like the firebird dragon of her bloodline marks. It was the skill of the Omarians, of which she was the last. But instead she stepped over them and headed back down the alleyway. She hadn't used her skills to kill anyone since the Skreaf. She understood that everything she'd gone through could have turned her colder, immune to others' suffering, indifferent toward life, but she hadn't. The effect had been the complete opposite – never more acutely than now had she sensed the life around her and understood the precarious confusion in which most people existed, and her lack of right to judge who should live and who should die. Right and wrong, good and bad had all run together like watered-down paint.

Halfway down the alley, Silho heard a thud behind her and spun around. Jude stood there, one foot in an extension rope attached to the rooftop of a building above, from where he'd dropped down. The red eye-lights of SevenM, his companion spider-like robot, locked onto Silho's face, feeding images back to Jude's mind. Jude made a quick gesture for her to come to him and she stepped forward. When she was within reach, he dragged her closer to him and wrapped his arms, mixed-metal prosthetic replacements, around her. He released the lowering-hold of the extension, shooting them back up to the rooftop, where he rapidly disconnected the anchor and re-coiled the line into his belt. As he ushered her behind the small icehouse in one corner of the flat space, Silho felt a flare of frustration; she hadn't needed rescuing and she didn't need shepherding. He knew that, he knew what she could do, but still insisted on shielding her, even more than Copernicus did. Once they were behind the icehouse, Silho lifted her mask, her breath misting the air.

"You left – I didn't know where you'd gone. Why did you turn off your locator?" Jude asked, his upper-level accent made heavier by frustration. "Kane told us to stay low until we rendezvous."

Silho noted he didn't use the commander's title. Things had changed between them, and not just because of her.

"I know," she replied. "But there is something I really need to do. Just like Diega. She left as well."

"Diega can take care of herself," Jude said.

"And I can't?"

"No, Silho. Clearly you can't," he responded sharply. "You turned your back on the enemy."

"They were neutralized."

"Yes, but for how long? Even you don't know the exact extent of your ability. Some people stay down longer than others. You said it yourself." He narrowed his eyes. "I don't know why you keep taking deliberate risks."

"I wasn't trying to take a risk. There were …" She hesitated. Jude already seemed on edge and any mention of Androts had become a trigger for him.

"What?" he prompted.

"Nothing … I just took a wrong turn," she said. "I was fine. I had everything handled."

Jude gave an unconvinced nod and lifted his eyes away from hers, looking into the darkness around them. The silence stretched on and Silho shifted, listening for sounds of approaching gangsters. She couldn't hear anything except the rain tapping across the rooftops.

"I'm just trying to keep you safe," Jude finally broke the silence. He lifted a hand to remove his glasses and Silho tensed. Jude never took off his glasses in public, always aware the bright blue of his eyes gave away his royal bloodline. His true identity as the heir to the Ar Antarian throne was still the secret of the tracker team. There was no one else there on the rooftop to see him, but it was still uncharacteristic.

Silho met his stare, his eyes shimmering like blue gems, lighter around his pupils, darkening almost to black around the edges. They cast a glow across the silver skin of his face, his features so strong and smooth, so perfect he almost looked like a sculpture, someone's definition of masculinity, someone's dream man – just not hers. She wasn't drawn to nobility or perfection – what captured her were scars and tattoos, dark eyes with a dark past. That's what felt like home. An image of Copernicus came to her mind and it sent warmth through her even in the freezing rain. She saw Jude's gaze was searching hers, looking for something that he couldn't find. A sudden determination in his expression made her discomfort surge.

"I have to go …" she said, turning away.

"No." Jude caught her arm in his metal grasp. "We need to talk." He stepped closer to her. "I need to tell you —"

"Later – I have to go," Silho said pulling away and backing up, pretending she didn't know what he wanted to say. "There's only a few hours until the fight-in. We can talk afterward – and don't worry about me."

She stepped away from him, heading fast for the edge of the roof.

"I love you," he called after her.

Her heart thudded heavily and she considered just pretending that she hadn't heard, but they were still standing too close for that to seem believable. She stopped and looked back at him, seeing in his eyes that he needed for her to say it back. His heart was exposed. She swallowed with discomfort.

"Same," she managed. "You're a wonderful friend ..."

He dropped his gaze, but not before Silho saw the hurt welling in them. Jude put his glasses back on and she felt a pang in her stomach. Hurting him was painful, but what option was there?

"You have to know – Kane is dangerous," Jude said, his voice low. "You don't understand what he's capable of."

"I know him," Silho said.

"No, Silho, you really don't." Jude gave a small, angry laugh, staring at her with pity and disappointment. He shook his head and sighed. "He's an excellent leader, a brilliant soldier – but he's a completely dysfunctional person. Not just dysfunctional – damaged, twisted – do you understand? I'm not just saying this for my sake, I'm saying it because you have to know the truth. He's very good at mimicking normal, it's why he's gotten as far as he has, but if you stay with him, he will hurt you. One day you'll cross his line and then you'll see what I'm talking about ... Silho, he's dangerous."

"Aren't we all," she said quietly.

"No, not like this," he insisted.

"Jude ..." She didn't know what to say. "In a few hours he's going up against Caesar for machine-breed rights. He's putting his life on the line for —"

"His life on the line?" Jude cut in. "If he really cared for the machine-breeds, he would have ordered us to go in weeks ago!"

Silho shook her head, her anger rising now. Jude knew well how hard the commander had been working on a plan to free the machine-breeds trapped in the gangster prison camps – how he'd looked at it from every possible angle – how he hadn't slept or eaten properly for so long because of it. Everything came down to the fact that they were severely outnumbered by the gangsters, even if Commander Santana and the United Resistance, all that remained of the city's former military, backed them. If they went into the camps it would be suicide. And now that the imprisoned machine-breeds were facing extermination, the fight-in was their only hope. Silho stared at Jude standing in the rain, and saw in his eyes the desperation and sadness haunting him.

"I'm sorry," she said.

He flinched and she realized it had been the wrong thing to say – again.

"Don't be sorry for me. Be sorry for all the children who are getting tortured while your commander figures out how to make himself look good."

"That's completely unfair," she said.

"That's how I feel," he shot back.

"I can't listen to this," Silho murmured.

"Then don't," Jude said. "Just go!"

SevenM clicked unhappily on his shoulder and Silho turned away. She walked to the side of the building and started climbing down the fire-escape ladder. Before her head cleared the rooftop, she looked back to Jude, and saw he was already gone.

Chapter 4
Silho

AQUAIS

SCORPIA (SUNNYSIDE)

"*This building stands as a reminder that demons walk among us. We must be ever vigilant ...*"

Words – that's all they were. But they hurt. They burned. Silho hated them as though each was a person with a twisted mind and ill intent. She'd arrived at the house with tension already burning holes in her stomach, and to find this here pushed her beyond her limits. She grabbed the rusted sign bolted onto the front gate of her childhood home and wrenched it off. She snapped it in half and flung it into the gutter, which was flowing fast with murky storm waters. Fury boiled inside her, threatening to explode out, but she caught it and pushed it back down. The sign had been written by people blind in a lie, believing that her father was a monster, a serial killer. They'd been deceived by the real demon, the Skreaf Bellum. During the war, Copernicus had released

41

an announcement across all levels of the city that her father, Englan Chrisholm, had been exculpated from his crimes. In reality, it hadn't had much of a response or impact. With the gangs and machine-breeds fighting, people were too busy trying to keep themselves and their children alive to worry about old news.

But for her, it had meant everything.

Yet unanswered questions had continued to haunt her, forcing her to resume the search into her parents' past. She'd expected to find little, but instead found nothing. For all intents and purposes, they had just stepped into existence as adults – her father as an artist, her mother into the military. Silho remembered even Hammersmith, her carer, who had mentored her mother, Oren Harvey, saying that he didn't know where she'd come from. It was as though they'd just appeared, then vanished again, like shooting stars. Silho had followed every possible lead, except one – and so the search had dragged her back, like the inevitable tide, to this place where the nightmare had begun. "Home," she whispered and felt the strength drain from her legs.

She breathed in deeply and pushed open the gate. It gave a grinding shriek. A broken path led through a garden, overwhelmed by weeds, to a cottage. Silho surveyed it through the greenish hue of her nocturnal mask. It was modest, tiny really, but had once been loved. Now it stood bashed in and busted out, defiled by words scrawled across every surface. This neighborhood, Sunnyside, had avoided bomb blasts while many of the surrounding suburbs were flattened.

This building still stands as a constant reminder that demons walk among us ...

Silho forced herself forward, every step taking effort as though she was dragging something heavy behind her. *Baggage*, that was what Eli had called it – he'd said that everyone has baggage, some more than others. Silho reached the doorway. Once a blue door with a dragonhead brass handle stood there, but now only an open cavity remained. Drawing her electrifier, she stepped over the threshold and swept the room. Then she lowered the weapon, taking in the ghost of the kitchen where she had sat and watched her father paint nearly every night of her young life. It seemed shrunken compared to the images in her mind. The last time she had been here, when she was six year-cycles old, an army of State Guardians had burst through the windows and door and arrested her father. They'd knocked over all the chairs. They still lay where they had fallen, broken and covered in thick dust and mold. The soldiers had dragged him away and she never saw him again. There were no goodbyes.

Silho picked her way across the treacherous, rot-devoured floorboards. One by one, she lifted the chairs and tried to straighten them under the table. She paused, preparing her mind, then turned and pressed her fingertips against a wall. She sensed the connection, and allowed the images of the past to flow into her. In her mind, life flooded back into the room. Color spread out, renewing every dust-dulled and broken surface. She sped through flashes of the near past, over the faces of people who had dared a peek inside this so-called chamber of horrors – the morbidly fascinated, the scientifically curious, and a few young kids on a dare who had run away screaming. She continued on – back – back – back in time – past the day of the arrest; she didn't need to see what was already indelibly burned into her mind. What she wanted was before that time – what she wanted was a better time – she wanted to see her dad again. She snap-stopped on an image of her childhood self sitting at the table with him. She let the memory play forward. He was teaching her to paint. He was talking and she heard his soft, reassuring voice.

"Now some red."

The child-Silho shook her head. "I don't like red."

The corners of Englan's mouth curved upward.

"You don't like red? Why don't you like red?" he asked.

"It doesn't taste nice."

"What does it taste like?"

"I don't know … like something bitter."

Englan nodded. "I understand, but sometimes we have to use colors we don't like to make a picture live."

"They're just pictures, Dada," she said. "They're not actually alive."

Her father smiled. "Of course, my love."

A knock sounded on the door and Englan looked up with a sharpness to his eyes that Silho had never noticed as a child.

"One moment," he called out. He lifted the painting and paints off the table and locked them into a hidden safe in the wall behind the stove. Once everything was back in place, he went to the door.

Silho skipped back again – rushing past six year-cycles of memories – over games and laughing, lessons and stories – all the way to herself as a baby where her father stood rocking her and singing in a language she'd never heard since, then everything went dark as she passed into a time before the house had been built.

Silho pulled her hands back from the wall. Grief struck with such renewed force that it took her breath away. She'd forgotten so many things about her father, and it was torture remembering everything again without any way to get back to him. Memories fade for a reason. Copernicus had tried to tell her that.

Silho's thoughts focused in on the picture her father was painting with her. She'd never realized at the time, but he was showing her how to make a realm portal. Since recovering from the burns she'd sustained defeating the Skreaf, she'd been trying to paint, testing if she had the skill, but her pictures were just that and nothing more.

Silho turned away from the wall and her eyes went to the stove. On the day of her father's arrest, all his hidden safes had been blasted open and found to be full of dead children, but it looked as though the stove was still intact. Silho went to it and dragged it out from the wall. The hidden compartment behind held the original lock. Silho reached for her weapon belt and drew out Solace – her mother's blade. It sliced the lock clean in half, and she let the pieces clunk to the ground. Expecting to find some kind of skeletal remains behind the door, Silho braced herself and wrenched it open. She narrowed her eyes. The safe was empty, save for one folded piece of paper. She reached in and took it out. In the center of the paper, someone had hand-scripted one line in black ink.

In my mother's house are many mansions – Silho Brabel.

Silho felt a strange rippling over her skin and instantly re-folded the note.

As far as she knew, her mother, Oren Harvey, had renamed her Silho Brabel in the desert, and her father had never known of it. So how could this be here? Not once in all the wall's memories had she seen Oren in this house. And what did the words mean – *In my mother's house are many mansions?* A creeping unease whispered in the silence. Could this be something the witches had planted – something dangerous?

Silho's com buzzed at her side with an incoming call signal. She viewed the caller ID – *Copernicus Kane* – and answered.

"Silho," Copernicus said. "It's time to move to the meeting point."

"Understood, I'm on my way," she responded, tucking the folded paper into her weapon belt. "Are you already there?"

"No, I'm here, outside the gate," he told her.

Silho froze, then she stood and edged to the window to peek around the frame. She saw Copernicus standing in the shadows near the front fence. Without any information of where she'd gone, without her locator activated, he'd managed to track her. He always did – and it sent chills of thrill and panic surging through her. It made her feel like running away, but at the same time, she would have been crushed if he stopped chasing. It was a little unbalanced, she knew that, but Copernicus didn't seem to need any explanations to understand how she felt, which was fortunate since she still found herself struggling for words when he was close – never sure if what she was saying actually made any sense, and whether she was talking to the man or the commander.

Her feelings for him now were so intense that she felt almost drugged-high when he was around and flat and empty when he was gone, as though he took all the color in the world with him wherever he went. Many times over the past months, she'd looked up from her research to see his eyes on her, and a thought had continued to replay in her mind – *While I'm chasing the ghosts of the dead, I'm missing out on living.* A few days ago, she'd begun to think that maybe it was time to let her parents go. She wasn't sure how to actually go about walking away – but she wanted to try. The thought was terrifying, but less so than losing him, and that had to mean something. It was the main reason she was here now – desperately searching for some kind of final door to close – but there wasn't any, just more questions.

At this moment here was only one thing clear to her at this moment: she would never come back here again. Silho felt like she wanted to say something, but what and to whom? She took one last look around, then turned and left the wrecked house. That was all it was now.

Copernicus opened the gate for her as she neared it. Half-light shadows darkened his face, making his scarlines glow and eyes burn with black fire. They consumed her, and even if she could have looked away, she didn't want to. All the pain of her argument with Jude faded now that he was close.

His attention shifted sharply to the end of the street, sensing heat and vibrations that Silho couldn't.

"Gangsters?" she asked, backing further into the shadows beside him.

Copernicus nodded. "They've been sweeping all the levels, setting off ebombs, trying to flush out the remaining machine-breeds."

"I know. I came across a few in Ishtamar," she confessed.

His jaw tightened with disapproval, but he didn't say anything.

He stepped out in the opposite direction from the gangsters and Silho followed him. They moved down the street, fast leaving Sunnyside behind and entering Knox, a former shopping district. Street lamps that had once twinkled now stood askew in the broken, caved-in paved roads. Every shop was trashed and looted; some were fire-ravaged, blackened. War had turned their colors monochrome – shadows and white. Mannequins lay, half-staggered in twisted positions, doll faces burned and crushed. Tangled among the fake dead were real corpses. The stench of rot made Silho gag. She held her breath, but could still taste it. Copernicus gave no outward reaction, and she thought that it must be a terrible thing to have witnessed so much horror that crossing paths with death became a casual encounter. She glanced at his gloved hands and wondered how he'd react if she grabbed hold and held on.

Copernicus halted so suddenly that Silho ran into his back. He stood, studying the shadows ahead of them.

"Go! Move – in there!" he told her, the sudden urgency in his voice sending her running in the direction he pointed. She climbed through the shattered front window of a shop, Copernicus just behind.

She heard it then, the dull rumbling of a gangster mass-mover, a prison-craft, flying low over the streets. She pushed further back into the destroyed shop, turning into a partially collapsed aisle. Her stomach lurched and she shifted into light-form vision. The silhouette of a person stood several paces away. Copernicus seized Silho's shoulder and dragged her behind him. He drew his electrifier and raised it, but didn't fire. Silho could see the stranger's flaring body-lights, but his silhouette was completely still. With his electrifier primed, Copernicus edged forward to the stranger. Silho followed, and when they were right in front of the man and he still hadn't shifted at all, she blinked back to normal sight. It was an Androt soldier, covered in body armor head to foot, a heavy artillery weapon hanging from one hand. Silho stared at his face. It was completely unmoving, the features frozen in an expression of anger and pain, and he wasn't breathing – but, by his body-lights, he was definitely still alive. Silho glanced at Copernicus, who was examining a wound in the machine-breed's chest. It was extremely deep and his clothes were saturated in white blood. Androts were usually rapid healers, so it was strange the wound was still open and extensive.

"What's happened to him?" Silho whispered.

"Shut down," Copernicus replied. "It's what happens when machine-breeds suffer catastrophic injury. They shut down their bodies to preserve their minds."

"I haven't seen this before," Silho said. Corpses of Androt soldiers had been turning up everywhere, but none like this.

"They've been dying rather than letting themselves be taken," Copernicus told her.

"So they could be reanimated?" she asked.

"Sometimes, yes, if their injuries can be healed."

"And this one?"

Copernicus shook his head. "Surprise attack, I'd say ... and by the looks of it, taken out by his own kind, otherwise the other Androts would have found him by now."

"Was he a traitor?" Silho asked.

"Maybe, or perhaps just a man tired of fighting."

Silho considered his words as Copernicus dragged a leaning shelf over in front of the Androt, blocking him from being seen from the street. The mass-mover roared closer, bringing with it the sound of marching boots. Copernicus and Silho quickly picked their way to the very back of the shop, where they hid behind several rows of high shelves. They crouched in the shadows, electrifiers aimed at the shop's front. The prison-craft roared closer, shaking the ground. Silho pressed back into the darkness as light-blasters shone into the shop and scanned across the interior. Gangster voices called out to each other. She glanced at Copernicus, waiting for his direction. He gave a slight shake of his head. *Hold.* She clutched her weapon tighter, waiting, until the thunder of the craft moved on, growing more distant as the search left their street. Copernicus lowered his electrifier and holstered it. He stood and looked down at Silho. His expression was cold and detached, fight-ready, but it softened as their eyes met. It was very rare to see behind his control and Silho felt suddenly overwhelmed by panic.

She stood, ripped up her face mask and said, "Don't fight Caesar."

"It's the gangster way," Copernicus said.

"I don't care. I have a bad feeling. There must be some other way – something I can do."

Copernicus shook his head. They'd already been over every other option and found them all lacking. Silho wasn't sure if she could, using light-form, mass immobilize the gangsters guarding the prison camps without taking it one step too far and slaughtering them all, and either way the effort would most certainly end up with her burning again. She could regenerate, but with extensive damage – it would take time, and then there'd be the backlash from Caesar to worry about. The fight-in was the only legitimate way to take control of the machine-breeds' fate.

"I understand how you're feeling," he said, "but the situation is what it is, and we have to continue. We have to free the machine-breeds. No one else can."

"I know but ... I just feel ..." She struggled to express her deep foreboding.

"Fear ..." He stepped forward and took her hand in his.

"It's more. Something is wrong ..."

"Silho," he said softly, "I understand, but you have to trust me."

He drew her close and she pressed against him, hugging him with all her strength as though someone were trying to drag them apart. He touched her face and lifted it to his. The words she wanted to say were lost to her, and a moment passed where she didn't know what to do, and she couldn't breathe, and she couldn't move. Then he leaned down to her. Her first reaction was to try to pull away, but Copernicus held her firm and pressed his lips against hers. Heat rushed through her body and she felt him respond, the embrace fast turning from consoling into something else. They kissed deeply, everything around them fading into insignificance until they were all that was left. She felt no more fear, just his lips, his touch and his body against hers. He guided her down to the floor, undoing his weapon belt and discarding it. The look in his eyes left no room for misunderstanding. Silho felt her heartbeats pounding too fast, so loud she barely heard her com beeping – insistently and persistently – until Copernicus pulled back and she had to answer.

"Eli?"

"Um ... Silho. It's not Eli – I mean it *is* Eli – as you know – you just said my name ... Can you – if you wouldn't mind – tell the Boss that I think the front-core coms are malfunctioning again and my menu has frozen." He sounded monumentally embarrassed. "I am so, *so* sorry, but I thought I should tell you. I can hear everything the boss is thinking and I assumed he didn't actually want me hearing ... what he's thinking ... at the present moment ... Not that there's anything wrong with what he's thinking – it's just – slightly explicit and – and there's nothing wrong with that – and – and I'm just going to stop talking right here."

Silho really didn't know how to respond. She actually felt like laughing, but Copernicus spoke into the com, his voice tight. "Thank you, Eli."

He blinked to access the prototype implant and gave it a verbal command. "End transmission."

He waited for a moment, then moved in close to Silho again, but before they could kiss, Eli's voice came through Silho's com.

"Ah ... Still here ..."

Copernicus clenched his jaw. He blinked open his menu again and disengaged manually.

"Eli?" he checked.

"Yes – just working on disconnecting. My menu is still frozen."

Silho could hear him working frantically on the other end of the com.

Copernicus disengaged again.

"Are you —"

"Still here," Eli confirmed.

"Now?"

"Yes ..."

"Now?"

"Sorry – yes."

Copernicus cursed. He grabbed the blade from his belt, and Silho flinched as he pushed the tip into his forehead, digging out the implant. He crushed it in one fist and dropped it to the ground. With blood streaming down his face, he looked so savage that Silho had to laugh. She realized it was a completely inappropriate reaction, but couldn't stop once she'd started. Fortunately, Copernicus didn't take offense. His fury melted into a smile and he dragged her back to him.

A rumble trembled the ground. The search was coming back around; the gangsters possibly picking up on their presence. Copernicus' eyes told Silho he was thinking the same thing. It was time to move. He helped Silho up, then grabbed his weapon belt and re-fastened it. Their eyes met and she could see the frustration in his expression.

"After the fight-in," he said, a promise in the words. He kissed her and she held onto him, not wanting to let go.

"Everything will be alright," he whispered to her. "Trust me."

He kissed her again and she nodded, wanting to believe him.

Chapter 5
Diega

AQUAIS

SCORPIA (ESTABANA)

Every time was the last time, until the next time. One too many drinks, a poisonous word, a feeling without a name and here she was, a liar again – proving right every wrong they said about her. She wasn't deluded. She knew it was sick. No shades of maybe to save her soul. This was all bad from every angle. Diega more than knew it – she felt it. It gave her the guilts. She couldn't face herself in the mirror for days afterward. And every time was the last time. *I promise.* Everyone knew not to trust a liar. When was she going to learn?

Diega's head hung low to her chest, sweat snaking cold rivers down her face. She could see her feet dangling above the ground. And below them, her blood, blue-black as the night sky, trickled down a drain. She dragged her head upright and it flopped back with little control. Her hands were bound above her with chains fasted to a beam. Beyond that, a tower tunnel stretched up to a sphere of light. *Too far to reach*. Somewhere up there was a club with music booming full-blast, but the only beat down here was her heart, slow and echoing in her ears.

Down here ...

In this dungeon reeking of pain and piss, bloody hand-prints on the wall keeping tally of the beatings. Diega's head dropped down again and she saw the man in front of her. One of her own kind – an Ohini Fen, with the swollen bulk and protuberant veins of artificially enhanced muscles. A black mask concealed his face. He raised the club in his hand, and as he did, he morphed it into a whip. He tensed. Diega braced, the colors of her rainbow skin flaring. She felt the rush of air and then it struck. Pain radiated through her body. She couldn't breathe around it. Agony ... and release.

She gazed back up to the light, barely feeling the other blows raining down on her, only returning to herself once her feet hit the ground and she toppled face-first into a pool of her own blood. Her punisher grabbed her. He ripped his mask halfway up and forced her mouth against his. The kiss tasted of metal. His hands were too rough and she did nothing to stop it – just closed her eyes, and she was back on the cliff watching the de-mon witch fall, only now she was falling with her – down to the Envirious Realm – where all the broken people go.

* * * * *

Diega pushed open the door from the stairwell to the main floor and staggered out into the club. The music pounded, vibrating the floorboards, as laser lights sliced the smoky darkness, over strobing figures, lost in the rhythm.

Before the war, the Helliox had been a borderline-illegal hole in the wall, kept in business by the Fen soldiers who frequented it, but never spoke of it. The sum of her people in one line – *what we know we never speak of*. But now ... Diega climbed a short flight of stairs and passed through a set of doors, finding herself standing on an open elevator platform, looking out over what the Helliox had become. From one basement room it had blown out to almost a full city block, a multi-leveled hive of entertainment. Somehow this place had survived and thrived when so much of Scorpia had crumbled.

The elevator lowered her past the neon flashing lights and sound-storm of an arcade city, past restaurants and bars, beauty parlors and pamper halls; past a barter mall packed out with hagglers. Below that was a gambling den, with a gigantic holo-screen projecting over the crowds. In the main fight arena, the tournament to decide who would stand up as boss of the fairy-breeds in the fight-in was well underway – only males allowed. Everywhere inanimate objects morphed and resettled, then changed again. Everything that could be shifted appeared blurred around the edges to Diega's eyes and those of her kind, though it wasn't just Fens crowding the Helliox – there were fairy-breeds of all types here – Sleagh Maith, Myrea Nene and Danan, as well as other less common types like the Grimshaws and Rhymers who had come out of hiding since the fall of the Ar Antarian king, who'd hunted them almost to extinction. Everywhere the whistles of the old language sang through the air. A sense of the forgotten was coming back. In some ways it felt like a victory and in others ways a backslide. Amongst the thronging crowds, there was not one non-fairy-breed face. The call for gangster law to reign had inflamed the just-below-the-surface racial prejudice of her kind. Diega looked up through the open top of the building to the stars above – with half the city lights knocked out, they'd never blazed so brightly and felt so close.

Diega stepped off the elevator onto ground level. Immediately she recognized a group of Fens from her neighborhood, La Crox, in Estabana. They were playing a game of Briscopa, traditional cards, around a table. She moved closer, but they saw her coming and closed their ranks, boxing her out. She was the bad daughter, the one who had abandoned her parents. She was a disgrace. Even here in this place. It was the hypocrisy of her people – sons could go, do and be whatever they pleased, whereas daughters only did as their parents allowed. A wild boy was a wild boy; a wild girl was a curse and a scar on the family's integrity. With all her being, she wanted to say she honestly didn't care what they or any others thought about her, but that would be another lie – albeit one she told very well. Everywhere she went, she always noticed who was looking and who was not, and she never passed a mirror without looking into it and hating what she saw.

Diega moved away into one of the bars, one with blue lighting and a crystal ceiling. The bartender took her order, holding her gaze for a few moments too long, a smile lingering on his lips. Someone pushed in beside her and put an arm around her waist. She whipped around to shove them off, but saw her friend, an ex-United Regiment soldier named Castana. He gave her an intoxicated grin. She still pushed him away, but only lightly.

"Dee!" He raised his voice over the pounding music. "It's been too long. I've missed you." His words slurred into each other, and he slipped an arm back around her. The bartender placed Diega's drink down in front of them, his smile gone.

"Allow me." Castana paid for the drink with a handful of pills – Moonshimmer and Intensity – barter and drugs were fast becoming the fairy-breed currency since the annulment of the sovereign. Diega reached for her drink.

"Wait," Castana said. He winked at her and hovered a pill above her glass. Her hesitation was a mere flicker. He dropped it in and she watched it fizz, then drained the glass in one go. Castana laughed.

"Never change," he murmured into her ear. He kissed her face, as the pain of her body and mind numbed. This was something that Jude had never understood, despite how close and intimate their relationship had become – she didn't take drugs to feel high, she took them to feel nothing. He'd never understood her at all.

Diega let Castana lead her out onto the dance floor where they joined the masses. His body pressed against hers from the front, another stranger from behind. She blinked and they were in the alley outside the club, both of them still pressed against her. Panic filtered through the drug haze. Where was she? Where were her clothes? Where was her mind?

Both men were laughing – not at her, but it felt like it. She shoved Castana away and landed a kick to the other's chest, knocking him sprawling. She staggered sideways onto the pavement, her hands closing over her clothes and weapon belt. She drew her electrifier and stood, aiming it first at Castana and then the stranger. Both men put up their hands.

"Easy, Dee," Castana said. "You know me. It's just a bad trip."

"*Fsx*," she cursed at him in Fenlen. "Don't trutting move."

She snatched up her clothes and kept the gun pointed on them as she retreated down the alley.

"*Sirca*," she heard the stranger say – it meant "crazy".

Diega paused just before the end of the alleyway and dragged on her clothes and belt. There still enough Intensity in her system for her not to feel the welts and bruises darkening all over her skin. Keeping to the shadows, she stepped out into Alamada Square, the center of Estabana. Outside the Helliox everything was far more subdued – an empty street, one small restaurant, with one small family eating inside by candlelight.

To the left and seven blocks down stood her parents' house. She hadn't been there for so long, since finishing her court-ordered military sentence and deciding that she wanted to continue her training as a soldier. She'd gone home that day looking for a new beginning, maybe even reconciliation. Even as she'd climbed the front steps, she'd realized it was bad idea. She'd opened the door, but knocked lightly as well. There were no locks or knocking between family, but she wasn't sure if she was still that. Inside the house was clean, but color- less – lived in, but abandoned. She found the two of them, her parents, sitting in the glass room, watching the stars. At her greeting, both glanced sideways with gray eyes. They looked like ghosts of themselves. Neither spoke, which wasn't sur- prising, but it still hurt.

She left them and went upstairs to the bedrooms. She pressed open the door to her sister Ariana's room. Everything was as it had been the day Ariana was taken – from the washed clothes folded on her bed to the home- work on her desk. In this room, time had frozen. She wanted to go inside, but couldn't bring herself to do it – so she went instead to her own room and found it completely bare. They'd thrown away everything. Tears seared her eyes, but she forced herself to walk in, military boots thudding on the boards.

She went to her hiding place in the cupboard and drew out the box. She opened the lid. Inside was the special bracelet with Ariana's name inscribed on it – a gift from their father for doing so well at school. Ariana had been effortlessly tal- ented in everything she did, unlike Diega, who had tried with everything she had, but never did as well. That day, the day Ariana had been taken, Diega had felt overwhelming jealousy of the gift, and even more so of her parents' praise. She'd stolen the bracelet out of her sister's room before they went out, liking the way it sparkled on her wrist.

She went down a dark set of stairs and never came back up ... The feelings flowed – impatience to anger, from anger to disquiet, from disquiet to fear, from fear to terror ... She was gone. The fun sister, the happy-go-lucky sister, the adventurous sister, the smart sister, the beautiful sister ... Gone. Forever.

The story she'd told from then till now was that Ariana had vanished in a crowd, but the truth, which she'd never told a soul, was that in the overcrowded Alamada Square she'd seen her sister walk away with a stranger – and she'd felt uneasy about it. She'd even started to run after her, but then she'd stopped, thinking for once Ariana would be the one in trouble for wandering off, for once she'd be the one their parents yelled at, the one being told she was an embarrassment ... And then she was gone, and all the regret in the world added up to exactly nothing. There was no way to bring her back. Because of jealousy, she'd let her sister die.

Diega had put the lid back on the box and taken it with her, leaving the house without saying goodbye. Her sister had been murdered year-cycles ago, but Diega was deader to their parents than Ariana would ever be.

Diega turned right and shuffled down the street, passing an overflowing dumpster. All rubbish collection had ceased since war broke over the city. A smashed-up speeder lay among the garbage. Diega went over and wrenched it upright. The engine was completely shot, but that had never presented a problem for her. She harnessed her electrosmith skills and sailed the speeder into the air. She zoomed, flying way too fast, the Intensity making time and space skip around her. Rooftops zipped past, gunfire sounded too loud, and then she saw the AOX building, the meet-up point, flash before her face. She collided with a ledge and crashed onto the rooftop, skidding along the rocks, only her military fatigues saving her skin from being shredded. She smashed into the other side, with the speeder on top of her. Hands wrenched her free from the wreckage and she looked up at Jude, staring at her through his night-vision glasses. His spider robot, SevenM, sat balanced on one broad shoulder.

"Diega!" He shook her. "What have you done to yourself?"

She shoved away from him and stood up, limping on a twisted ankle.

"Are you high again?" he demanded.

She snorted, sick to trutting death of Jude's holier-than-thou attitude. He was looking at her like a sickness that needed curing. She started to tell him to mind his own business, but he grabbed the narc-gone spray off his belt and squeezed it full into her face. It was absorbed straight into her bloodstream and sobered her immediately. A mountain of pain smashed down on top of her. She staggered to the edge of the rooftop and leaned against it, swallowing, feeling as though she was about to throw up. She grasped her anti-nausea serum and downed it, followed by a pain-cancel to kill the ache of her bruises.

"I don't understand." Jude spoke behind her. "You killed the Skreaf. You avenged your sister. Why are you acting even crazier than before? What's wrong with you women?"

Diega shook her head. He didn't understand. Everything was worse now – because of him, because of Copernicus and Silho and because she felt even more lost for purpose than ever, but she didn't want to give him the satisfaction of seeing through her. She just gave a rough laugh and said, "King Jude."

He knew how to press all her buttons, but she knew all his as well.

Jude moved in closer and said with pity that cut straight to her heart, "Diega – I still care about you."

Her eyes flickered closed. That was the worst thing to hear – *I still care about you. But I don't love you …*

He kept talking, but she didn't hear another word, just stared up to the stars, finding among the infinitude of glowing forms the star her parents had made for Ariana and sent into the sky to shine forever. She'd always wanted to make her own star from her sister – but never had. It would mean accepting she was gone. Beyond the stars, the immense forms of other planets filled the night sky, the most visible of them, Bandos, Eumaios and Praterius, said to have once been part of Aquais, struck free by a rogue meteor.

Diega's sight dropped down toward movement beside the building. Copernicus and Silho were walking along the street below. Even after all the year-cycles since she'd first met him and after all they'd been through, the sight of Copernicus Kane made her breathless, and she could still see why most people found him so frightening. It was partly appearance – his height and carved stone muscles, harder than any muscles had the right to be, as Eli had once joked. It was also his presence. He radiated an undercurrent of animalistic alpha-male … but mostly, it was his eyes. When they were angry, it was like the entire universal sky blackening over with a storm – the kind no one would ever go out in. It was primal. It was just plain scary, which was why everyone was still calling him Commander Kane even though the United Regiment had ceased to exist.

She could say she didn't still love him and want him and fantasize about him, that she wouldn't drop everything and everyone if he said he wanted her too – but that would be another lie. Those feelings had never gone away, and they hurt more than any physical injury she'd ever had. Hating Silho would be as easy as breathing, if the girl didn't make it so difficult. She wasn't conceited – in fact, most of the time she actually seemed completely oblivious to how strong she was, how stunning, how unique. Her *Tehron*, the shimmer of the star reigning in the sky on the day of a person's birth, which reflected always from their eyes, was ruby red. Diega had never seen another person with a red *Tehron*. There were no red stars in the Aquaian sky, which meant only one thing – Silho wasn't born on this planet. Diega knew all the other Fens saw it too – only her kind *could* see *Tehron* – but it was completely taboo to discuss it among themselves and held dire consequences if discussed with outsiders. So Diega kept her mouth shut. Telling Silho wouldn't change anything anyway.

In front of the stars a set of lights flashed, growing larger by the second. Diega spotted a craft, something unlike anything that she'd seen before, flying straight for them. Her first thought was *Eli*. Jude cursed and laughed behind her. She turned to smile at him and he smiled back. Eli Anklebiter – always bringing people together. Loving him was not optional. She just did.

Eli soared the craft in, grinning and waving at them through the front windscreen, not seeing the unilluminated AOX sign he was flying straight toward. Both Diega and Jude started waving their arms, yelling for him to stop – but he zoomed past and smashed straight into it. The new transflyer ricocheted back, the engines cut, and the craft plummeted to the roof, hitting with a resounding smash. Diega and Jude sprinted together toward the transflyer lying on its side. With the strength of his metal prosthetics, Jude heaved the craft back upright. Eli was hanging half out the pilot-side door, looking dazed. Diega helped him down to lie on the ground, all her personal distress forgotten in the shock of watching her friend falling from the sky.

"What was that?" she yelled at him, half-laughing, half-upset.

"You okay, buddy?" Jude asked, kneeling beside him. SevenM's many eyes scanned over Eli checking for injury.

Eli clutched his otter, which Diega always called an overgrown rat to tease him, and said in a small voice, "No ... I mean, yes ... I'm okay, I think." He let out a peal of laughter, then cut himself short. "Sorry ... sorry ... I'm just ... really sorry – I've never crashed before."

"Sometimes watching where you're going is useful," Diega told him.

"I thought you were waving to me," he said, then giggled again.

"We were – we were waving, as in, *don't crash into that sign*."

"Maybe something's wrong with me." Eli looked up at them with worried eyes.

"It's called stress," Jude said. "Go easy on yourself. We're all dealing with it – hopefully there'll be some kind of relief up ahead."

Boots thudded toward them, and Silho and Copernicus appeared beside Jude.

"What happened?" Copernicus demanded.

"He was waving to us and not looking where he was going." Diega gave Eli a light, playful shove.

"Are you alright?" Copernicus asked him.

"I think so."

They all helped him sit up and his otter scrambled back into his pocket.

"I just ..." Eli made a choking sound and burst into tears.

Jude thumped him on the back and Silho held his hand as he tried to compose himself.

"I'm sorry," he snuffled. "I'm a mess."

"It's fine," Copernicus said stiffly. "There's nothing wrong with expressing emotion."

Diega burst into laughter. "Coming from you, that's hilarious," she said. Copernicus was so repressed, controlled and hardened that he could barely smile, let alone cry.

"You don't cry," Eli said to the commander, then found a hankerchief in his pocket and wiped his nose.

"No ..." he said with a hint of discomfort. "Not – outwardly."

Diega laughed louder – *not outwardly* ...

"It's just you, Eli," she teased him. "You, pregnant women and small children."

"It's called having emotions, Diega," Jude said, taking it too seriously as always. "You should try it someday."

"Really? Thanks, your majesty," she snapped back at him.

"Okay, enough – time to fly out," Copernicus told them.

Eli scrambled up and they all climbed into the brand new *Ory-5*. Diega maneuvered herself behind the steering yoke, letting out the seat, her legs longer than Eli's.

Jude patted Eli's shoulder in the back seat. "Nice work, my friend – once again you've outdone yourself."

"I would say the same," Diega looked back at him in the mirrors, "but I don't want you to start blubbering again."

Eli laughed, looking much more like himself, even with the bloodshot eyes.

Hearing a distinctive snore from his pocket, Diega said, "Overgrown rat still not taking to her cage?"

"In short," Eli said, "no. I just couldn't get her to go inside tonight. Things shouldn't get too ... serious ... at the fight-in, should they?" he asked anxiously.

Diega gestured to Copernicus sitting beside her and said, "For him it will be serious. For us – there's always the chance of craziness as well, but the rat's a veteran at this by now. She'll be fine."

Eli gulped, both he and Silho looking decidedly ill at the thought of Copernicus fighting. Diega wouldn't have admitted it aloud, but she was feeling a similar disquiet at the idea. Copernicus himself looked as cool and controlled as always, and Jude just seemed ticked off at everyone, excluding Eli. Diega sensed it was going to be one of those days that she wished was over before it had even begun.

She started up the engine and Eli said, "Just watch the propulsion, it's very —"

Diega took off with a speed that shocked even her, smashing everyone back in their seats. They rocketed toward Sirenseron – the former royal palace, and topmost level of Scorpia.

Chapter 6
Croy

KULLRA FORNAX

NŸR-CORUM (THE FILTER)

The floating pier rocked with a deceitful serenity as Croy and Darius approached the gathering at the end of the jetty. Croy counted the number of personnel already on scene. They totaled twelve – twelve bodies dropping extraneous threads and fibers, twenty-four boots trampling over tracks, a hundred and twenty fingers smudging prints and contaminating evidence. The Conference had chosen not to listen to her when she'd explained to them about crime-scene integrity. They wanted things done the same way they always had been, even if it was the wrong way.

She grimaced at a sharp twinge in her knee. The idea of pain relief called to her, as it always did around this time. She liked to believe that one dayturn she would be strong enough to resist, but she had gone way past the point of making any more hollow promises to herself. Croy touched a hand to the pendant around her neck, a shaped piece of metal John L had given her. It was shrapnel from a Dray ship, from his maiden voyage as a Fleetsman. It had been a simple water run that had turned into a massacre, only John L and one other Fleetsman surviving. Though he'd fought in hundreds of battles against the Dray after that, he'd said it was always the one that woke him screaming from his sleep.

When they were near to the others, Darius called out.

"Oi."

Twelve faces turned their way, reflecting back a mix of emotions. Controllers Knightsbridge and Newton and their trainee, Micken Kisslefish, stood up at the end of the jetty. Kisslefish grinned, Newton's face darkened and Knightsbridge walked out to meet them, extending a hand to Darius.

"Mister Darius DeCavisi. How are you, my friend?"

"Fine," Darius grunted. He grasped Knightsbridge's forearm briefly, but didn't smile or meet his eyes.

"You ready for tonight?" Knightsbridge asked. He crossed his arms over his bulging chest and the seams of his shirt strained. The man had a fetish for undersized clothes, with fabric that rode up in ways and places that couldn't possibly be comfortable. Croy highly suspected it had something to do with trying to make his muscles look as big as possible, but his overplay reeked almost as much his body odor.

Darius nodded.

"It's going to be a good game," Knightsbridge continued. "Their centerstrike is out with ankle-swell. That means their whole left half defensive is going to crumble like wetwood. We'll kill them."

Croy stepped past the men and Knightsbridge gave her a sideways glance.

"Knightsbridge," she said. He muttered a reply, which might have been *hello* or equally likely *go to hell*.

She kept moving until Micken Kisslefish came at her with his grin. The young trainee had an oversized mouth and seemed to be in a permanent state of awkward over-excitement. Croy doubted he was old enough to shave, or to even grow a good crop of body hair for that matter, and could only guess, by his purple cloak, that he was the son of some Purple Wing who was indulging his kid's fantasies of becoming a Controller. Personality defects and defective breeding aside, Croy didn't have any serious problems with him. At least he listened and wanted to learn. He also wrote down everything she said and went around quoting her to people – a very flattering annoyance.

"Controller Croy!" The trainee launched in, parchment pad and charcoal roll in hand. "We've got a real live one today, don't we?" His nose plugs made his voice even more nasal than usual.

Croy glanced past Kisslefish to the end of the jetty. Her eyes found the corpse and she said, "Not exactly."

Someone had chained a dead girl between two anchor poles. The body bobbed half-submerged in the water. Newton was squatting beside the corpse and three Sketchers stood nearby scratching charcoal images from different angles of the scene.

Croy approached the body and Newton looked up at her with ice-blue eyes, several degrees too intense for comfort. He'd asked her out just after Roth left her and she'd declined – perhaps a bit too bluntly, taken off guard by his sudden, close, interest. Now both he and his partner, Knightsbridge, were harboring an obvious grudge against her. She just wanted to move past it and keep things professional, but they were holding on, as though no woman had the right to reject them. Newton pointedly stood and went to join the men, and Croy took over his place beside the body.

The girl was young – she placed her at maybe 14 to 16 annums. She was nude, her skin blanched of natural color, blue in patches and covered in goose bumps, not from the cold but the retraction of hair follicles after death. She also noted some swelling and wrinkling, especially around her hands. Croy stood and grasped one of the anchor poles. She leaned out, trying to see the corpse side-on. The girl's head hung low, her blue lips slightly parted, eyes staring, long fair hair floating in the water. Her arms were outstretched on either side of her body, the chains wrapping around her forearm and wrist. The binds had ripped her skin, but there was no blood, even from the wounds that were above the water level, which suggested to Croy that she had been tied there post-mortem. She leaned back in and glanced at the Sketchers. They had stopped their rapid strokes and stood watching her, hands blackened from the unset charcoal they used.

"All done?" she asked them.

"Yes, Controller," their lead replied.

"Alright." She spoke to trainee Kisslefish, who had come to stand right behind her, breathing down her neck. "Let's drag her up."

"Ah," Kisslefish said, then for once his cheery demeanor slipped. "You mean … with our hands?"

Croy couldn't help but smile. She turned away and heard an *ouff* as Darius shoulder-barged the trainee out of the way. Her partner glanced at the corpse then averted his eyes over the dark, rippling water around them. He hated dealing with the young ones, especially the girls. Once, under heavy alcoholic influence, he'd spoken to Croy of a girl friend from his childhood who had died badly after being attacked by a bunch of smuggler teens. He hadn't given any real details – except one line that had haunted Croy ever since – *They made her into an animal – the way she was screaming.* Croy had tried to ask him about it the next day and he'd pretended he had no idea what she was talking about.

"Excuse me, Controller Croy." A small team of Collectors clustered around them. "We've taken water samples, particles, fabrics and prints. Is there anything else you'd like us to get?"

Croy shook her head. "That will be all."

They nodded and moved away, heading back along the jetty. Croy heard Knightsbridge intercepting them to ask, "Did you get prints?"

"Yes," one of the Collectors replied.

"Particles?"

"Yes."

"Water samples?"

"Yes, and fabrics."

"Well, I want metals and minerals as well," he demanded.

"Controller Croy said she doesn't need anything else," the Collector replied.

"Well, Croy is not primary here, is she?" Knightsbridge snapped. "I am."

"Jackass," Darius muttered beside Croy.

"Leave it," she murmured back.

She dragged her chain cutters out of her kit pack.

"Kisslefish," she said. "Hold here." She indicated the girl's shoulder.

The trainee squatted down and gingerly gripped the corpse.

"Oh ... it's cold ..." he said.

"She ..." Croy corrected. "She is cold."

Kisslefish looked at her, not understanding for a moment, but then it clicked. "She," he repeated, and something shifted in his gaze – a realization – a sadness. He looked again at the girl and repeated softly, "*She* ..."

"Looks like she's been here for two to three turns" Croy spoke to Darius, judging the putrefaction.

"Kisslefish, up!" Knightsbridge barked behind them. He grabbed the trainee by the shirt and pulled him away. Croy noted the kid's calmness. Kisslefish might have been a Purple Wing, but he took getting pushed around surprisingly well. It made her think he was used to it.

Knightsbridge shouldered in beside Croy, trying to make her move over, but she held her position. She cut the chains around the girl's arms and they dragged her up and out of the water, laying her on her back on the jetty. The Sketchers moved around, recording the victim in the new position.

Croy's eyes were immediately drawn to the girl's injuries. Aside from the chain damage, she had significant bruising on her wrists, ankles and high on her inner thighs. There was one deep stab wound in her stomach and numerous shapes and lines – random unintelligible symbols – carved into the skin from her neck to lower stomach.

"Whoa," Kisslefish uttered, staring at the carvings.

"Does this guy have to be here?" Darius said, irritated.

Newton gave him a look that said *yes, unfortunately, he does have to be here.*

Croy studied the symbols. She didn't recognize any of them.

"I'm thinking stab wound was COD," she said.

"COD?" Kisslefish asked.

"Cause of death," Croy told him, and the trainee wrote it down.

"Based on what?" Knightsbridge demanded.

Darius hunched in and studied the injury. "Looks like a flat blade – most likely a 6 fable." He took a knife out of a sheath on his belt and held it up against the wound. "No – too wide – maybe a 5 or a 5-and-a-half, but the angle's not quite right for that either."

Croy took his word on it – he was the weapons expert. Her eyes swept the rest of the body. She spotted something and her skin prickled. She picked up the girl's wrist. It was branded with a deathcode. This body had already been to the Crematorium and been checked in by the Morticians.

"Darry —" Croy called her partner's attention to it.

Darius leaned in closer, putting a hand on Croy's shoulder. She felt his warm breath on the side of her face. Newton eyed them and his frown deepened.

"Why would someone steal a corpse from the Crematorium, mutilate it, then dump it?" Knightsbridge asked.

"It wasn't dumped, it was positioned," Croy said.

"Question still stands," Knightsbridge insisted.

"So *you* answer it, then!" Darius shot back. "As you pointed out, you're primary here!"

"I'm just asking," Knightsbridge said, with a much milder tone.

Croy looked at the victim's face, thinking. The girl's eyes were death-glazed, but still she saw they held some sadness. More than that – despair, confusion. Looking at the girl, Croy sensed fear, she sensed things had been fundamentally wrong. The girl had felt trapped, terrified – and hadn't completely understood why. Her eyes shifted back down to the wound and she said to Darius, "Could this be self-inflicted?"

He narrowed his eyes and moved around to view the injury from different angles.

"You're right," he confirmed. "She stabbed herself."

Croy stood up. She glanced at the Sketchers and said, "Can I have an image of the victim as she was found?"

"Right here, Controller Croy." The Sketcher closest to her stepped forward and handed her a picture of the body chained to the peer. Croy held it up and studied it. Knightsbridge shuffled around beside her to look as well.

"Arms outstretched, head above water level ... water ... why water?" Croy asked.

"To wash away the evidence?" the trainee suggested.

Croy shook her head. "To purify."

"To purify *what*?" Newton spoke up.

"Her suicide, perhaps," Croy said.

"Makes no sense," Knightsbridge argued. "If someone wanted to wash away what this girl did, for her sake or for their own, why would they jack her body from the Crematorium, slice it up and tie it to the end of a pier?"

"I don't know. It's just a theory," Croy said. "But I know where we have to start."

Darius swore and Croy nodded. If "creepy" was a place and had a face it would be the Crematorium and its clan of Morticians. A shiver ran over her back. Knightsbridge and Newton had suddenly gone very quiet.

"Where do we have to start?" Kisslefish asked, looking between them, too green to get it.

"You guys are primary on scene – do you want to go?" Croy asked Knightsbridge, not without some quiet satisfaction.

The musclebound Controller cleared his throat and spoke in a voice a few octaves higher than usual. "I'm not finished my initial assessment. I believe in thorough investigation before running off on a crazy hunch."

"Well how about you continue on with your *initial assessment*," Darius said, his anger exploding. "and we'll go off on our 'crazy hunch' and solve the case for you. How about that?"

"Darius, I wasn't talking about you," Knightsbridge said, backpedaling.

Darius laughed in his quiet way that had nothing to do with humor.

"You really don't get it, do you? If you're talking to Croy, you're talking to *me*. If you hate her, you hate *me*. She's my partner! There's no divide between us!"

He turned and strode back up the pier toward their draggers. Knightsbridge stared at his back, wide-eyed and speechless.

"Can I have a close image, face-up, and a full body with these marks visible?" Croy asked the Sketchers. They handed her the set of parchments and she folded them into her pocket, then spoke to Knightsbridge and Newton. "When the baggers get here, tell them to take the body to the Tower morgue for an in-house autopsy and to put a guard on it."

"You think someone is going to try to take it again?" Knightsbridge asked, incredulous.

"Probably not – but if they do, I don't want to be the one to explain it to VP – do you?" The mention of their boss was enough to quiet any further argument.

Croy slung her kit pack over her shoulder and headed after her partner. Kisslefish looked longingly after her. It was pretty obvious the kid would rather be with them than Knightsbridge and Newton, and she didn't blame him, but Darius had too many disciplinary marks against him to be allocated a trainee. That and he really didn't have the patience for it.

She found her partner sitting on his dragger, smoking a tigaro, simmering. She climbed on her own ride and looked back down the peer. Knightsbridge was ordering the Collectors around and Newton stood instructing Kisslefish on something.

"Why here?" she spoke aloud. "Why bring the body here? There's other water, contaminated, but more accessible."

"Guy's a jackass," Darius fumed about Knightsbridge.

"Forget it," Croy said.

"Forget him! Who does he think he's talking to? Crazy hunches? Who has the most closed cases and the most arrests *of all time*?" Darius said. "You and me! Everyone knows it. We walk into any place, anytime, and people move aside *for us*!"

"I don't think this is about our reputation," Croy said.

"Everything is about reputation," Darius argued. "You turned Newton down, so now they're trying to save face by pushing you, but I'm going to bash their heads in if they don't quit."

"Let it go, Darry. It really doesn't matter," Croy murmured, feeling the heaviness pressing inside her again.

"It matters," Darius said, "to me – you matter." He put his hand over hers on the handlebar of her dragger, but only for a second.

In her mind she was meeting Roth for the first time. He was a Conference assistant who had helped her and Darius drag Miriam Stover's body, stiff with rigor, off the crusher spikes where she'd been impaled after jumping off the Saint Lawless Borough suspension bridge. She was a canker-grass addict and stank of incense. Their eyes had met over the corpse ... *beginning at an end ... there was never any chance* ... Croy swallowed against feelings of painful sadness, manifesting as a dull throb in her chest – sadness because it was over, sadness because she had to start all over again and felt as though she had no emotional energy left. What sort of person was she even looking for? She glanced at her partner. There were feelings there for sure, there always had been an undercurrent, but she had never acted on it – afraid to make the first move and end up looking like an idiot, or worse, damaging their relationship. He was all she had in the world.

Darius revved up his dragger and took off, flying toward the circle of light at the top of the Filter. Croy pushed aside all the distracting thoughts and followed. They were going to the Crematorium, where she'd need all her wits about her, and then more.

Chapter 7

Copernicus

AQUAIS

SCORPIA (SIRENSERON)

Death had always spoken to Copernicus. From its silence, he heard echoes of the past; he saw answers in the bruises and blood. But these crime scene holograms told him nothing of patterns, of purpose or reasoning, fetish, fanaticism or passion. The images just hung in the air, together in time, yet fragmented. He knew there was a connection. He felt it, like a word on the tip of his tongue, a memory on the edge of remembering, but he couldn't see it. He clenched his jaw so tightly he tasted the bitter venom from the fangs behind his teeth.

The confines of the transflyer prevented him from stepping back for a wider overview of the holograms open all around him. Santana, a former United Regiment commander, now leading what was left of the military force – renamed the United Resistance – had asked them to attend this crime scene

at one of the UR refugee camps, but after the fight-in announcement, they hadn't had the time, so Santana had sent
through these images for his opinion. Copernicus understood
that hunting killers and bringing them to justice wasn't his job
anymore, but also that it had never really been just a job.

The first row of shots were grainy surveillance pictures,
taken by a slow rotation spyer, approximately five minutes
apart. They showed a scullion-gypsy family of four reuniting
after losing each other during the war. The overwhelming
relief, the joy, on their faces was so real and intense that
Copernicus even felt it stirring inside him. In the next image
they were all still hugging, heading toward the room where
the mother and daughter had been staying. In the shot after,
through the partially open door of the room, the family were
standing, their poses strangely rigid, their heads hanging low
to their chests. The final image: they were all dead. Santana's
team had taken post-mortem shots, clearer holograms of the
blood splatter and the injuries – three cut throats and one
fatal stab wound to the heart; three murders, one suicide.
Mother as the killer. Before dying, she'd scratched an X into
her own forehead.

The transflyer bumped as Diega pulled up for landing inside the storm-break tunnel on the western side of Palace
Sirenseron, as Jude had recommended. From growing up in
the Palace, he knew that going in from the west would give
them a chance to survey the rest of the grounds from a height
advantage in case of ambush.

Copernicus glanced over at Diega turning down the *Ory's*
engines. She had more bruising around her neck and arms.
She thought he didn't know what she did to herself, but he
could see it clearly. He just chose not to question it at this
stage. As someone who'd been bashed senseless too many
times, he failed to understand why someone would put themselves through it voluntarily, and until he could understand

it he didn't feel that he could speak with her about it. An autopsy of Diega's issues, as well as his own, would have to wait until they weren't under the immediate threat of death.

Silho leaned forward in her seat, looking over his shoulder to the holograms. Her warm fingertips brushed against his neck, sending nerves blazing like electric fire through his body – so hot it almost hurt. He'd never felt so out of control for a woman before – not even for the girlfriend who had cheated with Christy Shawe, the former gangster king, who had once been his best friend. He and Shawe had resolved old anger and reconnected during the battle against the Skreaf, and now he felt he could look objectively on this past. He remembered that even before the cheating, he'd always been sceptical of the word "love". He'd felt like it was an indefinable emotion that people forced into a fabricated word to make more sense of their lives. But now he actually felt it – *love* – so powerful that it was becoming increasingly difficult to focus on anything other than his need for her, not just to be near her, but with her. He needed to show her how he felt, otherwise he was going to lose his mind. All they needed was some time alone when somebody wasn't trying to kill them. He would make it happen – after the fight-in.

"Scullions," Silho said close to his ear. "They're seeing a vision."

Her words jolted him back to clarity. He hadn't picked it up, but he should have – the people in the crime scene holograms were scullion seers.

Diega glanced over at the images and demanded, "How do you get 'vision' from them looking at the ground?"

"I grew up in the Matadori," Silho reminded her. "We often camped near scullion settlements and towns, and I saw this all the time, groups of them standing together to strengthen their sight."

Copernicus looked back and saw Jude watching Silho with some resentment in his eyes. He used his viper bloodline skills to study Jude's heat pattern and the vibration of his thoughts. The Ar Antarian was burning up with anger. Copernicus had never seen Jude angry at Silho before – it had always been the aggravating opposite. So something must have changed. Something must have happened. Copernicus' jealousy twitched, but he reasoned if Jude was furious, that could only mean he wasn't getting what he wanted – *who* he wanted. Silho.

"So," Diega continued, "you're saying – here they are happy back together, then they see a vision – and the mother goes crazy? That must have been some vision. Maybe they saw the gruel the camp cook was making for their dinner."

Jude's silver skin flushed. "You're joking about the dead?"

"Sorry. I didn't realize you were so religious," Diega mocked.

"And I didn't realize you were so heartless," he shot back. "Seems to be the current trend with you women."

"Either way," Silho said, and Copernicus heard the tightness of her voice and sensed her body-heat flare up as well, "it's never a good sign when the people with the strongest intuition about the future start killing themselves."

Diega snorted. "Strongest intuition! Brabel, seriously – there's no such thing as *seeing* the future. They're a bunch of addicts, lunatics and charlatans."

Usually Copernicus would have shared Diega's cynicism, but something about Silho's words kept him quiet. Since they'd defeated the Skreaf and returned from Woulghast, he'd had a bad feeling, an ominous ill-ease, as though something was following them, but every time he turned around there was nothing there. He hadn't spoken to the others about it. They were already stressed and anxious enough as it was, and there was the possibility that his feelings were just a hangover from running so close to death in Woulghast – and that these hologram images just showed a random tragedy.

From the backseat, Eli stifled a half-giggle, half-cry. Copernicus glanced back at him. The imp-breed was staring at the holograms and looking green. Since becoming a tracker, Eli had been involved in many investigations of brutal murder, and Copernicus knew it got to him more than any of the others, but he'd never seen Eli so on edge before. The war had taken its toll on all of them.

"You with me, Eli?" he asked.

Eli immediately lifted his head and said, "No – I mean, yes. Yes. Definitely yes."

He took his otter out of his pocket and wiped his nose on her, before realizing she wasn't his handkerchief. He looked startled, embarrassed and apologetic to the otter, and Copernicus turned away pretending he hadn't noticed.

"Good. Let's move out, then," he said to the other trackers.

He jumped down from the craft and stretched out his legs, flexing his toes inside his boots. He'd spent the past few hours training and getting strapped up. He felt ready to face Caesar. He wasn't ego-blinded enough to think it wasn't going to be a difficult fight, but he was confident he could take him. Caesar's greatest advantage as a fighter was his speed – and Copernicus was faster. He'd proved that in the desert and he was sure the King of the Pride hadn't forgotten either – so he already had a mental advantage.

From beside him, Diega called, "*Eizenef aregz'amon*," and with a crack of magics morphed the *Ory-5* into a silver coin.

She started to push it into a pocket on her belt but Copernicus said, "No – hide it in your boot or somewhere. If something goes down and we lose our belts, I want to make certain we have transport."

Diega nodded. Jude pointed to the sphere of light at the end of the storm-break tunnel and said, "There's a viewing platform there that overlooks the palace gardens to the Hero's Walk and Oberon's Arena."

"Take the lead," Copernicus told him, and Jude gave what looked like a shrug of annoyance before complying. They moved out, their bootsteps echoing through the tunnel.

They came out where Jude had described – a thin balcony looking out over a vast expanse of garden and the great dome of the amphitheater glimmering in the new light of the sunsrise. The air behind and around the dome was blackened with the hordes of transflyers, mass-movers and flighted people descending in for the fight – and further still behind them, in the mists of the far distance, Palace Sirenseron rose imposing and magnificent into the clouds.

Copernicus sensed a sharp spike in Jude's heat and looked over. He appeared composed and expressionless behind his black-lens glasses, metal arms crossed over his chest and SevenM perched on his shoulder, but inside he was a mess. It was no wonder. He had more reason than any of them to be stressed. Not only was he half-machine-breed, about to be completely surrounded by gangsters who had spent the last months slaughtering and imprisoning his kind, but he was also half-brother to the Androts' fallen leader, Kry, as well as the heir to the Ar Antarian throne. He was the rightful king returning to the Palace, the home he'd fled from after his uncle found out his true bloodline and tried to have him killed. It was a lot to deal with in one hit. Copernicus considered that maybe this was the only reason behind his agitation, but the way Silho had been avoiding Jude's eyes suggested otherwise. His body tensed. He wanted to know exactly what had happened – right now – but he restrained himself from questioning Jude. The team had to focus and stay together, at least a little longer. After the fight-in, he and Jude were going to have a conversation, and if he found out he'd done anything to Silho, there was going to be serious trouble. Best case scenario: Jude would be out of the trackers and out of their lives, permanently. Silho kept saying she was handling it, but Copernicus sensed the situation had gone beyond her control. She didn't understand the way feelings could get twisted.

Eli was also watching Jude, but with concern rather than suspicion, and came out with the question most men, Copernicus admittedly included, were too afraid to ask.

"Are you okay, Jude?"

The Ar Antarian remained silent for several moments, looking as though he was wrestling with his words. Finally he said, "I've failed."

"What do you mean?" Eli asked.

"The Androts ... I should have done more to help them, to change things, but instead I hid."

"You weren't hiding!" Eli told him. "You went into Woulghast and saved the world!"

Jude pressed his lips together – it wasn't enough. Copernicus understood. Jude felt called to the plight of the Androts.

"And you've been doing everything you can to help the machine-breeds ever since," Eli continued.

"I should have done more!" Jude raised his voice. "I should have stepped into the war and tried to stop Kry or even helped him. Look at what's happening to the machine-breeds now! Caged, beaten, starved, slaughtered – for what? The innocent suffering for the madness of a few ..."

"And that's why we're here," Copernicus said. "To fight Caesar and win their freedom."

"And if you lose?" Jude asked. The question seemed to echo out over the vastness of the garden, amplifying Copernicus' silence. Before, Jude would never have questioned him.

Eli's stomach yodeled mournfully, Copernicus swallowed his ill-ease and Jude ran a hand over the Androt barcode on his neck. Copernicus eyed the mark – he'd told Jude he needed to cover it and that he needed to keep SevenM hidden. Clearly he wasn't in the mood to be told, but it was for his safety and the safety of the whole team, and Copernicus wasn't going to compromise that for anyone's emotional turmoil.

"You want to free your people? Put the robot in your bag and cover your neck," he said to Jude firmly enough for Eli to break out in red splotches.

For a moment he thought Jude was going to challenge him again, but then he relented just as Diega and Silho caught up with them.

Silho stared, awed by the vision of the palace before them. The red highlights of her hair glowed like strands of fire in the sunslight. Diega just drew her electrifier and said, "Are we doing this or what?"

"Arm up," Copernicus responded, and they all unsheathed their weapons.

As Silho drew hers, a piece of paper fluttered out from her belt. She lunged for it, but Eli moved quicker, snatching it out of the air. He went to give it back to her, but she hesitated to take it. Copernicus sensed something strange about her heat pattern, an unusual flare of mixed feelings. He took the paper from Eli instead and opened it, he saw the words – *In my mother's house are many mansions – Silho Brabel.*

"I found it," Silho told him, apprehension tightening her voice, "at the house. It has my name on it, but my father never knew that name. I thought maybe Bellum had put it there; maybe there was some kind of curse or enchant attached to it."

Jude immediately took Silho's shoulder, his anger at her forgotten. He turned her toward him to let SevenM check her. "Do you feel okay?" he asked.

"I think so," Silho said, not meeting his eyes. She stepped back from him, but Jude stepped forward again, keeping his grip on her arms.

"You need to say if you don't feel right."

Diega rolled her eyes and Copernicus fought against the urge to drag Silho away from him.

Eli stepped in fast. "I can run some tests? See who or what wrote it?"

"Good," Copernicus agreed. Eli took out a bag, and Copernicus dropped the letter inside. Silho's eyes lifted from the paper to his. Jude watched the exchange.

"Time to go," Copernicus said, he stepped over the edge and walked down the vertical slope to the gardens, while the others unfurled their hook-ropes and rappelled down.

* * * * *

Together the trackers walked, each wearing full military garb and body armor, down the Steps of Consequence, to a square landing that led through the Hero's Walk to Oberon's Arena where the fight-in would take place. The square was packed to capacity, and their presence drew immediate attention that spread like fueled fire through the masses. Soon everyone had turned to stare. Copernicus scanned over the crowd, over the people who would fight for the title of Boss, standing with their support groups. Most races and sub-races were represented, with the exception of marine-breeds, plant-breeds and spectral-breeds – and there were no machine-breeds of any type.

Copernicus kept the trackers moving, leading them to the edge of the crowd. It shifted and a path opened for them to walk through. It should have felt powerful, stepping up to a crowd of this magnitude and having it roll back and part before him – a sea of flaring body-heat, fear and hope, anxiety and excitement crashing in sparking red-orange waves – but it didn't. There were too many staring eyes, too many thoughts and feelings and questions pressing in on him, pushing down on him. He hated the attention, but circumstances were what they were and either he had to be here now or somewhere else, hiding – and he didn't hide. Copernicus knew he was many things – most of them ugly – but he was not a coward. He looked for Santana and his United Resistance soldiers, but couldn't see or sense any of them. It was strange that they hadn't arrived yet.

The trackers started through the crowd, which pushed back further to let them through. Everyone avoided Copernicus' eyes, but stared at his back when he'd passed, staying on him all the way to the front where the gangsters and their animals had assembled. Many of them he recognized. They all glared him down with expressions that said he was a rat and a dog and would never be anything but that. Their hostility rolled off him without leaving a mark.

Each of the gangs were accounted for, except for the Greenway Galleys. Christy Shawe's absence left a big hole, figuratively and literally. Copernicus had spoken to him just after the Lancaster Square announcement, trying to convince him not to attend. He'd told Shawe the truth – as soon as he and the Galleys got there, Shawe's ego would make him challenge Caesar, and then he would most definitely lose. His eyesight was poor and he had never been quick. Galleys were made to fight in groups, back to back, relying on their strength and endurance to wear down their enemy. If Christy could land a punch, it would be deadly, but Caesar was too fast for that, and although Christy's skin was armor-tough, Caesar's claws were the sharpest of retractile razors and he would keep at Shawe until he hit an artery and bled him out. Christy needed to keep his head down now and challenge later when circumstances were more in his favor. Fortunately, and for the first time ever, Christy Shawe had listened.

Finally the team pushed through to the front of the gangsters, where the Pride, decked out in their gold and purple, stood on the steps leading up to the Hero's Walk, a long ceilingless hallway that the gladiators used to pass through to get to the amphitheater. At the front of the Pride were Caesar's eight daughters and his cousin Smudge, with her black panther, Inski, sitting beside her. Woman and cat narrowed their yellow eyes, exactly in sync.

Behind them, the walls of the Walk were hung with the rarest and most valuable art of Scorpia, guarded by statues of all the Ar Antarian kings, the first to the last, from Oberon U to Miron U XI. Half of the statues had been smashed up and replaced with carved lions. The head of one of the stone kings rolled off as they stood there, and fell through a window in the Walk, crashing many stories to Level 2 below. A very distant boom sounded a minute later. Copernicus glanced at Jude. He could see Jude was angered, but on the surface still remained cool and composed. Diega, on the other hand, made no effort at all to hide her contempt, both for the setting and for the gangsters around her. She was keeping her electrifier primed. The colors of her rainbow skin flashed warnings, her eyes blazing with hostility. She was standing nearer to Jude than she had in a long time. Since the bust-up of their relationship, they had been like negatively charged magnets. Eli stood close to Copernicus' elbow on one side with Silho on the other. The Oscuri Trackers, fractured in places but united in purpose, stepped up to the Pride.

Moments later, the shadows of the Hero's Walk stirred and Caesar K-Ruz appeared, flanked by his great lions, his young son at his side, looking like a miniature version of his father. At the sight of the Pride King, sound just evaporated. Copernicus completely blanked his expression and straightened his form. He could see Eli's wings trembling under his shirt, where he kept them bound with bandages to stop himself spontaneously taking flight during moments of stress. Caesar came to the front of the Walk where he stood, unnaturally still, casting a huge lion shadow over the wall behind him. The very tip of the shadow lion's tail twitched and Caesar narrowed his darkly-rimmed golden eyes. Copernicus wasn't swayed by his theatrics and mind games. To him Caesar still looked like he had when they were kids – except now he'd grown a beard and a massive ego. On either side of where the Pride King stood, two gigantic holograms of Caesar sparked to life. Copernicus could see the gangsters had set up a city-wide feedback system that would project holograms of the event down through all the levels.

Caesar spoke with his smooth Crook'd Town accent. Without raising his voice, his words carried easily across the entire square.

"You, who have come here today, believe yourselves worthy to be the bosses of your people. You will fight for this honor and you will fight for your land. Every level of Scorpia 650 and above will today be allocated. All major skyways and mass-transfer elevators are neutral territory. No fighting shall take place in neutral territory. This is the gangster way and it will be respected or the gangs will punish you. Every level below 650 is no man's land – enter at your own risk – as is the Matadori Desert from the city wall to the boundary wall.

"I will lay the first claim to land – the Crook'd Town Pride claims Level 1 Sirenseron, Level 2 Standingbar and Level 3 Sejon – and all of Crook'd Town will remain ours from Oldfield to the Greenway borderline. Is there anyone here who wishes to challenge me on this?"

Copernicus sensed the heat of each of his team members flare, but he felt calm. The moment had come.

He stepped forward and said, "I challenge you."

Even the silence fell silent as though everyone was not only holding their tongues, but now also their breath. A hologram of Copernicus opened up beside that of Caesar.

"But not for land. I challenge you for rights over the machine-breeds. I make claim to their race, and I will fight for them. It is the gangster way."

Caesar's eyebrows flickered with surprise. He hadn't expected this, and if he refused it would look as though he didn't believe in his own law. Copernicus could see Caesar was thinking fast, but not fast enough. He met Copernicus' eyes and started to accept.

"I challenge you for Level 1, 2, 3 – *and* Crook'd Town!" Another voice boomed out over the crowd. Copernicus turned to see Christy Shawe and what remained of the Greenway Galleys stomping toward them. Immediately all the gathered gangsters raised their voices, yelling their calls and holding up their hand signs, their animals growling, shrieking and snapping. It would be a rumble of the biggest Bosses of their time.

"I accept," Caesar snarled.

Copernicus cursed. He felt like shooting Shawe dead on the spot. He was sabotaging their one chance to save the machine-breeds without resorting to all-out battle. The former gangster king was closing in fast on Caesar, making it clear this wouldn't be going down in the arena. It was happening right here, right now and there would be nothing civilized about it. Shawe would die.

Caesar gestured his son aside and backed further into the Hero's Walk, getting one of the walls behind him – smart compared to Shawe, whose only strategy was to clench his fists. In response, Caesar flicked out his claws with the sound of ten blades being drawn from their sheaths. He lowered his stance, ready to lunge.

Copernicus turned to the trackers and said, "Go to Plan B. We hit the machine-breed prison camps while the Pride is occupied. Move out! Go!"

They started to press back through the surging crowd, but then something in the wall behind K-Ruz seized Copernicus' enhanced sense of heat. It looked as though a fire had blazed to life inside the actual rock. The intensity grew until the painting hanging in front of the inferno exploded out, taking half the brickwork with it, and leaving a crater rift and sheer drop to Level 2 below. Both Christy and Caesar were blasted sideways, with burning debris crashing down on the Pride and other gangs inciting a howling, panicking stampede.

Amidst the chaos, Copernicus saw Caesar's little son with his clothes ablaze. He was running, screaming, fueling the flames – heading toward the broken wall and the drop. His mother chased behind him, but she was too slow, one leg smashed up by the fallout.

Copernicus took off, leaping up the stairs, ripping his jacket free as he ran. He caught the kid on the edge of the rift and threw the jacket over him, tackling him to the ground – rolling him over and over until he'd smothered the fire. Half a second later Caesar was there, grabbing the boy out of his arms, terror in his eyes. He dragged back the jacket. His son was sobbing, his clothes scorched and back burned, but he was alive. Caesar's eyes lifted to Copernicus, then the shrieking mother struck and threw herself down on top of her boy. The general crowd had dispersed, everyone yelling and fleeing. Those who had not escaped lay twisted, burning. The gangsters were starting to regather and return, not strangers to violence and death.

Copernicus heard Eli's sudden shout for him and spun around. His first thought on the explosion had been *bomb*, but now he saw they were actually under attack. Foreign soldiers stood among them, throwing flames and breathing fire, reducing people to piles of ash. Copernicus' eyes zeroed in on their firebird dragon bloodline marks. *Omarian.* But how could it be? The Wraith had said Silho was the last Omarian left. Clearly she was in error and now they were here with the intention to harm.

Copernicus scanned the confusion for Silho. He spotted Christy Shawe pinned under a fallen column but fighting to free himself. Diega stood close by, in the middle of the battle, trading electrifier shots for fire blasts with one of the Omarian attackers. Further behind her, on the other side of the platform, Eli, Jude and Silho had retreated behind a lion statue. He could see the main bulk of Omarians, directed by their commander, closing fast around them. The leader's eyes were fixed on Silho and he was moving in from the side, keeping in her blind spot. Copernicus sensed in that moment that they were there for Silho and everyone else was just white noise.

Bands of fear and fury tightened across his chest. He grabbed his electrifier and opened fire, blasting two of the enemy in the back. Others turned, coming at him, sending burning missiles roaring his way. He lunged sideways and rolled back to his feet, catching sight of the Omarian leader barging faster toward Silho. She was distracted by the forward-pressing attack, but SevenM, now perched on Jude's shoulder, saw him coming from behind.

The robot alerted Jude and he whipped around and ran forward to intercept the leader's path. The Omarian sidestepped his attack, then raised his hand, driving a dagger deep into Jude's chest, cutting straight through the heavy-duty armor. The Ar Antarian instantly fell. Eli saw him go down and tried to run to him, but the leader smashed him aside, ramming him face-first into the rock wall. Eli folded in on himself and lay where he fell.

The Omarian reached Silho and grabbed her from behind, his arm tight around her neck. She struggled violently, changing to light-form vision, but she couldn't shake him. Something was wrong with her skills. They weren't working and he was overwhelming her, a disturbing look of savage ecstasy on his face. Every instinct and emotion drove Copernicus forward. He flew toward them, boots crashing over rubble and bodies alike. The battle fell silent around him and all he heard was his own heart thudding. He leaped over a fallen column and saw, from the corner of his eye, Caesar jumping beside him. They landed without breaking their stride, closing the distance fast.

The Omarian leader turned and saw them coming. He hurled a fireball into their faces. It knocked them back, but Copernicus rolled immediately to his feet, numb to the pain, his eyes on Silho. He ducked beneath another blast and surged forward. A droning sound vibrated through the air, and all Copernicus' strength rushed from his body. He slumped to his knees, too weak even to stand. He'd experienced this before with Silho – light-form vision – but not like this, never this strong. Caesar thudded down incapacitated beside him.

The enemy leader gestured to his men to finish them and two Omarian warriors closed in, draining their life-force. Copernicus heard Silho scream for him, the sound echoing and fading, as the Omarian stopped in front of him, spitting sparks from his mouth, ready to exhale Copernicus' life-force when it surged through him and out. The warrior looked him right in the eyes and sneered, then the Omarian's face exploded as Christy Shawe's fist punched through his head. Gore splattered down on Copernicus. The Omarian draining Caesar lashed out and stabbed Shawe in the back with a dagger that looked as though it was attached to his arm. Shawe whirled around, smashed him to the ground and stomped him dead.

Free from the light-form, Copernicus staggered to his feet. He spotted the Omarian leader on the move, dragging Silho toward the shattered wall, toward the edge of the drop. He shoved through the mass of gangsters battling Omarians and ran toward them, but he was moving so slowly, his body weakened. He grunted, digging deeply into the reserves of his mental strength, pushing every last ounce of his remaining physical power into getting to Silho. He could see the leader's arm tightening around her neck, choking the life out of her. Copernicus' own throat constricted in response.

Another fireball crashed into him from one side, setting his shirt alight. He ripped it off and kept running, finally reaching the stairs. Just above him the Omarian was hauling Silho to the broken wall. It looked as if he was trying to throw her over the edge. She'd ripped bleeding lines in his arms, fighting to get free. Copernicus staggered up the stairs and, ducking beneath a blast of fire, lunged and grabbed Silho's legs. The leader kicked him in the face, smashing him backward. He barked a command at his soldiers and they advanced on Copernicus from all sides. He scrambled back to Silho, seizing her around the waist as the Leader thrashed her around, trying to push her through the rift.

Copernicus saw an Omarian dagger coming from his left and tried to block, but was too slow, drastically weakened by the light-form attack, with blood gushing from a wound in his forehead from the leader's pointed shoe. Caesar was suddenly at his side. The Pride King intercepted the blade, and with a slash of his claws, he took off the attacker's whole arm. Another Omarian trapped Caesar in light-form, but his hold was short-lived, as Diega shot him from behind as she ran up the stair. She blasted another round toward the leader's head, but he roared fire, consuming the shot before it reached him. Diega dodged the flames and started morphing everything around them into weapons to stab at the Omarian leader, trying to make him release Silho, but everything they did only made him tighten his grip, harder and harder, until Silho was making empty, dragging gasps, completely unable to draw breath.

Shawe crashed in over Diega and smashed the Omarian in the mouth. The impact shunted his head backward and burned Shawe's fist. Shawe shouted a curse, but the leader just smiled at them with bloodied teeth. It was a chilling, deranged smile. Copernicus knew a psychopath when he saw one, and the terror that shot through him forced him to his feet.

He grabbed Silho's shoulders and sunk his fangs into the Omarian's arm around her neck, but still it didn't budge. Silho grasped uselessly at his chest, her gasps coming fainter and fewer. Almost blind with panic, Copernicus started to summon an Illusionist enchant to try to confuse the leader, but the Omarian raised his dagger and stabbed Copernicus through the shoulder. Immediately he lost control of his arm. He could feel poison burning through him. He slumped back to his knees, still hanging onto Silho. His senses were fading, but he held on, refusing to let her go. Through misting sights, he saw her attacker slide a small picture from his pocket. He spoke with a rough snarl: "Behind the red star smiles the darkness – Omar Montanya." A blinding light flared inside the picture frame and the ground dropped away beneath them. The last image in Copernicus' mind was Silho's eyes, looking down at him, closing.

Chapter 8
Eli

AQUAIS

SCORPIA (SIRENSERON)

They first met on the corner of Jabiru and Egret streets. He was eight year-cycles old and had just launched his first self-designed, remote-controlled miniature replica transflyer. He was completely lost in the moment – running, leaping, laughing, flying the small craft through the streets. The feeling was pure childhood joy, and in that moment, he was sure without a sliver of doubt that he was going to be the greatest inventor of all time. In fact he highly suspected he might even be a god, or at least closely related to one. And then he hit face-first into a brick wall.

The impact slammed him onto his back, and he lay there gasping in shock. The brick wall shifted, it turned, and Eli saw it wasn't really a brick wall – it was a muscle wall, with a face. Fierce green eyes glared him down and a huge, meaty hand grabbed him by the front of his shirt. It dragged him up at a dizzying speed, bringing him face to face with a human-breed boy who must have been only a few year-cycles older, but had the muscles of a fully grown man. He had a scarred-up face and, along his arms, the horn-like shapes of the Galley bloodline marks.

"Smash him, Christy!" a squeaky adolescent voice, with a Greenway accent, yelled out from somewhere behind the boy. Only then did Eli realize that in his blind bliss he'd inadvertently stumbled into the gangland, and right into Christy Shawe, son of the Galley boss. Eli burst into hysterical laughter and passed out cold.

He woke several moments later to find himself sprawled on the sidewalk with a massive boot about to stomp down on his face. It pulled back just before it hit and Eli saw another human-breed boy, with viper bloodline marks and eyes like a starless night, dragging Christy Shawe away from him.

"Let him be, he's just a kid," the boy said, and there was something profoundly powerful about his voice that made Eli stare. His face was even more scarred than Christy Shawe's and his presence a million times more frightening.

Shawe shoved the viper-blood boy off him, but instead of proceeding to pulverize Eli's face, he stomped down on the miniature transflyer, smashing it to pieces. He spat on Eli and slouched off with his gang-mates – all but the black-eyed boy, who stayed behind. The boy crouched down and picked up the destroyed flyer by its tail. He looked it over, then his gaze lifted to Eli.

"Where did you buy this?" he asked.

Eli willed himself to talk normally, to make sense – desperate to impress. Instead he began babbling absolute gibberish while cackling uncontrollably.

The boy stared at him – *through* him – and somehow heard what Eli was trying to say.

"Can you re-make it?" he asked.

Eli pinched his lips together with one hand to stop himself from talking, and managed to nod once.

The boy stood and held out a hand to help him up. As Eli reached for it, Copernicus' face changed to Ev'r's.

She whispered, "My friend ... I'm finished. Keep going."

And she changed into the monster, into the Ravien, and lunged at him ...

Eli jolted from a sleeping nightmare into waking terror. His senses bombarded him, screaming, shouting, competing for his first dazed attentions – charred air, tangy blood, crying, yelling, electrifiers zapping, a tapestry burning above his head, cool tiles under his wings, and pain ... above all else *p-a-i-n*. It pulsated and swelled until it consumed all his other senses.

Grimacing, Eli rolled onto his side and maneuvered himself up inch by inch. Blinding agony stabbed through his right arm. He gasped and a wave of lightbrain threatened to level him again. He swayed, fighting to keep himself conscious. A warm stream of blood trickled into one eye. He swiped it away with his good hand. The other arm he kept frozen against his chest, not daring to move it again. He could see the bone was broken and pressing up against the skin. Sweat prickled his back and face. His fingers fumbled over his weapon belt, feeling for the shape of his anesthetic shots. He found the syringe and lifted it out. Gritting his teeth, he stabbed the needle into his broken arm. There was one more second of torture and then the pain faded out. The sweats and faints subsided, and he was able to see past his injury to the scene before him.

The Hero's Walk was devastated – artworks hung precariously askew, blood splattered the walls, and heaped piles of ashes covered the ground. The square was largely deserted now too, except for groups of gangsters running around, shouting commands, searching, confused. Eli scanned over the faces he could see – *no commander, no Silho, no Diega ...*

no Jude. A cold dread filtered through Eli's shock. He grabbed at his pocket to check Nelly and found her curled up in there, not sleeping, just trembling.

"It's alright, girl," he whispered to her, but his voice was shaking so much he could barely form the words. Not exactly reassuring.

He fumbled with a bandage from his belt, and rapidly formed a sling for his arm. As he struggled to his feet, snatches of memory returned to him. Something had attacked – he hadn't seen clearly who or what – the smoke and fire had half-blinded him. He'd just felt the heat and heard Jude yell, and he'd run toward the sound of his voice.

"Call the commander," he told his front-core, continuing to search up and down the long open-air hallway. The com system reached out, but immediately flat-lined. Eli blinked open the menu. He checked the commander's status and one word came up: *Deceased*.

"Not possible …" Eli whispered. "Reboot," he ordered the system, and waited for it to come back online.

Terrible feelings constricted his chest. Nelly crawled out of his pocket and wound around his neck, so stressed she started eating the collar of his shirt. More blood dripped into his eye and he grabbed the coagulator from his belt and sprayed the wound to stem the stream.

He heard a clatter of rocks behind him and Nelly darted back into his pocket as Smudge and Inski burst from the shadows. They almost knocked him down as they ran past.

"Smudge!" he called to Caesar's cousin.

She glanced back at him, her eyes confused and distressed.

"What happened? Where is everyone?"

She shook her head and kept going.

The front-core flickered back on, but the commander's status remained *Deceased*. Tears rushed to Eli's eyes and he started shaking. He was standing in ashes. This wasn't possible ...

"Focus," he whispered. "Do something."

Through misted sights he spotted the computer system the Pride had set up to project the fight-in. Eli limped to it and dropped down in front of the box. He hacked into the feedback function and sent the footage to his implant. A hologram recording of the attack opened and replayed in front of his eyes. He knew the attackers had been actual people, but on the recording they appeared as pillars of fire. He wasn't sure why, and tried dropping some quick filters and debugs over the footage to fix it, but nothing immediately worked. He saw Jude being engulfed by flames, then himself running in to try to help him, only to be swatted away like a mosquito. He watched the flames reach Silho, and the commander and others fighting for her, the chaos moving closer and closer to the broken wall, until there was an explosion of white light and it looked as if they all fell over the edge of the rift.

Eli blinked out of the footage and ran for the smashed-up wall. He stepped carefully out onto the crumbling edge and peered down. Several stories below, the remnants of the stonework had crashed onto a crossing bridge, beneath that was a staggering drop to Level 2. Eli couldn't see any movement on the bridge, but it was possible that the team was down there, buried by the avalanche of rocks. Eli zipped up his pocket so that Nelly couldn't unexpectedly jump out, then grabbed the blade off his belt and slid it down the back of his shirt, cutting the bandages binding his wings. Once they were free, he took a deep breath and jumped off the edge. Immediately the savage high winds snatched him up and tried to smash him into the side of the Hero's Walk. He fought against it with all his strength – struggling, pushing, straining to fly down to the bridge. He only barely made it, overshooting his landing and having to grabble one-handed before finally dragging himself up.

"Heat scan," he told his implant, moving his eyes over the rubble. It found nothing.

He changed scan-type to body shape and looked again. The front-core beeped as it picked up on something and zeroed in on the location. It was a man's form. Eli ran, scrambling through the ruins to the indicated spot. He grabbed up handfuls of rock, hurling them aside, digging desperately until finally he touched something cold. He seized hold of it and dragged it out from the debris. A metal hand attached to a metal arm.

"Jude!" Eli shouted, the sound swallowed by the wind.

He shoved rocks and dirt off Jude's face and chest. He found his other arm was crushed under a slab of rock, white Androt blood spilling out from where the prosthetic had half ripped away from skin and flesh. SevenM lay beside Jude. Both were unmoving.

"Jude, wake up!" Eli shook him, but he didn't stir. He wasn't breathing. Eli checked his pulse – nothing. With shaking hands, Eli grabbed the coronary defibrillation device off his belt. He turned the settings to full strength and positioned it over Jude's chest, waiting for the green light. It flashed on and Eli brought the paddles downward. Just before they contacted with Jude, SevenM struggled to lift his torso, teetering for a moment, then collapsing again. Eli stared in shock. SevenM moving meant Jude was still alive – but with no signs of life.

"Show neural patterning," Eli ordered his front-core. It brought up a display of his friend's brain. Everything was still functioning, but his body had completely shut down. After a moment of confusion, Eli spotted an injury in Jude's side. He hadn't immediately seen it because of the dust and rock fragments. It was a stab wound, and it looked as though the blade had been coated with some kind of necrotic poison. Jude's skin and muscles around the injury had blackened and eroded away. It was a devastating enough injury to have triggered his Androt half into shutting him down. But he was still alive – and that was all that mattered.

"I'm here, Jude, I won't leave you," Eli told him as he grabbed tourniquet pins off his belt and injected them all around the wound to stop the poison spreading. He was reaching for a bandage when he felt the bridge shiver and tilt with the ominous sound of straining metal. It was about to break away and drop without relief to Level 2.

Eli looked around wildly for something to help him lift Jude. He had explosives on his belt that could implode the boulder pinning Jude's arm, but Androts, even half-breeds, were extremely heavy – none of his equipment was made for supporting that weight. Eli spotted a window leading into a lower level of the palace grounds below the Hero's Walk.

"I'll be right back, I promise," he said to Jude.

He ran across the groaning bridge and darted through the window. There were still masses of people from the fight-in crowd fleeing on foot to Level 2, where the public elevator system was reportedly up and running. Eli scanned the crowd and one group of people immediately sprang into focus. They were impossible to miss. A family of Corámorán Giants, gargantuan-breeds, was lumbering toward the stairs. There were at least ten of them, but Eli only needed one. He half-ran, half-flew over the top of the crowd, finally reaching the Corámoráns. He ran alongside three of them, shouting, "Can you help me? Please – my friend is stuck! The bridge is collapsing!"

When he got no response, he sped up to the next cluster of four, "Please – my frie—"

One of them lazily swished his club and swiped Eli away. He skidded across the floor, under the feet of the crowd, and rolled out the other side, hitting the wall with a thud. He scrambled back up and looked across to the giants. Only one was left, walking slower, with her arms and legs in shackles. Eli flew to her side.

"Please," he called out to her. "My friend. He's not stuck – I mean, he's stuck – he's *stuck*. The bridge – it's falling. Please, will you help?"

She turned her head, and he saw himself reflected in the deep dark of her eyes – then she nodded.

Eli almost fainted with relief. The giant held up her chained wrists and he grabbed the cutter off his belt and freed her. She shook off the binds.

"This way!" Eli called. He led her back to the window. She busted through it and stepped onto the bridge, which rumbled and tilted more under each of her giant steps.

"This rock is pinning him!" Eli yelled above the wind, pointing to the slab crushing Jude's arm.

The giant lifted it and threw it aside with enough strength to make even the immensely powerful Christy Shawe look pathetically weedy. Eli carefully folded Jude's damaged arm across his chest. There was no time to set it. The bridge was sinking fast. The Corámorán sensed it too. She lifted Jude without straining and Eli snatched up SevenM. They made a run for the window, but before they made it, the bridge broke away and started to fall. The giant lunged for the ledge and hooked it with one arm. Eli buzzed his wings and grabbed onto her back. She dragged them both through and they landed down inside the chamber, breathing heavily.

Eli's eyes went to hers and he started to say, "Thank you so —"

A spiked club crashed down on the Corámorán's head, smashing her sideways. She crouched over Jude as the group of giants closed in on her, roaring and raining club blows down on her head and back. They were going to kill her.

"Stop!" Eli screamed at them, with zero effect.

He grabbed the electrifier off his belt and released a blast into the ceiling.

The giants bellowed at him, but he kept firing, forcing them back. When they finally retreated, Eli turned his attention to the bashed giantess. He didn't know why they'd returned to hurt her, and there wasn't time now to find out.

"Are you okay?" He grabbed her arm.

She blinked, dazed and bleeding, but managed to nod.

"We have to go and find a transflyer. Can you walk?" he asked her.

With a grunt she maneuvered her massive bulk upright, lifting Jude with her.

Eli led them up a flight of stairs, back to the top story of Level 1 and through the garden to the landing platforms where all the transflyers had been parked. He'd been hoping there would be something left they could use, but everyone had flown out. He looked back at the giant holding Jude like a ragdoll. He was so still.

A violent gust of wind shoved Eli back, turning him toward the city view. Scorpia, like the shimmering body of a giant beast, stretched out into the desert before him. His mind spun. What should he do? Who was left he could trust? One name came to mind.

"Call Commander Santana," he ordered his front-core.

The system buzzed and connected with the simpler com system the Fen sniper commander still used.

"Anklebiter?" Santana spoke.

"It's not me," Eli said, then cursed. "I mean – it's me. Are you in Sirenseron?"

"Negative. We're still on our way. There was trouble with the craft. Are K-Ruz and Commander Kane in the rink yet?"

Eli paused. "Something's happened – I need your help …"

Santana's voice darkened. "We're close. We can see the Palace now. What's your location?"

"East. Landing Quadrant."

"Sit tight. Almost on you."

The connection ended and almost immediately Eli heard the drone of the United Resistance craft, an ancient, blimpish mass-mover. He checked on Nelly as it touched down on the other end of the quadrant. She was busy biting holes in his pocket. Santana and a bunch of soldiers jumped out and ran across the zone in formation, their electrifiers drawn.

"What happened here?" Santana shouted when he was close enough. "Looks like a bomb blast!" He saw Eli's arm and cursed, then looked behind him to Jude and cursed louder.

"We were attacked. Enemy unknown. Jude needs help fast," Eli told him.

"We'll take him to the refuge center."

"No, I need my equipment. I need to go to our hide in Moris-Isles."

Santana's face twitched and Eli felt a sinking in his gut.

"What is it?"

"I got word from some Spotters. Your boarding house has been burned down ..."

The mention of fire stirred Eli's senses. Why were they being targeted? Was it connected to the witches? His mind jumped to Silho's note in his pocket.

"I have a hangar. We can go there instead," Eli said. "I've stored copies of mostly everything."

"Whatever you need," Santana told him. "Commander Kane?"

Eli flinched and Santana said, "Tell me on the way."

The Fen beckoned to the giant and the group of them ran to the transporter.

As they lifted away from the Palace, Eli replayed the attack footage for Santana and his team. This time, when the lights flared at the end of the recording, Eli recognized something that panic and fear had made him miss the first time around. That blinding blaze was a very unique type of light, and he'd only seen it once before – in Englan Chrisholm's cell as his portal had opened. Eli watched the attack a third time in slowed motion, and saw the commander and everyone not falling, but vanishing into the light – into the portal. Eli's heart lifted – he'd feared they'd been incinerated, but it now looked as though they'd actually jumped realms.

There was still hope.

Chapter 9
Diega

PRATERIUS

RAMBELDON FOREST (FAIRFIELDS)

Diega burst from the light into open air. She plunged, tumbling and crashing out of control. Blurred forms flashed past. Sharp points ripped her face. She plummeted down as the ground rushed up. And then she hit. A patch of long grass softened the blow, but still it knocked her breathless. She lay there with her face in the dirt, stunned, struggling to force air into her lungs. Finally she managed a ragged gasp, followed by another, and after a third, she rolled onto her back. The sky above was an unnatural shade of purple and the daylight stars, always visible to Fen eyes, were gone. It wasn't possible.

Diega clutched her chest and sat up. The high grasses obscured her sight on all sides. She drew her electrifier and raised herself to the height of the grass tops, checking all around her for the shimmer of *Tehron* that would tell her somebody was waiting in ambush.

Seeing none, she stood. The field around her stretched out and downward to the edge of a pinewood forest. Diega held her breath and listened. A bird cheeped, insects chirred and whirred, and a whispering breeze swished the grasses, stirring sweet scents of pine needles and vanilla flowers.

Diega slipped her com from her belt and whispered into it, "Connect tracker team." The signal didn't connect. She checked the device and found it had shorted out. Most likely the fall had been too much for it.

Ahead, the grasses rustled. Diega ducked low again, and heard a heavy groan. She aimed her electrifier toward the sound as the colossal meathead Christy Shawe hauled his muscle-suffocated carcass into sight.

He muttered a curse and reached a hand behind him, then started lumbering in circles as though he thought that would help extend his grasp. He turned Diega's way and spotted her. Aggression tightened his face, then he recognized her, and the tense lines relaxed, even though she still held the electrifier pointed straight at his head.

"Don't just stand there, sunshine," he growled. "Tell me what's on my back."

"I told you," she said through gritted teeth. "Don't call me *sunshine*, you trutting podsucking gadfly."

"Oh, I'm terribly sorry, princess," he mocked her, looking even more asinine than he usually did. "Is *buttercup* better? How about *sugar-pie*?"

Diega grimaced with the immensity of her loathing for Shawe. She tested her finger on the trigger. This was where Copernicus usually stepped in, told them both to shut it, but he wasn't here – and neither were Jude, Silho or Eli …

Scenes of the fight at the palace returned to her in blurred flashes. Everything had gone down so quickly. They were struggling to free Silho and then they were falling. She'd thought they'd toppled off the side of the Walk, but clearly not. She hesitated, then lowered her weapon.

"Where the hell are we?" she asked Shawe.

"Do I look like the trutting encyclopedia of the universe?" he said, still clutching at his back.

"No, you look like a shaved ape wearing pants," she muttered, shoving her electrifier into its holster. She trudged through the grasses to where the gangster struggled.

"Stop moving!" she ordered, then lifted the back of his shirt.

The sight that met her eyes sent a shot of weakness through her knees. She'd seen several lifetimes worth of distressing and gruesome wounds, but she'd never seen this level of injury on a person who was still alive. Shawe's lower back was a complete mess – the skin was gone, as well as several layers of muscle, leaving only bloodied meat. She thought she might even be seeing some exposed spine. Diega couldn't understand why he hadn't already bled out.

"What?" he said, glancing over his shoulder at her.

Diega stared at him incredulously. Did he really not feel how bad this was?

She took the compact mirror off her belt and held it up so he could see the reflection of his wounds. He spat out a long mouthful of curses.

"What happened? What did this?" Diega asked.

"What do you think? Trutting fire-breather stabbed me – he got Kane too."

A sick feeling lurched in her stomach. Shawe had phenomenally tough skin and he had still sustained this level of damage – what would it have done to Copernicus if he'd been hit? They had to find him, fast.

Diega checked her com again – still dead. She dragged out her body scanner, heat sensor and navigator, but found everything was similarly fried. All her tracking equipment was now useless. Even her electrifier, she discovered, had malfunctioned. They'd have to conduct a search the primitive way, line by line through the grass.

Shawe saw her looking around and said, "He's not here."

"How do you know?" she demanded.

The gangster looked her up and down with an arrogance in his sewerage-green eyes that said he wouldn't be explaining himself to the likes of her. "Because I know."

"Good for you," she spat back. She left him and walked higher up the slope. From that height she could see where she and Shawe had hit, but there were no other signs of disturbances to the grass. No one else had fallen here.

Diega moved back down to see Shawe ripping up his jacket and trying to use it to bind the gaping and horrific wound in his back. He grunted as material touched raw flesh. Just witnessing it sent shocks of pain through Diega's own skin.

"What are you doing?" she demanded.

"I'm belly-dancing – what does it look like, woman?" he said.

Diega was so sorely tempted to let him go, but at this moment he was her only ally in a strange place – a place where Copernicus was potentially lost and critically injured.

"If you put that straight onto the wound, it'll fuse with the scabbing and rip open again as soon as you take it off," she explained. "You have to have a layer of anti-adhesive underneath it."

"And where am I going to get anti-adhesive?" Shawe said. "Do you see any shops around here?"

"Just – stop talking," Diega muttered. She grabbed a pack of synthetic skins off her belt. She sprayed Shawe's wound with antiseptic and coagulators then applied the skins over the top. Somehow Shawe managed to keep his enormous mouth shut while she worked.

"We have to find the others," she told him, tying the strips of his jacket over the skins. "If Copernicus was stabbed, like you said he was, he'll be in a bad way."

She heard a gulp and looked up to see Shawe swigging Araki from his silver flask. She was telling him Copernicus could be seriously injured, even dead, and he was busy getting pissed.

"You don't care about anyone except yourself, do you?" she said. "You're just a trutting pisshead thug."

He looked back at her, his eyes hardening. "Sweetheart – honestly – I'm cutting you a break because obviously your early experiences of being bedded by every gangster in the city must have messed with your brain, but you're testing me."

"You don't know anything about me," she growled.

"Really?" He raised an eyebrow, then grabbed her collar and tugged it to one side, exposing the bruising on her neck. "Like it rough, do you, sunshine?"

Diega felt the vicious burn of humiliation. "Shut it!"

Shawe snorted. "Why would you go and do something as stupid as paying for that, when you could go down to the Isles and get someone to smash in your face for free?"

"I'll smash in your face for free if you don't shut it!" she shouted.

Shawe just laughed at her. A film of red closed over Diega's eyes. She felt her colors flare as she snatched the blade off her belt and launched herself at him – stabbing him right in the chest. The blade snapped in half and dropped to the ground between them. It was her favorite blade, the one Copernicus had given to her when he recruited her into the trackers. That had been the best day of her life.

Diega kneeled and picked up the broken blade. She whispered to morph it back onto the hilt. It didn't shift. It was then that she really noticed that her eyesight was differ-ent – the edges of the blade were solid. She stared around with growing disbelief. Everything was solid. Her skills were not working here – wherever *here* was – because they were definitely not in Scorpia.

Fear, fast translating into rage, ripped through her. She launched herself at Shawe, blindly striking and kicking him with the strength of every martial fight style she knew. She leaped back, expecting him to be attacking or injured – or something – but instead he was standing in the same position, just looking down at her with an expression that said he wasn't exactly sure what she was doing, but it made her look stupid.

"You're a real cracked nut aren't you, love?" he said.

Diega swore at him and attacked again, but this time he caught her midair, spinning her around and pulling her back roughly against his chest. He wrapped an arm around her and she couldn't budge, she could barely breathe. She felt his body, reeking of sweat and alcohol, pressed hard against her. In a blink she was back in Woulghast, bound and gagged with the witch closing in on her. Silho had saved her ... *Silho is dead ...* Diega zoned out – *if you're somewhere else it doesn't hurt ...*

When she finally opened her eyes, her feet were back on the ground and Shawe had released her.

"Back in the land of the living, then," he said, boredom in his voice.

She lifted a shaking hand and stabbed a finger into his face. "If you ever touch me again, I will kill you."

He just shook his head. "I don't *want* to touch you. I may catch something. But if you keep buzzing like a gnat, I'll have to swat you."

Diega found no words savage or hateful enough to express how she felt right then.

She turned and pushed through the grass, not thinking, just moving as far away from Shawe as she could. She heard him following and gritted her teeth. This place looked like Paradise, but with the loudest sounds being the regret inside her own head and the whistle of Christy Shawe breathing through his busted-up nose, it could only be hell.

Chapter 10

Croy

KULLRA FORNAX

NŸR-CORUM (THE CREMATORIUM)

The Crematorium, final resting place of Nÿr-Corum's deceased, was located at the southernmost extremity of the city, through Saint Smithy Borough, below the cask of the Mother Fire and straight down for as far as the warmth lasted – and then down some more. A stretch of freezing cold lay between the civilization of the city and the sub-civilization of the Crematorium. Its laboratories and factories were warmed by their own fires – fueled by burning bodies. It was a chilling kind of warmth. As Croy followed Darius' dragger, cutting through the biting updraft, she wondered what had come first, the Morticians rejecting society or society rejecting them. Either way, what had once been an elite and somewhat secretive bunch of scientists had now become a completely isolated and extremely bizarre sect of ... the word *people* didn't really seem to fit anymore. Once, Croy had tried to make Darius promise that when she died he would ensure, by whatever means, that her body didn't go to the Crematorium. He'd refused to talk about her dying, but at least she knew he'd heard her wishes.

"Almost there," her partner's voice spoke through the I-Sect in her ear.

"Can't wait," Croy muttered back.

They pushed their draggers to full capacity and cut through the last of the freeze. A gust of warmth buffeted Croy's face, the air thick with itchem-poly-magmylate, which the Morticians used to treat the bodies prior to cremation. Croy could attest that the stink of burning human flesh was truly awful, nauseating and putrid-sweet, and after smelling it once, it seemed to stain the sense of smell forever. The itchem was a powerful chemical mask. It made Croy's eyes water and her head spin, but even so it didn't completely overwhelm the stench billowing out of the Crematorium's chimneys.

Croy tried not to think about it. She tried not to think that she was inhaling fragments of the dead, but she couldn't quite shake the thought. Like the smell – it lingered.

Darius slowed his dragger and started to square off for landing. Croy glanced down at the rutted platform below them. The landing lights were all blown out and the indicating outline for inward passage had faded to nothing. Together the two factors spoke clearly. They were the first visitors here for a long time, maybe even since the slide-pipe was installed between the mortuary at the Tower and the Crematorium. Darius took the drop quickly and expertly, his ride leaning with his body and obeying his slightest touch and movement shift. Croy's dragger was more stubborn, shuddering with reluctance as she forced it downward. She knew it was somewhat juvenile to anthropomorphize a machine, but sometimes it felt as though the dragger really did have a mind of its own.

John L would have called her delusional – but with a smile and a shimmer in his eyes.

She touched down beside Darius and rested her boots on the ground. A fierce pain sliced through her leg from her toes to her scarred knee, sending a burning spasm through muscle and bone. Her whole body involuntarily jolted and went rigid. Then she felt something, a very strange sensation like things crawling all over her skin, then it changed, and she felt as though she were being shaken by the shoulders. An emotion rushed through her that she would have described as love or maybe desire had it not been completely out of place. The I-Sect in her ear emitted a deafening whistle, heated up, and exploded.

Croy yelled and tried to dig the burning shard of metal out of her ear as it melted into her skin. She staggered off the dragger, but her foot became stuck and she fell, crashing onto the ground with the ride on top of her. Shoving her finger deeper into her ear, she managed to snag a wire of the tiny device. She ripped it out and threw it, as Darius heaved the dragger off her and dropped down at her side.

"What happened?" he yelled. Croy flinched, the sound hurting her burned ear. She touched a hand to it and felt it throbbing.

"I'm fine ... fine," she insisted, finding her feet and pushing him away.

"You're bleeding." He grabbed a gauze patch out of his kit and pressed it over her ear. His other hand held her head steady. He was standing so close their faces were almost touching, and in this low light, the green-blue of his eyes seemed to glow. Croy took the gauze from him and stepped back. She checked the blood – it wasn't much, nothing to cry about.

"Damn machine." She nodded to the I-Sect and Darius went to pick it up. He held the smoking remains up to eye level and cursed.

"Have you ever heard of one of these blowing?" he asked.

Croy shook her head. "Unlucky first."

Her partner touched a hand to his own ear and shifted with discomfort, but he left his I-Sect in. It was their only communication with the rest of the city. He hauled Croy's ride upright and kicked out the stand.

"Not exactly the arrival we were shooting for," she said, looking around at the darkened entrance of the Crematorium.

Shadows hung heavy over the doors, obscuring angles and edges, making it seem like one black void stretching back into forever. The moaning winds rattled the buildings. They creaked and shuddered, fell silent, then shuddered again. Croy could feel the heat from the steam pipes beneath her boots, but it did nothing to warm her. She exhaled harsh gusts of icy air and felt eyes watching them from the darkness. The strange pain that had overwhelmed her as they arrived had now dulled to a buzzing in her head. She realized it was similar to the buzzing she'd experienced at the Strip, except this was a continuous prickling feeling rather than bursts of sensation. Strong emotions, disconnected from anything that was actually happening, continued to swell then sink inside her, and she considered the possibility that the Morticians were somehow involved in both the dayturn's incidents. The question was *how*, and *why*.

She glanced over at her partner. Darius stood surveying the entrance, disdain and anger narrowing his eyes.

"Do you feel something weird?" she asked him.

"Whole damn turn's been weird," he replied. "From the crazies on the Strip, to the sliced-up stinker, to now." He reached into his jacket and brought out the Predator 6. "Let's get some answers and get out of here."

Darius strode out, heading for the entrance. He took the lead as he always did, partially due to impatience with her slower pace, and partially due to protectiveness, even though he knew full well what she was capable of. Croy followed. She didn't draw her Firestorm, but was conscious of its weight against her hip. As they neared the front gate, a human-shaped shadow stepped into their path. Croy's steps hesitated, but Darius didn't pause; if anything, he moved quicker to meet the stranger head-on. Croy grabbed the torch out of her kit and sparked it up with her igniter. Flames flared in the end of the box. She held it up, sending a beam of light into the stranger's face.

The man – a Mortician – hissed and stepped back, shielding his eyes. Croy kept the beam trained on him and called out, "Controllers Croy and DeCavisi."

The Mortician lowered his arm and blinked into the light. Darius stopped a few paces from the man and Croy hurried to catch up, taking in the stranger as she walked. He was robed, his face sickly-pale and sunken, with heavy dark circles surrounding bloodshot eyes. He was completely hairless, with no eyebrows or facial hair. As she made this observation, a thought came to her – the body at the silo had still had long hair, and yet had definitely been dead for more than a few dayturns. As far as she'd been informed, the Morticians' procedure involved shaving the body as one of the first points of action. So why hadn't they shaved this girl?

Croy came alongside her partner as the Mortician spoke in a deep voice, as colorless as his face.

"May I help you?"

Croy's stomach lurched. He had the most powerful and awful breath. It was asphyxiating. It smelled like he was rotting from the inside out. Her hands twitched as she struggled not to cover her nose.

"We're here to ask some questions in relation to a body found earlier this dayturn in the Filter," Croy said.

"Ask," he replied.

"I'd prefer it if we went inside where there's more light." she told him.

The Mortician stared at her blankly, as though he hadn't understood.

"Move it, jackass," Darius commanded, giving him a shove with the muzzle of his Predator 6. "Inside. Now!"

The man drew back and wrenched open the front gate. Rust grated and the hinges squealed. He nodded and indicated for them to step past him. Croy followed Darius in, feeling her arm brush against the rough linen of the Mortician's robe. His stare burned into the side of her face. He shut the gate behind them, and Croy heard it lock as they passed through double doors into a hallway. It was very long, straight, and completely bare, except for the torches on the walls. Croy snuffed out hers and pushed it back into her kit. The Mortician came up behind them, his soft-soled shoes making no sound. He moved in a very unnatural upright way, with his hands clasped in front of him, looking more like a puppet than a person. It made Croy even jumpier than she already felt. She glanced at her partner. Darius was looking all around them, his nostrils flaring and eyes sharp. There were no signs of any others, but Croy could still feel eyes. The Mortician paused beside them, waiting.

Croy took out a parchment notepad and a stick of charcoal.

"Firstly state your name," she said.

The man stared vacantly.

"Name!" Darius demanded. "You know, that thing you inherited from your parents – or have you forgotten you had parents?"

"Klinsman," he said.

"Klinsman who?" Darius ask.

"Just Klinsman."

The Mortician watched as Croy scratched it down.

"Right. Mister Klinsman," she continued. "The body of a girl was found in the Filter this dayturn. The body had been chained between two anchor poles. It had the deathcode."

Klinsman's expression shifted for the first time. A crease appeared between his eyes and the skin shifted down where his eyebrows would have been.

"Our mark?"

"We have a sharp one here," Darius muttered not-so-quietly to Croy.

"Has there been a break-in recently?" she prompted.

"Yes," Klinsman replied after just the briefest of pauses and a shift of his eyes. "Yes, there has been."

"Why didn't you report it?" she asked.

"I am sure we intended to. I am sure the next time one of us went to the surface we would have. We only go every sixty turns."

"So in the meantime someone's running around town with a boosted cadaver – and that doesn't concern you?" Darius said.

The Mortician looked between them and said without any emotion whatsoever, "It concerns me greatly."

"What happened?" Croy asked. "When and how was the body taken?"

Klinsman swallowed slowly. "I assume an individual broke in and, as you said, stole it."

"You assume?" Darius said.

"I'm not aware of the exact details."

"How convenient."

"Okay." Croy pushed the parchment and charcoal back into her pocket. "We're going to need the name of the missing deceased and we'd like to see where the body was stored before it was taken."

"Why?" Klinsman asked, and Croy finally heard some color in his voice.

"Why?" Darius repeated. "Because we say so, that's why."

The Mortician's eyes went to Croy.

"Don't look at her – I'm the one talking to you." Darius snapped his fingers in a way that would rile even the most docile of people, but got little reaction out of Klinsman. "What are you freaks hiding?"

Her partner was getting close to losing control over his anger, so Croy stepped in front of him.

"Mister Klinsman, if you'll just give us the name and show us where the body was taken from, then we'll leave. Cooperation is not optional."

Klinsman swallowed again, his throat bobbing. "Follow me, then."

The Mortician led them further along the hallway at the same walking-dead pace, Darius zigzagging behind him with impatience. Finally they came to a room with a counter, and behind it a second, smaller room filled with parchments. Another Mortician – Croy assumed the parchment keeper – stood inside the office. He was dressed identically to Klinsman, with the same hairlessness and sallow skin. His eyes stretched with alarm as they approached.

"Wait here," Klinsman told them. He entered the parchment room through a doorway beside the counter and went to the man. They huddled in one corner to speak, casting cagey glances over their shoulders.

Darius narrowed his eyes at them. "What do you think they're saying?"

"Something along the lines of *did you notice a body was missing? – no – did you? – no – what do we do? I don't know, what do you think we should? No idea.*" Croy said.

Darius snorted. He stepped forward and banged on the counter with both hands.

"Hurry up!" he yelled.

The Morticians exchanged a few more words, and then Klinsman came back out.

"I'm just retrieving the file," he told them.

"Sure – and I'm just retrieving my Predator," Darius said redrawing his weapon. "'Fess up – you didn't know about the runaway cadaver, did you?"

Klinsman's eyes swiveled from left to right.

"Why say that you did?" Croy avoided the word *lie*, wanting to keep the situation as calm as possible.

"I'm in charge of entranceway security. I should have known," Klinsman finally confessed.

"Okay," Croy said. "Take a look at this." She took the sketch of the girl out of her pocket and showed him. "Any ideas who this is?"

Klinsman's pale eyes scanned over the image methodically, medically. Croy noticed he had sweat on his upper lip – still human after all.

Darius breathed impatiently through his nose.

"I think I know who it could be," the Mortician finally said. "But I must check."

He hurried back into the records room and vanished, along with the record keeper, through a second doorway.

Darius started to pace and after several minutes burst out, "What does he have to check?"

"He's gone to get someone," Croy said. She'd sensed that the Mortician had known immediately who the girl was. The door opened and Klinsman re-entered, this time with a different man. Both Morticians came out into the room, and Croy knew without being told that this new man was Klinsman's senior. He carried himself with an air of importance and he was, impossibly as it would seem, even creepier – almost to the point that he made Klinsman look like a poor impersonator.

When they were close enough he said, "Hello, I am Baraway Westor."

Croy was slightly surprised to hear his voice sounded quite normal, even cheery in a pompous way.

"Controllers Croy and DeCavisi," she said, flashing her badge because she had the feeling he would ask to see it. "What is your position here, Mister Westor?"

"Senior surgeon."

"And I take it your associate has explained to you why we've come?"

"Yes," Westor said. "My worker has explained. I was unaware there had been a break-in."

"You too, hey?" Darius crossed his arms, mocking them. "Is there anyone here who did know?"

"It has been a very busy time for us," Westor said. "And, to be honest, we do not have the highest security. People breaking in, or out for that matter, has never really been an issue for us."

Croy could see how that would be the case. She cut to the point. "Do you know who the girl is?"

Westor handed her a parchment file and she flipped it open to find a sketch of the dead girl, very similar to her crime scene sketch. Croy read the details.

"Victoria Kilner ... Suicide. When was she brought in?"

"A fort-turn ago," Westor said.

"So why wasn't she shaved?" Croy asked.

Westor's eyes shifted. He glanced down at the file. Croy studied him and saw he didn't know, but he covered himself well. "I can only assume that she was on the waiting list for preparation."

"How long does that usually take?" Croy asked.

"It depends on how many corpses there are," Westor explained. "As I said, we're very busy at the moment. There has been an influx of deaths of late. More than we've ever had."

Darius muttered something under his breath and Croy said, "Right. Thank you for your time. I'll have to take this file and we'll be back down when we need more information."

She feigned turning away, and Darius went with her. By now he understood exactly how she worked. Let the perpetrators think they're in the clear and then swoop back in – something John L had taught her. She paused and glanced back at the Morticians. They were looking at each other, Westor's eyes ablaze with fury. The anger sank back as he realized she was looking.

"Just one more thing," she said. "There were some post-mortem injuries to the body. Was she brought in like that?"

"Yes," Westor said without a pause to think.

"Who did it? Who mutilated her?" Croy asked.

"We don't know. We don't generally ask questions, but the only people who had access to the body were the girl's family and Controllers."

"And you," Darius added.

"Of course," Westor conceded tightly.

Croy nodded, turned away again, then back for a second swoop. Now Westor was looking openly rattled and irate and Klinsman had hunched in on himself so much it looked as though he was trying to sink through the floor.

"I almost forgot." Croy continued her pretense, to further throw them off. "Before we head away we need to see where the corpse was kept."

Westor stared at her. "I'm sorry, that's out of the question. Our work areas are not open to the public, and I frankly don't see how it would help in any way to see where it *used* to be."

"I wasn't asking," Croy said, maintaining her calm. "Just take us through or I'll have you and all your people detained while we audit this place from front to back. I'll remind you: you are not a separate entity, you are still under the jurisdiction of the Conference."

Westor narrowed his eyes, cold with contempt, and Croy could see this was a dangerous man to upset.

"Controller Croy," he said. "I've heard of you – Barastyna Croy – otherwise known as the Saint."

As always the sound of her first name made her cringe – she hated it – but she hid her irritation and said, "Well then, you know I'm not bluffing."

"What I know is that your *nickname* is well twisted with irony – you're corrupt. And your father was corrupt before you. Except he wasn't actually your father, was he indeed? Just a man who wanted to help an orphaned girl, out of the kindness of his heart – except John Lukashenko didn't have a heart, so I would hazard a guess he took his payment from your flesh."

"Son of a whore," Darius cursed and drew his Predator and aimed it at Westor's forehead.

Before he could pull the trigger, Croy grabbed the gun, wrenching it down and holding it there. She spoke with unshaken composure.

"Then I repeat – so you know I'm not bluffing."

She held the Mortician's stare and watched as the derision melted off his face. And then she had him. He backed away to the door and she and Darius followed him through the records room. Darius' teeth were gritted so hard that sharp ridges cut up on his cheek and veins were twitching in his neck. Croy doubted Westor realized just how close he'd come to having his brains blasted out. Unlike her, Darius never feigned anything.

The Morticians led them through several other hallways and rooms, where many more of their kind were working. They were all male – only men were accepted into their order due to their belief that women were not capable of the work they performed – and they all looked the same, flashing expressions of shock to see intruders in their inner sanctum.

In one workroom the walls were completely lined with jars of dead animals of all types in preservation liquid. Croy had never imagined there were so many different creatures and the sight sent a shiver of mixed disgust and fascination through her. She'd always dreamed of seeing an animal in real life – not animal skins, or animal meat or animals in jars, but an actual breathing animal. It was unlikely, since the Conference quarantine laws only allowed carcasses to be brought in through the gates.

Croy kept a hand on her Firestorm until finally they reached a large storage room, half-full with drums of itchem-poly-magmylate.

Westor paused in front of a door and said, "Through here are our cooled rooms." He gestured to the lines of pipes, which Croy had heard reached all the way through the rock wall of the cavern into the freezing outer tunnels. "Don't touch the pipes," Westor warned. "Your hands will turn to ice."

He took a key from his pocket and unlocked the door. Inside they were confronted with corpses on every surface. It actually looked as though the Morticians had run out of proper storage space and had started putting bodies anywhere they could. Croy had no idea there had been this many recent dead, and Darius' eyes said he was thinking the same thing.

They exhaled heavy mist, following Westor and Klinsman as they edged around the slabs, with barely enough room to move around the crowded dead. Each one was shaved bald, and as Croy passed them she looked specifically for signs of post-mortem assault or mutilation. From each body she caught a sense of their emotion before they had died. It was something she'd always had a natural intuition for.

Westor stopped in front of one storage chamber and eyed Croy coldly. "This was where the Kilner girl was placed."

"Open it," she instructed.

The Mortician stepped back and dragged open the drawer. There was another body inside. With so many extra dead, Croy cold see how they might not have noticed Victoria's corpse being removed – but still something wasn't adding up about the whole situation.

Out of the corner of her eye, she caught a flicker of movement behind a closed door.

"What's in there?" she asked.

"Just storage," Westor replied.

More shadows played beneath the door.

Croy drew her Firestorm and moved toward it. Taking the handle, she braced and yanked the door open. It was pitch black inside. Croy reached for her torch, and a figure lunged out of the darkness, trying to slam a metal bar into her head. She dodged the blow, which impacted on the door post instead, smashing away rock fragments.

Croy stumbled to the ground, her knee burning with pain. The strange buzzing sensation she'd been feeling flared up as Darius rushed past her. Croy staggered up to see her partner struggling with a younger man. Someone else was standing behind them in the doorway. The figure came forward and Croy saw it was a girl with long red hair. She was crying, so terrified that she was struggling to breathe. Darius smashed the kid in the face, hauled him around and put him in a choke hold. He managed to maneuver cuffs around the boy's wrists and lock them down. The girl started to make a high-pitched squealing sound.

"It's alright, Kellor, it's alright!" The young guy struggled to turn his face toward the girl.

"She wanted to go home – in the water – they don't like the water – they don't like the water ... home ... home ..." the girl said. She started shaking her head and rocking from side to side.

"Kellor, be quiet!" the guy yelled. Darius kneed him in the leg, pushing him down to the ground. The girl screamed.

Croy went to try to calm her, but she yelled even louder and started throwing herself against the wall, smashing her own head. She was shrieking, "You can see! You can see! You can see!"

Croy rushed forward and pressed the girl's neck in the way John L had taught her. It was completely unauthorized, but highly effective, and knocked the girl out straight away. She slumped to the ground. The guy stopped struggling, staring at the girl with horrified eyes.

"What did you do! Kellor! You killed her! You ... Kellor, wake up!"

Croy turned to the Morticians. They were watching with wide eyes, and behind them a mass of other Morticians were streaming through the door into the cold room.

"Who are these two?" she demanded, indicating the kids.

"I have never seen them before," Westor said.

Croy felt a buzzing in her head. This time it was exactly the same as at the Strip – a pulse – like words blurred out. She noticed all the Morticians' eyes changing. They all suddenly looked drugged up, when a moment ago they'd seemed clear. Croy glanced at Darius – he could see it too.

She moved fast, stepping back and snatching up the girl. She was just skin and bones. Croy slung her over one shoulder and aimed her Firestorm with her free hand.

"Alright, back up! All of you!" she yelled at the Morticians.

For a moment, no one moved and Croy thought she was going to have to start shooting, then the death-mongers started to shuffle backward. Darius dragged the young guy to his feet, and the four of them pressed through the crowd of dead and dead-like. Croy had been in a lot of dangerous situations, but she'd never felt this unnerved. Her mouth was dust-dry, and she could feel her hands trembling, but she kept up her hard front and shoved through.

Once clear of the cold room, they moved rapidly back the way they came. Croy felt completely lost, but Darius had a photographic memory for directions, so he took the lead. Behind them the Morticians followed in a dull-eyed herd, coming fast enough to make them break into a run. Croy noticed both Darius and the young guy were shaking their heads in a strange way. Panic pulsed inside her. They made it to the last corridor and crashed through the front gate, breaking for their draggers. As she reached her ride, a feeling raked through her of being drawn back toward the entrance. It felt like starvation – like she had to go back or she would die. Croy looked toward the gates and saw Morticians spilling out the front door. Westor was at the lead, his unseeing eyes drilling into her face. It was enough to force her onto the dragger, with the unconscious girl slung over the front. Darius and the boy were already lifting off the platform.

"Croy! Move it!" her partner yelled down at her.

She kicked her dragger to life and they shot up into open air, the dragger over-revving as though it were desperate to get her clear. As they sped away, Croy looked back down. All the Morticians had vanished, as though they'd never been there at all.

Chapter 11

Eli

AQUAIS

SCORPIA (UFFTOWN)

It was with the distinct feeling of giddy dread that Eli stepped to the borderline between Heely Gap and Ufftown. The imp-breed word *ToUp* had been etched into the Ufftown signpost, as it was in most imp-breed suburbs. Its literal translation into Urigin was *Enter If You Dare* or, as some people said, *Enter At Your Own Risk*. Before the war, said risk could have included being flour-bombed, bombarded, bamboozled, befuddled, hornswoggled, hoodwinked, swindled, frisked, frolicked, fast-talked, finagled, fleeced, flimflammed, tricked, tickled, wedgied, dacked, double-dealt, triple-crossed, robbed blind, or blindly led – just to name a few possibilities. But now ... It was hard to know what to expect. Eli wasn't sure how the imp-breeds as a community had dealt with the war. Usually his kind tried to make light of (and profit from) anything and everything, but, as far as Eli could see, there really were no amusing angles to mass slaughter and misery.

A tremor shivered through him. He couldn't stop shaking. He could barely comprehend what had happened. The team had just been reunited. Everyone had survived – and now the others had vanished and Jude was shut down, dying slowly from an unknown poison. On initial testing, Eli had found the toxin completely foreign, unlike any other poison he'd seen, and he'd thought he'd seen them all. So he'd set it up for deep analysis, then injected Jude with as much slowing serum as he had.

Leaving his friend alone in that condition had made Eli sick to his stomach, but there was no other choice. The one consolation was that Penman was there watching over him and SevenM, feeding back their status to Eli's system. Initially, Santana had said he and the other soldiers would stay as well, but then word had come through that the main United Resistance refugee camp was under attack, and they'd had to fly out. The news that Caesar K-Ruz had also vanished was destabilizing the city all over again. The remaining Androt forces were reportedly re-assembling against the gangsters. Eli could feel the tremors of explosions and battle-fire all over Scorpia and his chest was so tight and stomach so knotted that he could barely breathe. His gran'ma used to tell him that the Khaiti God gives the heaviest burdens only to those strong enough to carry them – she'd say *When you can't carry on, the Khaiti God provides,* but this was the same woman who occasionally accused her collection of miniature statues of conspiring against her, so Eli could only assume that either his God had mistaken him for someone else, or was having a good laugh at his expense. The truth was, he wasn't strong enough to carry this – his legs felt so gelatinous right now he doubted they would even carry *him* – and so he'd come here to Ufftown, his home suburb, in search of the wisest man he knew: Mr Beatlebee Bellbeater. If anyone could save his friends, it would be the ancient Greer.

Eli's gaze swept over the multi-colored cobble-pebble streets, lined with picket fences and small, misshapen stone cottages of every color imaginable and then some. Everything was painted, papered, glittered, bejeweled and fabric-draped, from statues to trees to the grass itself. But the streets were empty. Eli had never seen it so quiet and deserted. If not for the wisps of colored smoke rising from the cottage chimneys, he would have believed everyone had left. The silence gave him a very solid lump in his throat. The place was so empty, in fact, that he could see clear across town to the Wintress River and into Thrumburstone – a Glee neighborhood. The wide river forged a substantial divide between the suburbs, but for the two rival imp-breed bloodlines, no distance was distant enough. Glees and Greers didn't mix, they didn't even acknowledge each other's existence, and it was illegal, or at least it had been, for them to marry or breed. His parents had been the odd law-breakers, and now the racial war raged on his skin and in his blood. It was just typical that his family had to be the weird ones.

Eli hitched up his weapon belt. During the war he'd lost weight that he'd never really had in the first place and the heavy belt was sagging. He flexed the fingers of his broken arm. He'd quick-set the bone, but it still felt tender. It would have to do. There was no time for recovery, and no time to wait around trying to find his nerve; he just had to move on without it.

"Okay, girl," he said to Nelly, huddling in his pocket. "One, two, three ..."

Eli stepped over the borderline. A massive water balloon missiled through the air and splatted directly into his face, knocking him backward onto the ground, and providing a quick answer as to how his kind had dealt with the war – complete denial.

Eli sprang back up, spinning, ready to catch the next one. It was on this same street, many year-cycles earlier, that he'd been accidentally baptized before the proper time as a water balloon had drenched him just as a priest was blessing someone else. His gran'ma had been furious. Gran'pa had laughed so much he'd been ordered out of the house and had had to sleep in the garden shed that night. Now Eli heard snickering coming from everywhere around him – and one by one faces started to appear from around corners, over rooftops, through windows, all grinning with wicked delight. This, apparently fun, tradition was known to imp-breeds as the *unwelcome party*. Eli sighed and clenched his fists. Each of the party were carrying some kind of squishy bomb – flour, feather, dye, water – and yes – there was a stinkwater one too. This was going to get bad. And he knew his kind well enough not to bother to try to negotiate his way out, or run – running was the worst thing a person could do. He'd just had to grit his teeth and take it, and then hopefully they'd get bored and go away.

Eli crouched down and covered his head. He heard the laughter and mocking reach a crescendo and then the whooshes of air as they launched the bombs. He braced himself. Then the ground started shaking under his feet. He peeked up and saw the Corámorán, Flintlock Flystock, with whom he thought he'd parted ways, now stampeding toward him – closing the distance fast with giant strides. There was no time to move. Eli just rolled into a ball and cringed down as low as he could. He felt the running steps stop and then heard the *splat, splat splat* of the bombs finding a target. But, strangely enough, he wasn't soaked, sticky or stinking. Eli unballed himself and peered up. The gargantuan-breed had stood over him and taken the full brunt of the unwelcoming. The marks of the bombs looked pathetically small on her heavily muscled body, the water lines running down her arms looking no more than drips of sweat. The unwelcome party hovered in a circle around them, staring. Flintlock's nostrils flared, then she opened her mouth and released a sonic roar that blew them all backward. Eli flattened himself to the ground with his hands over his ears. When he finally emerged, all the Greers were gone. No sane person would ever accuse his kind of being unnecessarily brave, that was for sure.

Eli stood up and brushed off his pants. In most places he'd be brushing off dust and dirt – in Ufftown it was glitter and candy sprinkles. He looked up at the Corámorán. As far as gargantuan-breeds went, including the sub-races of Giants, Colossuses, Titans, Behemoths and Goliaths, Flintlock was positively tiny – but compared to imp-breeds she was absolutely enormous and, incidentally, stunning, with thick tresses of curls and the deepest, most soul-searching eyes that Eli had ever seen. The *Moi* or tribal tattoo on her chin and half her face indicated her clan and rank. Eli wasn't as well versed in the Corámorán as he was with other types of Giants, but he understood enough to see she was part of a high-ranking clan, but herself well down in the pecking order.

Her clan had smashed her up quite badly. It was believed that most gargantuan-breeds were immune to pain, but they could still get injured and killed. And Eli knew it was his fault that she'd been hurt. Before he could apologize again, Flintlock spoke, her voice rich and deep, heavy with the Corámorán accent.

"I followed you, Master Eli. Please forgive me if this was wrong."

"It wasn't wrong," Eli said. "But please don't call me 'master' – as I said before, we're equals ..."

"Equals," Flintlock repeated. She processed the word for a few moments before kneeling down and pressing her forehead to the ground in the gargantuan-breed manner of submission. "You freed me. You are my master and I am your wife ..."

Eli opened his mouth, then snapped it shut as her words hit him – *wife*. Realization sank in – the chains, the attack – in searching for a way to save Jude he'd inadvertently intervened in a Corámorán betrothal rite, entered into a challenge and, somehow, won ...

Eli thought about arguing the point, but then he noticed the enormity of her biceps, the spiked club at her side and the oversized electrifier strapped to her waist, and he decided that straight-out refusing a woman of this girth was potentially life-threatening.

"And I'm extremely pleased to have you ..." he stammered instead. "But you really don't have to be my wife if you don't want to."

Flintlock raised her head. She asked with some timidity, "And if I should want to?"

"Well ..." The physical logistics were somewhat mind-boggling. "Then I'd have to buy myself a really sturdy bed ... or ladder ... or something ..." As he said the words he realized they sounded a lot ruder than he'd intended. "I have a situation at the moment," he told her. "I'm not turning you away – I just – I have to focus on this ..."

"I understand," Flintlock said. "Tell me what to do and I will do it."

The air beside them blackened and shivered; it zapped with electricity. Eli stumbled back and Flintlock stepped protectively in front of him. He peered around her legs as Luther materialized. Sunbeams hit his shadowy form and it sizzled. He grimaced and lurched sideways into the shade. Usually Midnight Men could only appear at mid-dark, but being a half-breed clearly gave Luther some scope to play with. Eli felt a rush of emotion at seeing him and Moses. He came forward and might have even hugged them, if he didn't think Luther might accidently bite him in half. Moses licked Eli's fingers and whined softly. He sensed Flintlock keeping close behind him.

"Someone's taken the commander," Eli told Luther, and saying the words aloud stirred the panic inside him. "Diega and Silho, too ..."

Luther's eyes hardened with the news. He gesture-wrote in the air, "*I want to help you find them.*"

Eli nodded. "I know a man who knows everything. It's a place to start."

Luther looked past Eli to Flintlock and narrowed his eyes. Flintlock was studying him with equal suspicion.

"My friend, Luther. My ... wife ... Flintlock ..." Eli introduced them quickly before one of them attacked.

Luther's eyes darted to Eli and then back, and then he attempted the most awkwardly savage and inappropriately timed smile Eli had ever witnessed. It was just plain weird – even for Eli, who most of the time felt like the definition of the word – but Flintlock didn't appear to mind. She gave a grunted Corámorán greeting, then held one hand out to pat Moses.

Wings whirred behind Luther, and a Greer, late to the un-welcoming, zoomed in with a rogue grin and a squishy dye bomb ready in one hand. Luther flared up to a monstrous shadow and Flintlock roared, showing her dagger incisors. The Greer splattered the balloon over his own head and flew past with a look of horror frozen on his face. It made Eli wish he'd known these two when he was in school. It would have made life a whole lot easier. Still it was never too late to have two truly terrifying friends – especially now that he was faced with trying to save the rest of the team alone. A sob broke from his throat and Eli slumped to the ground, his legs giving up. He couldn't do this. He had nothing left.

Flintlock grabbed him by his wings and hoisted him onto her shoulder, where he perched like a particularly uncomfortable featherless bird. The shock of it shook him out of his breakdown. He was too nervous of offending her to refuse the offer, so instead he just said with restrained over-politeness, "Straight on. Many thanks."

Luther stepped back into the shadows, and as Flintlock started off, the impact of her footsteps shaking the ground, Eli thought of an appendix to his gran'ma's saying – "*When you can't carry on, the Khaiti God provides ... an enormous woman to carry you.*" He was quite sure she wouldn't approve of this addition, but he thought it had a nice ring to it.

He now sensed many eyes watching them from the shadows and from behind curtains. The news would spread like the plague. They headed down Firefly Avenue, passing a whole street of sweet shops smelling of warm candy floss and chocolate of every flavor, then another lot of game and trick stores, which instead of stairs to enter had bouncy slides and mirror-maze doors. Overhead an empty rollercoaster zoomed through the town. All the colors, sounds and smells were so overwhelming that Eli realized he must have been away for too long. Before it had just been normal, but now the whole place looked to him like someone had taken a load of happy pills, smoked a whole heap of funny grass, then decided to build a city level – which, incidentally, was a pretty accurate description of the founding history of Ufftown and all the other imp-breed suburbs.

In the town center, they finally found some Greers out and about – their skin dyed all different colors, their hair-dos strange and clothes mismatching by Urigin standards. Every person who saw them coming crossed the street or ducked into a shop to stare as they passed. They came to the corner of Woodworm Street and Eli tapped on Flintlock's head. She stopped in front of a narrow alleyway. On the other side was Bellbeater's Antique Bookshop. There was no way Flintlock would be fitting through, so Eli leaped down off her shoulder and said, "I'll be back in a second."

His new Corámorán companion nodded. She crossed her arms across her chest and turned to stand in front of the alleyway, as though to guard it. Eli raced between the two buildings, conscious that anything could get dumped over his head at any moment. He broke through on the other side and skidded to a stop. His gasp was so loud it startled a flock of brightly colored parrots feeding nearby. They took to the air and Eli's heart gave five echoing thuds before his breath rushed back to him. The street where Bellbeater's shop had stood, plus the next five streets behind, had been bomb-flattened. There was nothing left but rubble, scattered with hundreds of shimmering Khaiti green diamonds laid down for the dead. Eli scrambled up into the wreckage, searching frantically for the remains of Bellbeater's shop. He spotted the shop's sign, cracked and broken beneath a chunk of stone wall. Two diamonds had been placed nearby. Making sure not to touch them, Eli got in as close as he could to read the names etched into the gems –

Beatlebee Bellbeater I

Beatlebee "Swifty" Bellbeater IV

Tears rushed to Eli's eyes. Swifty had been one of his best friends when they were young – they had been roommates when they first moved out of home into a tiny apartment above a popped corn store. The store's machinery had regularly suffered malfunctions, flooding their apartment with oceans of popped corn. They'd also gotten their first "legal" job together, stacking books for Mr Bellbeater, Swifty's great-great-great grandfather. They'd then taken separate paths, and never properly said goodbye.

Eli lowered his head and cried for them, whispering the Khaiti blessing for the passed. He stayed there until something stirred behind him and he heard a *quark*. Eli looked over his shoulder to see a blackbird sitting on a pile of bricks. The poor thing had obviously been in some trouble – its feathers uneven and dirty, one wing hanging askew. Eli assumed it was a lost pet, maybe belonging to someone who had been killed.

He sniffed and wiped a hand over his eyes, then stood carefully.

"Hey there," he said, his voice thick with grief. He moved toward the crow with an outstretched hand. "It's okay. Are you hungry?"

He came right close to the bird and it climbed onto his arm, digging sharp claws into the skin. It stared into his eyes with a shiny blue gaze, then lunged forward and pecked him on the nose. Nelly darted out of his pocket chattering, scolding, and the blackbird flew upward. Eli grabbed his throbbing nose – it was a sharp reminder.

"The book!" he yelled. "Bellbeater's book on dark magics!"

Eli buzzed his wings and shot up into the air after the blackbird. It saw him coming and took off, leading him on a speeding chase through Ufftown. It darted through windows and out doors, up along buildings and down tiny winding streets. It crashed through one apartment, where Eli got tangled in the curtains and fell down onto a bed, on top of a person who was lying in it. He apologized profusely and tried to move away as fast as he could, only to realize the person, a girl with an extremely cheeky smile, was dragging him back in. He managed to evade her clutching hands and escape out the window, where the blackbird was resting on the ledge. It took off again, Eli just behind it, grabbing at it, his hands clapping empty each time. He just couldn't get hold. Something dark crashed in from his left, slamming into the bird and trapping it in shadowy hands. Eli touched down on the ground as Luther materialized with the squirming crow in his grasp. The bird gave one last indignant squawk and morphed into the book.

"Good work, Luther!" Eli said. He reached for the book, but was shunted to one side as someone else ploughed into him. He hit the pavement and looked up to see the imp-breed girl from the bed straddling his chest. She had a very pointy, keenly inquisitive face, bright eyes, and bouncing blonde curls covered with way, *way* too many bows.

"Hello!" she grinned into his face.

Eli tried to maneuver her off but she kept rolling back on, grappling with him and giggling hysterically.

"Sorry ... Sorry ... oh, sorry," she kept saying. Luther watched on, his eyes darting, not sure what he was seeing or what to do about it.

"Okay, okay, *okay!*" Eli said, shoving her off him and scrambling up.

The girl continued grinning, beyond oblivious. She came at him again, trying to hug.

"Enough!" Eli shouted. "This is not a game! I am not playing!"

The small Greer's face was sober for a micro-second and then she was laughing and grabbing at him again. Her hands went downward toward his pants.

"Hey!" Eli fended her off.

"You have one too!" Her eyes shimmered with childlike excitement.

"One what?" Eli backed away, confused and unnerved.

"A slinky minx!" She rifled in her pocket and dragged out a small and shiny black slinky minx, smallest of the animal cat-breeds. It meowed at Eli with the tiniest of voices.

"This is Mr Nimbles. What's yours called? Your slinky minx – I see it there. In your pocket," the girl said.

"She's not a slinky minx, she's a miniature freshwater ot-ter," Eli said, finally realizing what she was talking about.

"Ooh, I had a great-great aunt on my mother's mother's side who knew someone who knew someone else who had an otter," the girl told him, then started bouncing up and down in front of him saying *wee – weeee – weeeee*. Eli stared, incredulous that anyone could actually be this hyperactive, then he realized he'd been this and more when he'd first met Copernicus. The thought of the commander sent pain lancing through his chest.

The girl Greer stopped bouncing as suddenly as she'd started and said, "I'm Diamond LeSwer – and you, you are Eli Anklebiter. I know seventeen of your cousins." She held up one hand and started listing, "Sem Swish; Nehemya Hooperhopper; Samsmall; Samtall; and Tallsmall Spidersleg —"

"That's – that's great," Eli cut in. "Look I don't have time to talk right now, so —"

"Did you see, we're the same," she interrupted him. "Look – look – lookey – look – look." She held up her arm marked with the bloodlines of both Glee and Greer. "You and me," she grinned and raised her eyebrows. She started singing a song featuring the lyrics "you and me", which Eli had never heard and highly suspected she was just making up now.

"Great. Excellent. Awesome," he said with forced restraint. "It was nice meeting you. Now I'm going this way – you go that way – and good luck to you."

Eli turned and marched with Luther to the end of the street, where he stopped and took the book from the Midnight Man. The last time he'd had this book it had opened for him by itself, but this time it just lay there unresponsive, so with caution he flipped it open, searching the first few pages for a table of contents. Someone started breathing right behind him. He looked over his shoulder and Diamond LeSwer was there, with her wide, shining eyes and over-eager expression. Eli realized, this one was going to be extremely difficult to shake. First he'd try ignoring. He turned his back on her again and found the contents pages of the book. He scanned down the Ps. If he could figure out how to reopen the portal the commander and the others had gone through there was a chance to get them back. Diamond leaned over his shoulder, eating strawberry sour chews. Some saliva dripped on his neck. His heart leaped as he found the entry for *Portal* and the page number – 784. He flicked fast with trembling hands.

He opened it to 782, flicked over the page – but it was 785. He checked again. The page was missing – ripped out.

"Nooo." Eli clenched his fists, his panic surging back in. It blurred his thoughts in a way he'd never experienced before. He could barely breathe or think. He felt himself passing out and started counting back from forty-six, while his unwanted new best friend tried to force-feed a sour chew up his left nostril and pickpocket him at the same time.

Veins convulsed in his temples – one in his neck felt just about to burst.

"Go away!" he yelled at her. "*Seriously!*"

She regarded him with confusion. "To where?"

"I. Don't. Care!"

"Why?"

"Because you're aggravating me!"

"How?"

"By being here."

"Who's that – what's his name?" She looked at Luther.

"It doesn't matter. Just —"

"Shh. Wait. Listen." She cut him off. Eli paused, waiting, wondering if she'd heard something ominous.

"Listen," she repeated. "Closer, closer – closer." He moved nearer and, in the silence of their listening, Diamond released a squeaky toot of gas. Immediately a noxious odor engulfed Eli's senses. He couldn't believe it. He had no words at all. The girl was laughing uproariously, rolling around on the ground, until she stopped suddenly, looked up at him from her sprawled position, and said with all seriousness, "I love you. Marry me."

Eli saw a flash of an image of him and this girl, with her all-too-revealing pink tutu, standing at the altar. He stifled his first response of hysterical laughter and instead said, "Look! Ice-cream craft!" He pointed to the end of the street.

"Ice-cream!" the girl shrieked, leaping up and flying wildly away, falling for the very oldest trick in the book.

"Quick!" Eli said to Luther. He clutched the book against his chest and the two of them ran, winding their way back out of Ufftown to where Eli had parked the *Gypsy Rose*. The craft's exterior was unfinished, but the engine was running well enough to fly. Eli approached it, lost in a hurricane of thoughts, not registering the person standing near the *Gypsy* until Luther halted beside him and Moses released a rippling growl. Eli looked up and saw Smudge K-Ruz and her black panther standing in the shadows. He stared at the stunning pair – Smudge, lean and aloof, with glowing eyes and small dark marks all over her face and body. For him, she defined beauty, and under any other circumstances, finding her waiting here would have made him melt into a sticky mess on the ground, but today, with everything he was facing, he managed to just stand there looking vaguely constipated. He noticed that Smudge's eyes were bloodshot, her face tearstained. Inski pawed restlessly at the ground.

"I want to speak with Kane," Smudge said.

"The commander …" Eli struggled with the words. "He's gone …"

"The Fen?" Smudge asked.

"Gone too."

"The Ar Antarian?"

Eli shook his head. "It's just me left."

Smudge looked him up and down, her anxiety showing in the whites of her eyes, desperation crumbling her usually cool exterior.

"No," she murmured.

Eli spoke quickly. "I think they've all been taken through a portal by the people who attacked us, but I'm working on a way to get them back. I will get them back."

Smudge shook her head, and he could see she was still in shock.

"They're already fighting to replace him ..." Her voice was detached, "Julio will win. He's not Caesar. He has no control. He will have war with the machines until Scorpia is nothing but ash."

"I'll find them. I'll bring Caesar back," Eli tried to reassure her.

She looked into his eyes, and for a moment they were connected, then her gaze shifted to something behind him. Eli glanced back, then did a double-take – Luther was grinning at her with eyes like knives. He was staring and then looking away and all around in a staccato way. The ground started to tremble as Flintlock ran up to them – she started to roar, but Eli jumped to intervene.

"No – no – no, Flintlock – this is – this is ..." Eli's mind went blank.

"Smudge," Smudge said and Inski flicked her tail in annoyance.

"I don't know – I mean I know that – I know who you are – definitely – completely," Eli said, then a giggle escaped him. His eye twitched and a dye bomb exploded over his head, drenching him in purple goo. Diamond LeSwer flew past, laughing and farting.

Smudge's expression was a mix of disgust and disbelief.

"I should never have come here!" she growled and ran away.

"I'll be touching you ... I mean, getting in touch," Eli called after her.

To say the moment had been ruined was perhaps the grandest understatement ever uttered, but it really was the least of his worries, unless embarrassment suddenly became fatal. He used the flash-key to open the *Gypsy Rose* and climbed aboard. He put Bellbeater's book of dark magics into Nelly's carry cage and shut it, in case it morphed back into a blackbird. Flintlock and Luther stood waiting outside the craft.

"You two should go. I don't want either of you getting hurt because of me."

Luther gestured in the air. *No. I'm with you.*

Flintlock agreed. "I'm staying. I'll never leave you."

The words caused unexpected pain – maybe it was being back in the old neighborhood – but he saw a memory of himself as a kid, standing on the sidewalk in the rain, waiting for his father to come and pick him up. His father, Farleigh Freely, an especially shifty Glee by all accounts, had made contact with him – against his grandparents' wishes. He'd said Eli could come and live with him in Thrumburstone. He'd told him to pack his things and sneak out – to wait for him on the street corner – that he would come. So Eli had waited, with a suitcase full of comics and inventions, all day and half the night until his gran'pa came out and got him. He and Gran'ma had been watching him from the window the whole time. He'd never seen his father again and it made him wonder why he'd called in the first place.

If Eli ever crushed a child's heart like his father had crushed his that day, he thought he would actually stop breathing from guilt. He shook the memory out of his mind; he chose not to focus on these things for a reason. His real family were the friends who loved him – and they needed him to be strong for them again.

He heard a wrenching sound as Flintlock ripped out his backseat and threw it down on the sidewalk. The Corámorán climbed in, lowering the craft in a significant way. Nelly stayed quiet in Eli's pocket, not game to challenge the giantess in the way she would have any other girl trying to climb into Eli's craft. In Eli's mind, he heard Ev'r saying *Snack-size,* and his next step came to him. Clearly this situation was over his head, and he needed someone wiser to help him. He needed Ev'r Keets – and the formula he believed would change her back from Ravien was already rattling behind him in the cargo hold of the craft. It felt like fate.

He turned to Luther. "We're going to Golmaria to revive Ev'r Keets. She'll know what's happening."

Luther dipped his head and he and Moses vanished back into the shadows.

Eli turned over the engines. They shuddered and the craft lifted upward. He initialized the desert mapping system he and Silho had created together, and as they flew, the past replayed in his thoughts ...

* * * * *

Occasionally Eli carried on conversations with himself – especially if he had a new idea or high levels of stress – and he realized he was definitely doing it now, talking, plus laughing randomly. He wiped his expression clear and shot a furtive glance into the rear-vision mirror. Luckily, Silho was still consumed by the task at hand. She wore telescopic glasses and held Ev'r's desert map on her knee, managing to look both at the aged parchment and through the transparent base of the craft down to the Matadori plains flashing by beneath them. Using the re-routed steering column that Eli had set up for her, Silho navigated the borrowed craft toward their destination. She had insisted on taking the backseat, saying she needed more room to spread out the map, but Eli knew a compassionate lie when he heard one. Their friendship had developed into a little-to-no-explanations-necessary arrangement, and she understood that sitting in the pilot's seat would help calm his nerves. With the face of a pixie girl, and the stare of a war survivor, Silho was singularly lovely and phenomenally dangerous – and for a person who claimed to be socially inept, she was also painfully insightful. Eli had gotten used to feeling psychologically nude in her company. She was very much like the commander in that sense.

Eli found his gaze drawn back to the map. Intoxicatingly musty and ancient, he'd discovered it tucked behind the cover of a book, a personal journal, in Ev'r's bag. He had no idea who had originally created the map, but whoever it was had swung some serious power. The map was not the one-dimensional, fixed topographical sketch of the Matadori that it had first appeared to be. Once in the proximity of the desert, the inked borderlines and landmark icons had started changing, rearranging themselves to combat the rogue magics of the Matadori that worked to send travelers off-course. And it was highly protected, too, by an enchant so strong that any attempts to duplicate or transformate it were violently denied. When Eli had tried to pass the parchment through his scanner machine to create a holographic copy, the scanner had literally disintegrated before his eyes. The lingering smoke had reeked unmistakably of dark magics.

Silho murmured something to herself. She shifted the transflyer leftways and slowed their speed. Eli glanced down to the desert. A relentless wind rolled its sands into waves of yellow-orange mist, unearthing bleached bones and steely angles of crashed crafts and other great ships forgotten. Moments later they were lost again – that was the perfidiousness of the Matadori, its face a constantly changing mask, each expression more duplicitous, enigmatic, than the one before. This far out from the city, travelers could put no confidence in their tools of navigation or the sighting of landmarks, and especially not in their own senses. Even with Ev'r's map, Eli knew he would have been most hopelessly lost forever if Silho hadn't agreed to come along. She could read the sands. She saw the Matadori for what it was, and when it came up against the skill of Silho Brabel, all the desert's ferocity and bravado seemed quite pathetic, like a night shadow scared away by the sunslight.

Despite all the failed green lights, Silho's belief in his cause and, surprisingly to Eli, in his ability to find a Ravien cure had remained devout. She was the only one to really realize that this was more to him than an infatuation with an idea. In fact he'd been stalking hope for so long now that he was feeling something he'd never felt before – what it was like to hit a wall. All his life, problems and riddles, however complex and cryptic, had been like friendly faces in a crowd. Whatever it was, given enough time, he'd found a solution – but this ... Eli pushed the thought of failure out of his mind. He refused to abandon hope. It was all they had left of Ev'r – the ghost of hope.

Behind Silho, in the cargo hold, hundreds of little dart-vials of antidote jiggled in merry opposition to the actual mood of the journey. These were it – the antidote to finally free Ev'r Keets from her Ravien form. The thought brought Eli solidly back into the reality of their mission and he started to sweat again in earnest, as though his body was trying to drown him before he did anything to further endanger himself. On top of the sweats, he had also recently developed both restless wing syndrome and stress-induced alopecia – body hair only – leaving him a sweaty, shedding, twitchity, repetitious, ulcerated insomniac – as though he needed further turn-offs for the opposite sex. But this was it – this was definitely it ... Nelly sat on the front seat, staring at him with an expression that said his stubborn optimism was making them both look ridiculous. She huffed, curled up and went to sleep.

"Eli," Silho said, her voice startling him out of his thoughts.

"Yes, I'm here, I'm here, I'm here." He almost dove into the backseat.

She slid up her glasses and pointed ahead of them.

Eli turned back around to face the front windscreen. Nerves crawled all over his skin. They had arrived. They had finally found it. Golmaria. Fallen city of the Ravien.

The Ravien ...

One of the most dangerous monsters in Aquais. One bite and people transformed into one of their attackers. Luckily they weren't greatly ambitious as far as demon-monsters went. They kept to themselves and the rare accounts of attacks involved people entering Golmaria – for whatever lunatic reason they had – such as searching for a recently turned friend to try out an untested, potentially fatal potion that might or might not restore them to their previous form, with unknown side-effects and consequences. Eli exploded into fits of hysterical laughter.

"I can't do this. I cannot do this. I feel like I'm going to ..." Eli sucked in gasps of air, his chest heaving, "... pass out or implode or ignite or ... or ... or ... or ..."

Silho put a hand on his shoulder and said, "Easy. This is just a fly-by and a test – right?"

"But this is it – this is the one. Everything has to be right. I need to check the formula – the darts." Eli tried to turn around, but Silho held him firm.

"Already checked – seventeen times. They're loaded." She paused a moment before continuing. "I know you want this to be the one – but it might not be. We haven't done a live test."

"I know, but this is the closest we've been, and then finding the map in Ev'r's journal ... It just feels like fate, don't you think?"

Silho's returned expression was cautious. She opened her mouth to speak, but then closed it, just patting him on the shoulder and sitting back in her seat to unplug the diverter cable, throwing control of the craft back to Eli. He gripped the steering yoke and felt calm descending over him as he glided them over the city, dropping low just above the building peaks.

Golmaria had been built long before Scorpia and had nowhere near its size. It was a traditional design of all one level, with a cathedral in the center and all the streets spreading out from this like spokes of a wheel. And it was without one doubt the most spooky, evil-lurking-in-dark-spaces place Eli had ever seen – and he'd seen some serious spooky in his time. Why exactly the fine hairs on his wings twitched at the sight of this lost city he couldn't quite pinpoint, but it just seemed that the shadows weren't falling right. From their bird's-eye view it seemed to him that life here had just stopped. There were no signs of resistance, of a slowly fought war with ruined buildings, dead bodies and battling survivors. Everything looked perfectly untouched. The only indication that the city had died at all was the plant life that had re-conquered the streets, and the lack of activity on what should have otherwise been a busy day.

Eli spotted a child's bike lying on its side in the middle of a sidewalk. One wheel rotated slowly without a breeze. The people here had just ... *changed* was the only word that fit, knowing what he knew about Golmaria. What was even more disturbing was that it was broad daylight with both the blue suns riding high in the sky. What would this fallen city feel like after darkfall?

Eli shuddered.

"What was she thinking coming here?" Eli spoke of Ev'r.

Silho raised her eyes to meet his in the rear vision mirror. "About treasures and artefacts, I suppose," she said, but her tone told him there was more.

"What is it?"

"Well, the Lava Diavol Mountains are nearby. That's where she buried Ismail."

Eli nodded. Ismail Ohavor – a scullion-gypsy from Ev'r's family tribe – her dead love. Eli had found sketches of him in Ev'r journal, and sobbed his way through Ev'r's written account of their story.

"Eli ..." Silho's voice hesitated. "Have you thought that maybe she doesn't want to come back?"

Something twisted in the pit of his stomach. Ev'r had been through so much, and had been so scarred, that perhaps death had been a relief. He had asked himself on more than one occasion if his mission to save her was more about his obsessions than her actual wants, but every time he'd come back to the memory of her fighting the inevitable transformation to the last breath. She had wanted to survive, to live – despite everything.

"I think she'd want us to try."

Silho nodded, accepting the idea. She blinked and her eyes darkened as she jumped to light-form vision.

"Anything?" Eli asked.

Silho's eyebrows flickered and she gave a nod. "They're everywhere – inside all the buildings."

Eli's skin crawled, his wings twitching.

"But they're stationary."

"Sleeping?" Eli squeaked hopefully.

Silho shrugged. She didn't know the ways of the Ravien. No one did. They were entering some seriously untrodden territory here.

"Do they all look the same?" Eli asked, bringing the craft around for another wide circle over the city.

"All the same," Silho confirmed.

It meant they had no way of knowing which one was Ev'r.

"We'll just have to run the trial and then figure out a way of doing a mass drop," Eli said.

"Are you sure this craft is going to hold up against them?" Silho asked.

"I'm sure," he said, but wasn't even certain himself if that was the truth or a stress-induced lie. Silho climbed over from the backseat and sat beside him. Nelly had hidden in her cage and Eli could see her accusing eyes shimmering in the shadows.

"Take us down in front of the cathedral," Silho directed. "The biggest population is in there."

Eli gripped the steering yoke and took them down to hover in front of the cathedral door, the entryway blackened with ominous forms.

"And the priest wondered why his parishioners weren't attending church," Eli joked, but his voice was shaky.

"Hit the lights," Silho murmured.

Eli's finger hovered over the switch then flicked it up. He gasped. The cathedral was jam-packed with Ravien – all squashed in and squirming. In a sudden burst, the winged monsters spewed out, battering the craft, throwing Eli and Silho from one side to the other. The monsters' horrible faces smashed up against the glass. Eli triggered the craft's guns and opened fire. The dart-vials of antidote pelted out, sinking into the beasts. One Ravien hit the windscreen, turned into a naked person, then straight back into a monster.

Eli's heart leaped up and crashed down so rapidly that he didn't know if he was severely disappointed or actually having a heart attack.

"No good – pull out," he heard Silho yell, but found he couldn't move. She lunged over and grabbed the controls, shooting them straight upward at a dizzying speed until they were clear of the Ravien. She leveled them out high in the air and they sat there gasping, watching the Ravien looping up in the air, like the body of a huge snake, before darting back inside the cathedral.

Eli blinked and found himself lying in the back seat of the craft, parked in the desert. Silho was fanning him with the map, concern pinching her features. Eli giggled, then slapped a hand over his mouth to stop it. If there was ever a moment when he felt less like laughing ... Silho stopped fanning him and helped him sit up.

"Are you alright?" she asked.

"Never better," Eli lied on automatic.

"You need to give yourself a break," Silho said. "I mean it, Eli. You need rest, food, fresh air – a bath."

Eli sniffed himself – it was bad.

"The stench of failure," he said.

"No," Silho said firmly. "You successfully transformed a Ravien back to its previous form. That's never been done before. It's not even been imagined. Everyone says 'There's no point, so give up', but you've done it. It's a major step."

Eli felt his spirits lifting. "You're right. As soon as we get back I'm going to re-test the formula and see why the transmute didn't hold and then —" Silho's expression stopped him short. "After I sleep, eat, inhale some premium-quality air and wash my armpits ..."

Silho smiled and shook her head. A crackling sound drew their attention to the front windscreen. As they looked out, a cave-pocked mountain appeared literally before their eyes and then vanished again.

"The Lava Diavol Mountains," Silho said.

"Should we ..." Eli started to say.

"No," Silho cut him off. "It's the golden rule of the desert."

Eli paused for the answer.

"Don't go to investigate – ever."

"Noted," Eli replied.

"Let's get out of here."

"Agreed," he said. He jumped back into the pilot's seat and started the engines for the flight back to Scorpia.

Chapter 12
Diega

PRATERIUS

RAMBELDON FOREST (POND ODIOUS)

Diega moved through the pine forest, tracking the distant sound of a trickling stream. One of the first lessons she'd learned as a soldier was that water is magnetic to most living creatures. There is always someone to be found near water. She stepped with practiced caution, watching her feet for snares and traps, searching for tracks, while some distance behind her Shawe crashed through the trees, more unsubtle than a stampede of elephants. She'd been trying to ignore the sound. She felt so much hatred for him right now that the thought of even having to acknowledge his existence was too much, but at this rate he was either going to scare away anyone who could help them, or get them captured or killed. So she forced herself to stop and wait until he was close enough, then she turned and burned him with a glare.

"What?" he said, his mouth full of Barkers Mints.

The urge to punch him in the face swelled with tidal force inside her, but then she saw blood had seeped through the skin overlay and thick wrap around his wound and was fast saturating his pants. Her anger subsided. He was moving unsteadily because he had an injury that would kill most people instantly.

Her mind went to Copernicus before she could stop it, opening up a yawning void of fear that threatened to drag her down into despair, but she forced it closed. She looked Shawe in the eyes and in truth, though it made her sick to admit it, he didn't actually look stupid – he looked like he knew exactly what she was thinking. She thought he might try to hit her with some waste-of-air speech about Copernicus being the toughest guy he knew, or a born survivor, or tell her lies about how he would be fine, but instead he said, "You hear that stream, sunshine?"

"Where do you think I'm going?" she replied.

"In the opposite direction."

She snorted. "Somehow I think I know more than you about tracking ..."

"Yeah, maybe – with all your fancy equipment," he said. "But not without it. Fairy-breeds don't have trutt-all sense of direction."

"And you do?" she demanded. "Galleys have poor eyesight, plus you're too damn arrogant to admit it or get it fixed."

"My eyesight might be average," Shawe conceded. "But my hearing is a hundred times better than yours."

"Please!" Diega spat.

"Care to put a wager on it?" Shawe said.

Diega was sorely tempted – she never said no to a bet – but it wasn't the time.

"Just follow me," he told her. "And if I'm wrong, you get to say I told you so. I know that would give you all kinds of thrills."

"You have no idea," she muttered.

Shawe turned and headed back in the direction they'd come from. Diega grudgingly followed, on the slight chance that he was right. They couldn't afford to waste time just because of her ego. At first she thought he was leading them astray, but then she sensed the trickling getting louder and louder, until finally they reached a low row of shrubs that hedged a bank, leading down to a pond.

They crouched behind the blue-leaf plants and Diega took the telescopic sights off her belt. The advanced functions were all blown, but the basic magnifiers were still intact. She looked through it, scanning over and around the pond until the circle of sight found what looked like a wooden bed, with someone lying beneath a grass blanket. Diega registered movement beside the bed and adjusted the sights. Another person came into focus. From the full ballroom gown it was wearing, Diega judge it to be female, but it didn't look like any race she'd seen before. It had red skin scattered with large black dots and a very insect-looking face, with external mandibles and oversized, shiny black eyes. The stranger definitely wasn't an insect blood human-breed, and all the full blood insect-breeds had become extinct eras ago – at least, in Aquais they had. There were hooks growing from both the stranger's palms, and she was using them to weave some kind of basket, while chattering non-stop – presumably to the sleeping figure. Diega began to refocus the lens, trying to see if there were any weapons around the bed, but Shawe snatched the sights out of her grasp and looked through it.

"What is that thing?" he muttered. "Butt-ugliest woman I've ever seen."

Diega's anger flared. "Really? And what are you? The world's most beautiful man? Wait, let me grovel at your feet in awe of your radiating beauty." She snatched back the sights. "Don't touch my stuff."

She checked the stranger's camp for weapons and didn't see anything obvious.

"I'm going to talk to them," she told Shawe. "You stay here."

"Hell no. I'm coming with," Shawe said.

Diega refused. "One look at you and they'll run a mile. You know it. Just stay put."

Shawe set his jaw and stared her down, but didn't rise to follow as she left the shrubs.

Diega moved down the bank and across a section of spongy moss grass to the edge of the pond, directly opposite the beetle girl. She cleared her throat. The insect-breed looked up sharply, shrieked and darted behind the bedhead.

"I'm not here to hurt you," Diega tried to reassure her.

A few long seconds passed before a very high, proper voice came from behind the bed, speaking Urigin with a heavy clicking insect accent.

"Go away, please."

Diega felt a surge of relief that she actually understood her. Urigin was supposed to be the universal language, but Diega had wondered. "I will, I promise – I just need to ask some directions and then I'll go."

Two huge beetle-black eyes peeked around the bed-leg, followed by a face with red dots on each cheek.

"I'm a traveler," Diega said, realizing that to let on she was utterly lost and unarmed could be a very bad idea. "I took a wrong turn and lost track of my companion. Have you seen a tall human-breed man, with purple and blue viper bloodlines? He has scars on his face … Have you seen him?"

The beetle girl shook her head then nodded straight after.

"You haven't?"

The beetle nodded then shook.

"You have?"

The beetle shook then nodded.

"You haven't?"

She nodded then shook again.

"So have you or haven't you?" Diega demanded, her frustration rising fast.

The beetle girl shrugged.

"For the love of ..." Shawe's voice bellowed from the shrubs.

"Love?" the beetle squeaked. "Did that tree say *love*?"

Diega paused, then tried, "I think so."

The insect-breed gave a small smile and lifted a gloved hand to hide it.

"Wait, please," she said, then seized the lump in the bed and shook it violently, saying, "Wake up, Tickleback. Let Hypnos dance alone," then in a much less dignified voice, "Wake up, Fool!"

The grass cover on the bed rolled back and a sleep-dazed creature emerged. He sat up and fixed Diega with emerald eyes, even larger than his companion's. In a sudden flurry of fine, intricately veined wings and long gangly limbs, he sprang up, giving Diega a clear view of heavily muscled shoulders sloping down to a very thin waist and legs. The creature – the dragonfly – made a nervous gulping sound, hurriedly straightening his bow tie with one set of arms while trying to brush the grass off his suit with another. He tried to talk but coughed instead, sending a spray of sparks bursting into the air. He covered his mouth with all four of his hands and the beetle cast him a prudish look of disapproval.

She cleared her throat and introduced them, "I am Trilly Byrd of the cluster Nolly-Nolly and this —"

The dragonfly cut in, speaking in a deep, slow voice, "I am Tickleback Ickabod, Pond Odious, clan of the Devil's Darning Needles."

"Great – and I'm Diega Bluejay," Diega rushed the introduction then said, "I need to know – have either of you seen a human-breed man? Viper marks, scarred-up skin, dark eyes."

"Please wait," Trilly said again, then spoke to her companion in wing buzzes. He responded and they seemed to start arguing in clicks and taps that went on for a long time. Diega squeezed her eyelids shut, willing them to hurry up, trying to stay calm while time ticked loud in her mind. She expected Shawe to come bursting out of the bushes and crack their skulls together at any moment.

Finally Tickleback spoke, his small antennae swiveling. "We were told two stranger men like this had passed through Dallybrush some sets ago."

Diega's skin prickled. He was here – still alive. "What's a set?" she asked. "And where's Dallybrush?"

Trilly spoke fast. "Sun set to moon set – one set, don't you know?"

"Days?" Diega guessed. It wasn't possible that days had passed since Copernicus was seen here – they'd only just arrived.

She spoke her thoughts to the insect-breeds and Tickleback said, "Maybe you came through at separate time spaces?"

"Came through?" Diega said. "How do you mean?"

"The portal," he said. "You are not from here." His eyes moved over her.

"Where *is* here?" she asked, most of her not wanting to hear the answer.

"Rambeldon Forest," he said.

"On Aquais?" she ventured.

The insects looked at each other, then shook their heads in unison.

"Praterius," Tickleback said.

Diega knew it was coming, but still felt a dizzying jolt of shock. *We're on another planet.*

"Do you know which way this man was headed?" she managed to ask.

Tickleback nodded, but Trilly shook her head and said to the dragonfly between gritted teeth, "Don't say anything!"

Tickleback ignored her and said, "We were told he were taken by ..." he lowered his voice to the quietest whisper possible, "... the Neridori."

"The Neridori?" Diega repeated aloud.

"Oh my!" Trilly squealed and both creatures buzzed their wings in a nervous whir. Their agitation passed quickly to the trees that swayed and rustled without any breeze.

"Please don't say that too loud," Tickleback whispered.

"I'm sorry," Diega said. "Just tell me how to get to these —" she lowered her voice "— Neridori, and I'll leave you alone."

"They live in the Blackwater Forest past Wishing-Well Woods. It are very hard to find – a very long way if you don't know shortcuts," the dragonfly said.

"Is there anyone around here who could show me the way?" Diega asked them.

Tickleback took her in with deep, solemn eyes. "I know a way through the forest. I —"

Trilly interrupted with an impatient clap of her wings. "But we can't take you. It's far too dangerous – far, far too dangerous. We cannot go to Blackwater – no, no, no, no, no!" She stamped one petite foot. "We are not going anywhere."

Tickleback continued where he'd left off. "— I can take you there."

Trilly clapped her wings again and the dragonfly turned to her, saying in his slow, calm voice, "This friend needs our help and I will help her. We will do what is right." He turned back to Diega. "We will take you as far as we can."

Diega nodded with gratitude, but had no intention of letting her guard down. No one helped anyone without reason.

The dragonfly took a battered top hat from under the grass cover and perched it on his head.

"Follow Tickleback." He beckoned with all four hands.

Diega said, "Wait. There's someone else with me."

She heard Shawe standing up in the shrubs behind her.

Trilly gasped and scuttled backward, but Tickleback just nodded to Shawe and said in his gentle way, "Morning greetings, friend."

Shawe, ever the skillful diplomat, grunted a surly reply that sounded like "Trutt off".

"Follow Tickleback," the insect-breed repeated.

He gestured for Trilly to go first. She clacked angrily, then turned with a rustle of her billowing gown and set off. Tickleback whirred his wings and lifted off the ground, his long, thick tail balancing him like a rudder. He beckoned again and flew after his companion. Diega and Shawe exchanged a look and trudged after them.

Chapter 13
Eli

AQUAIS

MATADORI DESERT (GOLMARIA)

Eli had taken the data recorded on the day he and Silho
found Golmaria and created a prototype desert-navigation
program. This holographic mapping system now rotated
above the control board of the *Gypsy Rose*. Eli had linked up
the autopilot to the mapping system and felt the transflyer
auto-correcting their flight path every few moments, following the lines of the map. He wasn't sure if it would actually
work, but if it did, it would be the first programmable navigation map of the Matadori in history. If it didn't, they would
become inextricably lost, then run out of fuel and end up as
fodder for the desert hordes, if they didn't die from exposure
first.

High in the sky the suns were moving in toward their mer-
ging at the burning hour of the day. Even now, in winter, the
ferocity of the heat was beyond belief.

Though he wasn't steering the craft, Eli still kept a stranglehold on the wheel, if only to stop himself from replaying the fight-in attack footage for what would most likely be the billionth time. He'd already gone over it again and again, trying to bring into focus the blurs of flame he knew had been people, but nothing had worked. There was something about their attackers that the technology couldn't capture. Everyone else was clear enough, though. And maybe that was why he'd kept re-watching it, even when he knew he couldn't fix it – some irrational part of him hoped that if he watched it enough times maybe something would change – maybe Silho's eyes wouldn't blank out the way they had, maybe that bone-knife wouldn't stab through the commander's shoulder. But no matter how many times he replayed it, the footage remained the same.

He glanced at Ev'r's backpack sitting on the passenger seat beside him. It felt like a good sign – soon she would be wearing it again. The *Gypsy Rose* tilted and corrected and Flintlock shifted her weight in the back. It was Eli's experience that giants – all gargantuan-breeds, actually – fell asleep as soon as they stopped moving. It was the only way they could generate enough energy to shift around their mountainous bulk. But Flintlock had remained awake and alert the entire trip so far. Clearly she'd been trained against her nature – rarely a good thing. He shot a glance in the rear vision at the Corámorán and glimpsed something he'd missed before – the crest of the Menor crime family tattooed into her bruised wrists.

The Menors were part of what was known in alerion-breed tongue as *Yuna Kazo*, which translated in Urigin as "the Talented Families". Focusing mainly on upper-class criminal activity like gem and gold heists, art forgery and political blackmail, they considered themselves to be the gentlemen of the criminal world, superior to the gangsters – but blood was blood and murder, murder as far as Eli was concerned.

"You worked for the Menors?" Eli asked Flintlock.

She looked up, uneasiness shadowing her eyes.

"It's alright," he told her. "You don't have to talk about it if you don't want to. My kind – we always ask too many questions."

Flintlock processed his words. Giants were often thought of as slow-minded, but the Corámorán were, in general, intelligent. They had large bodies, but also large brains, compared to other gargantuan-breeds who combined a much bigger size with even smaller brain mass.

"Your questions. I like them," she eventually said. "Nobody else asks anything. Nobody else cares to ask."

"Yes," Eli said. "I used to have another gargantuan-breed friend, his name was Tiny. He said once that it was hard to be so big and yet feel so completely invisible."

Flintlock's eyes welled up with tears, "You understand," she said softly. "I had no choice. No say."

Eli lowered his stare so he didn't see her tears and start crying again himself. During the early year-cycles of his military training, he'd conducted a minor study into the gargantuan-breed practice of selling their children to pay debts, as well as in general barter and trade. When done in their own communities it resulted in the majority of children still having a happy family life, but when the Corámorán Islands and the gargantuan cities of Gont and Klimt had been destroyed by tidal floods some twenty year-cycles earlier, they had all headed into Scorpia. And here they were selling their children to non-gargantuans, who used them for slave labor and other more horrible things.

Flintlock spoke again. "I belonged to Troya Menor. Guard to his lady wife. I started off nobody and worked hard. Worked up."

Eli nodded. It was common for the giantesses to be put in charge of guarding the harems of the Talented Families. They were big enough to overcome most men, but were not usually tempted in the male way.

"His wife was Tracy Menor," Eli said and Flintlock grimaced at the name.

Eli knew the story from there. It was a classic case of the bigger they are the harder they fall. Menor was the biggest Talented Family *Ky-puten*, or Captain, in the city until everything fell apart and their closest competition slaughtered the entire family.

Eli decided to fast-forward the conversation over that bit, since remembering was clearly painful for her.

"Afterward you went back to your own family?" he asked.

"There was nowhere else to go. No one else would hire me. I'm too small," Flintlock said.

That made Eli laugh. "If you're too small, I must be microscopic," he replied. "I think you're absolutely enormous."

Eli had learned the hard way that most women didn't appreciate that compliment, but it made Flintlock smile for the first time. It was a radiant smile that erased all the hard lines of her face, but after a moment the expression faltered and she said, "Please don't send me back to them."

Eli felt a strong sense of sadness for her. He complained a lot about his own childhood, but it was really nothing in comparison to what others went through.

"I won't send you back. I promise," he said.

The transflyer seized up suddenly and savagely, pinning Flintlock against the seat and smashing Eli into the steering wheel. He pushed away and stared through the windscreen. Golmaria stretched out before them, just as creepy the second time around. Eli's wings twitched at the sight. He felt Nelly gnawing at his leg from inside the pocket. That was her way of saying *just leave it and go home*. But home, without the people he loved, was only a place with a roof and bed.

"Infrared," he told his on-board system and a heat grid flashed up across the windscreen. They flew over the city, scanning for Ravien, but there was no sign of body-heat anywhere – not even in the cathedral. It wasn't until they reached the outskirts of the city that the system registered something. There were huge pits all around the perimeter of Golmaria that had been dug down into underground tunnels during a time of atmospheric threat, and they'd never been filled back in. It looked from the body-heat scan as though the Ravien were now down in these holes. He slowed the craft to hover over the largest well.

"So I'm going to dump the antidote on them now," he said to Flintlock. His voice sounded almost cheerful, but inside he was one big knot. "They might attack us ..."

Flintlock straightened, readying herself.

Eli pressed the release button on the cargo hold and the new dart-vials dropped, crashing down into one of the boreholes. At first nothing happened, and then a group of Ravien clamored out of the tunnel and writhed on the ground. They started convulsing, then shifted back to their human forms. They held the change for several moments, enough time even for one of them to stand up and look around, but then they changed back to Ravien.

It was another failure.

Extreme disappointment pressed Eli down in his seat. The confines of the transflyer suddenly felt too tight. He couldn't breathe. He had to get out. He rapidly glided the craft away from the city and down into the desert, landing with a bump and a skid. He threw open the door and jumped down. The heat took his breath away and he staggered only a few steps from the craft before dropping to his knees. He stared out into the distant waves of heat, not seeing anything ahead of him. There was nothing to hope for. Nelly ran up to his shoulder and snuffled at his face.

Shadows fell over them, shielding them from the ferocious suns. Flintlock put a hand on Eli's head, and Nelly moved as though she was going to bite her, but then thought better of it and scurried back to his pocket to hide.

"I need to find someone to tell me how to save my friends," he told her. "I can – I can't do it alone. I just —"

Eli saw a buzz of movement beside the *Gypsy Rose*. He grabbed his electrifier and aimed it at the craft as Diamond LeSwer leaped into sight, calling out, "Surprise!"

Eli only just managed to stop himself from pulling the trigger.

Diamond flew the distance between them, blonde curls bobbing, shimmering in the sunslights, and flung herself into his arms. "I missed you so much!"

Flintlock immediately peeled her off Eli and held her high in the air by her wings, like a tiny insect.

"Who are you? What is your business with Master Eli?" she demanded.

"It's okay, Flintlock," Eli said. "She's ... she's ..." He really didn't know how to finish the sentence.

"Diamond LeSwer," the imp-breed girl said. She took Flintlock's other hand and started to do a strange midair jig. The giantess looked her up and down like she was crazy and dropped her to the sand, where she continued to dance and sing. Eli started to feel insane again, his heart beating too fast, his breath stuck in his throat. Something was very wrong with him.

"Something wrong?" Diamond said as though she'd read his mind, her face peering right into his. Her breath smelled like strawberry. "You look peakish. Are you peakish? I think you might be peakish."

"Stop saying *peakish*," Eli said. "I'm ..."

"Hungry? Thirsty? Having a nervous breakdown? Madly in love with me?" She grinned and her eyebrows darted up and down in unison like two hyperactive question marks.

"No, none of the above. Just stop —"

"— finishing your sentences?" she said.

Eli turned and fled further into the desert, where he collapsed into a gasping, sobbing heap.

The ground trembled as Flintlock ran to him, Diamond fluttering beside her. The tiny imp-breed girl threw her arms around him and began to sing a song, actually a lullaby that he remembered from his childhood – one that had always made him feel better. Flintlock joined in the comforting, patting him on the head like a small dog, until he felt strong enough to sit up.

"*Ie'est*," Diamond said in imp-breed. "Everything is okay. Tell me your problems and we'll wish them away together." Glittery streams of sweat ran down her face.

"This isn't something a wish will help," he told her. "My friends – one is poisoned and the others have been taken through a portal, and I can't find anyone to help me get them back."

"Why do you need help?" Diamond said.

"As I just said, to get them back."

"I heard you, but you don't need anyone to help you do that," Diamond insisted. "You're Eli Anklebiter. You're famous for fixing any problem."

Eli stared at her, taken aback by the words. "I am?"

Diamond laughed so hard she started snorting and couldn't stop.

"You're the foremost scientific mind in the entire city," she managed to choke out. "And you didn't even realize!"

"It's true," Flintlock said. "Your name is very well-known."

Eli was stunned. He realized people in the military and in some scientific fields would know who he was, but he had no idea that he was *famous* to the rest of the population.

"Really?" he asked.

Diamond continued snorting and Flintlock nodded. Eli remembered the commander once saying to him when they were still kids that one day everyone would know his name. He'd laughed at the time, hysterically of course, but hearing that praise from Copernicus had made him feel as though he could do anything. And he'd started acting that way, inventing more, dreaming bigger. It had changed how he saw himself. Despite Eli's issues, the commander had always believed in him. So had Diega and Jude – and Silho – yet here he was now running around trying to find someone to tell him what to do, when all he really needed to do was put his mind to it. He couldn't believe he'd been so stupid. He'd just panicked and fallen apart, maybe because a big part of him still felt as though their victory against the Skreaf had just been a massive fluke, and it was so easy to start doubting again. Enough! It was time to get himself together and start working.

Eli forced himself to stand. As he did, he caught a distant flash of the Lava Diavol Mountains, just as he had with Silho.

"Look! What's that?" Diamond shrieked and took off toward it, flying fast.

"Wait! Come back!" Eli called, but she didn't stop or even slow, so he was forced to fly after her, with Flintlock thundering behind them. Just as he came even with her, another zap of magics trembled the air and the mountains vanished, then reappeared directly in front of their path. He and Diamond crashed into the rocky mountainside and thudded down to the sand.

"What's up there?" Diamond sat up, her eyes shimmering with curiosity. "There's something glowing in one of the caves."

"It doesn't matter. We shouldn't be here. We have to go," Eli told her.

He took her hand to direct her back to the *Gypsy Rose*. She grinned at him and tried to kiss it.

Eli struggled and managed to drag himself away.

"Just come on!" he said. "I'm not playing around."

He turned and started back to the transflyer, but when he checked over his shoulder, Diamond was not following. She was up the mountain, disappearing into one of the caves, where he could see flashes of light.

"*Lai lai,*" Eli whispered in frustration.

With the saying *curiosity killed the imp* running through his mind, he flew back and up, landing in the cave mouth. Flintlock was still in the distance, but coming fast. He waved at her, hoping she could see where he was going, and then hurried after Diamond into the cool of the cave.

* * * * *

Keeping to the shadows, Eli picked a cautious path over the rocks, the thick earthy scents of the cave mingling with something else that set his teeth on edge. Nelly lay silent but awake, deep in his pocket. Eli zipped it up to make sure she stayed put. Finally he glimpsed the sparkle of Diamond's skin up in the darkness ahead. He climbed faster and found her, standing with her back to him, looking down at something. He ran to her side and whispered, "Diamond! Come with me – it's not safe here."

She didn't reply, staring, fixedly, at something below them. Eli followed her line of sight. What he saw was so strange and disturbing that it took him several moments to process it. Below them, in a hollowed-out chamber lit by flaming torches, there was a hole in the ground with a man lying inside it. His eyes were closed and skin was deathly pale. Eli would have thought him dead, except he could see the slight movements of his chest rising and falling. His stare lifted to the man's face and recognition jolted him. *Ismail Ohavor.* But he had died long ago – maybe even ten year-cycles now – so why was he here, breathing?

Eli blinked his eyes rapidly, wondering if he was hallucinating. Sometimes caves had trapped gases, or dormant magics, even hallucinogenic fungi particles in the air that could affect the mind. He scrunched his eyes closed, exhaled deeply to clear his mind, then re-opened them. It was still Ismail. Eli's shock became near-hysterical excitement that left him lightheaded.

"It's Ismail!" He gripped Diamond's shoulder. "He's here! He's alive!"

Her eyes filled with astonishment, a smile of wonder and hope spreading across her face, then she asked, "Who's Ismail?"

Eli shook his head. "I'll tell you later. Just – you stay here, and I'll go and get him. Okay?"

"Got it. You stay here and I'll go get him," she repeated.

Eli stepped onto the ledge and Diamond fluttered up to stand beside him.

"What are you doing?" Eli asked her.

"I'm going to get him and you're staying here," she said.

"No," Eli said. "I'm going." He pointed to himself. "You're staying."

"Oh. Right," Diamond replied. "But why am I staying?"

"Because it's dangerous."

"But why is it dangerous?"

"Diamond," Eli said, his patience starting to wear very thin. "Just wait here. Okay?"

The small imp-breed girl smiled and said, "Your breath smells like sunshine and rainbows."

Eli took that as a yes. He jumped off the ledge and flew down into the cavern. He landed lightly, but sensed the dense shadows stirring around him. The lantern flames flickered. One blew out. Eli crouched down to the dirt, realizing with a sick lurch that he'd rushed in without checking for threats. He cursed. After the amount of times the commander had told him not to let his heart lead his brain, he should have known better by now. He drew his electrifier and scanned the hidden corners of the cavern. When no dangers took form, he crawled to the grave and peeked inside.

It was still Ismail – lying like the breathing dead. A shimmer caught Eli's eyes and he leaned further down, seeing a manacle locked onto Ismail's ankle. It was linked to a chain that was sunk deeply into the side of the grave. The way the manacle had half-buried itself under Ismail's skin suggested he'd been there for an extremely long time. Nerves crawled across Eli's back and his stomach gurgled with foreboding. Every instinct told him to run, to get as far away from this place as fast he could, but this was Ismail – Ev'r's Ismail – and he wasn't going to leave him.

"Ismail," Eli whispered and something stirred in the hollow darkness above them. Eli stared upward until his eyes started watering, then he looked back to Ev'r's lost love and tried again. "Ismail."

The scullion-gypsy man didn't respond and Eli realized he'd have to go in.

Keeping his eyes fixed on Ismail, he gripped the edge of the grave and lowered himself down. He landed a few steps away from the prone man and crouched there, blinking the sweat out of his eyes, watching. All around him, the sides of the grave had been clawed and scratched, and he could see lines of deep red on the rocks where skin had worn to blood from prolonged effort. Ismail had been fighting to free himself – maybe for the full ten year-cycles.

Eli gulped. He inched closer to the scullion man until he was within touching distance. He reached out a trembling hand and gave Ismail's arm one fast tap, then whipped back. Nothing. His skin was gray and cold, but his chest continued to lift and sink.

Eli started to reach out again, then something thudded close to the edge of the grave. He froze and held his breath. Heavy, dragging footsteps closed in on them and Eli scuttled back, pressing himself as hard as he could into the side of the grave. A shadow fell over him and he tipped his head gradually back, up and up, until he saw – it – the hooded person standing above them. The burning tar of dark magics stung Eli's eyes and his immediate thought was *Skreaf*. The air left his lungs in a thin, shaking gasp. The witch jumped suddenly, landing in the grave between Eli and Ismail. Eli pressed a hand over his own mouth to stop from crying out.

The witch was hunched but hulking. The bulky layers of her robes and fur wraps made her look part-beast. Eli dug his fingernails into the dirt wall. His wings were twitching incessantly, trying to burst into flight, and he ached to let them, but what if he flew and the witch took Ismail away, hid him someplace else? He had to hold on, he had to fight for Ev'r's soulmate.

He slid a hand down to his electrifier and drew it inch by inch, extending it toward the witch's back. He held his finger on the trigger, his muscles shaking, waiting for her to reel around at any second and attack. But she didn't. She didn't turn and she didn't speak. She just stepped to Ismail's side and kneeled, lowering a basket of dead bats to the ground. She placed a hand with dirty, overgrown claws on Ismail's chest.

Her coarse whisper came from the depth of her hood. "Wake, my love."

Ismail stirred, looking up at the witch, the red glow of a night wolf behind the darkness of his eyes. Horror and dismay flickered in his stare as he woke from whatever dreamland he'd escaped to, back to this nightmare captivity, but the emotion fast died, leaving a defeated blankness.

The witch took his shoulder and forced him to sit up.

"A feast for you, my love," she croaked. "Eat."

She lifted one of the bats by its wing and Ismail snatched at it and shoved it into his mouth with a violent hunger. He started ripping it apart and gulping it down with hardly a chew, then he glanced up and spotted Eli. The scullion's expression didn't change, but he paused momentarily, with blood tricking down his chin, dripping into his overgrown beard.

"What? What is it?" the witch demanded.

Eli shook his head at Ismail, but the scullion man had already looked away.

"Thirsty," he grunted, his voice raspy and worn.

"You thirst, my love?" The witch crooned. "So do I. First you quench my need and then I'll see to yours."

Eli watched as she lowered her hood, revealing her face, a rotting mess of pus and decaying meat. Maggots and parasites writhed in the empty sockets of her eyes. The smell was powerfully repulsive, like a physical punch to the face. Eli covered his mouth and nose and gagged. He'd been around plenty of death and infested rot, but none of it living. Clearly she'd died and brought herself back with dark magics – zombification. As far as Eli knew only one dark witch, Darmel the Premonitionist, had immortalized herself this way, but this witch wasn't Darmel. Eli saw a brand on the sallow, sagged skin of her arms, the bloodlines so faded they were barely visible – *O'A*. He'd seen it before in Ev'r's journal. It was the inmate mark of O'Tenery Asylum. He realized this must be the Mocking Witch, who Ev'r had fought and killed to save Ismail. The one who had taught her everything she knew of dark magics. She wasn't a Skreaf, but she was still deadly powerful.

The witch ran her hand along Ismail's chest, all the way to his pants. Her fingers caressed over the fabric and she leaned closer to him, as though to kiss him. Ismail gritted his teeth, but didn't pull away, and maggots dropped from her face onto his shirt. Eli gripped his own mouth tighter, trying not to heave, as she licked Ismail's face with a swollen white tongue.

"Water," Ismail rasped.

The witch grabbed a fistful of his hair and dragged his head back roughly.

"First you'll give me what I want!" she shrieked.

Ismail started coughing, a deep, unhealthy rattling sound. He continued until the witch gave a displeased grunt and shoved him away. She lifted her hood to conceal her face, then stepped back, vanishing into the gray mist of the murk. Ismail slumped onto his side, his body racked with coughs. Eli darted forward, dropping to his knees beside him.

"Ismail!" he whispered, but the scullion just lay there rasping.

Eli holstered his electrifier and grabbed Ismail's shoulder, rolling him onto his back. The scullion's eyes were closed again, and his breathing had fallen into a slow and shallow rhythm. The witch had cursed him back into sleep. With his overgrown hair and beard splashed with blood, Ismail looked more wolf than man. He was a scullion-gypsy of the Blackwater Wolf family – just like Ev'r.

Eli shook himself out of his shock and grabbed the chain cutters off his weapon belt. He scrambled to the shackle around Ismail's ankle and snipped a link of the chain that was attaching it to the wall, but it regenerated straightaway and sealed back over.

Eli stared at it in disbelief.

"Magics. It must be cursed," he whispered, then cast a wild glance around them, expecting the witch to return at any moment. He grabbed for his weapon belt and pulled out every tool he could think of that would break a chain, but each time the chain snapped, it reformed just as fast. His heart hammered louder than his thoughts, which roared like a hurricane round and round inside his mind.

Ismail groaned, restless in his unnatural sleep.

Eli tried again, covering the chain with liquid ice, then smashing it. The chain broke and mended immediately. He stood up. Nothing was working to break the chain, so maybe he could send something to dig it out of the wall. He grabbed one of his newest inventions from a pocket on his belt. It was a burrowing drill, a small claw-like digging device, its design based on the hands of the Tangelan Burrowers, the technique copied from the burying-beetle human-breed bloodline. He'd initially thought of it for underground rescues or implantation of tracking or explosive devices into buildings, but it seemed just what they needed here.

He rapidly programmed it, then pushed it into the wall of the grave beside where the chain vanished. It blinked to life and he sent it through the dirt with a hand-controlled remote. It dug successfully, rapidly, following the length of the chain deep into the mountain earth and deeper still, on and on. Eli sensed the moments passing, counting the drips of sweat that rolled off his face as he waited for the drill to find the end of the chain and bring it back. Soon it became apparent – there was no end. The witch had thought of everything. Eli turned to Ismail; his face twitched and a growl rumbled in his throat, but his eyes remained firmly shut.

"I'll try the chain again," Eli said to himself, racing back and dropping down at Ismail's feet. He examined the manacle. It had the same green hue to it as the chain, which suggested it had been cursed as well. A horrible thought came to Eli: the only way out might be amputation. He had enough fast-acting drugs for it to be humane. If it was between that or staying here, he was sure Ismail wouldn't argue. He leaned in close and saw that Ismail's ankle had deep scarring all around where the shackle had embedded in the flesh. It looked like ... teeth marks ... as though Ismail had tried to bite his own foot off many times over – which meant it was growing back just like the chain. Eli's throat tightened.

"I'm getting you out," he told the sleeping man.

He felt over his belt and pockets, touching everything, desperately thinking of what options were left. His hand closed over something smooth and round that didn't seem familiar and he pulled out a Khaiti green diamond with the words *Beatlebee Bellbeater I* inscribed on it. His nerves jumped and he almost dropped it – touching someone's gravestone was extremely bad luck. He didn't remember picking it up.

As he stared down into the shimmering green, Ev'r's words on dark magics came back to him – *Any symbol can be used for good or evil depending on who is using it. It's not what the symbol is – it's what it can be in your hands. They intended harm – you intended help and your intention behind that particular symbol was stronger than theirs. It's a fundamental of magics.*

He was no wielder of magics, but the green diamond had saved him once before – and his intention to help Ismail was suffocatingly strong. He held the diamond up, summoned all his strength, then threw it at the chains, crying out, "Break!" The green gem bounced off and rolled into the dirt. The chains remained intact. Eli scrambled for the diamond and grabbed it back up. That hadn't gone as hoped, and Eli sensed time was starting to turn on them. The flame torches were flickering, the shadows creeping closer. The witch was returning.

Eli shut his eyes, searching it for answers. Ev'r spoke from his memories: *Skreaf magics are based on symbols.*

But what did the diamond symbol mean? In the desert that day he'd thrown his pendant at the Skreaf and yelled "Stop".

It had blocked them from attacking ... *blocked them* ... an idea took root and sprouted. Without pausing, he grabbed up his cutters and snipped the chain again. With super-speed he jammed the diamond between the two chain links before they could reconnect. The cut part of the chain started snaking about, desperately seeking a way back to the link, but the diamond was blocking it.

Eli let out a cry. "We've done it!"

He snatched some tape from his belt and bound the diamond firmly onto the end of the chain that was still attached to the manacle around Ismail's leg.

He started to try to haul Ismail into a sitting position, but then he heard scuffling behind him and his heart seized in his chest. He forced himself to turn and look. A tidal wave of relief crashed over him. Luther stood watching them with his python eyes, the shadows obscuring half his face. Moses appeared beside him, sniffing the air. He stood very rigid with his coat bristling, ears back, and the whites of his eyes flashing wildly. The wolf spotted the scullion man and his ears came forward. He made a small whining sound.

"Luther, help me get him out of here!" Eli cried out.

Luther gave a quick nod and used Cos magics to form a wind platform to propel them out of the grave.

As soon as they were out, Ismail's eyes flicked open, the curse to keep him sleeping broken. He gave a strangled gasp, one hand clutching his chest.

"He's going into cardiac arrest!" Eli said.

According to Ev'r's journal, Ismail had died from a stab wound to the heart. Eli ripped open Ismail's shirt, the material aged and rotten. He grabbed a syringe off his belt filled with a formula mixed to inhibit the body's natural stress response. The physiological process was different across races, but the formula was a good all-round mix that he'd discovered while doing a study into enhancing soldier concentration and accuracy during training and missions. It would slow the rate of Ismail's heart. He bit the cap off, spitting it away, then injected it into Ismail's arm. It had an immediate reaction, the scullion's body relaxing and his breathing coming easier.

Eli grabbed an oxygen vial off his belt and tried to attach it to Ismail's mouth, but the scullion swiped it away deliriously, his eyes rolling. He stared around at them, disorientated. A deep growl rumbled in his throat and Moses came forward, sniffing his face and whining softly. Seeing the wolf, Ismail's hostility melted away. He reached out a shaking hand to Moses and as he touched the wolf's white fur, he made a sound of shock.

"Real," he murmured, but then he jolted away. "She's coming," he rasped. "She's here."

Eli heard the thud behind them and his muscles froze. He didn't want to look. He really didn't. Beside him, Moses bared his teeth in a silent, savage snarl. Eli braced himself and looked.

The Mocking Witch stood there with a jug of water in one hand. She turned her hooded head one way and then the other, sensing something was wrong, but not knowing exactly what.

"My love?" she hissed and Ismail cringed. Her attention darted his way. She dropped the jug and it shattered.

"No!" she screamed, blasting them with a surge of stinking air. Eli drew his electrifier and started firing, getting off only a few shots before the witch hissed an enchant that ripped the weapon out of his grasp. She started to curse again. Ismail cried out.

Eli heard a clatter from above them and looked up to the ledge. Flintlock stood there beside Diamond, holding a boulder above her head. She hurled it down onto the witch, who used an enchant to break straight through it. Flintlock released a sonic roar that trembled the cave. She dropped down off the ledge and smashed the witch with her massive spiked club. The impact ripped the witch's rot-weakened flesh to pieces, but she re-formed in midair and doubled back whole. She tried to curse Flintlock, but was hampered by Diamond throwing what looked like a small metal square at her feet. On impact it unfolded and kept unfolding into a huge shield.

"Grab him!" Eli shouted to Flintlock as he tried to heave Ismail to his feet.

The giant lunged in and hoisted the scullion man onto her shoulders. She started to climb back up to the ledge, but the witch broke through Diamond's shield and sent a curse that ripped her back down. Luther flared up, bringing the ceiling crashing on top of the witch's head, completely burying her. She struggled to break out, but he held her with Cos enchants, mouthing to Eli, "Go!' Moses stood at Luther's side, snarling at the shuddering pile of rocks.

"Go!" Luther mouthed again.

Eli nodded. Luther could dematerialize, but Eli had no such skill – if he stayed, he'd be dead. He flew up beside Flintlock, who was climbing again and had almost reached the ledge. Diamond grabbed the giant's hand to help her over, getting in the way and actually slowly her down, but finally they were up.

Flintlock broke into a run, with Ismail slung over her shoulder and groaning in pain. They couldn't stop to help him; they just pushed on as fast as they could run and fly. The walls quaked around them, distorted screams howled behind and Eli searched ahead for the outside light, but the darkness seemed never-ending. Finally, when they'd already been running for far longer than he remembered taking on the way in, he saw a glowing spark in the distance.

"We're almost there!" he yelled to Diamond and Flintlock and they sped up their pace.

The spark grew bigger and brighter so quickly Eli soon realized it wasn't proportional to how fast they were moving – it was as though the light was traveling toward them as well. Except light didn't move unless it was —

"Fire!" Eli yelled. "It's fire. Stop!"

Lava Diavol translated into Urigin as *demon mouth* and Eli could now feel why – the heat propelling toward them was blinding even from this distance.

"The witch must have somehow blocked the entrance," Eli panted. He heard a curse hiss through the air around them and the shadows suddenly grew arms, trying to drag Ismail away from Flintlock, away from the fire and back to the witch. Flintlock battled to hold him as he gasped in pain, stretched between the two forces. Eli looked back; behind them the darkness was mutating, forming into an army of staggering, lurching figures. They couldn't go back. They couldn't go forward. Eli dropped to his knees, his eyes stinging from the heat of the fire. He grabbed a handful of burrowing drills from his pocket and a blast grenade. He bound them all together, set the timer for five seconds and threw the bundle up into the jagged ceiling. The burrowers set to work, sinking deeply into the rock. The shadow golems had reached Flintlock and were threatening to drag her down; the fire was looming, roaring, burning. Diamond held her face and screamed – a long high-pitched note. It was an excruciatingly long five seconds. Then a blast rocked the cave tunnel and Eli pushed Diamond aside as rocks crashed down where she'd been standing. Sunslight streamed down onto their faces. Eli fired the anchor hook from his zip gun and felt it find purchase above.

"Flintlock!" He threw the zip gun to her and she grabbed it, triggering the recoil. The pressure yanked her off her feet and upward into the escape tunnel, Ismail clutched in one arm. Diamond and Eli launched after her, flying fast as the fire collided with the shadows just behind them. The witch's scream chased them all the way through the darkness until they burst out into the desert.

As they did, an evil voice hissed, "I'll find you, my love ... I'll always find you."

It immediately took first place as the creepiest thing Eli had ever heard, but he didn't pause to ponder.

The group crashed down the mountain to the desert sand, and Eli spun back to search for signs of Luther, only to find the mountain gone – vanished. Above them the suns had almost merged and the sand had started to smoke and catch alight.

"Run!" Eli shouted and they raced through the fiery air toward the *Gypsy Rose* parked in the distance. The more they ran and flew, the further away it seemed to be, the sand itself seeming to be dragging them backward, the deceptive magics of the Matadori conspiring against them. One of Eli's boots burst into flames and as he hopped around trying to take it off, he realized his error. He grabbed the transflyer flash out of his pocket and shouted into it, "Engage autopilot, emergency pick-up mode!"

Immediately the *Gypsy Rose* burst to life, launching into the air and shooting toward them. It swooped in low and maneuvered sideways, the top of the craft opening like a mouth and scooping them up as it zoomed through. Eli slammed into the back of the cabin where the seat should have been. He groaned in pain, then Flintlock smashed down beside him, Diamond on top of her. Ismail lay between them, unresponsive, his eyes glazed.

The *Gypsy Rose* leveled off in the air and waited for further pilot input.

"Diamond!" Eli said, struggling upright. "Can you ..."

"Fly?" Diamond cut in. She scrambled over into the pilot's seat and kicked the transflyer up to top speed so quickly that Eli hit the windscreen and bounced back. He managed to collect himself and unzipped the pocket for Nelly to get out. She lifted her head up, looked around, then ducked straight back in. Eli spread Ismail out between himself and Flintlock. The scullion's eyes were scrunched tight shut and he was groaning in pain and coughing, the same deep unwholesome sound rattling inside him. Eli examined Ismail's chest. It was all scar. He'd suffered devastating injury around his heart, and there were dark magic symbols there too, etched deeply into his skin. Eli took out his stethoscope and listened to the scullion's heart. The beat was way too fast and extremely odd, and as he listened, he eyed the scars – it actually looked as if he'd had a transplant. Ismail writhed in agony, his breathing becoming more labored and erratic, and Eli was afraid full coronary arrest was imminent. He made a quick decision and unclipped the He-Ro, one of the robotic hearts he'd designed, from his belt. The team used them on heart attack and heart trauma victims.

"I'm swapping functioning of your heart to an external source," he quickly explained to Ismail, though he wasn't sure the scullion could hear him through the pain. He positioned the He-Ro over Ismail's chest and activated it. The unit injected its instant aesthetic, then attached hard against the skin and plunged its lines down, linking up with all the arteries of the heart. It clamped them and took over from Ismail's internal heart.

The scullion's body relaxed and he lay gasping, staring up at the transflyer roof with weeping eyes, the sunslight painfully bright for him after so long in darkness. He stared over at Flintlock and then Eli, started to try to speak, and then passed out cold.

"Master Eli, this man is very dangerous," Flintlock said, leaning close. "Leave him here in the desert."

"I can't leave him, Flintlock," Eli said, working fast, putting an oxygen mask over Ismail's face and injecting doses of fast-acting healing and regenerative agents into him. "He's a friend of a friend. We have to try to help him."

He continued to treat the tormented man while Diamond sped them through the desert, singing loudly with stress, some terribly rude song about underwear. When Eli had administered everything he could, including some more anaesthetic to keep the scullion under for a while so that the other medications could take faster effect, he stared down at Ismail's gaunt, pale face, a ghost of the strong, young man from the sketches in Ev'r's book. Ismail and Ev'r had been torn apart, then reunited, then she'd watched him die ... and now he was here and she was gone. Fate had dealt them a very cruel hand indeed – or maybe not. Maybe this was fate stepping in to give them another chance. If Eli could just keep him alive for long enough to bring Ev'r back, they could be reunited ... Eli imagined it for a moment, the look on Ev'r's face, but then the image melted into her becoming the Ravien. He shook the thought away, his mind going to Luther. He couldn't believe they'd left him and Moses alone to fight the witch, but there just hadn't been another choice. He murmured a prayer for their safety.

When he'd finished stabilizing Ismail, he checked the shackle around his ankle. It was still tinted green with the curse and impossible to remove. So Eli wrapped the remaining part of the chain, blocked by the Khaiti diamond, once around the shackle and fastened it so that it wouldn't drag. He left Ismail stretched out in the back with Flintlock watching him and climbed into the driver's seat. He had a tussle with Diamond for control of the craft, and once he'd wrestled the steering yoke away, she tried to sit beside him, then on him, then on the other side – with Mr Nimbles and Nelly hissing and chittering at each other at full volume from their respective pockets. He reconnected autopilot to his desert-mapping system and felt the *Gypsy Rose* take over, flying them back to the city – with more questions, fewer answers, more problems, fewer solutions, and one unpredictable and dangerous miracle.

Chapter 14

Croy

KULLRA FORNAX

NŸR-CORUM (THE TOWER)

Exhaustion defined them. They didn't sit – they slumped, debilitated. Their faces weren't tired, they were drained – of color, of expression, blank and bleary-eyed with heavily laden lids blinking ever closer to closed. Studying the prisoners now through the one-way glass, Croy saw they were clearly siblings, and from their tattered clothing and ragged physical condition, she judged they'd been in hiding for some time. From what she didn't know, since neither of them had uttered an intelligible word since arriving, but whatever it was, it had to be truly horrendous for them to seek shelter in the purgatory of the Crematorium.

Croy focused on the brother, a boy fast transitioning into a man with a broad chest and shoulders, a young face with old eyes – watchful, mistrusting. His sister, in contrast, was now calm – too calm. She looked completely disconnected and she was mumbling to herself. She was definitely cracked, but she wasn't the only odd thing about the pair – their actual posture was strange too. Tower Wardens had locked them in separate cells, but they sat on either side of the thick wall in an exact mirror image, pressed up against the rock as though they could feel the other one there.

The door to the interrogation cells opened and closed behind her, and Croy knew it was Darius by the scents of leather and tigaro smoke and the sound of his breathing. Growing up orphaned and rough in the industrial zones had taken its toll on his lungs. And the smoking didn't help. She kept saying it. He kept ignoring it.

"Found them," he said, and Croy turned quickly. For some reason, she hadn't expected these two to be in the system. Darius walked over to her, providing his own interpretation of the records parchment he was holding.

"Castor and Kellor Quartermaine, twin children of Ezra Quartermaine – Purple Wing, medical professor, nutjob and insurrectionist. Found guilty of high treason for conspiring with *Drays*." He bit down on the word. "He was tagged for execution, then vanished into thin air from inside a Tower cell. No witnesses, no traces. His children, aged eight annums at the time, have been registered as missing ever since."

"Until now," Croy murmured.

"Until now," her partner agreed. He showed her a sketch of the twins as children. She guessed they were now into their early teens.

"Why wouldn't they just turn themselves in?" Darius asked. "They would have been cleared and released – unless they helped their father get out."

"The girl," Croy said, "the sister, Kellor, she's not right. Maybe Quartermaine kept her protected, but once he was gone they were on their own."

"You think the brother knew she'd be exiled? Wouldn't he have been too young to understand about all that?"

"Think of what you knew at eight annums," Croy said.

Darius snorted. "Big difference between where I was and their sheltered life."

"Just because they were Purple doesn't mean they were sheltered," Croy reminded him.

She remembered seeing their father, Ezra Quartermaine. He had been a former Fleetsman like John L and occasionally the two had spoken, when John hadn't been able to avoid it. He'd told Croy that Quartermaine made him uneasy and she'd understood why. During her training and career, she'd been taken by surprise on many occasions by how normal and average killers could look, but Quartermaine was not one of these. He was crazy-eyed and wild-haired, and when he spoke he stood so close you could smell the sourness of his breath – it had smelled like blood. He'd finally come out with an outlandish claim that the Conference had secret laboratories where they ran terrible experiments on children. Their rebuttal was to have him arrested and condemned. Then they'd produced evidence of his contact with the enemy Dray.

Croy touched her ear. It was still aching and ringing badly from the explosion of her I-Sect, but worse than that was the stain of the strange emotions she'd experienced at the Crematorium. Since returning to the Tower she'd felt moments of extreme sadness and starving desperation that were unconnected to everything around her. She felt certain something far more sinister than the obvious was happening at the Crematorium, and these two might be the key to understanding what that was. And maybe their father was somehow connected.

The doors behind them swung open again and Croy and Darius turned to see their boss, First Controller Van Prichard, entering. He was second in charge of the entire Martial Corps, answering only to the admiral, who reported directly to the Conference. As John L had once described him, VP was a short man with a big presence. Windscars from his time as a Fleetsman reddened his face, their color clashing with the purple of his cloak. It was trimmed extravagantly in fur, and around his neck he wore the pelt of an albino fox, its head still attached. It gave Croy the shivers, because once the creature would have been beautiful, but now it was a scarf with a dead face and dull eyes, dulled even more in comparison with the sharpness of VP's predatory stare.

Croy avoided it. Her relationship with her boss had never moved past strange and precarious. It was VP who had convinced the Admiral to allow her to inherit John L's position as a Controller, even though he was only her adoptive father and not blood. It had effectively saved her life, but it was also VP who had dug up the proof against John L that had seen him charged and sentenced to death. There had been bad blood between them ever since John L had reportedly had an affair with VP's wife. Nothing had been proven, but Croy wouldn't have been surprised. John L loved women – all women.

Since her first day on the job, VP had never been anything but professional to her, but Croy couldn't rule out the possibility that he might be biding his time – keeping his friends close and his enemies closer. She'd witnessed firsthand his profound intellect and chilling patience for exacting revenge. So she kept her mouth shut as much as she could, hoping to fly under his radar. She had a lot to hide and even more to lose.

Behind VP, Controllers Knightsbridge and Newton entered with trainee Kisslefish. The door snapped shut behind them. Kisslefish was jittery as always, bright-eyed and stepping from one foot to the other. He flashed a smile at VP, who looked him over with little interest that immediately drained to none. Instead their boss turned his attention to Knightsbridge and said, "You have a button missing." He gestured to

Knightsbridge's tortured shirt, which was straining to contain his bulging pectorals.

Knightsbridge put his hand to the affected area and gave an uncomfortable, "Sir."

"The Quartermaine children," VP said, now looking to Darius and Croy. "Hiding at the Crematorium, were they?" He had a way of asking everything, even when he already knew the answer. John L had said he'd spent too much time as an interrogator.

"Yes, sir," was Darius' curt reply.

"And the Morticians were unaware?"

Darius spoke again. "So they said, though I don't trust those freaks for one grain-drop."

"Tricky bunch." VP shook his head. "Tricky indeed. And we're thinking the girl is responsible for the Kilner corpse?"

"She was a suicide." Knightsbridge stepped forward. "Newton and I were first on scene."

"Yet DeCavisi and Croy attended the Crematorium?" VP questioned.

"Because we hadn't yet finished our initial assessment," Knightsbridge replied with some awkwardness. A sheen of sweat slicked his face and there were spreading patches of wet under his arms.

"I see." VP scratched his chin. "You arrived first and finished second – yes?"

Newton and Knightsbridge glanced at each other, then lowered their heads.

"The Kilner corpse was found in the Filter. Did you see anything else unusual there?" VP eyed Croy in particular and she shook her head.

"Nothing, sir, aside from the ever-shrinking water level," Newton replied.

"Yes, it's a concern," their boss agreed, the lines of his face deepening. "So what's the connection between these two and the corpse?"

"At this stage, we have reason to believe the Quartermaines at least knew about the body being taken to the Filter," Darius said.

"How's that?" VP asked.

"The girl kept ranting about the corpse wanting to go home to the water."

VP's eyebrows flickered.

Knightsbridge cleared his throat and said, "The preliminary in-house post-mortem suggested that the stab wound was COD, with the additional injuries inflicted after death. Those symbols appear to be a chemical mathematical equation. On top of that, there were signs of sexual assault."

"The Morticians. Those freaks," Darius snarled.

"Not necessarily them," VP said. "There's the Quartermaine boy." He looked over the team. "Who wants to question him?"

"Sir, I will," Knightsbridge said quickly.

"And the girl?"

Newton stepped forward.

"They should be questioned together," Croy said, despite herself. After what had happened at the Crematorium she felt as though she needed to control how this went down.

"Really." VP's eyes carved her up. "Why is that?"

"The girl is mentally unstable and her brother is her crutch. Together they might talk, but not alone. Look at how they're sitting."

VP glanced over at them, then back to Croy with an evaluative stare that made her feel like she was being skinned.

"As you will, then," VP said to her. "Show us how it's done, Croy."

She thought she saw an odd glimmer of pride in his expression, while Knightsbridge silently fumed and Newton stared coldly.

Croy and Darius opened the door to Castor's cell and entered. With every step needles of pain shot through Croy's knee, but she hid it, not wanting VP or the others to know. The boy looked up at them, his face taut with anger, eyes wary.

"We'd like you to move into the next room for questioning," Croy said to him.

"Go up to hell!" Castor snarled.

"Little turd —" Darius made a move toward him, but Croy put a hand up to hold him back. The last thing they needed was Darry beating up a prisoner in front of the boss.

"It's up to you, Castor. We can question you separately if you like, but I'm not sure your sister's up to it. Do you really want her smacking her head against the wall until she kills herself?"

Castor's hostility dissolved and fear welled in his eyes. He stood up and shuffled with chained ankles and wrists to the interconnecting door. Darius opened it and they went through. Kellor tried to hug her brother as soon as she saw him, but her hands were chained. The sight upset Castor.

"Monsters!" he spat at them.

"Sit down." Darius shoved the boy to the ground and Kellor sank down beside him.

Croy could feel VP's eyes boring through the glass into her face.

"Castor and Kellor Quartermaine – you've been detained by the Martial Corps on suspicion that you interfered with a deceased body. I urge you to cooperate and answer truthfully the question you will be so asked," she said. "Why were you hiding at the Crematorium?"

"We weren't hiding," Castor threw back.

"No – you were just sitting in that freezer for the fun of it," Darius mocked him.

Kellor started talking. "Hunting – hunting them. They're there. I can hear their words – their bad words … bad words … bad words … bad … bad …" She started to get hysterical.

Castor dragged her close to him and whispered, "Kell, it's alright. Calm down. Just calm down. I'm here."

"Why were you hiding at the Crematorium?" Croy repeated.

"Why do you live where you live?" Castor demanded.

"Cheap rent, low draft, no ash," Croy lied. The truth was it was where Roth had wanted to live. The place had never quite felt like home to her.

Kellor stopped crying and looked at her – right into her eyes – and said, "I understand."

Croy felt a flash of disquiet and Darius looked between them.

"There's no law against living there," Castor said.

"Actually there is. It's called trespass – break and enter," Croy told him. "Listen, really I don't give a rat's arse why you were hiding out down there. We're not Security. We're not from the Orphans Home. We're Controllers – investigating a body that was stolen from the Crematorium, cut up and tied to the pier in the Filter. I know you didn't kill her, but why did you move her there?"

"We didn't," Castor insisted.

"He's lying," Darius said, his agitation and frustration rising fast.

Croy squatted down, looking at Castor, fear and hostility staring back at her.

"Your father was charged with treason, but neither of you were charged with anything. For all intents and purposes you're just victims. So tell us why you did it and I'll have you housed together. You'll be safe and your sister will get the medical help she needs. If you don't cooperate, I'll have you put in the orphan house and Kellor will be taken to the Waste.

She'll be locked up with screaming crazies on either side of her cage until they try her as incapable and exile her into the tunnels. She won't last five seconds. You won't ever see each other again. Mark me on this – I'm not a cruel person, but I understand what cruelty is."

Kellor started rocking, crying. Croy felt bad, but it had to be done.

Castor struggled, his eyes not shifting, not giving – but then he broke down in tears.

"I don't know why she did it. I went to get food and when I came back she was gone. I followed her tracks. She'd taken a drifter and that dead girl and gone to the Filter. She tied her there, but she didn't hurt her. She was already dead!"

"I was helping her," Kellor said with a sudden clarity that immediately lapsed. "She wanted to go home. They don't like water. I showed her the way."

"What is she talking about, *them*?" Croy asked.

Castor shook his head. "Make-believe monsters – she's not well."

"Guy's a genius," Darius sneered.

"Sod you!" Castor yelled.

Croy held up a hand to stop them.

"The symbols Kellor scratched into the body?"

"I don't know," Castor said, and she could see it was the truth. "It's some kind of formula. Our father was a scientist. He was always working on equations. She doesn't have a reason for doing things."

"Can we have some sweets now?" Kellor said, childlike. "We've been so good."

"Did you sexually assault the body?" Croy asked Castor directly, watching his face for a reaction.

His face registered instant shock and embarrassment. "You think I ... No ... No, I would never do that."

"It must have gotten awfully lonely down there," Darius spoke up. "Taking care of your nutter sister – living with all the corpses. They don't fight back much. And there's only so much you can do with your own hand." He made a crude gesture.

Castor's face reddened. The notion made him so angry that he couldn't even spit out his words. It was a naive reaction to the topic. Croy concluded that it wasn't him.

"What about your sister?" she said. "Could she have done something like that without knowing what she was doing?"

Castor shook his head emphatically. "No! She wouldn't."

"But she would carve symbols into someone's dead flesh and tie them to a jetty?" Darius said.

"For some reason she thought she was helping her … or saving her …" Castor said.

"From the monsters …" Croy murmured to herself, thinking.

"He's all alone down there now," Kellor said. "He can't fight them for much longer. He's hurt. He needs your help. Can you hear him calling you?"

A prickling feeling spread over Croy's skin.

"Who is she talking about? Who is all alone down there?"

Castor shook his head wearily. "She's just talking. It doesn't *mean* anything. There was no one there but us."

"And did you see anything strange?" Croy asked.

The look on Castor's face said it was the stupidest question he'd ever heard.

Croy rephrased. "Anything out of place – assaults, Morticians mistreating bodies … anything."

"Nothing," Castor said.

Croy nodded – if he had, he wasn't going to talk about it now.

"Your sister said you were hunting …"

"The monsters," Kellor spoke again. "they're down there – talking, talking, talking – shhh, don't tell Daddy

– he doesn't want me listening to them – he tried to stop them …" She lifted up her shirt, exposing her bare stomach and breasts. She had formula-symbol scars all over her body as well. Darius cursed and Castor yanked her shirt down.

"Did your Daddy do that?" Croy asked.

Kellor nodded, tears in her eyes. "I want to go home now, too. They don't like water … Or we could go up – up to the suns – like Daddy … up …"

"What's *the suns*?" Croy asked Castor.

He shook his head again, "Just something she's made up. She does it all the time."

Croy nodded. She glanced at Darius, then said to the twins, "That's all for now."

She stood, heading for the door, and Castor called out behind them, "What about us?"

Croy turned back. "You'll stay here for now while the case is processed and then I'll do what I said. You can stay together."

Castor put his arm around his now-crying sister and hugged her. Their crazy father had brought them into this world – dumped life on them – then taken himself out of it. Croy had always thought there should be some kind of compulsory psychological testing before people were allowed to breed. Though she was pretty sure if there was, she wouldn't have much chance of passing it.

They walked out into the observation room where the others were waiting. Trainee Kisslefish gave them a thumbs-up. Knightsbridge glared at him.

Croy gave a summary: "The girl took the body and positioned it, cut it up, but I don't believe either of them assaulted her."

"If the girl's a nutter, then how could she steal and fly a drifter?" Knightsbridge asked.

"Disconnected doesn't mean incompetent – sometimes they're even more capable," VP said.

"We'll start investigating the abuse angle further," Darius said. "We'll go back to the Morticians, and to her family."

VP scratched his manicured white beard. "No … the father is on the Conference." Croy caught him darting a glance at Kisslefish. "We can't question him and we can't interrogate the Morticians again without a warrant of specific accusation and that won't happen, so case closed."

"Case closed?" In questioning VP, Darius did what most would never dare. "So we're just letting whoever did this off the hook? What if those freaks are using bodies as their sex toys?"

VP shrugged. "They're dead."

"What if it was *your* daughter or wife … or mother?" Darius demanded.

"I said, case closed," VP repeated, his eyes drilling into Darius. "We all know the parameters of our work." He turned his attention to Croy and said, "I'm impressed." And from the way he said it, she wasn't entirely sure if that was a good or a bad thing.

The door to the room burst open and a Tower warden stumbled in.

"First Controller Prichard," he said breathlessly. "I have word from Admiral Bower – he requires your immediate presence. The Drays have taken down the *Teriscoria*."

A heavy silence fell over the room. They'd all been depending on the ship's safe return.

VP swore and charged out, leaving them alone with their dread.

PART 2

Chapter 15
Diega

PRATERIUS

RAMBELDON FOREST (DALLYBRUSH)

They crunched through the thick leaf litter of the forest corridor, stepping in and out of shifting shapes of shade and light filtering through the treetop canopy far above. Mossy vines constricted around the branches of the giant trees. Puffs of pollen-sweetened air stirred the undergrowth and flowers. They seemed to quieten as the travelers approached, whispering again as they passed by. The air was the freshest Diega had ever breathed. It was like a shot of pure mind-clearer straight to the brain. She'd never felt so awake, but had never realized until now that she'd been half-asleep, suffocated by pollutants.

Everything about this place was so natural and uncorrupted – and Diega felt sharply out of context in her heavy boots and fatigues covered in blood and dusty debris, reeking of smoke and sweat. She didn't belong in any sense. She tried again and again to access her morphing and electrosmith skills, but they were gone, blocked or invalid in this world. She felt naked and on edge without them. Just ahead of her, Shawe didn't seem to be suffering the same alienation, still moving fast despite his terrible injury.

He was an arrogant thug prick, but there was no way to deny it, Shawe was extraordinarily tough. He'd stopped at nothing to save his brother, gone literally to hell and back, and now Diega saw Shawe going after Copernicus with the same resolve. She hated to be moved by someone so completely foul, but the sight of him gave her strength and spurred her on. Her father had been the opposite – a defeated sort of person at the best of times, and when Ariana had vanished he'd fallen to pieces. Seeing him hunched in his chair sobbing, day and night, refusing to eat or speak or be comforted, just begging the stars to kill him too, had etched away pieces of her sanity. Nothing she had done or said had made any difference; he'd just looked at her as though he'd wished she was the one who had died instead of Ariana. And one day, during one of his hysterical breakdowns, he'd actually said it. His words and the guilt had driven her to run away to the gangland in search of people who were strong the way she wanted to be. She hadn't understood then that coldness comes with a price.

She remembered herself at thirteen year-cycles seeing Christy Shawe for the first time. He'd been rumbling with a bunch of his gang-mates and she'd thought then that he was the strongest boy she'd ever seen. She'd wanted him to notice her – to see her as well. But he never had. So much had changed since then – and so little as well.

Diega sensed the light dipping and looked up through the canopy. A purple sun rode high in the sky, with a second orange sun to one side and a white moon on the other. And no stars. Anywhere. It was highly disorientating for her, so much of a Fen's senses and self were taken from the stars. She realized this was the reason her skills were gone.

A low humming sound disturbed her thoughts as the dragonfly, Tickleback, dropped back to her side, leaving the beetle girl, Trilly, to lead.

"These are the three guardians of Praterius – the Thor, the Anvil and the Plenitude. As the Thor rises the Anvil sets and as the Anvil rises the Thor sets. The Plenitude never drops and no storm can blacken its light. Here it is always light." Tickleback smiled.

"Then why is it getting darker?" Diega asked.

Alarm flashed in the dragonfly's emerald eyes. He glanced ahead at Trilly.

"What?" Shawe demanded, having come close to listen in.

Tickleback paused, then spoke with a lowered voice. "A plague sweeps across the realms of the universe. The Indemeus X and his Arequium Mors are blackening the Zenzenya Lights and imprisoning all. The first signs of the apocalypse are a darkening of the light that only outsiders can see. After this – the Mors come."

Diega's skin prickled. "Who is this Indemeus X?"

Tickleback shook his head. "I don't know what he is, only what he means."

"Death?" Diega said. "Because we just fought the demon of death, and it didn't go so well for him."

"No, not death," Tickleback said. "Death is mercy and he has none. He cuts our connection with our Shais in Zenzenya Zinel. They are our eternal echoes in Paradise – and without them, we can't die, but we're not alive, and he takes us as slaves into his realm of Ursae for eternity."

"Sounds like a fairy's tale to me," Shawe grunted.

"How can he be stopped?" Diega asked.

Tickleback fixed her with his solemn stare and said, "He can't. There is nothing to be done, but to make peace with the manner of life and take in the seconds."

"If it moves, it can be stopped. If it breathes, it can be killed. And if it's looking for surrender, it'll be disappointed," Shawe said, quoting one of Diega's favorite sayings. It was painted across a wall in Warsaul, a suburb near the old Headquarters. She'd stopped to read it every single time she'd passed. It had always fortified her.

Her face must have shown something because Shawe said, "What?"

"You're quoting battle philosophy?"

"Yeah, so? You didn't think I could memorize things?" he asked.

"I didn't think you could even read."

Shawe snorted. "Typical, trutting, thinks-her-shite-don't-stink fairy-breed. That battle philosophy, I wrote it – yeah, I can write, too. What do you think about that?"

Diega had no idea how to respond, and had to give this one to him.

Shawe scratched at the binds around his wound, giving her and the dragonfly a glimpse of his back. The dark lines of poison had reached further up, corrupting more of his skin, but then they faded out. It looked as though the toxin had met Christy Shawe's armpits, then curled up its toes and died.

Diega saw Tickleback's eyes widening as he spotted the injury. Concerned the insect-breed might think it was something contagious and stop helping them, she said, "He was just stabbed."

"Yes, by an Omarian – injected with fireblood," Tickleback said.

"Omarian?" Diega and Shawe repeated in unison.

"Can't be," Diega said. "A person we know is the last Omarian."

She narrowed her eyes, trying to clear her blurred memories of the attack. Had she seen firebird dragon bloodline marks? Maybe ...

"Perhaps your person is the last Omarian on Aquais," Tickleback suggested. "Many more exist in their own realm, Omar Montanya."

"They took her, our Omarian – that's why we're here. Why would they want her?"

Tickleback shook his head.

"Forget why," Shawe said. "Just tell us how to get to them."

"A portal into Omar Montanya is the only way," the dragonfly replied. "But Omarians are a people you cannot fight. Brutality defines them and their prince, Lecivion Oflock, will destroy you in a glance. He is evil fighting evil, and evil always wins." He turned to Shawe and said, "To survive their poison you must surely be of godlike strength."

"Finally!" the gangster bellowed. "Someone recognizes my true worth." He grinned savagely. "See, sunshine – godlike. Remember that."

"We need an antidote to their poison," Diega told Tickleback. "Our other companion, the man we're looking for, was stabbed as well."

"An antidote," the dragonfly repeated, pupils dilating and shrinking as he thought. "I don't know of one, but for all our sicknesses here we go to the healing plants of the Eti River."

"The river," Diega said. "How do we get there?"

"There is a shortcut on the borderline of the Blackwater Forest, through the Head of Solomon, but Tickleback must warn you the Eti flows in what was once the Zanzarra Basin. It has now been corrupted, blackened and turned into the Murkmire Slough. It is a foul place, full of hidden treachery and mortal danger."

"Sounds like where I grew up," Shawe said, and Diega snorted.

"Here!" the beetle girl, Trilly, cried out ahead of them. "Here's the turn!"

She whirled to the left and vanished out of sight.

The others ran to catch up, taking the sharp turn and stepping into a clearing. In it stood a tribe of impossibly thin insect-breeds with mottled brown and olive-green skin. Some had partially missing limbs in various stages of regeneration. They stared with tiny eyes, then collapsed to the ground, lying in a heap, looking like a pile of sticks. Beyond the stickmen, four giant stone sculptures sat around a table, holding cards as though they were playing a game.

"Morning greetings, friends," Tickleback called out to them. They animated suddenly, their gray-brown faces stretching into gruesome but friendly smiles.

"The Bouldermen mark the first shortcut to the Woods," Tickleback told Diega and Shawe.

"I thought we were already in the trutting woods," Shawe swore, swatting at a tiny pixie dancing on his head.

"Not yet." Tickleback smiled.

He led them past the stone giants to the edge of the trees, where they stepped out into a field of tiny violet and dark pink flowers. Trilly was already halfway across the field, heading for more forest on the other side. All around her gigantic blue and purple snails with crooked houses built into the shells on their backs were munching their way through the flowers, leaving silver trails behind them. Diega and the others hurried to catch up with the beetle girl. They re-entered the forest on the far side of the field and headed toward the distant *shhh* of fast-running water. The sound intensified to a roar as they closed in on the source, finally breaking through the trees to a place where two rivers, rushing from either side, met in the center. Their waters crashed down a mammoth fall, churning into white froth on the rocks far below. Behind the thundering falls a city was built into the rocks.

"Illendriel," Tickleback told them, pointing to the shimmering city. "Second shortcut to the woods." He smiled and plunged straight off the bank, zooming all the way down into the water, vanishing into the froth. Diega peered down and felt her stomach turn.

"Scared, princess?" Shawe grunted beside her. He stepped off the edge and dropped like a bomb into the water below.

"Prick," Diega muttered and jumped straight after him.

Chapter 16

Eli

AQUAIS

SCORPIA (THE GRAVEYARD)

As soon as the hangar roof boomed closed above them, Eli leaped from the pilot's seat and ran to where Jude and SevenM lay on a makeshift stretcher. He found Penman hovering anxiously over them, holding one of SevenM's legs in a tentacle. The little 0318 gave a mournful beep as Eli checked Jude's heart rate – it was still slow but steady. A serene expression had settled on the Ar Antarian's face, almost as though he was asleep, but his silver skin was blanched white. "I'm here." Eli patted Jude's arm. "I'm back."

He turned to the compound analyzer, which he'd left testing the toxin, and saw immediately why it hadn't sent through any results. The poison had melted into the machine and completely burned it out. He'd never seen a toxin this voracious – and if it was doing this to the fortified metal of the analyzer, what would it do to simple flesh and bone? With a deep sense of dread,

Eli forced himself to lift the bandages over Jude's wound and look. The poison lines had progressed across Jude's body and the necrosis of the wound had widened, but not as badly as Eli had feared. Jude being half-Androt meant his more vulnerable Ar Antarian skin was infused with the special living metals of the Androts' bodies. It was extremely resilient and rapid-healing – Jude's broken arm was already completely fused – but even so the poison was on the move, reaching black tendrils of toxin toward Jude's heart and brain. The heart, and all the other essential organs, could be transplanted or replaced by real or robotic implants, but the brain – that was another matter completely. Certainly it could be repaired or modified in minor ways but a complete transplant had never been achieved. It was still a case of lose the brain, lose the person … Eli was determined not to let that happen.

He immediately started hooking Jude up to machines that would keep his body alive in the event the poison took everything out. Even though Jude was completely shut down, his body was still holding an equilibrium that needed to be maintained for him to survive. After he was satisfied Jude's vital organs were all supported, Eli ran along his workbench, rifling through piles of inventions until he found his advanced He-Ro series that he'd been working on. He chose one of tested success and attached it to Jude's chest. Should his heart fail, the He-Ro would immediately take over. After it was secure and activated, Eli moved on to injecting more slowing serums and healing mixtures into the wound until he felt sure that he'd done everything he could, then he grabbed a cushion from one of his chairs and positioned it carefully under his friend's head. He watched Jude for a moment longer before stepping back from the stretcher feeling ill to his stomach and shaky.

Penman stayed hovering close to SevenM, keeping his eyes on him. It was the first time he'd been anywhere near another machine-breed. His former owners had always kept him alone. Sensing movement, Eli glanced into Nelly's enclosure. The otter had put herself into it and was swimming in one of her pools. After the horror and heat of the desert, the enclosure had suddenly become more acceptable to her. Eli himself wished he could shower and try to scrub off some of the foulness he felt still crawling under his skin, but that would have to wait.

Shuffling sounded behind him and Eli turned to see Flintlock standing beside the bench where Ismail lay, still unconscious, but starting to twitch. Diamond was thankfully back in Ufftown, where they'd dropped her off and watched her walk with dragging steps into her apartment block.

Eli felt weary enough to collapse, but he forced himself to stay on his feet.

"How is he?" he asked, hurrying toward Flintlock.

The towering Corámorán considered his question and replied, "There's something very wrong with him, Master Eli, Something ..." she pointed warily to her chest. Eli nodded in agreement – something was undeniably wrong, but the question was what?

"Flintlock, see that body scanner over there?" He pointed to the large piece of equipment near to the bench. He'd been waiting for a reinforced hoist to lift it into place and form a makeshift, but functional diagnostic chamber, should any of the team need it. "Is that too heavy for you to lift?"

The Corámorán took three big strides over to the scanner and picked it up without so much as a strain.

"That ..." Eli had to pause for a moment to marvel at her strength, "is impressive ..." He snapped out of the trance and said. "Can you place it that side up over Ismail?" He pointed to the bench and Flintlock moved immediately to obey.

"We need to see exactly what's going on inside his chest," he explained, activating the scanner's holo-screen.

Eli positioned all the primary scanners over Ismail's heart and started them up. The screen flickered, fuzzed over then brought up an image. He stared, for a moment thinking the machine must be stuck on its last scan. This couldn't be Ismail's body – the heart was blackened, clotted and definitely deceased – but then he saw the heart was beating, or actually not so much beating as pulsing in a slumped and odd kind of way as though it was being animated via electricity not by voluntary movement. It took several more moments of fast thinking before Eli realized what he was seeing. He stepped back a little from the screen with shock.

"The witch put her heart in him – that's what's keeping him alive – but the heart itself is dead." He raised his stare to Flintlock who shook her head silently, her deep, solemn eyes reflections of his ill-ease.

"If it's dead, how is he alive?" she asked.

"Magics – dark magics," Eli replied, then a terrible idea occurred to him. "If it's still beating it means she's still alive – or at least still dead-alive ..." Fear for Luther twisted painfully inside him.

He pushed the retract button on the scanner and the machine's chamber slid back. He stood staring down at Ismail. The He-Ro was still firmly implanted in his chest, so at least if the zombie heart failed he could theoretically survive, but who knew what effects the dark magics were having on his body. Eli contemplated if he should try to remove the alien heart completely, but concluded that doing so without knowledge of what impact it might have on Ismail was ill-advised. What if the magics reacted to him removing the heart? What if it alerted the witch immediately or killed Ismail, or exploded like a bomb – who knew what curse the witch had put on it.

Eli blinked into his front-core implant and said, "Search – zombified organ transplants."

Immediately the words popped up in front of his eyes – "no results found for zombified organ transplants."

"Of course not, because that would be insane," Eli muttered. As he continued thinking, his eyes traveled along Ismail's bloodline marks and he noticed for the first time that he was an extremely strange blood mix – he had three lines, not two. Normally this would be impossible; usually it was the mother's blood and the father's blood showing up the two most dominant lines in their heritage. But he had three equally dominant lines. Sometimes, very rarely, scullion women could have one egg fertilized by two different men at the same time – and the baby would be a genetic composition of three people. In Ismail's case he was Blackwater Wolf, plus some variety of human-breed shark and bat-blood.

He considered the deep lines in the scullion's forehead and the parasites he could see crawling through Ismail's hair. It made Eli feel like madly scratching his own shaved head, but what troubled him more was what the state of Ismail's mind would be … obviously it would be a disaster zone – but what if he attacked them – then they'd have to lock him up and then how would he see them? Exactly as he'd seen the witch – as a threat he needed to escape from, and Eli didn't want that … But he didn't have time to build trust with Ismail to help him overcome the horror he'd been enduring. With the witch heart in his chest and the cursed shackle still attached to his ankle, Eli imagined it would be impossible for Ismail to even start to psychologically heal.

Eli hadn't done much research into long-term captives, it was more in the commander's field of interest, but he knew that often survivors would adjust to freedom quickly and successfully, only to later crash into depression and flashbacks, with the slow realization of the true impact of the imprisonment on their lives. All this interlaced with fluctuating feelings of guilt and anger, happiness, terror, self-hatred, confusion –

and sometimes also of missing their captivity, even if they'd suffered and hated it. The brain was a complex and frightening thing – a bit like a tamed wild animal that could turn on its owner at any moment. All that said, scullion-gypsies were known for their mental resilience, their ability to endure all kinds of ill-treatment and hardship and survive and thrive over most other races. So if anyone would be able to come out of such a situation with their sanity intact it would be a scullion.

Physically, aside from the zombie heart, the regenerative and healing formulas that Eli was feeding into Ismail's body via a drip were beginning to have a visible effect. His muscle and fat stores were starting to take a more pronounced shape, his ribs less visible every minute that passed. Ismail would wake up in a far better physical condition than how he went out, which meant he was going to wake up stronger, sharper and pain-free – more able to rip them apart if the urge hit. Eli reached for a fast-working sedative and placed it in the priority position in his weapon belt. They had to be prepared for the waking to go badly. A parasite crawled out of Ismail's hair and across his forehead and Eli immediately scratched at his own head, deciding it was way past time to shave Ismail's beard and head and douse him.

"Flintlock, would you please fill that tub there with water?" Eli asked the giant, who was still standing silently beside the bench. She instantly obliged, lifting the tub and heading over to the tap, while Eli got to work with his scissors and razor.

By the time he and Flintlock had clearly shaven Ismail and given him a thorough wash all over, the water was black, and Ismail looked completely different – less wild animal and more handsome man. He had a strong, heavy jawline and a powerful layer of muscle developing fast across his body. Eli examined the scars around his wrists and neck. The wrists looked like old bondage wounds and the neck as though someone had attempted to take his head off. Eli followed the scar all the way around to the back of Ismail's neck where, during the shaving, he'd noticed an interesting tattoo.

Eli bent down to examine it more closely. It was a military tattoo, but Eli wasn't exactly sure what type. He blinked, sending the information into his front-core and running a search. The information came back instantly and Eli jolted a little. The tattoo itself was the mark of a high-ranking Militia Corps soldier – and the cross through it was a symbol of dishonorable discharge. The Militia was one of the black lists, the secret units of the United Regiment that were not supposed to exist. The commander had told him it was the hardest of the lists and the training involved torture and brainwashing so that the soldiers were barely more than pro-grammed response machines. Militia soldiers were taught to compartmentalize their minds so that they could literally switch off their emotions and reasoning during missions and focus solely on the objective – then switch back on afterward. The commander had said sometimes they had trigger words and sometimes they could do it without, and Eli had wondered how this fracturing would affect a person psycho-logically. He'd wanted to do a research paper into it, but it was difficult to research people who technically didn't exist.

It threw another factor into an already tangled situation. With his complex genetic mix, scullion predisposition and invasive military conditioning, it was impossible to predict exactly how Ismail would wake up and respond to, firstly, his change in circumstances and, secondly, coping with what the witch had been doing to him. It seemed logical to Eli that during the long year-cycles of torment Ismail might have completely retreated into the part of his mind that was emo-tionless and programmed – the question was, did the other part of him, where he felt and reasoned, even exist anymore?

Who would wake – the soldier, the man, or the beast – or all three mixed into one confused and damaged person? Eli felt dizzy even contemplating it. He upped both the regenerative formula dose and the anaesthetic feed, so that Ismail would stay under for just a bit longer.

Flintlock had already begun to clean up the bathing and shaving equipment, so Eli turned back to Jude. As he did, he heard Penman beeping loudly, and saw the little robot start swooping in a crazy way around Jude's bench. Eli's heart seized as he spotted SevenM unexpectedly stirring and lifting shakily to his legs. Eli sprinted over to Jude's side, feeling borderline hysterical himself.

"Jude! Jude! Can you hear me?" He leaned low over his friend's chest.

SevenM's eyes flashed. He moved his pincer mouthparts and spoke for the first time ever, with a labored, robotic voice.

"Si-lho?"

The robot's eyes focused on Eli, feeding back to Jude's mind – awake and trapped inside his paralyzed body.

Eli swallowed, trying not to show his anxiety. Panic and stress would do nothing to help Jude now.

"She was taken through a portal with the commander and Diega, but I'm sure she's fine. I know it ..." He let the lie happen.

SevenM tried to talk again, making a few sounds before staggering and dropping to one side, his eyelights dying out. Penman let out a distressed shriek and Eli felt the burn of tears. He stared down at his friend, longing to hear his voice.

"Everything will be okay," he whispered both to himself and Jude. Or, at least, it would be when he figured out who had attacked them, and with what poison.

Eli forced himself into composure. He moved quickly to his computer and opened up the attack footage, throwing his every filter, scrubber, sorter and shaper at it, with absolutely no result. He rubbed his eyes. His throat was so dry he couldn't swallow at all, but he didn't want to stop even to drink. There wasn't time. A bottle appeared right beside him, followed immediately by Diamond's grinning face. Eli turned his head so quickly he almost snapped his neck. "How?" was all he could manage to stutter. Flintlock also grunted in surprise behind them.

Diamond just grinned wider. "I'm very fast," she told him. "What's this – what are you doing?" She pushed in beside him. Nelly looked up from her bowl of fish treats in her enclosure and snapped at Mr Nimbles, who was glaring at her.

Eli stammered, still trying to figure out how she'd gotten past his security, "I'm ... I'm trying to clear this footage. I have to see who attacked us at Sirenseron."

"Okay ..." Diamond said. "Allow me."

She stepped in front of him and took over the hologram keypad, typing so rapidly even Eli had trouble keeping up with what she was doing. The images shuttered and cleared – the pillars of fire becoming people and those people men with the firebird dragon bloodlines mark. Eli gasped, shocked Diamond had found the solution so fast and even more shocked at what he was now seeing. "They're Omarians," he murmured. "I don't understand." He'd noticed in the past that Silho's outline in record footage was always slightly blurred, but he'd never connected it to her half-Omarian blood. He couldn't believe what he was seeing.

"That's a portal," Diamond said beside him, as they watched Silho and the others being dragged into the painting.

"I know – but how do you know?" Eli asked her.

"A lot of research and reading. That's what happens when everyone thinks you're too weird to play with, isn't that right, Mr Nimbles." She scratched her minx on the head and he purred. Eli felt her words cut deep into him. He stifled the urge to tell her he didn't think she was weird, in case it incited another bout of hugging and kissing.

"Most portals can only be used once and then they're blown. Some, very few, can tolerate more use," she said, pointing out the footage of the exploded painting on the Hero's Walk wall.

"Then we'll have to find a new portal," Eli said. "Any ideas?"

She pursed her lips and shook her head. Eli's thoughts jumped back to the blackbird book. He ran over to the craft and retrieved it, starting to flick through the pages as he ran back. He knew the *Portal* page was missing, but maybe it would have something on Omarians. He found the word in the contents and opened up the book in front of them, but the Omarian section was ripped out as well. He cursed, and his thoughts leaped again to Englan Chrisholm – he had painted hundreds, even thousands of pieces, potentially all portals. At the time, the news had claimed all his works were burned when he was arrested, but surely some had survived?

Eli accessed his main computer system to search for anything on Chrisholm that might give them some clues and he saw a message pending. He opened it and read a brief note from Santana – *all today, all homicide–suicide.* Holograms flashed up in the air before him – scenes of death with one connecting factor – in every picture an X, or many, had been scratched or drawn into the walls or floor, or into the victims themselves. Silho's words in the craft came back to him – *It's never a good sign when the people with the strongest intuition of the future start killing themselves.* "They're all seers," he murmured to himself.

"What are they seeing?" Diamond questioned beside him.

The Xs in the picture seemed to jump out at him and Eli's skin chilled. It hadn't even crossed his mind that all this might be connected to the witch Darmel's prediction. He remembered it exactly: *The end of days is near. An ever-living enemy is rising. You must spread a warning. You must prepare a means of travel and escape this land. There is no hope of survival.*

The situation suddenly jumped from possibly containable to apocalyptic and Eli felt like throwing up. He grabbed the black book again and searched for *Indemeus X*. He found a page number and flicked forward with trepidation – yes – it was missing too. He slammed the book shut. Someone had anticipated this situation and stolen the pages. But who? Eli's investigative brain kicked into autopilot over his swelling panic and he spoke to his front-core system: "Fingerprint scanner."

He scanned his eyes over the pages beside those that were ripped out and the system picked up on a distinct matching set in each missing section.

"Run a search," he ordered his system and it flicked through several million images in a microsecond before settling on one name.

"Ezra Quartermaine," he said to Diamond.

A profile picture loaded up. A man with out-of-control, frizzy gray hair and dead-cold eyes. Instantly Eli felt a stirring of disquiet.

He ran another search for information on Quartermaine, but it came back with absolutely nothing, as though all his traces had been scrubbed clean.

"Nothing," Eli reported, seeing a dead-end looming up ahead.

"I disagree," Diamond said, as she pickpocketed him compulsively. "You can create a touch map with his prints." Eli glanced at her. He'd never heard of a touch map.

"Here." She took over again and typed in a set of codes around the fingerprint. "The fingerprint recognition FR10 system was installed city-wide to grant access and verify ID, yes, but it also has a surprising side-effect ..."

She made a last entry and stepped back as a city grid map opened up with hotspots popping up across it, indicating where this Ezra Quartermaine had left more of the same prints. There was a massive concentration around a spot in Duskmaveth-Aendor, a spectral-breed neighborhood on Level 497 Zilah. It wasn't as far down as Moris-Isles, but far enough to be a no-go zone for most people, including Eli. Spectral-Breeds were secretive and unpredictable at best, with sub-species such as Midnight Men, Deaths and Specters positively fatal. Just one touch of a Specter could freeze a person to instant death. What was this Ezra Quartermaine doing down there with the pages from Bellbeater's book? Who was he? How much did he know? And whose side was he on? "You're brilliant," Eli said to Diamond. He'd never even thought of creating a touch map, and he'd designed the whole FR10.

She grinned and started jumping up and down while Eli transferred all the information to his front-core implant and his external portable system as back up.

"I have to go to Duskmaveth and speak with this Quartermaine. We're in the dark. We need to understand what's happening here. I also need to get an antidote for the poison in Jude's system and find a way to access a portal," Eli said. "He seems like our best – well, our only – lead." "I'll help!" Diamond volunteered immediately.

"No, it's too dangerous. You're definitely not coming."

Before she could argue, he turned back to the attack footage, which was paused beside them. Behind the foreground scene, Eli caught sight of Smudge's beautiful face. He sensed Diamond watching him looking at Smudge and he glanced at the little imp-breed girl. He knew that expression – he had felt the way she was looking many times before – and had never wanted to inflict that on anyone else. He shook his head.

He could not be dealing with this right now. "We're taking you back to Ufftown and this time you have to stay there. Seriously," he told her.

"But I want to stay with you." She gazed at him with ever-hopefulness. "I know I'm not *normal*, but I can help."

"I know you can," Eli said. "But you could also get killed. I can't watch you as well as watch me. I'm not *normal* either and it's all I can do just to keep myself together. Don't feel bad – I've had a lot of therapy to get where I am."

"Me too," she said "We're the same." She pulled up her sleeve and showed him the scars on her arms from the blood-transfusion therapy she'd endured. He flinched in horror. His grandparents hadn't even entertained the thought of putting him through blood therapy – it was so brutal and cruel. Diamond started singing and hopping around and all he could think of was what she must have already suffered and of where he would be if the commander hadn't befriended him, encouraged him, helped him through everything. "Okay – you can stay, but you have to do what I say." he told her.

The realization dawned over her face. He started talking, trying to contain the blowout, but then she was leaping at him, kissing him and squealing, "I love you, I love you!"

"Master Eli!" Flintlock called urgently behind them and Eli turned.

Ismail's eyes were opening. Eli's stomach did a backflip that felt like it landed wrong. He gestured to Diamond to calm down, then made a careful path over to the scullion, keeping his hand on the sedative in his belt. Flintlock started to draw her electrifier, but Eli shook his head. The first object-ive with Ismail was to separate them from his tormentor, and start building trust. Eli stopped beside the bench and Ismail turned his head weakly, staring at him, realization filtering in moment by moment. Eli saw sharp ridges press up on Ismail's cheeks as he clenched his jaw, and his eyes took on a bestial edge, dark with warning. Eli felt like he needed to speak – fast.

He cleared his throat and managed, "Ismail, my name isn't – I mean – it is Eli, and this is Flintlock and Diamond. You've been the captive of a dark witch for a long time, but you're safe now. You're free. You're not a prisoner here – we're just trying to help you."

A growl rumbled in Ismail's throat and his nose wrinkled up savagely, but behind the aggression, Eli saw terror. Diamond burst into frightened song and Eli slapped a hand over her mouth. Quickly changing his approach, he said in his most formal military voice, "Soldier. Specialist Investigator First Class Eli Anklebiter standing and present."

Ismail's expression immediately changed. The hostile lines smoothed out and the red glow behind his dark eyes dulled down. Gripping the sides of the bench, Ismail hauled himself into a sitting position and Eli stepped back a few paces. Flintlock's hand hovered over her weapon.

"Ex-Commander Ismail Ohavor." Ismail spoke in a deep, gruff voice and Eli felt a wash of relief sweep over him. They had communication.

Ismail looked down at the He-Ro embedded in his chest. He touched a hand to it and Eli spoke fast, afraid he'd rip it out.

"Soldier, I recommend you leave that in. You've suffered high-degree trauma to your heart. It's currently non-functional."

Ismail lowered his hand away from the He-Ro and looked back up at Eli, his face a controlled military mask. Then something beyond Eli caught his attention. The scullion froze. Eli turned to see what he was looking at – and saw the attack footage paused on an image of Silho, the Omarian's arm around her neck. Ismail slid naked off the bench. He staggered, then righted himself, ripping out his drips and moving unsteadily toward the hologram. He stopped in front of Silho and stood there transfixed. Eli felt a jolt of memory. Ev'r had written in her journal about her and Ismail meeting Silho and her carer Hammersmith in the desert, how the big scullion man had formed an instant friendship with Silho. Ev'r had said it had felt as though they were having deep conversations without saying a word, and if Silho was older Ev'r might have been jealous.

Eli carefully approached Ismail, unsure what the scullion's next reaction would be. He gestured for Flintlock and Diamond to stay behind him. Diamond was holding her own mouth closed, muted sounds coming from behind her hand.

After some time of silence, Ismail shook his head as though waking from deep thought and looked over his shoulder. His face was still inscrutable – in soldier mode – but then he spotted Ev'r's bag sitting beside Eli's main workspace, where he'd placed it when they'd first arrived back. The scullion's reaction was immediate and violent. Emotion rushed into his eyes and he inhaled sharply. He went for the bag and snatched it up, holding it to himself desperately close.

"Zara," he uttered and tears welled in his eyes and streamed down his face, lined with pain and heartbreak. Eli swallowed around the growing lump in his throat.

"Ismail," he said, forgetting himself for a moment and moving toward the crying man.

Ismail's eyes locked onto him and he felt an itch inside his skull that he recognized from past experiences as a telepath trying to access his mind. He instantly raised the psychological blocks that he'd learned back in United Regiment basic training. It kept most telepaths out, but the itch cut immediately into a deep ache as Ismail tore through his defenses and into his thoughts and memories. The room changed around him, the walls and space vanished into a rush of darkness and lights, sounds and flashes of images from his past – all dragged forward toward Ismail, who stood before him, radiating. He didn't siphon just one thought or memory, as was common telepathic strength, he took them all – by far the most powerful telepath that Eli had ever encountered.

Seconds later Ismail released him and Eli fell backward onto the ground. Flintlock stood over him with her electrifier pointed at Ismail.

"Flintlock, no!" Eli said as the Corámorán's finger tensed on the trigger. "Stand down!"

He'd always wanted to say that and it made Flintlock drop her aim. Diamond was bouncing around, uncontrollably shrieking. Eli sat up and spoke quickly to Ismail who was staring at them overwhelmed and trembling with shock.

"Ismail – I know you just saw into my mind – so you must already know this. We have every – I mean – no intention at all of harming you. We're trying to help. I'm a friend of Ev'r's – Zingara's – you saw …"

"Ravien?" Ismail whispered, the lines in his forehead deepening. He searched Eli's eyes for answers and Eli said, "Yes – but – I'm going to find a cure and bring her back. It's only a matter of time." Despite his own doubts he made the words sound completely certain. He stood carefully and pressed a button on his holographic keypad, bringing up his file on the Ravien antidote.

"See," he said to Ismail. "There's a cure to be found – and I will find it. There's still hope."

Ismail's bloodshot eyes moved over the figures and equations and Eli wasn't sure how much he was understanding of it, but by his expression, Eli guessed at least enough to see how advanced they were. And as Ismail read, Eli saw a shift in his expression. All the emotion drained away until his face was once again a military mask.

"Specialist Investigator Anklebiter, what is the procedure for procuring the cure?" Ismail asked, and his voice was flat, almost robotic.

Eli felt a shiver in his spine – the emotion had become too much for the scullion and he had quite literally switched himself off. It was quite disturbing to witness.

"The procedure," Eli managed to gulp out. "I'm afraid it has been stalled by the current situation. The Omarians attacked us. They've taken Silho Brabel and the rest of my team, including my commander, Copernicus Kane, and they poisoned Jude ..." Eli paused, feeling another pang of pain that made it difficult to continue speaking in a neutral way. "My first objective is to fly to Duskmaveth-Aendor to follow a lead to try to bring them back – to try to launch a rescue. Once my team has been recovered I can focus on the antidote, until then – I can't. As a Ravien Zingara is not in any immediate danger, whereas my team is."

Ismail processed the information then said, "If the Omarians have captured your squad, the probability of their survival is too low to be considered a viable risk. I suggest you write them off as a loss and proceed to the next objective, obtaining the cure."

"I can't just write them off," Eli said, trying to keep himself from slipping into the emotionality, but failing. "They're my friends."

Ismail eyed him warily. "I sense you've lost perspective, soldier."

"Well, to be honest I never really had much to begin with," Eli said, completely dropping his attempt at being military. "I won't abandon my friends to die and I won't abandon Ev'r – Zingara – either. I know you must remember Silho – can you really just strike her off as dead?"

Something flickered in Ismail's deadened stare and Eli thought maybe he shouldn't be trying to trigger him to switch over again. While he was the soldier he was standing straight and focusing sharply – as the man he'd been hunching, shaking and blurry-eyed. Maybe he should allow him to slowly unravel himself at his own pace, as he felt the strength to do so.

"My objective is clear to me," Eli said, "first my team and then the cure. My question to you is – will you stay to assist us or will you leave? If you stay we have a better chance." He posed the question knowing it was a dangerous one, but necessary to begin to convince Ismail he was actually free. He held his breath in anticipation of the answer, scared Ismail would say he was leaving – and then what?

Ismail considered the question, then slung Ev'r's bag over his shoulders and grunted, "Ready to deploy."

"Ah ..." Eli said. "Maybe some clothes before we start off."

The scullion looked down at his naked body.

"There's a barrel full of unused uniforms over there. They were the commander's. It's the only thing I have here that might fit you," Eli told him.

Ismail gave a nod, some confusion behind his eyes, and moved toward the barrel. Eli felt quite sure the scullion was shifting between lucid and lost quite rapidly over and over, but he was keeping most of the struggle behind his military control.

Eli wanted to ask why he was choosing to come with him, but stopped himself in case it made Ismail change his mind.

"Are you okay, Master Eli?" Flintlock asked him. "Did he hurt you?"

"I think he needs mouth-to-mouth resuscitation. I volunteer." Diamond grabbed him.

"No," Eli fended her off. "I don't need resuscitating, I'm fine. He just read my thoughts."

"Don't let him go with you," Flintlock said, her eyes shimmering with fear.

"It's alright," he told her. "I think I can contain him, but please, I need you to stay here and guard Jude. Diamond, I want you here as well, be my eyes in the system, help me when I need it."

He braced, expecting a barrage of complaint and disagreement from them, but Diamond just squealed, "Yippee!" and Flintlock gave a stern nod, clearly still not convinced of Ismail, but not about to question Eli's judgement.

"I'll check Jude one more time – can you two please load all the equipment in that pile there into the transflyer." He pointed.

They moved to obey and he ran to Jude's side. He put a hand on his friend's shoulder. The skin felt as cold as the metal of his arms.

"I'm going into Duskmaveth to find some information, but I'll be straight back." He tried to keep the tremble out of his voice.

There was a chance he wouldn't be coming back and, if he did, that it would be too late. He imagined what Jude must be feeling, stuck and helpless. He didn't want him to be scared. Eli felt the sting of tears – he blinked them back, glancing away to the *Gypsy Rose*, trying to compose himself. Diamond was standing beside the craft. She waved at him, then sniffed at her own fingertips and pulled a disgusted face. "Here's something that might give you a laugh," Eli said to Jude, trying to sound upbeat. "You know how I'm always talking about finding someone who I have things in common with, who loves me for who I am? Well, I actually met a girl. We're exactly alike, she loves me – and I can't stand her." He gave a small laugh. "It's highly disturbing to think that what I actually want is someone who doesn't like me and who I have no similarities to … and even more disturbing that I'm only just figuring this out now … Plus I may have accidently gotten married." He laughed again, but the sound immediately faded out.

This was normally where Jude would say something wise and reassuring. Eli stared at his friend. He just wanted him to open his eyes and be okay – and he wanted the others to walk through the door … but neither was going to happen unless he made it so.

Eli stepped back and activated a security shield over Jude, SevenM and Penman. Before Nelly could react he shut the door to her enclosure. She stared at him through the glass, her whiskers drooping.

"I'm sorry, girl," he whispered to her. "It's too dangerous. I love you."

He forced himself to turn and run to the *Gypsy Rose*, where he gave final instructions to Diamond and Flintlock.

"Don't worry about Nelly," Diamond said. "Me and Mr Nimbles will take good care of her."

Eli gave a small laugh while Nelly glared at him with a look that said *not them, anyone but them*. He understood her reluctance, but at least they were enthusiastic. Diega had always called Nelly an overgrown rat and the commander had almost thrown up in his mouth every time Eli had let her eat from his plate. Thoughts of the others spurred Eli to move, when all he wanted to do was drop. He jumped into the pilot's seat as Ismail climbed warily into the passenger's side. For a moment Eli was shocked to silence. Washed and clean-shaven, wearing a uniform, Ismail looked like the military commander he had been. Eli was curious about the reason for his dishonorable discharge, but now wasn't the time to ask too many questions. *Too many questions – too soon … That would be the title of his autobiography – if he ever wrote one.* Ismail held Ev'r's bag against his side.

"How's the external attachment feeling?" Eli asked the scullion as they buckled up.

Ismail touched a hand to his shirt, where the outline of the robotic heart could be seen.

"It's functioning," he replied.

"Good," Eli said. He held out two formula vials with slow-release syringe tops. "These are refills for the ones you currently have implanted in your He-Ro. One is a pain-cancel and the other is regenerative. You've already had significant muscle and weight gain since the escape, but I'd like to see even more. I'm giving these to you so that you're in charge of changing them," Eli said, wanting to give Ismail at least the impression of having control over his health.

He held them out to Ismail, but the scullion just looked at his hand and when he raised his eyes to Eli's the soldier was gone and the man was there.

"There's no point, imp-breed. I'll never be free of her," he said, his voice low, defeated. He dropped his eyes to his ankle, where the shackle was still firmly attached beneath the pants.

"Well you're free now," Eli tried to keep his tone positive, despite the anxiety squeezing his insides. "And we're going to keep you that way."

"She's hunting me ... I can sense it." He touched a hand to his chest – to the zombie heart beneath the He-Ro.

"Doesn't mean she'll find you – or recapture you."

"No, she won't retake me," Ismail replied, darkness in his words. "But I won't be able to escape her alive. That is a certainty."

"Have you had a vision? Are you a seer?" Eli asked, feeling even more rattled.

"I am, but I see no visions, because there is no future," Ismail replied.

"I'm not – I mean – I *am* going to help you," Eli promised him. "I'll make sure you and Ev'r are reunited."

"We will be," Ismail said, "in paradise."

He started to tremble again, the shock resurfacing, and as soon as it did, he visibly switched over to soldier, his eyes blanking out. He sat in the seat, staring directly ahead of him – the purely procedural side of him, waiting to execute unquestioningly whatever mission the emotional part of him had set in motion. Eli swallowed his unease. He triggered the opening of the hangar roof and looked up as it opened into the darkness above. He shivered, feeling exhausted and frightened of what lay ahead. Ev'r spoke in his mind, *No rest for the wicked.*

Chapter 17
Diega

PRATERIUS

RAMBELDON FOREST (WISHING-WELL WOODS)

Diega resurfaced in an isolated pond, the waterfall and city nowhere in sight. She swam to the edge of the pool where Shawe was hauling himself out. Tickleback's voice echoed from somewhere ahead of them.

"Come on! We're close to the Wishing-Well Woods."

Diega clutched handfuls of grass and dragged herself up, surveying their new surroundings.

"Great, more trees," Shawe muttered at her side.

The ground suddenly shuddered and they both stumbled, losing their footing. A colossal spider stepped into their path, standing taller even than most of the towering trees. Diega's gaze followed eight extremely long, thin legs up to an oval body far above. The spider was bobbing with frustration, trying to navigate several thousand small offspring through a white picket gate up ahead in a clearing.

Shawe's face paled and he stared up at the monstrous arachnid, wordless for once.

"Scared, princess?" Diega whispered to him, and he spat a mouthful of curses at her. She chalked up one point to her.

Tickleback appeared from the trees ahead and said, "Don't be fearful. Followmont Longfellow is not dangerous."

As though to verify this, the frazzled spider, who apparently had a name, lifted one foot and ripped out the only small tuft of hair still growing on his head. The strands floated to the ground like feathers while his children continued to jump around making yipping sounds, refusing to obey.

"Morning greetings, friend." Tickleback flew up to the spider. He returned a moment later to say, "He says we should go first. He'll be a long time."

Followmont Longfellow stepped aside, wearily gathering his children around him, while Diega and Shawe moved by. Neither ran, but only because the other one was watching.

They passed through the picket gate, and immediately Diega felt a change in the atmosphere. While Rambeldon Forest had seemed almost dream-like, these Woods felt darker, as though many predatory eyes had now turned their way. Beyond the gate, the land immediately dropped into steep, dirt steps and a path cut through the middle of a tangle of thorny shrubs, dotted with miniature pink, white and yellow flowers. Multi-colored pebbles covered the ground.

"Take a stone, throw it into the Well and make a wish," Tickleback said, propelling downward so that he could pick up a rock.

Diega and Shawe glanced at each other.

"I don't believe in that trutt," Shawe grunted. "Keep moving."

"Take one," Tickleback insisted, pressing a stone into each of their hands.

"We don't have time for games," Diega told him.

The dragonfly regarded her with his deep-seeing eyes. "This is no game."

He turned and led them out onto a small wooden bridge arching over a stream. As they walked, Diega glanced over the railing into the waters and saw, staring up at them from below the surface, the faces of aquatic nymphs, riding eels and loaches. One of them jumped up and spat a mouthful of water into Shawe's face, then darted away, laughing bubbles.

"Little gadfly!" Shawe tried to vault over the railing into the water, but Diega grabbed his arm and managed to drag him back.

"Leave it, we don't have time!" she reminded him.

"Once I ruled the streets, now they're spitting in my face?" he shouted.

"We're not on the streets anymore, if you hadn't noticed," Diega said.

His furious gaze dropped to where her hand was clutching his bicep. A cocky smile replaced the anger and Diega dropped him like fire.

"Don't be shy," Shawe said. "I know you like what you see."

She tried to think of words strong enough to reject the notion on every possible level, but took too long and ended up just looking caught out. Another one for Shawe. He laughed and swaggered away.

Soon they reached the other side of the bridge and a thatched-roof well. Tickleback paused to make a wish and threw in his pebble, while Christy belched and walked past without a second glance. Diega chucked her stone in, and, despite herself, made a wish to find Copernicus alive.

The bridge dropped to a path that led them from the Wishing-Well Woods into the Blackwater Forest. It was even gloomier here, the black-trunk trees growing closer together, blocking the light. Diega noticed there were no insect noises – no noise of any kind, in fact.

"Oh my!" Trilly's gasp broke the silence and Tickleback stopped suddenly.

Diega looked around and saw they'd walked out into the middle of a clearing full of wax sculptures.

"We have to go back," Trilly hissed, then started to tremble, tears misting her big, black eyes. "Oh me."

Tickleback eyed the sculptures of what looked like giant bees and said, "This is where we must leave you, my friends." He lifted his top hat. "I would come with you into the Hive, but they'd kill me on sight. You have a far better chance alone."

"Wait?" Diega said. "Are these … bees?"

"Shhh," Tickleback hushed her. "Their Queen Alphra calls them the Neridori. Be very careful. Should they take you to her, do not say anything unless she asks you."

"Wait!" Diega called him back. "What way do we go to find the Hive?"

"You won't need to find it," the dragonfly said. "It'll find you. Good luck, friends." His emerald eyes fell on Diega. "Don't forget us."

He waved and they were gone in a whirlwind of gangly harlequin legs and black and red dots.

Uneasy, Diega scanned the wax sculptures, with their long spears and pointed stings. Shawe drew his blade and sniffed the air.

"It smells like —"

"Honey?" Diega suggested.

"Rot," he growled.

A faint hum began in the distance, growing rapidly louder. Diega looked toward the sound and her heart gave a loud, jolting thud. A fast-traveling mass of gold and black was closing in on them.

"Trutt," Shawe swore.

They glanced at each other, then straightened and faced the oncoming army.

Chapter 18
Croy

KULLRA FORNAX

NŸR-CORUM (SAINT AGNES BOROUGH)

She moved against the crowd, pushing through masses of Martial Corps personnel thronging in the Tower corridors. Everyone had been called to the High Deck. A Conference representative was flying down to make an announcement regarding the *Teriscoria*. Croy was supposed to attend, but the pain in her leg had become unbearable. She had to get out and get a fix immediately. Before now, she had never once gone to her supplier during a work shift – it was messy and dangerous – but she really had no choice now. It was either go or collapse.

Croy glanced back at Darius. He stood halfway down the corridor talking closely with his latest fling. The girl was grinning, showing too much tooth and casting him coy looks while tracing a finger down the seam of his shirt, over and over. Croy didn't know her and had, a long time ago, stopped bothering to introduce herself to Darry's girlfriends. She knew she came across cold, maybe even hostile at times, but her partner turned girls over and out like a conveyor belt, his passions flaring volcanic, then dying out frozen. He could never find exactly what he was looking for, and Croy believed that had everything to do with him losing his parents so early. She understood, because it had been the same for her – except that she'd had John L and Darius hadn't had anyone.

Croy touched a finger to the new I-Sect in her ear and disconnected the signal. She'd call Darius after she was fixed – it was always better to ask forgiveness than permission.

Croy turned sharply out of his sight and moved down a flight of stairs, clutching the rail to keep herself upright. With people all around her, she fought not to let the pain surface, but once she reached a lower, isolated corridor, she leaned against a wall and let out a cry. She wanted to stop and sit, but knew that would only make the pain worse, and then she wouldn't be able to stand again, so she forced herself on.

Somehow Croy made it out to her dragger and maneuvered herself on. She did have some painkillers in her stash at home, but it was too far to fly in her condition – so instead she took off for the much closer respectable markets in Saint Agnes Borough, where her dealer lived, hiding beneath a legitimate mask.

By the time Croy reached the Kazismir markets, which mainly dealt in dyes, fabrics and perfume, she was drenched in sweat and almost crying in agony. She spotted Septimo standing in front of his stall haggling with two men. They were dressed in expensive fabrics and appeared of high repute, but Croy recognized them as smugglers. They cast suspicious looks her way and Septimo glanced over his shoulder, taking her in for a moment before turning back to his deal. With Septimo, it was always business first. Croy looked away and waited, clinging to the guardrail, as the men finished their dealings and exchanged their wares. The Change of Shifts siren sent up a scream that echoed throughout all the boroughs as Saint Mariread's Timeglass, suspended high in the center of the city, ran dry and flipped over to the nighturn. This original Timeglass was the largest ever made and the reference by which all others were set. It ruled time without mercy.

Once the smugglers were out of sight, Septimo came over to her with that smile on his face that's she'd always found so enticing. He never seemed to age, always keeping the same boyish swagger and cheekiness that she remembered from when they were young. He was the one the girls were told to stay away from, with good reason – a reason that was immediately forgotten as soon as he smiled. Septimo wrapped his arms around her and she leaned into him. He smelled too good. Perfumes were his cover trade – all of them way beyond what she could afford. Another stab of pain sent her staggering. Septimo grabbed her around the waist, checked for who was watching them, then half-carried her to the shop behind his stall. It wasn't a tent, like the shops on the Strip, it was a proper rock structure. Septimo's mother was sitting in the entranceway, a suspicious woman who had lost her mind when she lost a daughter, even before Septimo was born. She wasn't one to trust with a turned back; the knife scar just above one of Croy's shoulder blades attested to that. The woman was crazy dangerous and the only reason she hadn't been exiled into the tunnels was that Septimo had paid off the Conference Judge – and kept paying him. Sometimes Croy wondered how Septimo could care so much for a woman who barely recognized him, and even attacked him if he went too close, but she didn't question it. She understood, even though she'd never experienced it herself, that the mother-bond was powerful. To the point where, even though she had no memory at all of her own mother, sometimes she still had feelings of missing her.

Septimo's mother hissed at them as they moved past her into a backroom. Once there, Septimo closed the curtains in her face, shutting her out.

While the front stall and shop face were the picture of legitimate business, back here with the floor cushions, dimmed candles and incense smoke it looked as though they'd stepped straight into Saint Smithy Roughtown. Septimo lowered Croy down onto one of the cushions and sat opposite her. He took out a pipe and lit it up. This smoke was sweeter than Darius' tigaro and made her feel lightheaded. Septimo watched her through the haze, waiting.

Croy grabbed the bundle of parchments from her jacket and dumped it down between them. He gathered them up, but didn't go through them. After all these annums, he knew her information was always good. There was a time she'd felt guilty selling the secrets of the Martial Corps to a criminal, but that time was long past. She did what she had to. John L had taught her that.

She rolled up her pants past her knee and tentatively loosened the bandage as Septimo took out a syringe and dragged liquid into it from a large decanter. He handed the needle over to her and watched as she injected herself. After a moment more of agonizing pain, her knee went numb and she slumped back, sinking into a gray fog.

When she finally raised her eyelids, heavy and sluggish, Septimo was still smoking, flicking through the papers she'd given him. He felt her stare and looked up, narrowing his eyes, reading her.

"What's wrong?" he finally asked.

"Nothing."

He exhaled a cloud of smoke and said, "Tell me."

"Just the job." Her words ran into each other and she shifted on the cushion, feeling disconnected from her own body. "A few crazies. A few guys ..."

"Guys?" Septimo raised an eyebrow, his gaze sharpening. He put down his pipe and leaned forward. "Who? Smugglers?"

"No – like one guy and then another guy – Controllers – colleagues."

"Well, what can you do? You're popular." He drummed his fingers on the surface of his side-table. "What're their names?"

It was a simple enough question, and she seriously considered telling him about Roth and Knightsbridge and Newton, but she wasn't gone enough not to realize that would have consequences. Underneath the smile and charm, Septimo was a brutal smuggler, leader of his mob, and ruthless to the core. She knew he saw her, or at least her information, as a valuable asset, and he protected his assets.

She shook her head. "I'm handling it. It doesn't matter."

He leaned back in the cushion and sighed deeply, still watching her.

"What?" She pushed the hair out of her face.

"I can't help you if you won't tell me anything."

"Really it's nothing. I'm just tired."

"So lie down and rest." He smiled.

"I should head off," she said.

"You just got here."

It was way too warm in there and her eyelids were feeling heavy again. She knew she had to go back to work and hear about how a bunch of Purple Wings were going to prevent Grays from rioting because they were starving and thirsting to death. She highly suspected none of the plan would involve sharing the masses of food and supplies from the Purple Wing stores, and that was too much to deal with.

She lay back a little, not wanting to think about it, and sensed Septimo moving closer. She felt his hand on her shoulder as he sat down right beside her. The cushion sagged inward, pushing them together. She leaned away a bit, stretching out and looking through the gap in the mat door to the markets outside. There was a guy walking with two children. He grabbed up the little girl and whooshed her through the air making zooming sounds – perhaps he had aspirations for his daughter to become a Fleetsman. So many did and so few made it. Croy felt Septimo watching her closely.

"You want kids?" he said, his voice soft.

She shook her head. "Why bring someone into this ..."

"That's what I say," he agreed.

He stroked a hand down her face, then leaned in and kissed her with an intensity that made her ache. It made a nice change from Roth, who had always seemed like he could barely stand to be near her.

"The *Teriscoria* has been destroyed," she murmured.

"I know," he said, kissing her neck. He moved on top of her and started undoing his pants.

"I'm supposed to be at work," Croy said, making only a token effort to get away.

"Work." He pushed up her shirt. "Forget it – come work for me."

She laughed. "Doing what?"

"This," he whispered and slid his hands up between her thighs until she gasped.

He started to rip down her pants when suddenly a gun pushed around the curtain and pressed against Septimo's temple. The smuggler's eyes widened and he sprung to his feet, his own gun drawn.

Croy staggered up and saw Darius standing in the doorway, his eyes locked onto Septimo. She stood between the two men, Darius blazing and Septimo cold.

"You brought a friend?" the smuggler said to her, his voice dangerous.

"No," she said emphatically. She couldn't lose him as a supplier, she'd spent too long building the trust. "He's my partner."

Septimo looked Darius up and down and she saw he was recognizing him. Croy dared a glance at Darius' face to make sure he hadn't seen the parchments.

"Get out, both of you," Septimo warned, gesturing with his weapon.

Croy moved fast, pushing out through the curtain and grabbing hold of Darius' arm. She dragged at him until he backed up and followed her past the stalls and along the grid-way. Once they'd gone a short distance from the market, he pushed her roughly and yelled, "What are you doing? You said you weren't taking anymore. You swore!"

"I lied!" she yelled back. "That's what addicts do!"

His anger simmered down at the words. She'd never admitted it before.

"You're not an addict. You're in pain," he said, and hearing him make excuses for her hurt her almost as much as the scars. Both of them knew there were other, legal, medicines she could take for her pain. None of them worked as well, but they still worked. She'd just gotten hooked on mortacane and couldn't stop.

Darius changed the topic. "All kinds of hell have broken loose at the Tower. Everyone has new assignments. They want to contain the panic. They were asking for you at the meeting. I had to cover."

She didn't say sorry or thank you because that would have made him angrier. Instead she asked, "Where have we been sent?"

"At the moment, nowhere," he said. "We still have this nighturn off, and next shift VP will give us our new territory." He shook his head and said with barely contained hatred, "The Drays ..."

"I know." Croy nodded. She understood why he hated them even more than most. They'd killed his parents and made his childhood a living nightmare – and now they were trying to take everyone else out too.

Darius shook off the anger and said, "I have to go to my game. So just – go home. Just go home."

He gave her a cutting look and started to walk away, leaving her.

Croy hugged her arms around herself and lowered her head. She felt like crying, but no tears came. Septimo stood watching her from the front of his stall.

Halfway down the grid, Darius halted. He turned and walked back to her.

"What's wrong with you?" he demanded, his anger flaring again. "What were you thinking letting some filth like that touch you?"

"The job today – it shook me," she said, and it was true in a sense, but not a honest answer to his question.

"Yeah, well – me too," he surprised her by admitting. "But you heard what VP said, case closed."

"It shouldn't be."

"Of course not! But what can you do? Another day, another murder. It's our job. Just shake it off. You're stronger than this. It's just because that sodwit Roth left. Why do you care so much? He didn't treat you right anyway! He wasn't good enough for you. I don't understand!"

He was looking at her straight in the eyes, which was rare for him. Usually he avoided all eye contact, even with her. There was hurt in his gaze and it twisted a knife inside her. She moved closer to him so that their bodies were almost touching. Her hand brushed against his. His eyes lowered to her lips and, for a moment, Croy thought he was actually going to kiss her, but then he stepped back and looked away, as though he was scoping for someone. When he looked back his eyes had hardened up.

"Come on. Come and watch the game," he said gruffly.

"It's alright. I'm starving. I'm going to get my package," she replied. The last thing she wanted was to stand around faking interest in sport with Knightsbridge and Newton when the world was crumbling around them.

"Then we'll fly together till the field," he insisted. He took her hand and dragged her away from the railing, then put his arm around her as they walked. She liked the sway of his hips against hers, but as soon as Septimo was out of sight, he moved away again, and they walked separately to their draggers.

Chapter 19
Silho

OMAR MONTANYA

MOUNT SIRIA (THE CASTLE SCORN)

Silho gasped as life rushed back into her. Every breath was raw agony, but the pain was ecstasy – because she was alive. She was breathing. She coughed and tasted smoke – and remembered. *Copernicus ...* Silho tried to sit up, but the chains around her arms and legs held her down. She struggled, thrashing against her binds until a burning hand touched her chest, draining all her strength in one violent jolt. She couldn't move at all. Light-form. She'd used it a thousand times without understanding what a torture it was to be on the receiving end.

A face loomed over her, darkened to indistinct shadows by the light above it. It lowered closer and Silho saw a man with long black hair and a gaunt, battle-hardened face. He had the empty eyes of a demon, one eyelid hanging heavier than the other. Silho blinked into light-form vision, hoping to siphon back her strength, but she was met with a burning pillar of flames that she couldn't access. It blistered her eyes and she was forced to blink out.

"Who are you?" she demanded.

"Lecivion," the man said, his voice flat, detached, as though it was someone else's name and someone else's life, for which he cared not at all. "Prince of Omar Montanya, and all of the scorchlands. And you, Silho Brabel ... I've been waiting a long time to finally meet you – in person."

Silho remembered Raine had said Omar Montanya was the Omarian realm. Her eyes went to the so-called Prince's bloodline marks – firebird dragons! Shock radiated through her, but she kept it contained beneath a layer of cold fury.

"Well, untie me and let me shake your hand," she said, the threat embedded in each word.

His mouth twisted into a half-smile, half-snarl. "I think we both know how that would end."

"Do we?" Silho said. "You ambushed me at Sirenseron. Let me up now and we'll have a fair fight."

"Oh, but this isn't a fight." Lecivion said. "This is you doing what I say. Now lie still." He stabbed a needle into her arm and she groaned as a burning ache spread through her body. She saw other Omarians pushing machines closer to the bench where she lay. It was the first time she'd seen anyone from her father's bloodline, but she felt no recognition of them – just hate.

They started hooking her up with tubes, electrodes and monitors.

"What are you doing to me?" she demanded. "Why am I here?"

"You, Silho Brabel, are being converted into a vortex portal, within which our world will be placed – out of reach of the Indemeus X," Lecivion told her.

A desperate scream echoed around them and Silho managed to turn her head toward the sound.

Below the raised platform where her bench stood, a space stretched out into the gray distance, every square of it occupied by more benches and more women chained down and hooked up to machines – thousands of them. Mostly they were motionless, but Silho caught movement here and there. One woman, near the front, was surrounded by Omarian soldiers. She was fighting her binds, and screaming, "Help! They're going to kill him, they're going to kill him!" over and over. Her terror and panic tore at Silho's soul, and she raised her own voice in response.

"Get away from her! Leave her alone!"

Lecivion looked down at the scene without a flicker of emotion crossing his face. One of the Omarians near the screaming woman looked up. He shook his head and called something out to Lecivion in a language that Silho remembered her father speaking. Lecivion nodded and his soldier blinked to light-form vision, instantly draining the woman to ash. He breathed out a blast of fire, which zapped back through his lips. Then the soldiers started clearing the space away, brushing the ash into a bin as though it was no more than common dust. The callous brutality awakened Silho's rage. She set her eyes on Lecivion, and if a thought could have killed, his heart would have stopped on the spot. He turned to her, feeling the ferocity of her gaze.

"What's it to you? Did you know her?" he asked, his tone mocking.

"What are you doing to them?" Silho demanded.

Lecivion continued to adjust the machines around her as he replied, "Well, in brief: we have one female – you – and we need another, for the other side of the vortex."

"What do you mean, *another female* – another Omarian?"

"You are not Omarian." Lecivion said sharply, his eyes snapping to her. "You're a half-breed – let's be clear about that – which is why we need another half. You see, you're somewhat of a rarity – the first female to be born with any measure of our blood. Before you, even though we took women of all races, they only ever produced full-blood Omarian sons. We were all dominant – we consumed – until your mother ..."

She heard some color coming into his voice – a shade of red and black – hate and anger ...

"So we know it's possible for another female half-breed to be born ... it's just unlikely, but if we have enough women, of enough races, surely one will produce a girl. If there were any of your mother's kin left, of course, we'd start with them, but she was the last one ... *Draigar*." He snorted and smoke billowed out of his nose.

"My mother was a Pyron," Silho said. They were a rare race, but there were others.

Lecivion gave his cold smile.

"Surely you're above swallowing every lie that's stuffed down your throat. Oren Harvey was Draigar – she tattooed the marks of a firelighter into her skin, and into yours – but her blood ran true to what she was ... always." He clenched his jaw.

"What's it to you? Did you know her?" Silho used his own words against him.

Lecivion stared at her and flames surged inside the black of his pupils.

"Yes, a man knows his wife – or at least he likes to believe he does ..." His gaze went past her into his memories. He walked to the edge of the platform and gripped the railing, the metal immediately glowing with heat. "Do you understand what it's like, looking out over the worlds and seeing out-stretched hands in every direction? Not outstretched to give

– but to take – always to take – when people need you to save them – you're all they see – but then it's over and you're no longer relevant – and they forget – all the gratitude – all the promises ... Your mother's world was overrun with ratha demons. We went in and saved them, and your mother was a gift to me, a willing gift, so I thought – a princess – but Oren Harvey cared for nothing and no one but herself. She used me, then she used your father to fulfil her exact needs, then she left us both to rot – and that's the truth of it."

Silho shook her head, his words stirring up a storm of emotions inside her. "Are you angry because she lied or because you loved her?" she asked, already knowing the answer, but wanting to hurt him with the truth. His kind of anger and jealousy, the type that drives a person crazy, couldn't be twisted from anywhere but love. Silho had come to understand that the opposite of love wasn't hate, it was indifference.

Lecivion narrowed his eyes at her. "You took nothing from your father," he said. "You're her all over again." He lifted something from near her head and held it in his hands. Solace – Oren Harvey's blade. He must have found it in her weapon belt, which was now nowhere to be seen. He turned the Solace over, examining the markings on the hilt, then pushed it into his belt.

"Is this punishment for what Oren did?" Silho said. "Because she's dead now ... this is not hurting her."

Lecivion snorted smoke and shook his head. "No and no. No more talking now, I'm tiring of your voice."

"My feelings exactly," Silho returned. She blinked to light-form vision and looked back to the other captive women. Through her chained, outstretched hand she drew in a blast of energy from their body-lights. Not enough to hurt any of them, but enough to break out of her binds and jump off the bench. She snatched a sharpened tool off a side-table and threw it at Lecivion. It stabbed into his shoulder and he shouted, bringing Silho crashing to the ground with one gesture. Rough hands grabbed her and dumped her back on the bench.

"Well, then," Lecivion said extracting the metal shaft from his shoulder as his soldiers tied her back down. "I didn't think you could draw from this far away – not many could. I thought too little of you, but now I know." He spoke the last words as a threat. "There's no need for you to be mind-living in this – in fact, it's undoubtedly better for you not to be …"

While his people re-inserted the tubes and machines, Lecivion locked her neck into a device so that she couldn't turn again to look at the other women. Footsteps sounded and another group of soldiers moved up the steps of the platform to stop behind Lecivion.

"What?" he demanded without turning to face them.

"Her people are still on the move. Some followed us to Praterius, others have found Quartermaine's tracks."

"So finish them," Lecivion said. "Surely you don't need me to tell you how, Imperator Hycinion?"

"No, sire," the other Omarian said. "But I questioned whether I should withdraw more troops from the cause – under the current circumstances."

"What circumstances?" Lecivion's voice was deadly calm.

The soldier said, picking his words with extreme caution, "The worsening situation. It appears the disease of the Indemeus X is spreading, sire. There have been sightings of strangers walking the scorchlands – the half-living with dead masks covering their faces. News from the south says these demons are turning people, whispering to their minds and sending them mad with violence."

"And what of it?" Lecivion demanded. "Let these demons walk. Let them turn the commoners. I told you – as I told everyone – we will have the other female in plenty of time. The Indemeus will not take our world." There was an edge of manic fanaticism in his voice that allowed for no other opinions.

"Yes, sire," the soldier wisely agreed.

"Send two outfits – one to Aquais, one to Praterius – eliminate anyone looking for Silho Brabel. As I specified, no traces," Lecivion ordered.

"As you will, sire." The soldiers moved away and Lecivion turned his attention back on Silho.

"You won't be able to stop him," she said. "My commander – he'll track me."

"I stabbed him with my *kien* and injected enough poison to kill ten of his kind, so he's most certainly dead by now. But how interesting. You refer to your lover as your *commander*. Perhaps you're not so much like your mother after all. I did wonder, while watching you all these year-cycles, how you would end up ..."

"What do you mean – watching me all these year-cycles?" Silho said, refusing to hear that Copernicus was dead.

"Did you think we didn't know you existed? Your father did his best to conceal you, but his best was pathetic. In all this I pity him the most. Oren Harvey broke him to pieces ... He honestly thought she loved him." He shook his head.

"So if you knew I was there, why didn't you kill me – why were you just watching?" Silho demanded.

"You were the first. I really didn't know what to expect from you. Many times along the way I thought you were finished, but you kept going – even against the Skreaf. I must say, I gave you no chance of surviving – you shocked me."

"You're Skreaf hunters – you could have wiped them out, but you stood back and watched as they almost destroyed Aquais?" Silho said, another wave of fury rising inside her.

"You say that like Aquais means something," he mocked her. "It's nothing but another speck among a billion others."

"You're deranged," Silho spat.

Lecivion held out his hand and one of his soldiers gave him a syringe full of yellow serum.

"Time to go, Silho Brabel. Go into the beyond knowing that you've served a purpose."

He advanced on her and Silho held her position, every muscle tensed and waiting. She had to get the timing exactly right. As he leaned in, pushing the needle into her forehead, she whispered almost inaudibly, "Of all the things you've said to me here, one thing stands out the most."

"Really," Lecivion said, his breath hot on her face. "Do tell."

"You said you thought too little of me ... and you were right."

In a rush of unexpended power that she'd drawn from the other trapped women, Silho broke up again out of the binds and neck lock. She ripped the needle out of her forehead and stabbed it into Lecivion. He screamed and threw a blast of fire at her before she could depress the plunger. She felt her skin scorch, but didn't pause her attack. She grabbed up a metal tray and lunged off the bench, smashing him across the face. He stumbled and fell backward off the elevated platform. The other Omarians threw fireballs at her, and tried to trap her in their light-form. She was outnumbered, and her surprise advantage was blown – her only option was to flee. When she'd first broken out of the binds, she'd spotted a doorway to her left. Smacking at the flames still burning her hair, she vaulted over the railing of the platform and hit the ground running, with Lecivion's voice shouting behind her, "Get her – alive!"

Chapter 20
Eli

AQUAIS

SCORPIA (DUSKMAVETH-AENDOR)

Eli's expectations of Duskmaveth-Aendor had centered around one word – spooky. He'd envisioned decrepit buildings, gothic gloom, dust and webs and haunted shadows. So when he and Ismail stepped into a suburb of ultra-modern structures, blinding lights and cleanliness almost to the point of sterility, his jaw dropped a little. Being dissipaters, spectral-breeds didn't need stairs or doors or windows, so all the buildings were architecturally mind-bending, glowing alien structures, alarming and ethereal, twisting high into the black ceiling of the subterranean level. It definitely didn't feel like a lower-level suburb. It felt as if they were discovering a new and advanced civilization, except for one thing: there was not a soul in sight. The streets were completely empty, eerily so, and the silence was deafening. Eli stood in the middle of a white road and looked around, feeling like the last person left after some kind of apocalyptic happening – or at least the second-last. Ismail stood beside him, Ev'r's bag on his back. On the way there, to stop himself talking about Ev'r and provoking Ismail into emotional breakdown, Eli had babbled through ten year-cycles' worth of political history, including the Skreaf uprising, intermixed with his personal life story, all of which Ismail had already siphoned from his thoughts but had sat through again without comment or complaint, his expression barely changing the entire time. Eli glanced at the scullion; with his fatigues and weapon belt, a spare which Eli had stored in the transflyer, he looked every bit the elite soldier he had once been. Really, the scullion cut an impressive figure, so much so it was easy to forget, even so soon, that he was the same person they'd dragged out of the pit. He was making a fast physical recovery, his skin nowhere near as pale and his body bulking up fast. Eli could see why Ev'r had been drawn to him – he felt a slight platonic man-crush himself – maybe because Ismail's brooding and silently furious presence reminded him a bit of the commander. At that thought, a spike of grief made Eli flinch. They had to keep moving. His front-core signal had dissolved into interference as soon as they had entered the level, the surges of Cos magics proving too much for the experimental system. Fortunately, his external system was still up and running. He checked their navigation against the touch map, which was leading them to where that concentration of Quartermaine's fingerprints was located.

"It looks like it's at the end of this street," Eli said.

Ismail didn't respond. He just waited until Eli set off, then followed, scanning his electrifier left and right, checking their surrounds in a methodical way. It made Eli wonder about the extent of his skills. "Does your telepathy work from a distance or just close up?" he asked.

Again the scullion said nothing, his dark wolf eyes roving around them.

"Where do you think they all went?" Eli said. "All the spectral-breeds?"

Ismail gave him a dubious look, then he went suddenly for his weapon belt, grabbing the binding band that the military used to stop spectral-breeds from dissipating if they needed to arrest them. Eli blinked: he and Ismail were now standing in the middle of a massive crowd. There were spectral-breeds literally everywhere – in the streets, on the buildings, in the air. Eli gulped. He took a step back and bumped into a Skilsy Wraith. It stared down at him with hostility in its gray eyes. He pulled away, brushing against another, then spun and stumbled, falling straight through the vaporous body of a Phantom. They were all pressing close and no one looked happy to see them.

Eli scrambled to his feet and said, "Hi folks. We don't mean to disturb."

When they didn't respond, he murmured to Ismail, "Maybe put the band away."

"Disperse!" Ismail shouted out to the crowd, but they just closed in tighter. Eli noticed several Specters among the gathering and gulped again, keeping his arms firmly at his sides.

"It's not like it was," he whispered to Ismail. "The military no longer has power in these places …"

"It never really did," Ismail growled back. He drew his electrifier and armed it. Eli's skin prickled as Cos magics swelled around them and the ground started to tremble.

"It's not alright – I mean, it *is* alright," Eli called, trying to calm the mounting threat.

His com buzzed and he snatched it up. Diamond's voice came through, amplified.

"Attention, spectral-breeds, this man is Eli Anklebiter, known to have saved many of your kind during the Skreaf witch invasion."

Upon hearing these words, the crowd actually stopped and Eli could see thousands of pale faces looking over and through each other at him, the hostility of their eyes starting to fade. He did his best to look heroic, putting his hands awkwardly on his hips, then dropping them immediately, feeling ridiculous. The spectral-breeds said nothing, but gradually the crowd started to thin as they vanished in groups and pairs, until once more Eli and Ismail were alone. It was only then that Eli felt how fast his heart was racing. He wiped the sweat from his eyes and murmured, "Gone ..."

"They're still here," Ismail murmured, looking around. "Everywhere."

Eli squinted and caught a glimpse of fast-flowing ethereal shapes all around them.

"Are they thinking about attacking us?" he said, his anxiety lingering.

"I don't speak any spec-breed languages," Ismail said. "But I don't think so. They're just watching."

"Diamond, how did you know what was happening?" Eli asked through his external com.

"I've hacked your frontal lobe implant. I can see what you see," she replied.

"Oh," Eli said, and then "Oh," once more because he hadn't realized the system was hackable – and he was the designer. He was starting to see a slightly disconcerting theme emerging.

"But don't worry, I can't read your mind because the actual system has crashed. It's just an optical portal at this stage," Diamond continued, sounding a lot more coherent than she had up until this point. "By the way – I love you."

Just out of reflex Eli almost said it straight back, but managed to stifle the words with a cough, then said, "Carry on," and disconnected the signal.

He and Ismail continued down the street until the navigator brought them to a grate in the road dropping into darkness. Eli stared down with trepidation. If there was one place that childhood horror stories had completely spoiled for him, it was dark storm drains. Ill-ease squeezed his neck.

"Down here – I think," he said, restraining a bout of terrified laughter.

Ismail's iron composure didn't waver at all. He just bent down, wrenched up the grating and started climbing through. Eli followed, inching down the rungs, his hands slippery and the smell of wet rust heavy in his nose.

He kept moving until his feet found solid ground. Ismail was waiting there, his eyes glowing red in the dark. Eli fumbled his night-vision specs and dropped them to the ground. As he ducked down to grab them, he heard a series of clicking sounds echoing in the enclosed space. A red glow flared all around them, and when Eli stood, he saw the light was projecting from Ismail's eyes. The scullion continued to make the clicking noises and Eli realized what was happening. The echolocation skill from Ismail's bat blood was coupling with the nocturnal sight capability of his wolf blood and producing a projection of their surroundings. What Eli was seeing wasn't just a lit-up space, but Ismail's mental translation of the space, based on the click echoes, projected through his eyes. It was complex and seriously impressive. "That is truly amazing," Eli spoke his thoughts in a slightly entranced voice. He'd never known another person who could do that.

Ismail didn't respond. He just moved to a doorway in one of the walls and stepped through, clearing their path right and left with his electrifier. He gestured to Eli, who gripped his own weapon and followed.

Using the navigator as reference, they descended deep into the underbelly of Duskmaveth, closing in on the place of massed fingerprints. When they had almost reached it, a flash of reflection up ahead made Ismail pause. The red glow of his projection swept across the face of a Midnight Man.

"Luther!" Eli whispered and started to step forward, but Ismail's hand clasped firmly onto his shoulder. On second look, Eli realized it wasn't Luther, but an actual full-blood Midnight Man, and he was not alone. There was a cluster of four or five standing there, sleeping together until mid-dark, when they would wake to feed on the near dead. Eli checked his chronograph – a half hour to mid-dark, which meant they had half an hour to get the information and get out. It didn't sound like enough.

They crept past the sleeping Midnight Men, the navigation finally bringing them to a fortified door. It had a complicated custom-made locking system, designed to keep out intruders of every race, including dissipating spectral-breeds. Eli knew that people didn't use this level of security unless they had something serious to hide. With a heavy sense of dread, he knelt down and injected a syringe full of a nanobug virus from his belt into the system. It spread out, distracting and redirecting the inbuilt security, covering Eli as he hacked in and took control. He found the unlocking codes and triggered them. The door shuddered as the locks shunted open.

Eli stepped back and Ismail kicked open the door, rushing in first. Blue lights flickered on and Eli heard Ismail call, "Clear." Keeping his electrifier up, Eli stepped around the doorpost and peered around at a large empty space. The concrete floor was stained with rust where equipment and benches had sat for a long time before being cleared out. Only a smell lingered, a sterile stink that turned Eli's stomach. He glanced at Ismail, but the scullion seemed unmoved. He strode to the center of the room and stopped there to stand watch, well and truly in military mode. Eli wondered for a moment how much insight Ismail had into his behavior while he was in this changed state of mind, if he remembered why he was doing what he was doing, or if everything was blanked out except the mission objective – which in this case was finding the tracker team. Ismail's face gave nothing away and again Eli was reminded of the commander. It gave Eli some insight into why Ev'r had gotten involved with Copernicus, albeit briefly, when they were much younger.

Eli walked further in, looking around for clues as to who this Ezra Quartermaine was and what he'd been doing there. He spotted a tech-port in one wall where a computer system had been plugged in and felt a surge of excitement. He ran to it and hooked up his own system, setting up an extractor to harvest the code remaining in the socket. Most people thought once they'd unplugged their computer and removed it all traces of their work would be gone, but in reality a huge amount of data was permanently stored in the tech-port and could be accessed with the right programs.

As the data started to flow into his system, Eli saw it wasn't going to be as easy as extract-and-read – everything was double-, even triple-coded, and embedded with several destroyer viruses designed to self-destruct the information if anyone unauthorized tried to open it. This was going to be tricky and delicate. He reached out to begin the unlocking process, but his com buzzed at his hip, startling him. "Yes?" he answered.

"Don't enter that code!" Diamond said and Eli froze. "You can't cold-hack the viruses or you'll whiteout your whole system. They're advanced cybernetic necrons disguised as simple destroyers. You have to impregnate them with back-up fillers first so when they blow, everything is duplicated."

"Right," Eli said, again feeling stunned by her depth of knowledge and ashamed he'd written her off so quickly. "Has anyone ever told you you're brilliant? Because you're brilliant."

Diamond paused. "Just you – now."

Eli started typing fast, then said with excitement, "The fillers are working – everything is translating over, but the decryption is running really slowly."

"There's nothing you can do except decrypt in smaller sections," Diamond replied.

"Okay – thanks." Eli disconnected the com to preserve battery life and continued manually decrypting sections of data as quickly as he could, until a good portion was decoded. He let the rest keep running while he accessed the voice search function and said, "The Indemeus X."

A full-length hologram of corrupted code flared up in front of him and he typed again, rapidly striking the holographic keyboard, throwing repair filters and patches onto the data until at least half was readable. He sped through the words.

"Anything?" Ismail spoke up behind him.

"Nothing on who or what the X is …" He continued reading as he spoke. "But it looks like Ezra Quartermaine is or was a scientist working on a number of theory-based projects directed at combating the X and his underlings, the Arequium Mors."

"What theories?" Ismail questioned.

"Well, the first theory involves someone named Shah-Jahan RaAhura having, it looks like, ancestral power to defeat the X – but that's marked 'untested'. The first tested theory was Project Nÿr-Corum – it was a breeding program between human-breeds and something called Dray. They were trying to breed in resistance to the Arequium Mors mental influence. They must be telepaths of some sort, I'm guessing. The project was a failure, hypothesis disproved." Eli glanced back at Ismail. "Any of this making sense to you?"

Ismail shook his head, his expression grim.

"This *scientist* then started Project Spectral Defense, trying to mix human-breed and spectral-breed DNA to develop the same resistance … Oh, here he writes that he's discovered the

Arequium Mors are actually a variety of spectral-breed. This project also failed." A series of disturbing holograms of twisted cross-bred human-spectrals appeared before them, all the test subjects languishing behind glass and bars in conditions of abject misery or hideous death. Eli's mind jumped immediately to Luther. From the dates of these images, Luther would be the right age to have been a subject. Eli felt nauseated and when he spoke again his voice was shaky.

"The final recorded project is titled 'Project Vortex Portal', and it looks like Ezra Quartermaine teamed up with the Omarians to test a theory about creating a vortex between two portals strong enough to contain an entire planet, which is completely impossible and insane. I mean, the physics ..." His mind raced around figures and numbers, spiraling into an infinity of impossibilities. "That's all that's decoded so far of the projects —" He looked at Ismail and saw the scullion's eyes were fixated onto something on the holographic screen.

Eli looked back and startled away several paces. A full-sized image of a man had opened up. He had shoulder-length black hair, a narrow, hard face, and orange-black eyes with slit pupils like a dragon. They were void of all feeling. A long, thin dagger was growing out of the man's arm, marked with the firebird dragon bloodline. Eli immediately recognized him from the attack.

"This was the man!" he said to Ismail. "He took Silho. He was choking her."

Ismail strode over and stood eye to eye with the image of the Omarian man. "Lecivion," he snarled, and Eli saw him switch out of soldier mode. Anger, hate and sadness flooded his eyes all at once and his lips curled back around sharp incisors. "You know him?" Eli asked, feeling a spark of hope.

"I've seen him in my visions ... before ..." Ismail flinched, his hand shooting up to touch his chest.

"Heart pain?" Eli asked quickly.

"I told you, imp-breed," Ismail murmured, closing his eyes trying to regain composure. "She's hunting me."

"I won't let her get you," Eli repeated.

Ismail shook his head slowly, started to speak but then decided against it. His body trembled and sweat slicked his face. Eli put a comforting hand on the scullion's shoulder. Ismail looked down at the hand and then up at Eli with warning in his stare, but Eli didn't remove it. The commander had taught him a lot, but he'd learned by himself that a genuinely caring touch after harsh treatment can break down all kinds of walls.

"What is it to you, imp-breed?" he asked. "Why do you care so much? What do you want from me and Zara?"

"Nothing," Eli responded. "As I said, Ev'r's my friend."

"There's no such thing as friends," Ismail echoed something Ev'r had once said. "And nobody does anything for nothing."

"I do," Eli replied.

"Why?" Ismail demanded.

"I don't know," Eli said, honestly. "I just – care. Diega, my tracker colleague, my friend, said I have a hero complex." He smiled at the thought of Diega teasing him, but the smile faded. Where was she?

"So that's why I care … but why are you here helping me?" Eli asked the question he'd been trying to stop himself from asking.

"For Zara." Ismail said. "If you're killed there's no chance for her …" Desperation filled his stare, but then his eyes blanked out to hard and vacant. "Proceed with the objective, soldier. Available time unknown," he said, his voice back to military.

Eli nodded – Ismail was right, time was against them, they had to stay on track. He looked back to the screen.

Information was starting to filter in around the image as the system continued to decode its data. It looked as though Quartermaine had set up the picture to document the Omarians' abilities.

Eli read aloud. "The male Omarian is born with a needle-like section of bone known as the *kien* that he can access by breaking his own wrists ..." He flinched as the hologram demonstrated the process. "If used to stab, it injects a slow poison that burns like fire." Eli spotted a crucial word. "Antidote!" He went in very close, the light and words reflecting across his face. "There is only one cure – Omarian blood poured over the entry wound ..."

To cure Jude they needed Omarian blood ... To get the blood and to find the commander and the others, they needed ...

"Portals. Look up portals!" Eli instructed the system. A sea of data, formulas, equations and theories appeared instantly. Eli waded in. Partway down, science gave way to paranoid rambling as Quartermaine clearly became more and more convinced that the Omarians, in particular Lecivion, were planning to double-cross him. His plan of counter-attack was to attempt to assassinate Lecivion. He had tried to make a portal into the Omarians' realm using his theories but had failed, and had changed plan to finding an existing portal instead.

"Quartermaine writes: *I've located two remaining portals in Scorpia constructed by rogue Omarian Englan Chrisholm. One hanging in the Superior Hall of Nineva in Adliden, the other lost in the depth of LaNoria ...*" A map appeared beside the writing, showing the locations of both paintings. Eli's immediate thought was *no wonder these two Chrisholm paintings survived the mass burning that claimed all the others*. Adliden was the only underwater level of the city, Nineva one of its suburbs, and LaNoria was the notorious Level 4, completely sealed off from the rest of the city many years before Eli was born after some sort of infectious outbreak.

The information didn't say whether Quartermaine had gone to search for the portals or anything further, other than one more line which Eli read out.

"The access enchant to open the portal to Omar Montanya is 'behind the red star smiles the darkness – Omar Montanya'."

As soon as Eli said the words, he realized he'd made a terrible mistake. A shock wave ran through the air with a gust of burning heat. The ground trembled. Ismail growled and Eli gulped. They both sensed some kind of presence gathering force around them.

"Move!" Ismail said. "Disconnect everything. Evac now!"

Eli yanked his system free. He gathered everything up and shoved it onto his belt, then raced behind Ismail toward the door. They crashed back out into the consuming dark of the tunnel and Ismail started clicking, projecting a path for them as they ran. Eli glanced wildly over his shoulder and saw the motionless forms of the Midnight Men, sleeping still, but for how long? Eli had lost track of time inside the laboratory. He ran on, his wings flapping uselessly, crashing against the sides of the tunnel. In front of him, Ismail skidded to a sudden stop as a square of white light flared in front of them.

"Other way!" he ordered Eli, whipping around and shoving him back in the direction they'd come. They fled, but soon running bootsteps were echoing close behind them, herding them back toward the dead-end of the laboratory room. Eli had thoughts of locking themselves in and trying to set up some kind of barricade when Ismail grabbed him to a stop.

"In there," he said, pointing to the still silhouettes of the Midnight Men just ahead.

"What do you mean?" Eli gasped.

"I mean – in there!" The scullion crushed Eli's arm in a vice grip that would have made him yelp if he wasn't frozen numb with fear. Ismail dragged him to the Midnight Men, where they inched around behind the deadly spectrals. Shadows cloaked their forms, shreds of gore hanging off razor claws. Bones and skulls and random objects cluttered the ground beneath their feet. Eli's mouth felt desert dry. He glanced at his chronograph. It was past mid-dark. He stifled a strong urge to burst into laughter. The footsteps pounded nearer and Ismail dragged Eli further back to hide in the shadows.

A group of five Omarians ran into sight, coming to a halt beside the Midnight Men. One scanned his fire torch across in front of the Spectral Breeds, the flames rippling through the darkness. The Omarians looked at each other with uncertainty, contemplating the strange spectrals. Eli sucked in his breath, trying to channel invisible. Ismail had closed his eyes so that their nocturnal glow wouldn't give them away. The Omarians shuffled around and murmured to each other, distracted by the Midnight Men, not noticing them crouching behind. Eli willed them to just keep going toward the laboratory. It would give him and Ismail a chance to make a run for the ladder. They seemed to start backing away and Eli felt a flicker of hope, but then one Omarian lifted his hand and hurled a fireball straight at the sleeping spectrals, setting some of them ablaze. The Midnight Men woke with horrible screeching screams like nails scratching down a blackboard. They flared up, their Cos magics shaking the tunnel and bringing chunks of rock down on Eli's head. They flew at the Omarians, who responded with fire and light-form.

Ismail seized Eli's arm and dragged him around the chaos. They broke out and bolted down the tunnel. Eli could hear steps pursuing them. Ismail fired electrifier shots over his shoulder into the darkness. The steps slowed, but as soon as Ismail stopped they came again, faster. Ismail glanced at Eli, his wild eyes glowing red, reflecting Eli's thoughts back at him – if the Omarians got them in their sight with light-form, they'd be sunk. Eli pushed his legs, the muscles screaming, chest burning, but the steps behind them advanced. They could hear the Omarians' ragged breathing just behind them, feel the fire on each gasp. They managed to keep one turn ahead until finally they reached the last corner before the ladder.

"It's here!" Ismail said.

A form appeared right in front of their path and Eli slammed to a stop, seeing a Midnight Man – and then a wolf.

"Luther!" Eli yelled.

Luther ran toward them and Eli thought for a moment he was going to hug him, but the spectral-breed flew straight over them, crashing into the Omarian just about to throw a fireball. Luther and the Omarian grappled with each other, Moses snarling and barking, snapping at the man's legs. Ismail grabbed Eli, but he pulled away; he wasn't going to abandon Luther this time. The Omarian shoved Luther back and caught him in light-form vision. The half-Midnight Man gasped and sank to his knees, convulsing. Moses leaped at the Omarian's neck, but was snared as well. The wolf howled and contorted horribly in midair. Ismail was shouting, Eli screaming – both were blasting their electrifiers, but the Omarian was consuming the shots with his fire.

It looked hopeless, until a thought jumped to clarity in Eli's mind. He grabbed the light blaster off his weapon belt, flicked it on and shone the beam right into the Omarian's eyes. Immediately, the man flung an arm over his eyes and shied away, releasing Luther and Moses. Before the Omarian could recover, Ismail opened fire with his electrifier, blasting him apart. The man exploded into a ball of flame. Eli hit the ground, shielding his face, and when he looked up he saw the Omarian was ash and Luther lay sprawled out in front of him cradling Moses. Eli scrambled to them. The wolf was unmoving and tears were streaming down Luther's face. Ismail dropped down beside them and lifted the wolf's muzzle. His head hung limp, eyes rolled back in his head. Luther sobbed. Ismail touched Moses' side and sent a cracking electro-current into him. The wolf stirred back to consciousness and gave a faint whine. Ismail put his head down to Moses' face and the two touched foreheads, connecting for a moment – a wolf and man who shared the same bloodline. More bootsteps sounded behind them. "Luther, take Moses back to my bunker," Eli rushed. "There are people there who will help. They're friends – go!"

Luther staggered up, terribly weakened himself, struggling to hold the wolf's bulk. It took him several attempts to dissipate before they both vanished. Ismail and Eli's eyes met, then they sprang up, lunging for the ladder and climbing as fast as they could. Eli buzzed his wings, but the tunnel was so constrictive he couldn't launch into flight and had to rely on the speed of his hand. When they were halfway to the surface a fireball rushed after them, and Eli gasped, feeling the brutal heat biting at his legs, before it sank back down. They were just out of range, but immediately heard Omarian boots on the rungs climbing after them, getting closer. The next fireball would consume them. They took the second half of the ladder at an impossible pace, scrambling and dragging themselves up and up until Ismail slammed into the grating above and threw himself out. Eli tried to follow but failed, his legs slipping out from underneath him. His chin slammed into the ladder bars and he bit down on his tongue, the pain almost blacking him out. He dangled by one slipping hand and heard the roar of fire behind him. Gritting his teeth, he swung up, reaching desperately for the top of the ladder. Feather-soft hands with an unyielding grip latched onto his wrist and wrenched him upward out of the hole. He collapsed onto the sidewalk as a column of fire blasted up right behind him.

Eli lifted his head and saw a pair of gray feet in front of him. He scrambled up, surrounded on all sides by Skilsy

Wraiths. Behind the Wraiths more spectral-breeds were re-materializing – masses of them, standing statue still, staring at the grate, where the clunks of the climbing Omarians echoed below.

"Keep moving!" Ismail called to Eli from where he was pushing through the crowd, getting away from the grate.

"Thank you," Eli said to the Wraiths around him. "But you should go. They're fire-wielders – they'll set you alight."

The Wraiths regarded him with enigmatic gray eyes and held their position.

"Soldier, move!" Ismail shouted again and Eli ran to catch up, weaving his way through the silent Spectrals as the sounds of their pursuers grew louder and nearer to the surface.

"They'll kill them all," Eli panted to Ismail.

The scullion shook his head. "Specs aren't as fragile as they look."

As he said the words, an Omarian face lifted up through the hole and yelled at them. At the same time Eli sensed Cos magics surging through the air all around. There was a screech of steel and wrenching of concrete – a boom and a blast and then a deafening crash that quaked the ground so fiercely Eli was thrown off his feet. He spun around to see the spectrals had lifted an entire building and slammed it down on top of the grate, crushing the storm tunnels and the Omarians deep into the ground below. It felt a bit like overkill, but Eli had no complaints.

Eli dragged him up and they ran on until they left Duskmaveth-Aendor and found themselves beside the Brownstone River, close to the public elevator where they had entered the level. Panting, Eli grabbed his com and called Diamond, who answered immediately with a deluge of babbling and crying. She'd seen the whole thing through Eli's eyes, but been unable to do anything to help.

"It's okay, we're alright," he comforted her. "Slow down. It's okay. There's a half-breed Midnight Man coming to you with a white wolf. Both have been drained by the Omarians. You have to help them – do you understand?"

He heard her gulping, then she said with a trembling voice, "Mr Nimbles likes dogs ... They smell like mud."

"Do what you can for them," Eli said.

"I will."

"Can you send me through Jude's stats?"

"Sending now," Diamond told him.

Eli ended the transmission, reading Jude's status report as it showed up in his system. His heart rate had slowed more and some of his organs had shut down as the poison progressed toward his brain. They had no time to stop and recover. Eli glanced at Ismail and gasped.

He had slumped down to the ground and was clutching his chest in agony. Eli dropped to his knees, rapidly checking the He-Ro for the pain and regenerative vials; they were both still three-quarters full. He shouldn't have been feeling any pain at all.

"She's after me," Ismail gritted out, now switched out of military mode. "Leave. Continue on. Save Zara." He gripped Eli by the front of his shirt. "Save her!"

Eli grabbed onto the scullion's hand and saw a flash of images leaving his mind and entering Ismail's. It was Ev'r just as she'd turned to Ravien – *'My friend ... I'm finished. Keep going.'* Eli heard the memory of his own scream as she'd changed.

Tears filled Ismail's dark eyes and his grip on Eli's shirt loosened. "Go," he uttered, slumping back defeated. "Leave. I'll end myself before she finds me. I want to do it alone."

"No, I'm not going anywhere without you," Eli told him. "I know you don't think you'll ever really escape her, but that's just the captivity talking. You've been trapped for so long, part of you must have had to reconcile itself to the idea that it would be forever. Your body and mind are now just re-adjusting to being free."

"Only in death … are we free," Ismail murmured.

"True – but we're also, well, dead – so it's not really the best option, and just remember. You win against the witch with every free step you take," Eli said.

Ismail just shook his head, nowhere close to being ready to reason through his feelings. A quick thought shot through Eli's mind. He opened up Ev'r's bag, which was sitting beside Ismail, and drew out the Morsus Ictus. Ismail saw it and his eyes widened. Eli was about to speak, to say it was a symbol of Ev'r being with him, of her strength and resolve, of their bond, but words seemed wholly unnecessary. Ismail felt it immediately.

"You have to fight. Even if you don't believe you'll win," Eli told him. "You've survived so much – you have to keep going."

Ismail stared at the blade, and said, his voice starting to flatten out, "When the witch comes for me – and she will. Take me out. If you care at all for Zara – you'll do it."

"I won't let her take you, but I'm not going to kill you either," Eli told him.

"You have no idea how powerful she is."

"Maybe not, but we got you out, didn't we?"

Ismail had to nod to that and something shifted in his expression, but only for a moment and then his face hardened back to soldier mode. He stood, accepted the Morsus Ictus from Eli's outstretched hand and sheathed it.

"Proceed at will," he said, swinging Ev'r's bag onto his back, while Eli stood up on shaking legs.

"I think the next step is Adliden," he said, "to try to retrieve the portal."

Ismail gave a nod and said, "To Adliden."

Chapter 21
Diega

PRATERIUS

RAMBELDON FOREST (THE HIVE)

Diega stared up at the seething swarm of Neridori, and saw herself and Shawe reflected back a thousand times in the mirror sheen of their black eyes. Thick plumose hairs and black and gold armor covered their bodies and faces, each set into the hardened grimace of a combat soldier. Like Tickleback, these insect-breeds had two sets of arms, and in both they held sharpened spears. Long spike-stings grew out of their lower backs. Diega clenched her own blade, preparing to fight, but the Neridori didn't attack, they just circled for a while on thin, transparent wings before sinking down to land in a circle around them. They stood upright on two legs, all of them taller than Diega, then in one united sweep they stabbed their spears inward at her and Shawe.

One spoke in Urigin, the words almost drowned out by the buzz of its voice. "Hand over your weapons."

Shawe looked as though he was about to refuse, but Diega shook her head at him. With a grunt of reluctance he lowered both his blades. Diega followed him, unclipping her weapon belt and throwing it down. Several of the creatures came forward to frisk them roughly. Christy objected when they took his flask, but quietened as a spear jabbed at his neck.

"Now march," the same guard commanded, and the spears closed in on them, forcing them to turn and move through the forest.

With each step, a background humming grew louder, first to a *bssss*, then a *bzzzz*, and finally, as they reached the towering gates of the Hive, the all-imposing *ZZZZ* of a million giant bee wings, whirring together in the thickly sweet air. The Neridori standing guard opened the gate as they approached, and they entered into the shadow of the gigantic Hive rising up ahead, its walls made of vertical wax combs and hexagonal cells. All around the palace, Neridori worked at a frantic pace. Some were collecting pollen from towering yellow flowers, others removing what had been collected and taking it away. Further down the path, thousands of Neridori worked on the side of the palace, spitting gooey globs of wax from their mouths and smearing it over the walls to reinforce and extend. Others worked to cool the wax, spreading water over the walls and fanning it with their wings. On the top of the Hive, a solitary Neridori danced in a series of sweeping, graceful figure-eight movements, directing the workers.

The guards pushed Diega and Shawe all the way up to the palace entrance and forced them to walk through a mass of waiting Neridori, thousands of glossy black eyes staring them down. Diega stepped carefully, her head lowered, conscious of the spears and stings all around.

The entrance hall of the palace was a vast wax chamber, the walls decorated with glowing gold, orange and yellow swirls that made Diega think of wings in motion. Wax vases and ornaments stood on pedestals around the space, and in the center sat a massive sculpture of what looked like a hugely obese slug with tiny wings. The guards moved the captives up many flights of steps before they came out into an open chamber full of Neridori, scurrying and buzzing frenetically around something in the center of the room.

The guards forced them down to their knees, and Diega glimpsed, through the frenzy of bodies, a wax lounge where what she guessed must be Queen Alphra lolled, even more grossly blubberous and hideously flaccid than her sculpture. She was just a small head on a mountain of white, rolling flab, sparsely covered in bushy gold and black hair. At her head, servants spoon-fed her nectar, which she slurped up with an eelish tongue lashing out from interlocked mouthparts. At the other end, another group worked catching the white eggs as they plopped out in a constant mucusy shower, while another even more unfortunate group of subjects cleaned up the excrement and other offensive excretions slopping to the floor. The odor of the room was syrupy sweet, with a disturbing underscent of old meat.

Diega spotted, kneeling on the ground behind the queen, a group of bees who were stockier, and more muscular and masculine-looking than any of the others she'd seen so far. One of them looked up and a guard struck him over the head.

A guard from the group that had captured Diega and Shawe cautiously approached the queen and bowed low to the ground, wing tips touching the floor. Alphra regarded her with shifting, beady eyes.

"What?" She spoke louder than all the others, though the word was still blurred by the buzz.

The guard answered. "Your Majesty, Queen Alphra, Great Mother and Sustainer of the Hive, may this unworthy servant present these trespassers found in the woods."

The queen gestured impatiently.

A spear poke to Diega's back made her shuffle forward on her knees. The queen leaned toward her like a tidal wave of blubber to get a better look. Her stare, black and cold, bored into them.

"Why were you trespassing on my land?" the queen asked, a definite threat behind her words.

"Forgive us, your majesty," Diega said, playing nice. "We are travelers from a faraway place and we lost our way."

"We're not lost, we're looking for someone," Christy chimed in.

"You dare speak, drone?" the queen said with such hatred Diega winced. Clearly this insect-breed had some kind of immense dislike of males.

Alphra lifted one flabby arm and jabbed it at Diega. "Are you responsible for bringing this ill-formed drone into my land?"

"Who are you calling ill-formed?" Shawe objected. "I'm guessing you don't have any mirrors here, because you're one ugly-looking slug."

The chamber exploded into a buzzing uproar, drowning out Diega's attempts to apologize. A swarm of guards closed in on them, spears stabbing, their intentions clear.

"No!" Alphra commanded. A glint came into her eyes. "Lock them up."

The guards converged on Diega and Shawe, forcing them from Alphra's chamber down a series of tunnels to a prison section of the Hive. They threw them into an open cell and, before Diega and Shawe could scramble up, rapidly sealed the entrance with wax, plunging them into darkness.

"Shawe!" Diega used his name like a curse word.

"What?" he demanded. "You think I'm going to let that trutting gadfly call me ugly!"

"Yes, Shawe! Under these circumstances, yes!" Diega yelled. "Now you're the trutting gadfly because we're locked up in here – thanks to you!"

"As if she would have given us anything anyway!" he shot back. "I saved us by getting us out of there."

"Well, thank you so very much for saving me!" Diega said. "Now, how are we getting out of *here*?"

Shawe paused, then he swore and charged at the rubbery wax seal over the door, ramming it again and again, bouncing back every time.

Diega slumped to the ground and closed her eyes; her whole body was aching with fatigue and hunger. She cursed herself for not eating and drinking along the way when she had the chance – now all her supplies were lost with her belt. The only thing she had left was the silver coin in the hidden pocket of her soak, the *Ory-5* in its morphed state, which they could have used to escape – if her skills were working – but they weren't, so it was nothing more than just a coin. For several minutes she stayed completely still, trying to think, while listening to Shawe charging and bouncing back over and over until it became so ridiculous that she had to shout, "Stop that, you stubborn lunatic!"

When he didn't stop, she sprang up at him, grabbing a handful of shirt and muscle. He groaned as she accidentally punched the wound in his back. He dragged her off him and shoved her toward the cell wall. She slammed against it, her fingernails digging deeply into the wax. It surprised her how soft it actually was.

"Hey, the wall's pliable," she said to Shawe, squatting down and digging out another chuck of wax.

Shawe came toward the sound of her voice and stumbled over her, half-falling onto her back, just managing to keep himself up with one arm.

"Get off me!" She struggled to shove off his crushing weight.

"What are you doing lying on the ground? Having a nap?" he barked.

"I'm digging through into the next cell. Get off!"

He rolled away and demanded, "How's that going to help?"

"We might be able to keep digging until we find an open cell."

"Which could take forever."

"I'm sorry, do you have an appointment somewhere?" Diega snapped. "Or a better idea?"

"Yes … I'm going to cut that slug into little pieces and feed her to herself!" He sprang up and started back into uselessly charging the door.

"Imbecile," Diega muttered. She continued chiseling out chunks of the wax with aching fingers until finally, hours later, she broke through to the other side. Diega put her ear up to the small tunnel and listened, but all she could hear was Christy breathing like a dragon on the other side of the cell.

"Can you stop breathing – permanently?" she hissed at him.

Sounds of a gasp and fast-stirring limbs came through the hole and a buzzing Neridori voice demanded, "Who's there?"

Diega slid back. The last thing she needed was a sting to come through the wall and through her head.

"Who are you? Tell me … please." The voice spoke again, quieter, desperation clinging to the words.

"Diega Bluejay," she said. "Who are you?"

There was silence for a second and then the voice replied, much closer to the hole, "Drone 9898989898989898 … Are you real?

"Yes, I am," Diega said.

"Really?"

"Yes."

"Really?"

"Yes."

"Really?"

Diega paused. Shawe muttered a curse.

"Are you there?" the voice shrieked.

"I'm here," Diega said. "Why are you locked up?"

"I'm unchosen ..."

"What does that mean?" she asked.

"Not chosen."

"Yes, but why does that get you locked up?"

The drone replied, "The queen chooses some of our brothers to be her mates and the rest of us are put here."

"For what? Until when?" Shawe spoke up.

The drone paused. "Until forever."

A chill crept along Diega's back. She hadn't seen any feeding slots in the cells they'd passed.

"Do they feed you?"

The Drone answered in a sob. Christy swore again and started pacing.

Diega rubbed a hand over her forehead, thinking. The drones in Alphra's chamber had looked like they had the same sting capabilities as the females, so why weren't they busting out? The only thing she could think of was that they were brainwashed. Somehow she had to break through the conditioning and make this drone do what she wanted. She closed her eyes, trying to remember what Copernicus would say when he was interrogating someone and breaking into their thoughts.

"Tell me your name," she finally said.

"I don't have one. I'm a drone unchosen. Drone 9898989898989898."

"You must call yourself something – other than a number," she insisted.

The drone paused, then ventured, "Sesame?"

"Sesame, are you hungry?"

He whimpered.

"I want to help you get food, but first you have to help me get out of here. You have to use your sting to cut a hole through the seal on your cell and then through mine. Then we can go and free the others. We'll get everyone out, and you can all eat."

No reply came through the wall.

"Did you hear me?"

"Out?" Sesame said. "We don't get out."

"Trust me," Diega said. "You can. I'll help you."

"We're not allowed. We stay where we're put," Sesame replied automatically.

Shawe cursed again. Diega closed her eyes and fought for calmness. She took in a deep breath and then said, "Do you really want to die?"

"No," Sesame whimpered.

"Do you want to be free and fly away?"

"Fly?" the drone whispered. "We could fly?"

"You can do whatever you want. You don't have to stay here."

"But we ha—"

"No!" Diega cut in. "You don't have to do anything except escape."

"But the queen ..."

"Forget her. She's sitting down the hall gorging herself sick while you and the others are starving to death. Listen to me. Your brothers need you, right? They need you to lead them out. If you don't, they'll all die as well. What if they're as scared as you are right now?"

"We're not allowed out. We stay where we're put," Sesame repeated, but to Diega it sounded as if his resolve was weakening.

Diega lowered her voice and said, "You're strong. You can fight her. You don't have to die like this ..."

Sesame started to speak, then broke down into long, buzzing sobs. He cried for so long Diega thought he would never stop and she and Shawe would die listening to the sounds of this creature's misery, but finally he quietened.

Diega pressed her ear to the hole and heard him standing up and shuffling forward. There was a sound like a knife blade puncturing rubber, then more movement in the corridor. A sliver of light fell across Diega's face as Sesame broke into their cell. She leaped up and pushed out through, into the hallway, Shawe right behind her. They stared at the emaciated drone standing there, trembling and swaying and blinking into the light.

"Trutting hell," Shawe muttered and Diega agreed. The sight and smell of the drone made her feel like gagging, but she held it together, scanning along the seemingly endless corridor of sealed cells. If Copernicus had been taken by the Neridori, as the dragonfly had said, he'd be in one of these.

"Can you tell which of these cells have been recently sealed?" she asked Sesame. The drone whimpered and wrung his fuzzy hands, his antennae drooping low.

"It's okay." Diega tried to comfort him. "You've already taken the biggest step, it's just getting all the others out now, including a friend of ours. He was captured a few days – sets – ago."

The drone glanced around, hesitated, then pointed to one cell.

"Can you open it for me?"

He gave a small nod and hobbled over. He punctured the rubbery wax with his sting. Diega grabbed the sides of the hole and wrenched it apart. A fist flew through and punched her right in the face, knocking her onto her back. She held her bloodied nose and looked up into the golden eyes of Caesar K-Ruz. The Pride King's attention immediately snapped to Shawe. The two gangster superpowers glared each other down, before Shawe lunged, crash-tackling Caesar back into the cell. Diega heard the sounds of punches being thrown. The noise would alert the guards for sure. Cursing, she climbed in after them.

Chapter 22

Eli

AQUAIS

SCORPIA (ADLIDEN)

Eli stepped out of the pipeway and onto a ledge. They'd found a blocked-off water main leading into Adliden and followed it here to the top of the submerged, subterranean level. On one side of the ledge a craggy rock-wall towered above them. On the other side, the ground fell away into a precarious, ninety-degree drop to a fast-flowing river far below. The rushing brown rapids roared, crashing into the rocks and spitting up wet slivers. The air hung lifeless, its salt and seaweed tang leaving an off, bitter taste in Eli's mouth. He glanced at Ismail.

The scullion hadn't spoken a word since they'd left Duskmaveth, just stared ahead of them with empty eyes. It was clear, he really didn't believe he had any hope whatsoever of staying free of the witch and surviving. In his mind, death was the only way to escape. Eli knew he couldn't just snap his fingers and make Ismail believe in something different, his thoughts long entrenched and reinforced by torture and imprisonment – all he could do was try to keep him moving. Eli forced himself to focus on the plan – get to Nineva, get the portal, go to Omar Montanya, rescue Silho, the commander and Diega, return with some Omarian blood and heal Jude ... There were so many holes in the plan it might as well have been a colander, but he chose not to think about that.

They followed the ledge downward to a path that ran beside the river, its muddied sandbank melting into the waters and slowing the flow. The stiller parts of the stream were full of marine-breeds – tuskfish, sandfish, twohand fish, wibbling-wobbling jelly boulderfish that plonked into the water to hide. Flocks of gliding rainbow coralangels hovered over heavily whiskered cats with fur and scales, batting at tiny butterfly fish flittering past on delicate wings. On the opposite side of the river, crustaceans squatted on the bank, sifting through the sand with clamp-like claw hands. Thick, orange shells covered their skin and their eyes sat on stalks on the top of their heads. They looked up sharply as the strangers approached. Some leaped onto two legs and darted into burrows in the sand, immediately sealing them over. Others just stared with their stalked black eyes. One clicked its pincers together in a *snip-click* sound. The message was clear enough – *stay away*.

"Is it just me, or does everyone seem a little unfriendly here?" Eli said to Ismail.

"The war's touched them too," the scullion muttered grimly. He fixed his stare on Eli. "Machine-breeds against the gangsters?"

During the flight there, Eli had recounted more of the recent civil war that had brought the city to the brink.

"Yes," Eli said, surprised and encouraged by the fact Ismail was asking a question. "Kry against Caesar K-Ruz."

"It was only a matter of time," Ismail said. "Before the machine-breeds revolted."

"Maybe I'm naive," Eli replied. "But I can't understand how such a powerful group like the machine-breeds could have been oppressed so much in the first place ... They have strengths like rapid healing and resistance to magics that no other race has ... I mean, I know the historical account of the situation, but it just doesn't seem plausible."

"That's because it's the *official* historical account, written by the oppressors," Ismail said, some feeling coming into his voice. "It's not the actual account. You don't need to do much to control someone stronger than you – you just need to know what their weakness is and be ruthless in exploiting it. The real story was that the Ar Antarians began to take control after they stole a group of children whose parents were influential Androt leaders. Then they used simple threat to manipulate the parents and turn the race against itself. The machine-breeds never recovered after that."

"I've never heard that before," Eli said. "But it does ring true."

"You think scullions allowed the governments to write their history for them. We wrote our own history! Not that any of it actually matters," Ismail said, and Eli saw a momentary flicker of emotion in his eyes.

"Where were you born? Was it in the city or in the scullion settlements?" Eli asked, trying to encourage him to keep talking. Ev'r hadn't written anything about Ismail's earlier life in her journal, just documenting from the start of their relationship when Ev'r was twelve and he fifteen. They were actually cousins, third or fourth removed, which was why they had the same last name.

"My background is irrelevant to the mission," Ismail responded. "I suggest you focus, soldier."

"Well, to be honest, I've never been much good at focusing on one thing," Eli said. "Me – I was born in the back of a transflyer. My father was going to take my mother away to some place where they could live together, but then I was born early and he took one look at me and changed his mind! My grandparents raised me."

Ismail grunted, eyeing Eli's mixed Glee and Greer blood-line marks on his arms, blue stripes and purple dots.

"I noticed that you had two fathers – were you close to either of them or your mum?" Eli pressed him again.

"As I said, my background is irrelevant," Ismail answered.

Eli took that as a no and said, "I never got to know mine either really. I saw Mum once or twice when she came to ask my grandparents for money, but then she married some rich guy and never visited again. Dad ... he was kind of in the picture for a moment there, but not really. Kind of hurt a bit," he admitted.

Ismail gave him a hard stare and said, "Do you know what happens to Militia recruits who bring up their past?"

"No, but I can imagine it's not pleasant."

"They're shot. Dead. On the spot," Ismail said, flatly. "There is no past. There is no future. There is only the mission."

Eli absorbed the information with dulled horror and decided to restrain his normal imp-breed urges and stop before he had an electrifier to his head. Hunger snarled inside him, gnawing at his stomach. He grabbed some supplies off his belt. A packet of dried fruit and some energy bars. He opened one pack and started to offer it to Ismail. The scullion whipped around instantly, his eyes shining red, a savage, wolf-like expression on his face. The beast had surfaced.

Eli had seen that look on the packs of starving dogs that roamed the scullion settlements just outside the city walls. He used to go there and throw them bones and meat cast-offs, which the cooks at the United Regiment cafeteria would put aside for him. Without hesitating, he threw all the food away from him onto the ground. Ismail lunged at it, dropping to all fours and furiously tearing open the packets. He shoved the food into his mouth, swallowing almost without chewing. After he'd finished it all, he grimaced and threw everything back up. After only the slightest of pauses, he started eating the vomit.

"No!" Eli called out despite his better judgement not to get between a hungry wolf and his meal. "Soldier – stop – desist!"

Ismail jolted. He straightened up to his knee and stared down at his vomit-covered hands. His face was blank again as he switched back to the soldier.

Eli crouched down where he stood so that they were on the same eye-level.

"It's okay." He stayed crouching and shuffled toward Ismail at a cautious pace, until he was close enough to hand the scullion a wipe from his belt. Ismail accepted it and cleaned off the sick, then Eli took his flask off his belt and poured some anti-nausea serum into it. He handed it to Ismail and said, "Sip it, it'll help settle your stomach."

Ismail first sniffed at the flask, then snatched at it and gulped the contents down, unable to consume anything slowly at this stage. Eli kicked himself for not foreseeing the reaction. Ismail looked so healthy now, thanks to the healing formulas, that he'd completely forgotten not long ago he was eating raw meat and dirt just to stay alive.

Ismail finished the whole flask and then handed it back. They both stood up and Ismail's eyes were so vacant and staring that Eli wondered if he'd completely retreated into shock.

"Are you okay?" he asked him.

"Confirmed." Ismail responded. "Proceed." He turned, walking in a trudging, mechanical way – but moving nonetheless.

They followed the path back up a slight slope, walking for some time until they reached a heavy tarnished metal door blocking their way. Rust smothered its hinges and there was an inscription carved in the rock above the frame – one word – *Talak*.

"The marine-breed god of the waters," Eli murmured.

He checked his navigation. It looked as if this door was the only way to get down to the lower parts of the level where the painting was located, in the amphibious city, Nineva.

"Do you think it's just water behind there?" he asked, envisioning opening the door and being swept away by a torrential current. Ismail put his ear to the door and listened.

"No, it's hollow," he said. He grabbed the rusted turn-circle and started wrenching it down. A few big turns later, the door screeched open. A gust of air smelling of warm salt water wafted out.

Ismail armed his electrifier and stepped over the threshold down into shin-high water, and Eli followed, the water level significantly higher on him. A dim light shone up ahead and they waded toward it, their splashes echoing through the tunnel. Soon they came to the source of the glow. Someone had cut out a section of rock and replaced it with glass. Behind that, a strange marine-breed creature hung suspended, completely still as though frozen, in light blue water. There was something written on a plaque, mottled with age, fixed under the window. Eli narrowed his eyes and ran a hand over the words, chipping away some of the rust so he could read them.

"*Trak Hrak Racktak*," he said aloud. "Marine-breed language – I've got a translator."

Eli reached for it, but Ismail said, "If you trespass ..."

"If you trespass ...?" Eli prompted.

"That's all it says."

The scullion pointed and Eli turned to see another light up ahead. They moved through the water toward it and found a second glass window with a creature behind it. This one had oversized red eyes and a gaping grouper mouth, its face covered in long, green, tentacle-like whiskers. The scaled body extended out behind it like a whale.

It also had a plaque that Eli read: "*Mrak Splak Racktrak.*"

"If you trespass in these waters." Ismail put the two together.

"There's another one," Eli said. He waded up to the third circle of light, noticing the ground under their feet starting to change from firm rock to a spongy moss. He peered down into the turbid swill below them, but couldn't see anything. They stopped at the light. A creature stared out from behind the glass. It had a long shark-like head and small gray eyes with black pupils. Its body looked like a human-breed's, except its hands were sharp knife-like fins and the flipper feet pointed outward. There were five lines in its neck – gills.

"No writing." Eli leaned forward and as he did, movement caught his eye. The gills of the creature had expanded.

"It's alive." he said.

As the words left his mouth, the creature lashed out, cutting through the glass and slashing toward Eli's neck.

He just managed to leap aside before it struck. Water dribbled from the fractured glass and it started to split in more places. The ground trembled.

"They're underneath us!" Ismail fired his electrifier into the water, but a fin-hand darted up and slapped the weapon away.

"Run!" Eli yelled. He buzzed his wings and shot forward as a knife-like fin stabbed upward right where he had been standing.

As they fled, the shark creatures rose from underneath their feet, slashing with razor fins and sending high-low calls echoing through the tunnel. They gave chase, moving with rocking, lunging steps, seemingly awkward, but surprisingly fast and agile. Ismail swerved and leaped, trying to dodge the fins. One stabbed up through his lower leg and he yelled, ripping the Morsus Ictus off his belt and slashing down with it, severing the creature's limb. Another door appeared up ahead and Ismail charged it, hitting it with so much force that it flew open.

They ran out onto a ledge and skidded to a stop in front of a dead-end. A wall towered forever up in front and beside them, made of smoothed white coral with no footholds to climb. On the other side was the steep drop to the river below. They heard a roar behind them and turned to see a wave of water racing down the tunnel, collecting up the sharks and speeding toward them. The glass had given out.

There was only one way to go.

"Down!" Ismail commanded and jumped off the ledge. Eli half-flew and half-skidded down the slope behind him in a storm of mud and sand. They hit the ground and rolled a few times to the edge of the rushing river. On the ledge above, the creatures had reached the end of the tunnel and were waterfalling down the drop in one gray-white mass.

Eli and Ismail exchanged a glance, then both plunged into the river. A speeding rip swept them away, dunking and pummeling them. Eli gasped, fighting to keep his head above the water, his wings too wet to fly. He looked back and saw fins pursuing them. Ismail swam powerfully, grabbing Eli aside just before he crashed into a boulder.

"I forgot!" Eli yelled above the roar of the river. "You have shark blood. Can you talk to them?"

Ismail shook his head. "They're not listening. They're too hungry. I could send out an electro pulse that will stun them, but it will take me out as well."

Eli spat out a mouthful of briny water and said, "No. Plan B?"

"I can feel something else swimming through the water ..." Ismail told him.

"Something that won't eat us?" Eli said hopefully.

As the sharks closed in, Ismail started whistling, and after a few moments, a head popped out of the water right beside Eli. It had a yellow face with a long equine snout, a spiky mane and round orange eyes, ink spot pupils in the center. More of the same type of creature emerged, swimming alongside them, changing color from a warning neon yellow to a friendlier brown with black stripes. One of them whinnied and Eli yelled, "Seahorses!"

"Grab one!" Ismail shouted. "Quick, before they run!"

Eli lunged for the closest horse and touched its scaly side. It shied away. He moved faster, grabbing its mane and dragging himself onto its back. Ismail was doing the same, and was only half on when the horses bolted, galloping through the water fast with feathery fins, curling tails and hoofed feet. Eli clutched two handfuls of mane to stay on, as they thundered down the rapids, water spraying in his eyes and mouth. He yelled to Ismail, "We have to get to the Superior Hall in Nineva."

Ismail whistled to the horses and they whinnied.

"What did they say?" Eli asked.

"They said 'hold on'!"

Eli noticed then that the rapids had flattened out and there was a dull roar coming from up ahead of them, growing louder as they closed in fast on a waterfall. As they reached the edge, Eli clenched his teeth and squeezed the horse's sides with all his strength. The herd catapulted out of the river and for a moment hung in the air, before tumbling at a nightmare speed down the falls. They crashed into the water below and Eli was ripped off the seahorse's back. A hand grasped his arm as the herd propelled themselves back upward to the surface. Eli gasped in air and Ismail dragged him up behind him onto his horse. The waterfall joined the river with an ocean, and an underwater current grabbed them and dragged them out further and further away from anything resembling land. The sea swelled and the razor-fin sharks kept coming, leaping down the falls. Waves rose up like gigantic beasts all around the seahorses and the creatures ducked under the surface. Eli felt the pressure of the waves breaking over their heads like a giant's pounding fist. He blinked through the salt water and saw hundreds of glowing lights below them. Instead of resurfacing, the horses propelled downward toward the light.

Chapter 23
Croy

KULLRA FORNAX

NŸR-CORUM (SAINT BONIFACE BOROUGH)

The Old Docks in Saint Boniface Borough was a meeting spot, a place to congregate, to find someone or lose yourself in a crowd. It wasn't exactly rough. Grays took their families there all the time to socialize and watch the Fleetships and other flyers entering and leaving the Saints' Door. It was the only way in or out of the city. Still, the docks weren't exactly brawl-free either. Rowdy pubs lined the main stretch of gridway, crowded places where people gathered for a good time which occasionally ended badly. It was also one of the largest pick-up points for daily rations. Being a Controller, Croy could have had her packages delivered to her house or the Tower, but she preferred to go for them herself.

The Docks had always been her favorite place in the city. Her one dream and ambition, since childhood, was to become a Fleetsman. She'd taken the test over and over, thought she passed many times, but failed every one. It had been nearly two annums since she'd last tried out. She wasn't ready to give up the dream. It still called to her like a desperate hunger, but the constant knockbacks had taken their toll. She couldn't completely explain the desire to fly – except that maybe John L had brainwashed her from an early age with all the stories about his time in the Fleet. All the adventures in the outer tunnels – the dangers, the excitement, the animals, the foods, the relationships – even the Drays. He'd become an expert on their enemy, yet he'd never spoken about them with any malice. Croy could remember not feeling any surprise when John L had been accused of conspiring with the Drays and sentenced to death. Terror, but not surprise.

On most of her trips to the Docks, she'd throw on her gray cloak and go undercover, but after everything that had happened this dayturn, she didn't feel in the mood for being jostled and manhandled by an overcrowd of edgy Grays, so she kept on her black uniform cloak and the crowd peeled open in front of her. Silence had a way of preceding her steps, but she was used to it. The Grays didn't trust the Corps, the Corps didn't trust the Grays and no one trusted the Purple Wings, who were so busy bribing and backstabbing each other they barely noticed anyone else existed outside their circles. Today there was a feeling in the air – strangers were interacting, talking to each about the fallen *Teriscoria*. It was the temporary banding together before the inevitable falling apart. Across the drop space, along the New Docks, Fleetsmen were harnessing up the city's third-largest ship, plus an army of smaller guard ships that would be escorting it. Seeing this mass assembly Croy couldn't help but wonder if all their defenses were being drawn out on purpose.

She reached the ration stores and went through the door, nodding to the row of Tower Guards keeping the crowds in check. There was a line-up, which she bypassed, heading directly for the counter. The stores manager, a short man with a twitchy moustache who was almost wealthy enough to leave Gray status, had her package waiting by the time she reached the desk.

"Controller Croy – the Saint!" he announced loudly. "Always an honor!" He gave a slight bow.

Croy grunted and took the package. She liked a polite person, but an arse-kisser couldn't be trusted. She noticed how much larger her ration package was compared to that of the Grays at the counter beside her. They noticed it too, but no one commented. She handed over her tokens, but the manager tried to refuse them, clearly wanting to be in her good favor.

"It's the law," Croy said, forcing the tokens back across the desk, to his obvious disappointment.

She shoved the package into her bag and left. She could have shared her food with the family beside her, but then what about all the others in the line? Acts like that could start a riot. When the time came and food ran out, she'd make sure whatever she'd been stockpiling went first to the Gray children – to feed as many as she could for as long as it lasted. Until then, she needed to keep up the status quo.

Croy limped back out onto the Docks and felt twinges of pain radiating down from her scars. That shocked her. She'd just had a fix – it should leave her pain-free for several turns at least. She'd been injured before she had memory, just after her parents had died and John L had adopted her, and she'd carried the pain always, but it'd never been this bad – and it was getting worse. The thought left her shaky – but more than anything she was hungry. An all-consuming starvation threatened to overwhelm her. She couldn't wait any longer. She rushed to the edge of the stores building and squeezed herself into the dark space between it and the pub next door. She ripped open the package and dragged out handfuls of overflat bread, shoving it into her mouth. The walls of the pub trembled with the sounds of music and dancing, laughter, and games of darts and darrows. Whether it was denial or a lack of understanding that made these people celebrate during their descent into a nightmare, Croy didn't know, but if it kept them from panicking it was worthwhile.

Urged by thirst, she stopped eating and dragged out the decanter of water. It was pitifully low. She held the bottle up and eyed the contents, her thoughts jumping to Victoria Kilner's body floating at the end of the jetty. She lowered it without drinking and looked over the food, startled to see she had already all but demolished it. Her stomach strained uncomfortably full and yet somehow she still felt hungry. The possibility occurred to her that she was getting sick – or at least, more sick. She just wanted to go home and sleep. Croy gathered up her bag and dragged herself out of the space, stepping back into the crowd.

A harsh, jarring sound immediately seized her attention. In the crowd up ahead, two men rushed at each other, grappling for a second before the stronger one slammed the other to the grid and started bashing his head into the steel. A boy rushed in to help the man and the attacker punched him away. A girl and a woman screamed. Croy grabbed her Firestorm from its holster and ran to the fight. She barged through the onlookers and dragged the aggressor off the victim. She kicked his legs out from under him and he went down to his knees with a clunk. Then he started to rise, glaring up at her, with a look in his eyes that chilled her nerves. He looked blind with rage, completely lost to his anger. Croy positioned herself in front of the victim as the attacker stood and drew a crudely made shank from his pocket. He started toward her and Croy aimed her Firestorm at his head.

"This is a warning. Stop where you are. Lower your weapon or I will shoot you," she said.

He kept coming. Croy held her place and repeated, "Drop the weapon now or I'll shoot you."

Still he kept coming, shuffling forward, past fearful on-lookers, until suddenly he lunged.

Croy pulled the trigger and blasted him back. The attacker landed dead on the ground, half his face and head missing. Croy turned immediately to the victim. His wife and children had gathered around him; the boy's nose was broken and bleeding badly. Croy checked the man's pulse. He was still alive, but had a terrible head wound. She didn't like his chances, but occasionally people were surprisingly resilient. She grabbed some gauze out of her kit and pressed it to his wound.

"Hold here," she said to the sobbing wife.

Croy tapped her I-Sect and connected with the Tower.

"This is Croy. There's been an incident at the Old Docks – one dead, one unconscious, one injured. I'm off duty."

"Back-up dispatched," the switchboard informed her. She tapped out of the connection, then stood and faced the crowd.

"Anyone see what happened?"

No one spoke. They were all Grays – all wearing the same deliberately blank expression. They'd just seen her shoot and kill one of their own, so she didn't blame them for not trust-ing her.

"You see what happened?" she asked the victim's son, who was holding a piece of fabric to his bleeding nose.

"No," he said thickly. "That guy started on Dad for noth-ing. Will he be alright?" He blinked back tears.

"Who is he?" Croy nodded to the dead attacker.

The boy shook his head. "No one we know."

Above them came the drone of draggers closing in fast. The Controllers burst through from the gridway above and the crowd stepped back as they lowered to land. Controllers Mirth and Sirsha touched down and jumped off their rides.

Croy knew them quite well – they'd graduated the same annum from training.

"The Saint." Sirsha slapped her hand in a flashy way. The guy was always showing off and dropping names – harmless, but obnoxious. It was as though he'd never quite gotten over the shine of being a Controller, as though every day was his first day. Mirth was far more grounded, but unfortunately seemed to have been born without a sense of humor. She had a permanent offended scowl on her face, as though someone had just farted and she was smelling it.

Croy indicated with her Firestorm. "This one went this one with no apparent provocation. He turned on me, I gave him two warnings – then I put him down."

"Got it," Mirth said, then spoke to the crowd. "All of you back up, unless you want to join him."

The crowd pushed back and she went to inspect the dead man. Sirsha stayed beside Croy, standing with his arms crossed as though they were on a social outing, "There's been a few of these random attacks this turn – people must already be twitching."

Croy ignored him, annoyed he was chit-chatting while the victim was bleeding out beside them. She crouched back down with the family. At most, the Controllers would drop him at the local healer, but a local wouldn't be able to do much for him. He'd need a Tower surgeon if he was going to have any hope, but he was just a Gray and didn't have the right to access a surgeon – unless he was part of an investigation.

She spoke to Sirsha, "Take this man and his family to the Tower. Have him seen to immediately. Tell them I need him for a case."

"Whatever you say, Saint Croy," Sirsha said. "Whatever you say."

Mirth returned to help her partner. As the body baggers were flying in, Croy slipped away into the crowd.

Chapter 24
Diega

PRATERIUS

RAMBELDON FOREST (THE HIVE)

Diega lunged into the cell and tried to break up the fight between Caesar and Shawe, but they were locked together, their hands around each other's throats. Shawe was cursing and K-Ruz snarling, with his nose wrinkled up like a wild cat. His shadow lion paced the wall behind them, tearing at the air.

"Stop!" Diega hissed, jumping on Christy's back, trying to wrestle him away, but with no success. Even kneeing him in his wound did nothing. She toppled off and jumped up to try again when something caught her eye. In a patch of light thrown from the door, she saw a hand. Fear lurched through her, and she had to force herself forward, peering into the dark corner of the cell.

She saw him then – Copernicus – slumped against the wall. His heavy muscles had eroded, his skin sagging around painful boils erupting all over his body, spreading out from the festering wound in his shoulder. His handsome face had sunken in like a skull. The sight slammed into Diega, driving her to her knees. The sounds of the fight behind her stopped and Shawe appeared at her side. He was staring at Copernicus, looking at him full in the face, not avoiding the pain. Since her sister had vanished, Diega had never felt this much agony when nothing was physically wrong with her. If she'd had any drugs on her, she would have smashed them down without hesitation. This was too much – *it's not him ... it's not him.*

"Save your tears, he's still alive," Shawe said.

Shocked, Diega scrambled forward. She placed a hand to his chest and felt it rising. Copernicus stirred faintly under her touch. With an immense struggle he lifted his head and opened his eyes and she could see he was still there, still fighting. She automatically grabbed for her weapon belt, but it had been taken. She had no serums or painkillers to give him. Shawe was leaning in closely.

"Mate, you look like you're three quarters done," he told him. "But apparently there's some river close by with healing plants. Me and your girlfriend here will get you there."

Copernicus moved as though he was trying to stand, and Shawe grabbed him by the shoulders, hauled him up and held him there. Copernicus' boots slid out from underneath him and he staggered, fighting hard just to keep upright. It was very clear he would die fighting, but would die all the same if they didn't get him immediate help. Diega fought her own weakness and stood, going to support Copernicus' other side, but Caesar stepped in.

"Don't hold him like that," he said. "You'll rip the wound further open and speed up the poison."

"What do you care?" Shawe growled.

"He saved my boy's life – I owe him."

"You owe him now, do you?" Shawe mocked. "You're all honor, you are."

Caesar snarled, flashing sharp incisors.

"Shawe, if he wants to help, then let him," Diega said. She looked him in the eye and said, "Please."

His savage expression held for a moment, but then he relented. He looked away and that was as much agreement as he was going to give.

"K-Ruz is right. Holding him up like this is just going to speed the blood circulation and cause the wound to hemorrhage faster," Diega said. "We have to carry him with the least amount of contact." It felt wrong talking about Copernicus like he was a victim, but there was no other way. "If you two lock hands he can sit between you and you can carry him like that."

Shawe looked her up and down and said, "You're crazy, right? You really think me and him are going to hold hands?" Both he and Caesar snorted, like two big boars.

"Yes!" Diega said. "For Copernicus! Because *you* would never have found your brother without him ... and *your* son would be dead."

The two gangsters stood in uncomfortable silence, staring at each with rippling animosity. Shawe made the first move and held out his hands. Caesar grabbed onto them savagely. They both flinched with disgust and fury, but kneeled down so that Diega could help Copernicus to edge back and sit on their linked arms. They lifted him up.

Scuffing footsteps sounded outside the cell. Diega lunged for the seal while the others backed into the shadows. She inched the split open and peered out.

"Drones," she told the gangsters. "A lot of them."

"Already?" Shawe asked. He and Caesar came forward with Copernicus and peered out around her. "Trutt, there's millions of them. How are we going to escape with that lot tagging along?"

"More easily than if it was just us," Caesar said. "They'll make a good cover." His sharp eyes moved over the scene, formulating strategy with every glance.

Diega pulled back the seal and the others maneuvered out. She followed them, coming to stand in front of Sesame, leading a multitude of ragged, starving Neridori and a number of other random creatures.

The drone whispered into her face, "I told them ... I told them we don't have to stay where we're put."

A sudden violent roar trembled the ground and walls and everyone instinctively ducked for cover, Shawe and Caesar balancing Copernicus between them.

"What the trutt is that?" Shawe cursed as the sound and vibration came again. Diega recognized it.

"Snoring," she said.

"Rest time," Sesame spoke up. "After the last meal, just before the Anvil sets, the queen naps and all the workers rest."

"Good. I'm going to go cut her up," Shawe growled and Sesame winced.

"No," Diega said and she turned to the drone. "Time to fly. Assemble your people."

"Fly?" he and the other drones chorused.

"Yes, fly. That's why you have wings!" she said, "Start stretching them."

Sesame hesitated, then whispered, "I have to go to the queen's chamber."

"Why?" Diega demanded.

"Our brothers, the chosen, we can't leave them. We have to get them out as well."

"We can't risk it," Diega said.

"I have to!" Sesame insisted, staring at her with fearful eyes. "Their death is worse than ours and I won't leave without them ... Neither will the others ... I'm sorry."

Diega glanced at Shawe and Caesar. Neither offered any immediate alternative and she could think of none herself. They had no choice but to help him. They needed the drones for their escape and couldn't risk Sesame bumbling into the chamber alone and raising the alarm before they were clear of the Hive.

"Fine," Diega said. "I'll go with you."

"Trutt that," Shawe said. "I'm going."

"No, you need to carry Copernicus. If I get caught you two can still go on."

His face said he didn't like it, but he saw the situation for what it was.

"Don't do anything stupid," he told her.

"That's like one raindrop telling another not to be wet," Diega snorted. It was an Ohini Fen saying that lost some of its shades of meaning in the translation.

Shawe smirked and arched an eyebrow as though she'd just said something suggestive. "I don't think it's the time or the place, sunshine."

She just sighed and shook her head. Caesar looked like he wanted to vomit on both of them.

"If we're not back in five minutes, or if anything goes down, fly out without us," she told the gangsters. She took one last look at Copernicus and saw his eyes were on her, then she turned and left.

Chapter 25
Silho

OMAR MONTANYA

MOUNT SIRIA (THE CASTLE SCORN)

She didn't just run for her life – she flew on her feet, pursued by men and fire – Omarians – crashing along the black rock corridors of the Castle Scorn. Every hallway looked the same, every turn ended in another, with nowhere to hide and no one to help her, until the last corridor narrowed to a tunnel and became a maze. Its walls were too high to climb and Silho felt like she was running in circles, with the voices of her pursuers echoing from every direction. Then one voice came through clear and sinister.

"There's no way out of here, and there's nowhere to hide. I'm coming for you, Silho Brabel."

Lecivion – it sounded like he was right above her. Silho crashed through the maze, fleeing the feeling of his hands and the flames in his eyes. She'd seen death in that fire. Finally she found a fracture in one of the walls with a hollow space behind it big enough to crawl into. Even as she scrambled inside, she realized she was trapping herself, but her mind was spinning so fast she didn't see any other choice.

Silho huddled in the dark, gasping and trying to get control over the fear that had blurred out her rationality. The fierce heat of the place was terrifying, smoke and sulphur choked the air, and the sharp ache of her burns and injuries were starting to overwhelm her. A flashback flared in her mind, of when she was trapped inside the Mazurus machine, burning alive. She clutched her head, trying to block it out. Somewhere beyond her panic, she heard the Omarian voices closing in on her – it sounded like they'd formed an organized search and were moving methodically through the maze. She knew she had to move – now – but couldn't force her body into action. Light-form, her greatest strength, was useless here and she felt completely helpless. Her mind went to the trackers, to Copernicus. For a moment she thought she heard his voice somewhere in the maze, but when she focused her listening, the words were gone, just an echo in her mind – *Claude animus meus*. Close my mind.

It was the Illusionist enchant Copernicus had taught her so that she could focus her mind and survive the Skreaf. She whispered the words and as soon as she did, the sounds of the Omarian soldiers, of her rushed breaths and even the pounding of her pulse faded out, until it was silent in her mind and she felt her resolve and reasoning returning to her, her training kicking back in. She realized she was still gripping her head and lowered her hands, holding them out in front of herself. As she stared at them, a thought came clear to her – while light-form may have been her strongest skill, it wasn't her only skill. She could touch the walls and see what they saw and everything they'd seen in the past. She could find a way out of this maze and out of Lecivion's castle.

Silho placed her hand on the wall beside her, but immediately pulled away – the black rock was scorching hot. Silho forced herself to touch it again, and she found, although it was burning, *she* wasn't burning. It actually didn't hurt at all, and her burns from Lecivion had stopped aching, already healed. Silho breathed in deeply and easily despite the smoke. She'd been too panicked to realize before, but it occurred to her now that her body was made for this environment – and here she was stronger, not weaker. She'd said to Lecivion that he had thought too little of her – now she had to believe that herself. Instead of letting the memories of being trapped and burning cripple her with fear, she focused on that fact that she had defeated the Skreaf – and if she could destroy an army of demons, she could survive one crazy Prince.

Silho focused on her hand touching the rock and allowed her skills to channel in. Through her mind, she sprang from her hiding space, out to another wall and all along that, searching for a way out, until she found something that made her pause the flow of images. It was a break in the maze, a hidden doorway. She ventured through it in her mind and found it led out into a wide corridor, lit by globes of lava embedded in the rock. It was her escape. Silho zoomed backward, plotting the path that she needed to run to get there. It wasn't far, but the Omarians were closing in fast. She only had the briefest window of opportunity.

Silho smashed out of the hollow and tore through the maze, two turns, three ... halfway along the fourth she came to a sharp stop in front of the hidden doorway. Omarian voices sounded just beyond where she stood. The wall in front of her looked completely solid, but she trusted what she'd seen and stepped into it and through, out of the maze and into a corridor made of the same porous black rock. It stretched into the distance on both sides. Silho pressed her hand against one wall and jumped along in her mind, checking which way to go. On one side she found Omarian soldiers heading toward her, but the other way was clear.

She turned and ran with a steady pace, not pushing herself beyond her limits, wanting to reserve strength to fight or sprint when she needed to. She kept a fingertip skimming along the wall, checking ahead of herself the whole way. She wasn't sure if Lecivion knew the extent of her skills, but she hoped he didn't. Glancing up, she searched the ceilings for I-eyes and spyers, but didn't see any glimmers of reflection. It was possible that this realm didn't have the same technology, but that wasn't to say they weren't tracking her through other methods. The thought spurred her on.

At the end of the corridor, the path split into two. She saw through the walls that one way led back to the warehouse facility from where she'd escaped; the other side headed into cave-like tunnels at the heart of the Castle. She took that side and ran into the cave-tunnel, the heat intensifying the further in she went. Silho stifled her first reaction of fear and took deep breaths of the fierce air, reminding herself she wasn't burning. The echo of Omarian voices spoke from deeper in the caves and Silho pressed into the shadows, following a path down toward the sound. In her mind she was thinking, if she could somehow isolate and incapacitate a soldier, she could steal his portal painting – provided they all actually carried one, not just specific people. If she could get a portal, she could jump back to Aquais. The memory of Lecivion stabbing Copernicus forced itself into her mind and her panic crept back up on her, but she repeated the Illusionist enchant and regained her control. Copernicus was alive. He and the others were searching for her. That was the only thing she'd allow herself to believe.

She slowed her pace as the voices grew louder, until they sounded just beyond the next corner. Silho edged forward and peered around. Two Omarians stood beside a chute in the wall, grabbing things as they slid out and throwing them over the edge of a cliff down to a river of surging lava below. The lava radiated a scorching heat and cast a red-orange glow all around the cavern. Silho squinted through the hazy shadows, trying to see what the men were disposing of. It looked like bags of something. She inched further forward, moving her head to see around the back of one of the soldiers. She focused as another object came through the chute – and then she saw it – a face. Silho's throat tightened. They weren't bags, they were women and baby boys – corpses – all the failed attempts to produce another half-Omarian female like her. The sight sickened Silho to the heart of her. At first she felt paralyzed, just like when she'd first gone out with the team into the war zones after her recovery. There were so many horribly injured and screaming people that she'd literally not known who to help first, and had just ended up turning in circles and crying. Copernicus had seen her and said, "Pick a place and start there, that's all we can do."

He'd pointed and she'd gone, and begun, and he was right – it was the only thing they could do, when it was so difficult to determine who needed help the most. Remembering Copernicus' words calmed her again.

The chute rumbled and clanked and another woman came tumbling out. As she thudded to the ground, Silho caught a twitch of movement. She was still alive. The Omarians grabbed the woman up roughly as though she was no more than a pile of garbage. Moving on instinct, Silho seized a rock and rushed out at them before they could throw the girl over. She smashed the closest soldier in the back of the head, instantly dropping him. The other one saw her coming and tried to trap her with light-form. She dropped to a crouch and grabbed him by the legs, dragging them out from under him. He hit down hard and she leaped up, landing a kick to the side of his face, but it wasn't enough to knock him out and he struggled up with a roar, raising both hands. The Omarian bone blade broke out from one of his wrists. Silho knew that if he got her in light-form, she'd be dead. So she did the first thing that came to her mind. She rushed him, slamming a shoulder into his chest and knocking him off the edge of the cliff. For a moment he looked shocked and then he plummeted out of sight. Breathing hard, Silho knelt down beside the survivor, who had slumped over onto her stomach. She was naked and had the rainbow skin and golden star bloodlines of an Ohini Fen. It made Silho's mind immediately jump to Diega. She took the woman's arm and carefully rolled her over onto her back. She was cut open, low down, from one side of her stomach to the other. The wound was grotesque and the colors of her skin had faded out almost to white.

Silho went to rip off her jacket to bind the wound, but found she wasn't wearing it. All her clothes were gone, replaced with a surgical-type gown with nothing underneath.

"It's okay. You're not alone," she whispered, trying to tear some of the fabric off the gown. "We'll get you help. Everything will be fine."

The Fen looked up at her with desperate eyes, gasped out and died.

Silho stared, her hands releasing their grip on her gown. Behind them the chute thudded and another dead woman rolled out, then a baby, then another woman and another and another ... Silho watched them pile up, feeling numbed by the horror of it. How many women had Lecivion abducted? How many families were searching for daughters, mothers, sisters, never to see them again, never to know their fate?

The echo of tumbling rocks broke Silho out of her thoughts, and she turned fast toward the sound. She touched the ground and leaped forward in her mind, back upward to the entrance of the caves – to where a troop of Omarian soldiers were entering the tunnels. There was no choice. She had to leave the bodies and run. She jumped up and started to go, but then doubled back fast. She'd forgotten to check the unconscious soldier for a portal. She rolled him over and patted him down rapidly, but found only one small knife. With such powerful skills and inbuilt blades, Omarians didn't have much need for external weapons, and there was no sign of a portal. Silho took the knife and ran to the other side of the cavern, where she found a narrow ledge jutting from the rock wall. She followed it, blinking down at the fiery molten rock rushing beneath her. She almost lost her footing and forced herself to concentrate ahead, where the path wound around to another tunnel leading up.

As she stepped off the ledge and into the tunnel, a wave of dizziness swept over her and she staggered, slumping against the rocky wall. She felt a sharp pain in her side and touched a hand to it. Her gown felt damp. She looked down and saw in the dim glow that half her dress was red with blood. Her fingers found a wound in her side and she groaned with pain. She hadn't realized, but during the fight, when she'd rammed the soldier, he must have stabbed her with his bone blade before he'd fallen. Silho cursed and her sight started darkening. She was losing too much blood. Gripping the wound tightly, Silho touched the wall with her other hand, still holding the Omarian's knife. She searched for where to go and saw in the memories of the rocks another doorway up ahead, leading into a hidden room. It stood empty, but there were marks on the floor that suggested crates had once been stored there. Silho staggered up toward the doorway. She needed to try to stem the blood flow before it was too late.

She stumbled through into the room, its rock floor smoothed out and walls lit with the lava globes. Before she could take a step further, her knees gave way and she dropped to the ground, the weapon clattering down beside her. She had a high pain tolerance, but this was too much even for her. Fighting to keep consciousness, she tried to bunch up the gown to hold against the wound, but it was already drenched and the blood seeped straight through. Gasping, she fell forward on her hands. She'd never thought, after surviving so much, that she would die so easily. Tears stung her eyes and she dug her nails into the rock, trying to force herself up, but her body didn't have the strength. With heavy eyelids, she looked toward the door, part of her certain that Copernicus would appear and save her.

Moments passed and he didn't come, and in the numbness of her mind, she realized he never would – she was on her own. No one could save her but herself. Her eyes closed and she slumped down, hands pressed against the floor. Images flickered and flowed behind her eyes as her mind looked into the memories of the walls. Silho drifted, clinging to the last of her strength, while the blood pooled around her. Suddenly the images stopped on the memory of a girl walking down one of the castle hallways. Silho recognized the wary green eyes and tangle of curly blonde hair, much longer then than Silho had ever seen it in pictures. Her mother, Oren Harvey. Silho immediately noticed that Oren had no bloodline marks on her arms. In the memory, her mother turned through a doorway and stopped, seeing a man standing in the room with his back to her. He glanced over his shoulder and Silho recognized the hollow eyes and angular face, the arrogant expression.

"Oren," Lecivion said.

Her mother didn't move, just stood watching as Lecivion stepped toward her – heel-toe, heel-toe with his pointed black boots. He stood staring down at her face and spoke quietly, but there was a danger behind the words. "I hope you understand that everything I'm doing is for your own good. If you're allowed to continue to visit your land, you won't ever start to view Omar as your true home."

"I understand." Oren replied immediately, but her voice was flat, and Silho could sense her restrained anger.

"Good. Now kiss me. I hate it when we argue." Lecivion leaned down and pressed his mouth against hers. Oren allowed it and even smiled when he pulled back, but when he put his arms around her and drew her close, her smile hardened and eyes turned to fury over his shoulder. He stepped back again and Oren blanked her expression.

"I must go, but we'll eat together tonight ..." he leaned in close and whispered, "and share my bed." He kissed her face and stepped around her, leaving the room.

For a moment Oren stood there, fused by her anger, then she grabbed a piece of cloth from the bed in the corner. She wiped it hard across her lips and face where he'd kissed her, then she knelt down beside the bed and reached under, pulling out some loosened rock and lifting a small black chest from a hiding place. She opened it and very carefully removed an object – a framed painting of flames. She looked up at the wall, directly into Silho's eyes, and whispered, "The flames."

Silho jolted back to her hidden room, where she lay on the ground bleeding out. Oren's words echoed in her mind and she heard the truth inside them. She had nothing to bind the wound, but she could cauterize it. She managed to lift her head and looked around the room, spotting one of the lava globes. She tried to crawl toward it, but her legs wouldn't move. After several attempts she slumped back down, slipping fast toward the darkness of death. She saw a flash of her mother leaving her in the desert with Hammersmith. Oren had been clutching her stomach in the same way Silho was now, with blood seeping from between her fingers. She'd uttered, "... *war has fractured my soul, it has stolen my name and purpose. I am an alien to myself and a stranger in my own skin ... Don't become me.*"

Silho's eyes flickered open – the black rock ceiling spun above her. *Don't become me* – Oren spoke again. Silho summoned all her remaining strength and rolled onto her stomach. She dragged herself hand over hand until she reached the wall, then she fought until she was kneeling up. It took her many attempts, but she finally raised the Omarian knife high enough to stab into the globe in the wall, smashing it, the lava gushing out. She let the burning stream run over the small blade until it was glowing hot. With shaking hands, she gripped the handle and lowered it toward her wound. As white metal contacted with skin, Silho felt an agonized surge of pain and heard the sizzle of her own flesh, but she pressed the blade harder knowing that this pain was life.

When she finally lifted the knife away, the bleeding had stopped. The skin was burned badly, but she could see it was already starting to heal, sealing the wound as it did. Silho could only assume that being half-Omarian, she was immune to the bone blade poison which Lecivion had spoken about. She slumped against the wall, crouching low. Her heart was racing, cold chills shivered through her and she couldn't re-member ever feeling so thirsty, even after half a lifetime in the desert – but she was alive. She rested her head on her knees and tried to regather some strength.

Her mind strayed back to what she'd just seen in the walls and to Lecivion's words about her mother ... *she was the last one ... tattooed the marks of a firelighter ... princess ... Draigar.* Silho had never heard of that race before. She raised her head and looked at her arms. She had noticed that after her recovery from the Skreaf, the flames of her blood-line marks, the part she had inherited from her mother, had healed fainter – but she'd assumed the fading was just a side-effect from being burned so badly. She'd never considered that maybe they were faint because they weren't real – but if they were just surface tattoos, they wouldn't have healed back at all, unless Oren used a different sort of tattoo – maybe even involving magics. But then why could she heal like a Pyron, unless resistance to fire was also a skill of the Draigar? Maybe that was why Oren had chosen to pretend to be a firelighter?

Silho wanted to access the walls, to find more memories of her mother and to see exactly what had happened, to maybe even find her father here – to see when they'd first met. Who had her father been to Lecivion? Just a soldier? A friend? A brother? She wanted to know everything, but already she'd lost so much time. She had to get out of here. She stretched her legs, testing them, then using the wall, dragged herself up. Her head spun, and she closed her eyes, forcing herself into focus. Through her fingertips she accessed the walls and leaped through the castle, searching for something she could use to escape. At first she was looking for a portal, but soon realized that she didn't know the words Omarians used to make them open, so she abandoned the idea and searched instead for a doorway out of Scorn. Silho raced through thousands of images until she halted over one picture. Her pulse skipped. Disbelief spread through her.

Chapter 26
Croy

KULLRA FORNAX

NŸR-CORUM (SAINT MARIREAD BOROUGH)

When she finally reached home, Croy found her front door standing ajar, with the locks intact. Fear spiraled through her. She drew her Firestorm and edged her way inside, pausing in the tiny space of her sitting room. Objects had been disturbed. They were out of place – or rather, rearranged. She recognized the pattern and smelled a familiar perfume wafting in the air. She holstered her weapon just as her ex-boyfriend, Roth, and ex-friend, Angeline, came walking out from her bedroom. Roth was carrying a box of his possessions. They both halted when they saw her. The moment dragged on. Croy wanted to look away from them, but didn't. Roth's expression tightened and his eyes demanded her not to make a scene. He moved protectively closer to Angeline, who bit her lip and looked teary. Croy shook her head. How had it come about that even though she was the one they had cheated on, this girl came out looking like the fragile victim and Croy like the menacing maniac?

"We're here collecting the last of my things," Roth said, all business.

Croy swallowed back a reply. She went into the corner that served as her kitchen. She opened a cupboard and threw the rest of her package inside. Keeping her back to them, she looked out the window, a cool breeze brushing over her face. She wasn't exactly sure what she was doing – perhaps perfecting the art of looking unconcerned while her heart was ripping in two. John L had once said she was silent on the outside but inside she was a storm, and at one time she'd felt like that, but lately she just felt defeated.

Croy glanced back at them. Angeline was watching her with concerned, sad eyes while Roth threw more things into the box. His elbow swept over one of the shelves, knocking something to the floor. It was a fossilized megator egg that John L had given her, from one of his early expeditions. It hit the rock floor and split in two. Roth started to pick it up, and Croy felt her anger exploding. She rushed over and snatched it away from him with more force than was necessary.

Roth made a snorting sound and muttered something.

"If you have something to say, just say it," Croy said, breaking her own resolve not to speak.

"It's not worth wasting my words," he replied.

"Then don't," she said. "I already know what your thoughts are anyway."

After a moment of silence, he demanded. "How can you live like this?"

"Like what?"

"In this shrine. Every surface is filled with him. You're obsessed with him. I know he was your carer, but this is unnatural. And the worst thing about it is that he was a bad person – a traitor – why waste your time exulting someone who doesn't deserve it and never did?"

"Roth, maybe we should just —" Angeline tried to intervene.

"No!" he snapped at her. "I refuse to feel guilty about this when it's clearly her fault. Admit it," he demanded from Croy, "you can't love anyone else because you're in love with him – you're obsessed! That's why you can never make a relationship work."

"Keep telling yourself that," Croy said.

"I will because it's the truth."

"It's your truth, not *the* truth. The truth – plain facts? You cheated. I'm not stupid – I know people fall in and out of love all the time. I never expected you to want to stay with me forever, but I did expect honesty. You should have just broken up with me, not gone sneaking around. Maybe it was exciting for you two or something, but don't try to pin your wrongs on me. I have faults, but I never would have done this – to either of you."

"Maybe I should go," Angeline said.

"Maybe you shouldn't have come," Croy threw back at her. "You know where the door is. You came in and out enough when I wasn't here."

"I'm so sorry," she whispered. "I'll wait outside." She hurried to the door and left.

"You're unbelievable!" Roth turned on Croy.

"And you're a liar!" she yelled back, losing all control. "Get your stuff and get out – once and for all!"

"I'll go because I can't stand to be anywhere near you, but just so we're clear – this is still *my* house. I'm only allowing you to stay here because Angie feels sorry for you."

His words, each of them, cut inside her.

"I paid for half of this place." Croy tried to keep her voice steady.

"Please." Roth snorted. "Your wage barely covered the front gate. I had to pay for everything!"

"Because you're a Conference assistant and you make so much more than me – yes, I remember. I could never forget, you reminded me enough times."

"Because I fought to get where I am and I wanted you to do the same – to have some self-respect, some drive or ambition, other than your ridiculous fantasy of joining the Fleet. But no, instead all you wanted was to stay in your same bog role with that idiot DeCavisi."

"Don't talk about him. Don't even say his name!" Croy warned.

"Sorry, did I step over the line and mention the love of your life, did I?" Roth fumed.

"So I'm in love with John L and I'm in love with Darius and that's why you had to cheat with her?" Croy shook her head.

"I fell in love with Angie because you pushed me away, and now I'm going to marry her and have a real relationship. Don't make trouble for her at the Tower or I'll make trouble for your beloved Darius – you know I can. Stay away from her. I mean it."

"Just get out!" Croy shouted.

"I'll come into *my* house whenever *I* want," he growled back.

He grabbed up the crate and left, slamming the door behind him.

Croy waited to hear their footsteps on the gridway. When they had faded to nothing, she rushed to her bathroom and sank down in one corner of the cramped space. She covered her face with her hands and fought to slow her breathing. Blades of pain cut through her leg. She tried to stretch it out, but couldn't – the pain was swelling, erupting, a burning dagger slicing through flesh and bone. She lunged for her toilet

313

pail and struggled, with shaking hands, to unlatch it and push it aside. She grasped her stash from underneath and dragged it out. Croy grabbed one of the pre-filled syringes and tried to inject herself, but her hands were trembling too much and her eyes were blurred with tears. She blinked them back, furious at herself for letting Roth hurt her again so much. Darius was right, she was stronger than this, but it was hard to dismiss Roth's criticism completely when part of her wondered if it might be true – maybe she hadn't been loving enough, maybe she had been too cold …

"Stop," she hissed at herself. She forced her hands steady and plunged the needle into the scar tissue. Very gradually the pain dulled to numb. Croy dropped the rest of the syringes back into the hiding place with her other contraband and the stash of John L's papers that she hadn't turned in with the rest after they locked him up. She dragged herself to her feet and limped out into the sitting room, where she stood in the center of the space, looking around. It felt emptier, lonelier. She could feel the silence pounding in her heart. This wasn't home. It was a prison.

Croy rushed to the door and ran out of the house. She raced to her dragger and took off, at first flying with no direction, but then she found herself heading back to the place she always went when things turned bad. Croy landed on the deck of the Dower Brothers warehouse, where over twenty annums ago the Dower Brothers had lost their minds and axe-murdered all their Gray workers. It had been abandoned ever since. Despite Nÿr-Corum's lack of space, nobody wanted to use it. They said it was haunted. John L had thought no one would find him there – his one mistake. Controllers had shot him as he ran away, and he'd fallen over the railing into the Mother Fire below. Croy lowered to one knee beside the place where her father had fallen and rested her head on the cold metal bars. Her body relaxed and the tears came. Once they started, she couldn't hold them back.

"John …" she whispered, "I'm not doing so well … I miss you …"

She clutched the shrapnel pendant – the last thing he'd ever given her. He'd told her, never take it off, *as long as you wear it, I'm still with you* … The thought gave her comfort.

Croy's I-Sect buzzed in her ear. She sniffed and wiped a hand over her face, then tapped to open the line.

"Croy," Darius' voice came through with the sounds of cheering and chanting in the background. They'd obviously won their game. "What are you doing?" he asked.

"Nothing," she lied, trying to disguise the thickness of her voice. "You won?"

"Game was dirty," he replied with disgust. Darius preferred losing a good game to winning dirty. "Where are you?"

"Nowhere." She used the rail to help herself stand. The knee was already hurting again. Panic stirred insider her, but she kept her voice steady. "Just on my way home."

"Do you want me to come over?"

More than anything she wanted to say *yes*, but instead she said, "No, I just want to sleep."

A woman's voice spoke in the background close to Darius' ear, something about going back to her place.

"Are you sure?" Darius asked Croy, and she heard him taking a drag from his tigaro.

"Yes, I'm sure. I'll just be sleeping anyway."

"Right." Darius said. "Call me when you wake up."

Croy tapped out of the conversation and looked over the edge. When she needed her partner the most was when she pushed him away the hardest. Maybe Roth was right. Maybe it was all her fault.

* * * * *

Croy reached home just as the high winds siren started to scream. A massive frozen-air hurricane was hammering at the Saint's Door. She lay in bed, shivering under her blanket, watching the shadows flowing across her ceiling, the winds shaking her whole house. It was too dangerous to light a fire in these conditions, and she felt sorry for the Controllers who were out on shift this nightturn. The wild winds made people go crazy at the best of times – and these were the worst.

She closed her eyes, physically and emotionally exhausted, but she couldn't sleep. Her mind kept dragging her back through the argument with Roth over and over again. She thought of everything she should have said but didn't, and everything she did say that she shouldn't have. Her knee had started pounding with pain and her stomach was cramped with hunger, but finally she managed to drift into a restless sleep of realistic nightmares. She lay there in her bed with a dead-eyed Mortician standing over her holding a scalpel. He snarled and stabbed it down into her knee. She woke screaming into another dream where she now stood over Victoria Kilner scratching symbols into her flesh, except the girl was still alive and screaming, her face becoming John L's as he ignited into flames. He was yelling for her help, but she was lying on the floor, one of her legs severed at the knee, spilling blood. She couldn't stand, she couldn't get to him. She saw a flash of eyes, the darkest that she'd ever seen, and heard a whisper ... *Shah* ... *Shah-Jahan* ...

Croy woke, lathered in sweat, her shirt stuck to her skin. She ripped back the blankets and sat up, gulping, feeling sick to her stomach. She staggered into the bathroom and kneeled beside the toilet pail, but nothing came up. Hunger pains crunched her in on herself. Something very strange was happening to her and it crystallized in her mind at that moment that the Crematorium was at the heart of it.

She forced herself up and was dressed before she fully realized what she was doing. She slung her kit over her shoulder, pushed the Firestorm into its holster and battled her way out into the howling winds. Objects sailed past her head, smashing into houses and gridways. She made it to her dragger and had to force it to start. The ride coughed and lifted up with the greatest of reluctance, as if it knew where they were going.

Chapter 27

Eli

AQUAIS

SCORPIA (NINEVA)

The herd of seahorses raced the predatory shadows chasing them through the deep waters, carrying Eli and Ismail past the sunken wreck of a public transporter and downward toward a dome of light – a vast underwater city encased in a transparent film – Nineva.

By the time the seahorses neared the dome, Eli's lungs were screaming and the sharks' jaws snapping right behind their feet. The horses darted into a glass tunnel at the top of the dome and the water started churning. Eli felt an artificial tide dragging him and Ismail off their seahorse's slippery back. They fought to stay on, but lost their grip, the powerful current sucking them through to the end of the tunnel, where a trapdoor opened and dumped them in a cascade of water down into a pool inside the dome. Ismail dragged Eli to the surface and hauled him, coughing and gasping, to the edge.

Eli hauled himself out and kneeled there, rubbing the salt water out of his eyes.

When he could see again, he looked around and saw they'd landed in some kind of grand entrance chamber in a palatial coral building. Eli checked his navigation. They were not far from the Superior Hall where the portal hung; they just had to get there. Amphibious marine-breed of all varieties, walking in and out and around the chamber, cast the pair suspicious looks. Outside the transparent film, a mighty blue whale swam alongside the building. It stopped and opened its monstrous jaws. A crowd of marine-breeds poured out from inside its mouth. They began to enter the chamber, dropping in from the sealed-off tunnels above, as Eli and Ismail had a moment ago. He watched the creatures fall, their flippers changing to legs just before they touched the ground. Some of them were marine-breeds and some of them were human-breeds of aquatic blood.

"Incoming," Ismail muttered from where he stood beside him.

Eli staggered to his feet and saw a group of armed guards approaching fast. He recognized them as Johanians, a type of deep-sea marine-breed that had come to Scorpia after their city, Latlas Seaport, had been destroyed. Fins protruded from their backs and arms, which were covered with blue wave bloodline marks. Their scaly skin held many scars, and gills sliced the sides of their necks. Each carried a trident spear, their clothes made of green sea-plant clothing. Their expressions were of grim mistrust, but their round shark eyes moved over the strangers with a cautious interest.

"*Vak marak pak martak,*" the guard at the front of the group called out.

"He's asking why we're here," Ismail translated to Eli.

"We mean trespass – I mean – we *do not* mean trespass," Eli replied, as the group circled them. "We were just out walking, exploring – and took a wrong turn."

The last thing he wanted was to let on that they were there to steal something.

The guard replied in Urigin, exposing gold and silver teeth, "Really? Because you don't look like explorers. More like soldiers, I'd say," His eyes focused especially on Ismail, on his shark bloodline marks. The other guards around him nodded in agreement.

Eli tried to cover. "Well, we were both soldiers, before the war. We were attacked by some razor-fins – in a tunnel." He pointed to the transparent ceiling where the sharks were still circling in the waters above.

The guard didn't look up, just eyed Eli then said, "I see. In that case, you can stay and rest a time. They'll tire in a day or so and then you can leave."

"Thank you," Eli said. "We really appreciate it."

"Your gratitude is acceptable, but of course you'll have to hand over any weapons you're carrying," the guard continued. "Unless you have a problem with that?" His eyes bored into them.

"No, not at all," Eli said, while cursing inside his mind. He took his electrifier and blades off his belt and handed them over, then stood still while the Johanians checked the rest of him, taking his lightblaster and rope.

Eli glanced at Ismail. He'd given over his spare electrifier and all the other weapons, but not the Morsus Ictus. The blade was nowhere in sight. The Johanians patted him down – twice – and didn't find it.

Once the guards stepped back, satisfied they were clean, their captain indicated to a cluster of female marine-breeds who had appeared behind them and said, "Follow the women. They will show you to a place where you can bathe, feed and rest and they will alert you once the hunters have gone."

The women bowed and Eli nodded back. It seemed like the perfect opportunity – follow them, and then when they leave go and find the portal. Except nothing in life was ever perfect and he could feel the eyes of the guards consuming them as they left the entrance chamber.

Their guides took them through a series of hallways fashioned from smoothed coral and into a bathing room lit with large, glowing pearlescent shells. Three sides of the room were the same white coral as the hallways, with the fourth made of seamless glass. It gave them a view of the lights of another city far below Nineva. This city, which Eli assumed was Nereus, the best known of Adliden's suburbs, didn't have the transparent dome stretching over it – it was a pure underwater kingdom, and alarming in its beauty. Even though they were still in Scorpia, below a man-made sea with mechanically propelled waves, Eli felt as though he was actually under one of the fantasy oceans from the fairy's tales his gran'pa used to tell him.

Between them and Nereus lay another wreck, this one a ship, its tattered sails swaying in the undulating water. A diffuse light shone through its hollow window eyes, as though the ghosts of lost sailors were still feasting in a parlor aboard. Marine-breeds swam in pairs and groups between the amphibious Nineva and Nereus, a multitude of glowing starfish lighting the sea sky above them. Under other circumstances, Eli could have spent hours entranced by the scene, but their reason for being there hammered at his mind and he turned his back on the window. He looked over the various soaps, cloths and lotions that the girls had set out for them. Some of them were shaped like flowers and fruit. Eli's stomach growled. His supplies hadn't gone far to fill the void. As though on cue, the women returned with platters of food and jugs of juice.

"Let us take your clothes," one of them said, starting to undress Eli. "We will wash them for you."

He clung to his shirt and said quickly, "No thanks! Really, that's okay." If growing up in Ufftown had taught him anything, it was never to let anyone take your clothes "to wash them". "I don't take off my clothes – ever. It's part of … my religion."

The marine-breed women looked confused, but didn't argue. They glanced at Ismail and he folded his arms over his chest to indicate he wouldn't be getting nude either. They lingered for a moment longer and then filed out, closing the door behind them.

Without warning, all the taps and shower heads in the room spluttered on and started spraying out warm fresh water, filling up the numerous white rock tubs around the walls. Steam rose, twisting to the ceiling. Ismail opened his mouth and dragged out the Morsus Ictus, which somehow he'd been hiding inside there. Eli couldn't understand how he'd done it without choking himself or cutting up his throat, but somehow he had.

"Extremely impressive," Eli said.

The scullion shoved the blade into his belt and moved to the door. He opened it a fraction and peered out.

"Confirmed presence. Five armed hostiles," he whispered to Eli.

"What?" Eli asked, moving to peer around the scullion. All he saw was a glimpse of the women still standing in the hallway.

"They're not hostiles. They're just marine-breed girls," he said.

"They're not girls, they're guards," Ismail replied. "And they're keeping us here."

"Why? What would they want with us?" Eli asked.

"I don't know. Their electro-shields block their intentions from me, but in my experience the Johanians are pure mercenary."

"You think they'll try to sell us out?"

Ismail's face darkened, something flickering in his stare, and Eli knew he was thinking of the witch.

"Is there any way around them?" Eli tried to peek past Ismail again.

"Not out there," Ismail said, carefully closing the door. He scanned the room and his gaze settled on one of the tubs. Ismail moved to it and started using the Morsus Ictus to cut the seal joining the tub to the ground. He worked fast until, with a heavy grinding, he shoved the tub to one side, exposing a large open pool underneath it.

"Hold your position here while I scout an exit," Ismail said to Eli and without a further word leaped in.

Eli stood on the edge staring down into the dark waters. Several minutes after the bubbles stopped surfacing, he was well and truly panicking. He didn't know what to do. What if Ismail had gotten stuck somewhere and needed help? Should he jump in, should he stay there? The door started opening and he rushed over to block it. The marine-breed woman on the other side peered in, looking shocked and slightly angry that he was barring the door.

"Is everything alright? We heard a sound …" she said.

"No … I mean, *yes*! Yes! Absolutely everything is perfect. It's just that my friend is … bathing his body … naked, of course … and he's very shy and embarrassed – so if you wouldn't mind just waiting for a few more moments before coming in, that would – that would be great." He grinned.

The marine-breed gave him a very suspicious up-and-down look but said, "Very well," and stepped back a few paces.

Eli gestured his thanks and slammed the door shut. He raced back to the water and took a wild leap in. As he did, Ismail surfaced, and Eli ended up sitting on top of his head. Ismail dragged him off into the water, giving him a look.

"Sorry," Eli said, treading water. "I thought you might need assistance."

The door to the room started opening again and Ismail barked, "Dive!"

Both of them dropped down beneath the surface and Eli felt Ismail grab him by his jacket, then with a whoosh, the scullion took off, dragging him through the water.

Ismail swam fast through a pipe and out into a larger desalination processor. The water here was hot and filled with the muted thud and clanking of cogs and rods. One slammed down right beside Eli's head. He could feel the pressure building in his lungs and his panic rising. He grappled for Ismail and felt him increase his speed. They were definitely swimming upward now and they finally broke through the surface into darkness. Eli gasped in the hot, salty air. "I've decided I hate water," he rasped. "Never going swimming again, ever."

Ismail didn't respond. He started clicking, using his echo-location to project out an image of their surroundings. They had surfaced in a large pipe, with rungs in one side leading upward. Ismail swam for them and Eli followed. They climbed to the top and cautiously opened the hatch there. Eli looked out at a desalination plant in full swing. They ducked back down as a group of workers bustled past. Once they were out of sight, Ismail carefully maneuvered out of the pipe and down onto a grid platform. He held the hatch open for Eli to follow and he scrambled out.

At the sound of more workers approaching, they dropped down behind some machinery. Above them, the light from the starfishes shone through the glass roof of the factory. Eli held his navigator up to a beam of light and found it had blanked out. The machine was water-resistant, but not water-proof. Thinking quickly, Eli blinked, engaging his front-core. The system was back up after its lapse in Duskmaveth. He sent a thought command to the implant to call Diamond and almost immediately her voice spoke into his ears.

"Eli, I'm here."

"My navigator has shorted," Eli whispered. "I need a copy of the portal map sent to my front-core – urgently."

"It'll be quicker for you to command the implant to harvest the image straight from your memory," Diamond told him.

"It can do that?" Eli asked.

"Definitely," Diamond said, then talked him through the process step by step. Soon he had the map open in front of his eyes, including their location and the best route to take.

"We're close," he whispered to Ismail, his hopes lifting. "Through that door and straight down the corridor."

The scullion nodded.

They waited for a clear path, then made a dash for the door, bursting from the processor plant out into a long white corridor. They moved cautiously along it, keeping silent and pausing at every sound, until the walls started to widen out, white rock becoming glass as they entered the Superior Hall, a vast oval chamber with a glass domed ceiling and artwork covering every inch of wall space.

Distracted by questions of how to determine which painting was the portal, Eli started to step into the chamber without first clearing it. Ismail dragged him back into the shadows of the doorway. He pointed to a gathering on the other side of the Hall. It was the Johanian guards who had taken their weapons. Their leader was speaking with several other official-looking marine-breeds in uniform. They were standing around a painting, which was a mass of small pictures making a larger image. It reminded Eli of the painting in Englan Chrisholm's cell.

"That's it!" he whispered. "The portal."

He turned to Ismail and saw a reflection of light flare in the darkness of the scullion's eyes. He spun back around to the painting. The images had vanished into a blaze of white. Figures were taking shape in the glow, growing larger and clearer, until a group of men crashed out of the frame into the Hall. The light died, out leaving the portal blackened and destroyed. *Firebird bloodline marks, deep brown skin, green eyes with flames flickering behind them – Omarians.* Eli and Ismail shrank back as the fire-wielders gathered opposite the marine-breeds. There was a moment of eyeing off and staring down, and then negotiations began, questions and answers, intra-group conferring and outer-group confirming.

"They're selling us," Ismail whispered beside Eli and he nodded. He could see it from their gestures – *one tall – one short – flapping motion, wings.*

Soon an agreement was reached – an amount demanded by the marine-breeds and given the nod by the Omarians. The Johanian leader started giving directions, pointing the way to Eli and Ismail, but then one of the officials motioned for a pause. He made an unmistakeable Urigin gesture, holding out one palm and slapping his other palm against it – *payment first.* The Omarians shook their heads, their refusal met by a counter-refusal – *no payment, no prisoner.* The Johanians clearly had not the first clue of who they were dealing with.

Without warning, the Omarians attacked. With a flick of their wrists, they incinerated the marine-breeds into white ash, including all the guards and their leader with the silver and gold teeth. The air smelled like fried fish and Eli gagged before he could stop himself. The Omarians' blazing eyes snapped in their direction.

"Quick, go!" Ismail barked, giving Eli a shove.

They broke out of the shadows and tore back the way they'd come. Eli glanced over his shoulder and saw the Omarians thundering behind them. It felt like a nightmare on rerun, except this time they had no weapons, no Luther and no spectral-breeds to save them. All they could do was flee. Their boots thudded, their breathing fast and ragged until they reached the door to the desalination plant. Ismail kicked it open and they crashed through. A processor worker ran at them and Ismail punched him across the face, knocking him flat, while Eli locked the door behind them. Ismail dragged over a heavy drum and pushed it underneath the door handle. They scanned the workspace searching for a place to hide, but there was nothing concealed enough, and all the steel vats looked like potential ovens. They heard clanking boot-steps on the grids around them as more workers ran their way, brandishing metal bars and shovel-like weapons. Right behind them, the door handle rattled, heat radiating through from the hallway. With both sides and all exits blocked there really was only one way to go.

"Climb!" Ismail instructed.

He clambered up onto one of the desalination machines, heading toward the glass ceiling. Eli followed, hands slipping on condensation-coated steel, his wings too damp to fly. Ismail leaped off the machine and grabbed hold of a ceiling support beam. He swung until he had enough momentum to wrap his legs around the beam. Then he let go, hanging upside down. He grabbed the Morsus Ictus off his belt and raised his torso in a sit-up, about to stab the glass.

"Wait!" Eli yelled out. "If you puncture it, the pressure will bring the roof down on our heads!"

"It's still a higher survival chance than being burned alive!" Ismail responded.

He struck the glass, and even though it was heavily re-inforced, the Morsus Ictus sliced straight through. He hit it again three more times in quick succession, and water started trickling through the cracks. Eli heard an ominous creak and groan and saw fracture lines spreading out across the ceiling.

"Not good. So not good," he whispered, watching them spread. In a few seconds an ocean-load of water would dump down on them. Eli's hands flew over his weapon belt and jacket, searching for something, anything, that might help them live through this. The gathering processor workers had started shouting and throwing their metal bars at Ismail, trying to knock him down, while the Omarians continued ramming the door, the drum rocking precariously, a second from tipping. An alarm, like a whale call, blared into life.

Still hanging upside down, Ismail stretched out his hands to Eli and gestured, "Come on! Jump!"

Eli buzzed his damp wings and made a leap for it.

Their hands clamped together and Ismail held him dangling over a long drop to a desalination pool full of machinery below them.

Eli yelled, "The pressure will be too much! We won't be able to hold on!"

As he said it, an idea flashed into his mind. He grabbed at his belt with his free hand and pulled out a small transparent oval capsule. It was another project he'd been working on before the Skreaf attacked – a commission outside of his military work for a friend who'd wanted to start up his own company. It was a safety insert for transflyers to replace the largely ineffective air-tubes. Eli had come up with an idea for something that was essentially a large bubble made of intelligent superfiber that was triggered on impact and expanded to form an exact-fitting protective layer around the person. He'd completed a few successful dummy runs, but hadn't gotten to the stage of a live test. He'd only kept the capsule in his pocket because he liked clicking the lid on and off for stress relief. He hated to use something that hadn't been fully cleared, but really their options weren't extremely numerous at this stage.

"Ismail!" he shouted above the noise of the alarm, but before he could tell the scullion his idea, the ceiling collapsed and they started to fall in a gigantic gush of water. Eli clenched his fist to trigger the release of the capsule. It instantly blew out into a huge bubble that latched onto Eli and wrapped around him. It felt like diving into a bowl of cold jelly. He and Ismail's hands were still linked, so the superfiber judged they were the same organism and encased him as well. The thing Eli hadn't accounted for before then was breathing inside the superfiber. His mouth, nose and ears were completely sealed over by the transparent material and panic trembled through him. He couldn't breathe at all.

The water collided with the machinery below and he and Ismail struck down, protected by the bubble, before being dragged into the flood. The pressure tide sucked them upward and when the bubble finally stopped rushing and spinning, Eli stared down at the ruined facility below. The Omarians were nowhere in sight. He couldn't believe he and Ismail had made it out alive. He felt the scullion's hand squeeze down on his, and thinking it was a gesture of encouragement, he squeezed back, but then something hit them hard from the side. They were shunted through the water, the bubble spinning, giving Eli a glimpse of something speeding their way – a massive set of open jaws full of, sharp, ragged teeth. A razor-fin shark. It struck, biting down on the superfiber and bursting it. The sudden release catapulted Ismail and Eli upward through the water, while the fiber started to encase the razor-fin instead, which would have saved them if the rest of the vicious predators weren't rising in a shadowy mass just below them.

The closest shark rushed in and Eli saw a flash of light. He blinked, blinded for a moment, then spotted the motionless forms of Ismail and the razor-fins all sinking downward into the darkness below. After a second of confusion, Eli realized Ismail must have released his stunning electro-pulse. It had halted the sharks, but knocked him out as well, as he had said it would. Eli swam downward, pushing himself after the scullion. He kicked desperately, finally managing to catch up and grab Ismail's shirt. Eli's lungs had started screaming for air and every inch of progress toward the surface took immense effort. It became agonizingly clear that they wouldn't make it. Eli thought fast and, remembering what had happened when the superfiber burst, he snatched the distress flare off his weapon belt and broke it open. The kickback of the ignited charge ricocheted along his arm and through his chest, but he held on tight.

The flare exploded, rocketing them upward with a massive whooshing rush. Eli clung on for his life's worth, swallowing several lungfuls of sea water and almost blacking out. Ismail's shirt started to rip. Eli clutched desperately at him, trying to get a new handhold, and seized one of his ears. It was going to leave a mark, but better that than the alternative. They broke the surface, riding the explosion high into the air, then slamming back down into the water. Eli gagged, coughing and gasping through his raw throat. He wrapped an arm around Ismail, trying to keep his face afloat. The lights had blacked out at the surface in an imitation of night and all Eli could see were the shadows of waves, larger than buildings, rising up all around them. He felt them lifting up and grasped Ismail tighter, shouting, "Help! Help us! Is there anyone there?"

He heard a whistle above the crashing water and glimpsed the silhouette of a boat on the peak of a wave just beyond them.

He waved frantically, and the boat waved back with an enormously long arm and paddle hand.

It skimmed down the wave and rushed up toward them, snatching them out of the water as a monster shark lunged up. Eli screamed and tucked his legs in, just seeing red teeth and a dark hole below him. Spikes shot out of the boat creature's skin, making it entirely unpalatable. The creature swatted the shark away with a huge hand and thumped the surface of the water in warning.

Eli felt himself slipping out of the boatman's grasp. He fell and landed in its warm boat body.

"The portal. It's gone," Eli whispered and collapsed, out cold.

Chapter 28
Diega

PRATERIUS

RAMBELDON FOREST (THE HIVE)

Diega and Sesame crept along the wax tunnels back toward Queen Alphra's chamber while her thunderous snores roared around them. They reached the entrance and crouched low. The queen's resting guards covered the floor and walls.

Diega turned to the drone and whispered, "Stay here."

"I have to come," Sesame insisted. "They won't believe you."

"Then keep behind me," Diega ordered.

She took a deep breath and stepped into the room, silently picking her way over the sleeping guards to where the drones knelt, staring at the ground. Diega tapped one on the shoulder and he buzzed with fright. Sesame slapped a hand over the drone's mouth. The guard closest to them stirred and Diega held her breath. It buzzed something, then lapsed back to sleep. The sounds of the queen's snores ripped through the air. Sesame whispered to the drone, then removed his hand. The two of them alerted the others. Diega gestured to the door and the drones nodded, rising to their feet with difficulty after being forced to kneel for so long. They hobbled out of the chamber, but Diega paused, spotting Copernicus' weapon belt and her own, along with Shawe and Caesar's stuff, lying in one corner in a pile of offerings to the queen. She inched her way to them, stuffed the gangsters' belongings into the belts, then fastened both of them around her waist to free up her hands.

As she stood, her eyes were drawn back to the monstrosity of flesh that was Queen Alphra. Her body lengthened then scrunched with every snore. Diega felt like grabbing one of the guards' spears and stabbing her through, but then a million Neridori would be on their backs and escape impossible. That was what separated her from Shawe – logical thought before action – unless someone laughed at her. That was the one thing that made her lose all reasoning and set her off every time.

Diega turned toward the exit, catching sight of movement on the other side of the queen. Immediately Diega dropped to the ground and peered around the edge of the sofa. A large group of Omarian warriors stood watching the sleeping monarch. Diega made a split-second decision and yelled as loudly as she could. The queen woke with a start. She saw the intruders right in front of her and released a deafening buzz that shook the whole hive. The room erupted into movement and sound. The Neridori guards swarmed around the Omarians, stabbing with stings and spears. The Omarians struck back with light-form and blasts of fire. Diega didn't pause to see who was winning. She lunged from the chamber and out into the corridor.

"Go! Go! Fly!" she yelled at Sesame and the other drones as she overtook them, racing back to where the others waited. She saw the gangsters supporting Copernicus up ahead.

"The Omarians are here!" she shouted to them. Shawe cursed and Caesar growled.

Sesame buzzed behind Diega and a swarm of the drones massed around the group, grabbing hold of them and the other non-flighted creatures rescued from the cells. Diega felt Sesame clutch her around the back and chest, holding her with both sets of hands. The drone beat his wings frantic-ally, struggled a moment, and lifted them off the ground. They swooped upward through a skylight into the cool forest air and purple dusk of the setting Anvil.

Diega had a brief aerial view of the Hive courtyard below her, now a battlefield where writhing masses of black and gold concentrated around patches of red and fire. Omarians and Neridori clashed on the ground and in midair. The fierce insect-breeds released buzzing screams, attacking the fire wielders, plunging their stings into them without hesitation, even though it meant their own death as well. The Omarians were greatly outnumbered, but they were also more powerful. The battle looked as if it could go either way.

One Omarian looked up and spotted the group escaping. He leaped onto a Neridori guard's back and forced it, with his dagger to its throat, to take flight. He pointed in Diega's direction and the guard hurtled toward them.

"Sesame, fly faster!" Diega yelled up at the drone.

Sesame gasped, beating his wings desperately, but he was an unpracticed flier and weak from starvation; the Omarian on the guard caught up with little effort.

Diega felt a blast of fire at her back. Sesame screamed and crashed into the treetops. A branch ripped Diega out of his grasp. She slammed into a heavy trunk and ricocheted off. Knocked breathless and half-senseless, she scrambled trying to get hold of something to stop herself falling. She grappled with a bunch of leaves, but they ripped and she plummeted from the sky. Sesame swooped in, trying to catch her, but another fireball scorched his hair and sent him scattering. Diega had a moment to think that this was it, this fall would kill her. She braced for impact and saw the ground racing up at her.

Caesar dropped from the void above and snatched her out of mid-air. He landed solidly on his feet on the forest floor. The drone carrying Shawe dived down beside them. As they zoomed past, Shawe grabbed Diega's hand, yanking her off her feet and back into the air, her legs dangling below. Another drone picked up Caesar and the pair sped them through the forest, keeping low and out of sight, dodging the black tree trunks as they flashed in front of them. Diega's stomach churned, the wind shrieking in her ears.

With a crash of leaves the Omarian and Neridori guard burst down right behind them. Shawe's drone shrieked. It zig-zagged faster through the trees, trying to avoid the inferno blasts singeing their backs. Trees on all sides went up in a blaze, and the fire started to spread rapidly through the forest. The Omarian managed to steer the guard in beside Shawe. His Neridori slammed into the drone and the Omarian snapped his poisonous bone blade out of his wrist and stabbed it into Shawe's arm. The gangster yelled a curse, but didn't release his grip on Diega. She clung on desperately, digging her fingernails into him and trying to climb up his arm. She could barely see with the wind rushing in her face. The Omarian came back in for another try. He raised his blade and Shawe punched him across the face with his free hand. Hot blood spurted from the Omarian's nose. He sent a fireball into Shawe that would have incinerated most people, but Shawe's tough skin didn't burn so easily.

Diega felt a disturbance in the air and heard Shawe groan – the Omarian had him locked in light-form.

"Freefall!" she screamed at their drone and he obeyed, dropping like a rock from the sky. It broke the connection and Shawe gasped as he regained his control, but the Omarian was still on them. He zoomed in above them, concentrating his attack on their drone instead, who buzzed hysterically, weaving and bucking, dodging fire and light-form and almost dropping them. Diega knew he wouldn't last long against the Omarian and squinting through watering eyes, cast wildly around for something to help them. She spotted K-Ruz riding on the other drone some distance ahead.

"Caesar!" she yelled to him, her voice immediately snatched by the wind. She thought there was no chance he would hear, but his acute feline senses picked up on the call and he whipped around. He spotted them and spoke to his drone, urging it back. It did a quick turn and flew back their way, on a collision course with the Omarian. The warrior saw them coming and paused his attack on Shawe's drone. Diega watched upward as the two Neridori zoomed closer and closer. The Omarian raised one hand, preparing to in-cinerate Caesar, but the Pride King raised his hand as well and Diega heard the *shing* of his claws coming out. A second more passed – the two creatures were almost on each other. The Omarian threw a fireblast at Caesar, who ducked it and slashed out with his claws, severing the Omarian's head. The body rolled off the Neridori guard and plummeted down to the forest floor. The guard made a sudden dodge out of the drone's path, narrowly avoiding a collision. Without sparing them a further glance, it spun in the air and sped back toward the hive.

Sesame flew in underneath Diega and she dropped onto his back. She groaned from the pain in her arms and wrists from hanging for so long and her senses blipped, specks of light dancing across her sight, but she managed to blink them away.

"We have to find the gateway into Murkmire!" she yelled to Sesame.

"I don't know where the gateways are," he buzzed. "I've never been out of the hive."

"Then take us to the others who escaped. We need to find someone who does know."

The drones flew them onward for some distance before Sesame dropped to the ground, where the rest of the drones and other freed prisoners had gathered. Diega jumped off his back and landed with Shawe and Caesar beside her. The wound in Shawe's arm was already blistering up and cracking open, but he barely seemed to notice it. He moved fast toward Copernicus, clutched in the arms of another terrified-looking drone.

"He's not well. He's not well at all," the drone stammered as Shawe and Caesar took hold of Copernicus again. He was struggling to keep his head up, still fighting the poison, but Diega could see he was slipping fast.

"Does anyone here know how to get to Murkmire?" she called out to the gathering, her voice hoarse and frantic.

"To the swamplands?" someone called back. "Inchmeal knows the way – the way Inchmeal knows." An enormous grasshopper sprung out of the crowd, staring at them with intense, dark brown eyes, antennae pointing forward.

"You know how to get there?" Diega repeated.

The creature gave a chirping response, "Indeed, indeed, indeed, indeed, follow Inchmeal to the gateway – to the gateway follow Inchmeal."

He turned and disappeared with a giant bound.

The group crashed through the forest after him, each of them sensing the fire presence of the Omarians closing in behind. Caesar snarled softly, tasting the air and disliking the smoke.

The insect-breed led them into a clearing where swans were gliding over a golden-water pond beneath a gigantic head carved in rock. The eyes of the sculpture were glistening, giant pearls. Water flowed from its open mouth into the pond.

"The head of Solomon," Diega murmured.

"Swim through the mouth to Murkmire ... To Murkmire swim through the mouth," Inchmeal told them.

Diega splashed into the pond, with Shawe and Caesar dragging Copernicus just behind her. The trees around the pond had started to sway and groan, and the wind rose, biting at their skin, wailing as though the whole forest were crying. Smoke stifled the air. Diega reached the head first and grabbed the rock mouth. She hauled herself up onto its lip.

The head began to shake.

"Quick!" she called to the others and helped them haul Copernicus in.

She heard a shout and looked up to see the Omarians appear at the water's edge. She felt their light-form grip her, the strength draining from her body.

A swarm of drones led by Sesame bombed down on the Omarians, the distraction allowing Caesar and Shawe to climb into the mouth. In a sudden movement, the head tilted back, sending Diega and the others crashing down over smooth, algae-covered rocks into blackness.

Chapter 29
Croy

KULLRA FORNAX

NŸR-CORUM (THE CREMATORIUM)

Croy fought a savage upblast of windstorm to bring her dragger down on the landing pad of the Crematorium. Instead of leaving it parked outside, as she and Darius had done earlier, she dismounted and wheeled it toward the entrance door of the main building. She couldn't risk a cyclonic wind sweeping away her only method of escape. Despite the hum of the I-Sect's signal-pending in her ear, she felt profoundly alone. She could barely move around the fear, dragged forward only by the insistent buzzing sensation in her head, which had grown stronger the closer she'd flown to the Crematorium. Now that she had arrived, the sensation had changed again, the buzzing lessening, becoming more a feeling like someone had hold of her wrists and was hauling her in. Her instincts told her to run, yet the touch felt so familiar, and there was such a sense of great urgency behind it. Every time she hesitated the grip tightened, so she limped on, leaning heavily on her dragger, bracing against the freezing winds. As she neared the gate Croy drew her Firestorm and prepared for a Mortician to step into her path, but she reached the entrance without interception.

Keeping the dragger in front of her as a shield, she pushed the door open and wheeled the vehicle inside the building. She paused, holding her breath, listening, waiting, staring down the length of the long, hollow corridor. Nothing. She kicked out the parking stand and primed her weapon, then started down toward the records room. Thick chemical clouds of the itchem-poly-magmylate saturated the air, but she could still smell an undercurrent of decay, like a puff of Klinsman's breath on every gust of wind. The flame torches flickered wildly.

A door banged shut behind her and Croy whipped around, aiming her Firestorm at an empty corridor. A heavy silence filled every space.

She turned back and kept moving, gritting her teeth, struggling to keep her breathing slow and hands steady, as she retraced their steps from a dayturn earlier. She found the records room empty and passed through it, heading for the cool rooms. There were no signs of Morticians anywhere until she neared the storage room that opened directly to the coolers, then she heard the grinding shriek of metal striking metal.

Croy kept low and ran to the closed door of the storage room. She slammed her back into the wall beside it, first clearing behind her, then inching the door open to peer inside. The first thing she saw was red. Red on the walls, on the ceiling, on the floor, then all the gore of cut-up Morticians strewn everywhere. Masses more of the hairless, white-cloaked death mongers stood surrounding a person, a man, trapped in the center of the chaos. He was swinging an axe, fighting them back. He sidestepped a stabbing knife, grabbing the attacker by the arm and flinging him aside. Through the throng of bodies, Croy caught sight of the man's face. His features and body structure seemed human, but his skin was different, darker and marked with a pattern across his arms, and the shine of his clothes was unlike any fabric she'd seen. It blended with the shadows. A cage-like device had been attached around the stranger's head and face. He swung the axe with brutal force and split a Mortician clean in half. As he swung again, another Mortician stabbed a scalpel into his side repeatedly. Each time Croy felt the pain as though she were the one being stabbed.

More of the death mongers grabbed the man around the chest, legs and waist, trying to drag him down to the ground. His muscles strained, clearly powerful, but the sheer number of Morticians was overwhelming him. Croy felt a sense of being suffocated and crushed, and panic shot through her. The man's dark eyes raised to door and he looked straight at her. She felt a buzzing in her head, and heard words that echoed through her mind ... *to me ... to me ...*

Strength rushed through her. She charged into the room. One Mortician whipped around and threw a knife at her head. She dived sideways out of the way as it struck exactly where she'd stood. More were turning to her, all their eyes strange, staring but unseeing. Some of them started to move toward her. Croy raised her Firestorm and shot without hesitation – blasting through them row after row until the only two people left standing were herself and the stranger. Fire and gun smoke saturated the air. Croy kept her aim on the man, her eyes locked with his. Breathing heavily and bleeding profusely, red blood like a human, he lowered the heavy axe to the ground with a clunk. Croy felt more pulses of buzzing and pain seared through her leg, sharp enough to make her cry out and stumble. Shadows flickered over the ceiling.

Clattering came from the cold room behind the stranger. Croy's first thought was of victims and survivors trapped inside there. Still keeping the man in the Firestorm's sights she backed to the cold room door and shot a glance through the transparent panel. It was a moment before she registered what she was seeing – all the bodies, the corpses, were twitching, rising, standing and starting to stagger to the door where she stood.

Impossible, but it was happening before her eyes.

Croy looked back at the stranger. All around him dead Morticians were starting to stir. Soon they'd be swallowed by a mass of reanimated dead, and her Firestorm was all but out of flint. Sparks from one of the burning bodies ignited a puddle of itchem on the ground from a punctured barrel. The fire spread fast to the rest of the barrels – enough to make the whole place explode. They had to get out – now.

"Move – toward the door!" Croy instructed the stranger, gesturing with her weapon. He tried to comply, but could only shuffle, his ankles chained together. Blood gushed from the wound in his side, fast saturating his clothes. He looked up at her, and she felt what could only be described as love – like seeing someone she'd been missing for a very long time standing in front of her. It completely overtook her, and even as she realized with distant horror that this man wasn't human, she found herself running to him as burning corpses rose all around them and the door to the cold room started to dent inward. The man was trying to swing the axe down on the chains around his legs, but couldn't get the angle right. Croy holstered her Firestorm and grabbed the axe from him, freeing him with one hit. She grabbed him around the waist and he leaned against her as they broke for the door. One of the dead Morticians grabbed Croy around the ankle but she kicked free and they fled, running to keep ahead of the shambling dead and the roar of fire gathering strength behind them. The place was about to go up like one big cremation oven.

Finally they reached the last corridor and Croy saw her dragger up ahead. They ran for it, almost there, when the Mortician leader, Baraway Westor, flew out of the shadows and smashed the stranger onto the ground. He tried to stab a scalpel through the man's head. Croy drew her Firestorm and blasted him off but even though he was burning and hanging in bits, he still staggered up and tried to rush them again. Croy lunged onto her dragger and the stranger swung on behind her. She grabbed her knife and threw it, taking out Westor's legs, then kicked the dragger to life. They crashed through the door, zooming across the landing pad, into the open air.

Croy looked back to see the dead spewing out the front gates, staggering over the strip and tumbling over the edges, falling soundlessly into black nothing below. It was the most hideous and disturbing thing she'd ever seen. She sped up, and they had already reached the lower edge of Saint Smithy Borough by the time she felt the tremor of the Crematorium exploding.

Croy flew toward her house with the Dray's arms wrapped around her waist and his hot breath on her neck – this beautiful monster.

Chapter 30

Eli

AQUAIS

SCORPIA (ADLIDEN)

The slow swishes of the boatman's oar arms lulled Eli into a half-sleep haze where he drifted for an unknown time, finally to wake with a jolt, tasting the tang of dried salt water on his lips. His sudden movement disturbed Ismail, who was sprawled out beside him. The scullion's eyes blinked open and he pushed himself up, a growl rattling in his throat before his military composure overcame his wild side. They both stared into the wide, flat face of the marine-breed who had come to their rescue, and now rowed them through calmer river waters. The boatman had a puckered mouth, and skin that matched the blue-brown of the water with yellow flecks the same color as his eyes, sharp and shrewd. He was watching them intently.

Ismail squinted and Eli felt the telepathic itch of the scullion trying to break into the boatman's mind, but his head suddenly tilted sideways as though he'd been physically re-buffed. Eli's first thought was that a mind would have to be enormously powerful to keep Ismail's skills out.

"Identify yourself," Ismail demanded.

"I'm Imrad the Twibowl, aren't I," the boatman replied, blinking transparent eyelids in and out. He gave a shrill whistle, then added, "And you?"

Ismail just stared him down.

Eli said, "Eli Anklebiter and Ismail Ohavor." He couldn't take his eyes off the boatman. According to the current research literature, Twibowls had become extinct year-cycles ago after a natural disaster poisoned their home waters. Eli had seen the horrendous images of the dead and hadn't been able to get them out of his head ever since, but clearly the research was wrong. This was truly one of the most amazing beings Eli had seen, ancient, brilliant and perhaps the last of his kind.

"Many thanks for rescuing us," Eli said.

"Rescue?" Imrad chuckled. "Rescue, indeed. You whistled me in, didn't you, so mayhaps you saved yourself, mayhaps true?" He smiled.

"Mayhaps – I mean maybe," Eli said. He realized the Twibowl must have heard Ismail whistling to the seahorses. His mind returned to the destroyed portal. It left them only one other option – LaNoria. He closed his eyes and lowered his head. Their realistic chances of getting into the sealed-off level, finding the portal and then getting out were zero – but they couldn't just abandon the others. That wasn't an option.

Eli looked up at the Twibowl, who was watching him closely with interest, while Ismail watched the Twibowl closely with suspicion.

"I wonder ... well, we're looking for —" Eli started.

"Don't tell him anything!" Ismail cut in.

"It's okay. You can speak," Imrad said, with a long, slow swish of his paddle arms.

"Can we?" Ismail responded coldly. "How generous of you."

"We have to ask. What else can we do? The portal is destroyed." Eli said.

"Portal?" Imrad repeated.

Eli rushed in before Ismail could stop him, "We're trying to get to another realm, to rescue our friends, and there's a portal in LaNoria. It's the last in the city. It's just getting there and getting out that's going to be the issue."

"Well to LaNoria I can help you with," Imrad said. "I can take you to an entrance, but out … that I don't know."

"Why would you be so eager to help us?" Ismail said.

"Just so." The Twibowl smiled. "Just will."

"No one helps anyone without wanting something in return – what do you want?" Ismail demanded, echoing his previous sentiments.

"I want to sing." Imrad pursed his lips and started singing, with the most beautiful, haunting voice, the saddest song about a soldier trying to find his way home. It brought tears to Eli's eyes and as he wiped them away, he noticed Ismail glaring at him.

"Why did you swim back for me?" the scullion asked with a lowered voice, while Imrad kept singing and whistling. "You should have kept going. You jeopardized the entire mission!" He clutched at his chest, cursing.

Eli heard a muffled beep beneath Ismail's shirt and said, "Your vials are getting low. Here —" He took the refills, which he had tried to give Ismail earlier, out of his belt.

The scullion hesitated, but then took the vials. He opened his shirt and checked over the He-Ro until he found the vial chamber.

"I swam back for you because soldiers never leave soldiers behind," Eli told him as Ismail removed the emptying vials and replaced them.

"Illogical romanticism gets you nowhere except dead, soldier," Ismail responded. "Your heart is bigger than your brain. Besides it's not the truth anyway, your mind just told me so – and I want to know the real reason."

Eli considered his words – he was right – military honor had nothing to do with him not leaving Ismail behind.

"I'm not going to abandon you because Ev'r loves you," he said.

"You don't know anything about her or me," Ismail dismissed him.

"I know ... her journal ... when you were alive her writing was full of hope and future and promise, and after you died – that all vanished. You meant everything to her."

Ismail's face contorted with pain and he looked away. When he spoke, his voice was shaky. He'd switched or been jolted out of military mode back to the man. Unsurprisingly, the mention of Ev'r seemed to be a consistent trigger of the shift.

"And do you think I didn't care for her?"

"I'm sure you did."

"No!" He clenched his fists. "We were going to get married. Her father had me captured. He sold me to the Militia."

"I'm sorry," Eli whispered.

"There was no way out," Ismail emphasized the words. "I tried *everything*. And no matter what they did to me, the worst torture was knowing that she would think that I had left her – that I didn't love her. They threatened to kill her if I ran. Do you understand what it's like to have to hear that, and not be able to do anything about it?"

Eli gulped and shook his head.

Ismail's eyes were starting to blank out as the memories became too painful. He said in a monotone, "I heard she wasn't doing well. Her father was going to marry her off to a boy – I knew he was cruel. I heard there was a witch granting wishes.

They called her the Mocking Witch of O'Tenery Asylum. One soldier had gone bald – she gave him a head full of hair. Another wanted a girl who didn't want him – next thing she was madly in love. What I wanted ... was for Zara to be safe, happy and free. The witch told me everything came with a price. She said I'd have to give my life ... and I said, *take it*." Ismail closed his eyes. "I thought she meant to kill me, but instead she enslaved me, so I stabbed myself, not realizing that would break her spell over Zara and make everything worse for her."

"Dark magics twist everything," Eli said. "Even the greatest acts of love."

"If me dying now, this second, could bring her back, I would. I wouldn't hesitate. Do you understand now how much I love her?" Ismail looked up at him.

"I understand you love her so much you're willing to die for her – but do you love her enough to live for her?" Eli said.

Anger flickered into Ismail's dulled eyes, the man still just below the surface. "What are you talking about, imp-breed?"

"That's one part of your journey together that I understand – I mean – *don't* understand," Eli said. "Why did you let yourself die out there in the desert after you'd been reunited with Ev'r, why didn't you come to the city to get treatment? I know you were a fair way out, but you must have known you were sick for a while ... and with your skills and hers, you would have been able to make it back – you would have survived."

Ismail's face had paled and his eyes were burning, and Eli thought that this time he might not have just accidentally stepped over the line, but leaped over it with both feet. He expected the beast to emerge any moment, but Ismail managed to restrain himself; he even surprised Eli by responding.

"I knew it wouldn't last." He stared out to the river, looking into the past. "We were happy, but I knew it was only a matter of time before it changed. The witch would never let us be. I thought … with me gone, she would finally be free of her …"

The logic of if was so damaged that Eli's mind ached. He understood what sort of life had brought Ismail to this thinking, but still, it made him want to cry.

"I'm only telling you all this, imp-breed, so that you can explain to her …" he said, his stare boring holes into Eli's face. "I saw in your mind the lengths you've gone to to revive her. It's beyond my understanding why you'd care for strangers, but I'm … grateful … that you do."

"I think it would be better if you explained it to her yourself, because you'll be there too," Eli said, stubbornly. "Hero-complex, remember."

"I'm dead," Ismail told him. "There is no hope for me." He lowered his eyes to the cursed shackle locked around his ankle.

"Hope is infinite," the boatman spoke up, "and time not always a traitor." He gave a long whistle that echoed into the silence around them – and was answered by a chorus of other Twibowl whistles. He wasn't the last one left, there were others who had survived. Despite everything, Eli smiled, his spirits lifted by the thought of it.

When he looked back at Ismail, he jolted. The scullion's eyes were completely white and his body was shaking.

"Ismail!" He lunged over to him. He grabbed his arm and Ismail snapped out of the trance, his eyes rolling down to normal.

"What was that?" Eli asked. "A vision?"

Ismail looked genuinely shocked as well and lost for words. Finally he managed to say, "I haven't seen the future for year-cycles."

"That's because, as you said, you felt there wasn't a future – but now that you're —"

"I saw Silho," Ismail cut in. "She's somewhere near fire."

"The Omarian realm," Eli said, his heart picking up pace at the mention of Silho. "Is she...is she okay?"

Ismail ran an exhausted hand over his face and murmured, more to himself than Eli, "We should have tried to help her, but we just left…"

"What do you mean," Eli said, not understanding.

Ismail snarled his lips, "Hammersmith – that Blue-Ten addict – that selfish, weak trutt. I saw into his mind. He sold her out to that – *Lecivion*. He planted something in her back so that the Omarians would always be able to find her wherever she went … and now they've come and taken her, and … she's dead. I saw her dying in a sea of flames."

The words shook Eli, but he refused to believe them and muted his grief. "After everything that's happened to you – you're still affected by a girl who you met briefly in the desert so many year-cycles ago. Maybe I'm not alone in caring?"

"Silho wasn't just a girl … She was …" He shook his head, unable to explain. "*Consan*," he said in scullion-tongue, and Eli understood it to mean a stranger who is family – kindred. It was a complicated scullion belief where people were linked through time and rebirth.

"Well, I know Silho well," Eli said, trying to sound positive. "And I know she'll fight to the last, so I'm going to keep searching for her until I find her or I die … these are not just my work colleagues, or even just friends – they're my family – Silho, Copernicus, Diega, Jude, Ev'r."

"They're all dead. I saw it." Ismail told him, flatly, all the fire and feeling in his eyes burning out to a blank stare as he switched back to soldier mode.

"No," Eli refused. "I don't believe it."

He closed his eyes, needing to zone out for a while to regather his control.

When he opened them again, he saw they had left the inhabited areas of Adliden and had entered murkier waters, where coral trees grew along the banks beside abandoned homes made of shell and rock. A thick, brown silt covered everything as though it had all recently been flooded. Eli sensed they were coming close to the end of their journey and he still had no plan for their escape from LaNoria. He blinked open his front-core menu and called Diamond.

"I wasn't asleep – just resting my eyes," she said immediately.

It put a flicker of a smile on his lips. "It's okay, you're allowed to sleep," he said. "But I need some information. What do you know about entries and exits from LaNoria? The short version."

After a moment of silence, in which Eli wondered if they'd actually found one topic that Diamond didn't know about, she said, "There are several ways in, but they all require magics and there's only one way out that won't get you killed. There's an old elevator – an antique, really – that used to run between the old asylum, which was the Galleria Majora before it was destroyed, and Level 4 – remember, they were trialing it as the new asylum before the contamination?"

"No, I didn't realize," Eli admitted.

"Well – the elevator is shut down and sealed off, but if you could get inside it and hack in, you could get it started, and then it looks like there's a clear run up, based on the grids I'm looking at."

"Excellent," Eli said, feeling his spirits lifting. "Can you send me through the location of the elevator?"

"I can do one better, I can send you through the location, with the quickest route from the portal."

"Brilliant, Diamond – I keep saying it, but really brilliant. You're amazing."

"So will you marry me?" she responded brightly.

"Ah … well," Eli said, struggling for words. "I'm going to see if we can live through this first and then … reassess afterward."

The plans started loading into his front-core and he saw the route maps flashing up in front of his eyes. The distance between the portal and the elevator really wasn't that far.

"You know that LaNoria is a white-out zone, don't you?" Diamond said. "We'll be completely cut off."

"I know," Eli responded, trying to sound upbeat. "But we'll be out soon. Don't worry."

After a pause Diamond said in a small voice, "Eli?"

"Yes?"

"Don't forget to fly."

It was a complex imp-breed saying that at the core of it meant something like "keep breathing because I love you". His gran'pa use to say it to him. He missed him.

"You too," he whispered and ended the transmission.

Before Eli had a chance to memorize the maps, Imrad dragged his oar hands in the water to bring them to a halt beside a rocky plateau leading into a cave.

"Through there, my weary travelers," the boatman said, pointing to the cave. "You'll find an entranceway."

"My friend said that LaNoria can only be accessed by magics," Eli said.

"Then your friend is very right," Imrad replied.

"Is it safe?" Eli asked.

"Absolutely not," the boatman said and Eli gulped. He stared into the blackness inside the cavern and nerves crawled in his skin. Ismail was sniffing the air with distrust.

Eli forced himself to stand and step out of Imrad's boat body. Ismail followed, and when they were both out, the boatman rowed around to face them, saying, "Sometimes this world falls against evil and sometimes it stands. I hope this time it stands."

"So do I," Eli said.

He and Ismail turned and walked across the rocks to the shadow of the overhanging cave mouth. They stepped inside the ragged shade. Eli looked back to wave at Imrad, but the boatman was gone, the river was gone, and a black wall stood blocking their exit.

"Dark magics," Ismail snarled.

Eli turned and saw himself reflected in the scullion's eyes. He saw the monster hand reaching around his face a second before it wrenched him backward into the wall.

Chapter 31
Croy

KULLRA FORNAX

NŸR-CORUM (SAINT MARIREAD BOROUGH)

By the time she'd almost freed the Dray from the cruel head cage, her hands were shaking so badly she could barely grip the last steel hook embedded deeply in his flesh. She had to hold one hand with the other to finish the torturous task. Throughout the ordeal he hadn't uttered a sound, just sat forward in the seat with his head lowered. The only indication he was feeling any discomfort was the tightness with which he gripped the sides of the chair and the sweat pouring off him. Croy's knee was aching horribly from crouching for so long on the hard floor of her house, but the presence of the Dray distracted her from the pain. Always in the past when she had thought of the Drays, she'd imagined some kind of grotesque shadow-form, twisted and inhuman in every way, but nothing about this man suggested demon or monster. His eyes were darker than any she had seen and they shone when the light reflected off them, but they were full of emotions that she recognized and wisdom that she wished she had. He even had parasite-scars and windscars marking the hard muscles of his body, just like a human Fleetsman.

Croy noted that the bruises on his legs from the chains were fresh and the puncture wounds from the cage were not infected. It suggested he was captured just recently, yet some of his other injuries looked dayturns old, or older. She dropped the last of the hooks onto the floor near to the swabbing alcohol and her Firestorm, which she had placed right beside her leg.

She wiped a hand over her face – the freezing storm was still howling outside, but the Dray was radiating heat like a fire. She wasn't sure if it was actually him or the clothes he was wearing. The top had been ripped and hung off him, but the pants were intact. The fabric looked like some kind of animal skin, with heavy black scales that seemed to blend with the darkness. Croy had tried to cut away the rest of the top to stitch some of his other wounds, but had found that her knife, made from the strongest steel in the city, hadn't been able to penetrate the material. It made her wonder what had torn his suit up – clearly nothing human-made.

After struggling to her feet, Croy gripped the cage and lifted it completely off the Dray's head. Sensations bombarded her, feelings so intense that she immediately dropped the cage to the ground with a clatter. She recognized the emotions. She'd felt the same way just after John L had died and she had dreamed of him alive again, only to wake to find him gone. It was that feeling – that ache and void – that longing to see someone again and knowing it would never happen. It surged through her so powerfully that she found herself gripping onto the Dray's arm, just barely stopping herself from actually climbing onto him and hugging him. This was a dangerous stranger whose true intentions she didn't know. With

355

supreme mental effort she managed to release him and back away, but only a few paces, where she crouched down and lowered her head so as not to see him. She shook from the effort of keeping away from him and her chest ached with it. The cage had obviously been some kind of barrier to his power.

"Switch it off! Make it stop!" she demanded through gritted teeth.

"I can't," he spoke, his deep voice piercing right through her to where she hid in her mind. "It's the *rete* calling you in."

"Into where?"

"Into me – into your family line," he said.

Croy shook her head. "I don't understand." The shaking was worsening and her body was dragging her forward, toward him.

"Come closer. I'll explain everything," the Dray said.

"No!" Croy responded.

She sensed movement and looked up. He had stretched out his hand and she could see some kind of exotic marking imprinted in the skin of his arms. She couldn't stop herself, she reached out a shaking hand and placed it onto his. He closed his grip and gently drew her closer until she was sitting at his feet. He leaned down and touched his head to hers. The warmth of him, the scent of him rushed through her. She heard his voice in her mind.

It's alright. I'm here.

She fully realized that a stranger being *there* shouldn't be comforting, yet it was. She reached up and put her arms around his neck and all the fear drained out of her, leaving only silence in her mind, and something else she could see – a line stretching out into darkness.

He released her and she leaned back, kneeling beside him. Immediately she felt it – the pain in her knee was gone. She'd never been able to kneel on it like this. She shifted gingerly

– but still felt nothing. The shock and extreme relief brought tears to her eyes.

"Who are you?" she whispered.

The Dray looked down at her, his eyes shimmering like flames over dark waters.

"Shah-Jahan RaAhura ... Captain of the *Scorpian Manticore*." He flinched and pressed back in the chair, holding the stab wound in his side. He closed his eyes and seemed to drift into sleep.

Croy watched him for a long time before standing and walking, without any limp, into her bathroom. Feeling as though she was moving in a dream, she unlatched her toilet pail and from her hiding spot dragged out John L's papers, stashed beneath his leather jacket and his last packet of tigaros. It was some of his research into the Dray. Just before Controllers had raided John's house she'd hidden the papers, hoping the Conference wouldn't have enough evidence to convict him, but VP already had more than enough. She stared down at the parchments covered in John L's black scrawl. Until now she'd never more than glimpsed over it, some part of her always wanting to believe he was innocent and not wanting to see anything that proved otherwise. She realized now how stupid this was. She scanned through the writing and found what she'd been looking for, she had a memory of seeing it once before, the name RaAhura – *Vesuvius RaAhura* – *Captain of the* Scorpian Manticore – perhaps Shah-Jahan's father? She read a note beside the name – *the Captain is the core of the family. The strongest of them all, who holds the* rete *together. Through him and by him all cerebral communications pass. Without him the clanship falls apart.*

"Cerebral communications?" Croy whispered. What did that mean? There were many parchment sheets of writing, but the words blurred before her eyes and she found she couldn't read them. She placed the parchments down and went back out into the lounge room. Shah-Jahan still sat with his eyes shut. She could feel his pain pulsing through her, as well as hunger and thirst.

She went to her food stores, took out a decanter of water and some bread and carried them to him. She touched his arm and his eyelids blinked open. She offered him the water and he took it and drank deeply.

"Why are you here? What happened to you?" she asked him. "Where's the rest of your family?"

A shadow crossed Shah-Jahan's face. "The Arequium Mors drove the human ship, the *Chimera*, into the *Scorpian Manticore* and since then they have been hunting me, through humans, through animals – whatever they can possess. The entire family was at risk. I had to leave and cut the *rete*." He swallowed painfully. "I found my way into the city through air pipes in the Crematorium."

"The Arequium Mors crashed the *Chimera*?" Croy repeated, trying to understand what he was saying. "What are they?"

"You saw them – the shadows, minions of the Indemeus X – his heralds and hounds."

"Who is the Indemeus X?" Croy asked.

"A demon," Shah-Jahan told her. "Set to drag our universe into his underworld. It's foretold I can stop him ... though how, I can't see."

"They made the dead move ..." Memories from the Crematorium shook her.

"That's what they do. The Arequium Mors can't hurt anyone with their own hands, but they wield high influence. They can't affect Drays, only those with less complicated minds, like humans."

"If they can influence humans, why couldn't they influence me? I felt them trying," Croy said. "My leg ... the pain."

Shah's eyes moved over her face and she could feel his hands on her even though they held the decanter in his lap.

"What is it?"

"Do you want to hear the truth or a lie that won't hurt?" he whispered.

Croy had a feeling like the house was about to collapse in on her.

"Truth," she said, though she wasn't completely sure.

"You're human, but you have an implant of Dray bone in your leg – connected at the knee – all the way down there." He pointed to her scarred knee. "It's blocking them."

Croy's mind absorbed the shock and rejected his words, "I fell when I was little, between a gridway. They said I wouldn't walk again but I did, I fought for it. John L told me …"

"John L …" Shah-Jahan repeated. "John Lukashenko?"

"Yes," Croy said, feeling disquiet rippling all over her skin.

"This man and other human men came to my people with a treaty, offering medicine and advancements in technology. We formed an alliance, believing they were speaking on behalf of all humans, but then we discovered they were using us – harvesting our dead to use in experiments on human children – human women – injecting and splicing blood and bone."

"I don't understand," Croy said, her voice faint.

"At first we thought they were trying to create a weapon against us, but then we discovered they were working for someone else – someone more powerful …"

"But there is only us and you."

Again she felt his comforting touch through her mind. "This is not the whole world – there are above lands – people, city, desert, sky – suns …"

"Above is hell." Croy said. "The saints escaped down here from there after demons cast them into the fires for their beliefs."

Shah-Jahan spoke gently, "They came down looking for a place to start again when in the above land humans started breeding into animal bloodlines to survive. Your forefathers believed against it, so they left and told that story of hell so no one would try to go back up. Their intentions were pure, but fast corrupted by greed and jealousy."

Croy studied Shah-Jahan's mouth and dark eyes but she couldn't see a lie or any maliciousness anywhere there. He was telling the truth. She felt shattered, lost for words and thoughts.

"The twins from the Crematorium … The girl knows about this?" she managed to ask.

The Dray nodded. "The boy has a bone implant in his spine, the girl in her head. They were both done later – you were the first. Their father was one of the men who came to us."

"You remember their names?"

"We never forget anything," Shah-Jahan said.

"Who?" she said, bracing herself for the answer. "Who were these men?"

"John Lukashenko, Ezra Quartermaine, Rogan Kisslefish, Zeman Kilner, Van Pritchard …"

Croy swallowed and closed her eyes.

"They had a laboratory somewhere here in your city. We tried to stop them, to talk to them, but they didn't listen. They cut us off. They killed my captain." He clenched his teeth with pain.

Victoria Kilner's dead face appeared for a second in Croy's mind.

"The corpse the twins stole – was she … one of us?" she whispered.

Shah nodded. "I felt her in the *rete* before she died. She could hear the Mors, but didn't understand what they were saying, what they meant. Her father told her she was crazy. It drove her to death."

"And what were the Morticians doing with her?" Croy said.

"The Mors were trying to influence the death tenders to take the Dray bone from the girl and splice it into themselves so they could find where I was hiding there."

"But the twins took her first."

He nodded and shifted with discomfort, and Croy felt a wave of nauseating pain radiating from him. Shah leaned forward in his seat and she stood and examined his back, finding another older but severe injury low down. She lifted the alcohol to swab it.

"Did the Morticians use the body?" she asked.

He understood her meaning and said, "No."

"The father?"

"A man who experiments on his own child is not a father – or a man."

"A monster," Croy uttered. "John …" She closed her eyes. He'd taught her everything she knew. She thought he'd loved her, but she was just an experiment. A heavy weight pressed down on her chest. She felt no anchor holding her to reality, but then the line she'd seen in the depths of her mind tightened and she felt him there – Shah-Jahan – holding her, keeping her and fortifying her.

She opened her eyes and looked down at him.

He spoke. "If the Drays are allowed entrance into city, they can save the humans from the Arequium Mors. If not, the Mors will drive them all to kill each other. That's what they feed on."

"After the sinking of the *Chimera* and the *Teriscoria* there's no chance of people accepting that," Croy said. "They wouldn't believe. I wouldn't have believed if I didn't – feel. I need evidence to convince them. You said they had a laboratory here – where?" She hoped it wasn't the Crematorium, which had just gone up in flames.

He shook his head. "We were never told."

Croy's mind went to Kellor Quartermaine. She would know. Everything she had said, though it had seemed like insane babbling, now made sense.

"The twins are being held in Tower. I'll go to them and get the information."

"It's too dangerous. I'll go with you," Shah said and tried to rise, but sank back down clutching his side in pain.

"It's better if you stay here," she said to him. "If any humans see you, they'll attack, even without the Mors influencing them."

"They'll be hunting you to get to me," Shah-Jahan said, his voice heavy with weariness.

"Then I'll have to move fast," Croy said. "All the rest of the food is in there." She handed him the bread. "I'll be back."

He held out his hand to her and she took it, his warm touch radiating courage and strength through her.

I'm with you, he spoke in her thoughts.

Croy grabbed her Firestorm and left. Everything outside her house looked the same, yet everything inside her had changed.

PART 3

Chapter 32

Diega

MURKMIRE SLOUGH (FORESTS OF MISTY)

Diega tumbled out of the cave tunnel and slammed down into boggy black mud. She lay half-stunned, staring up at a brown sky, electricity convulsing inside low-hanging clots of dark green clouds. Masses of tiny, biting insects swarmed through the air, fouled by noxious gases burbling and belching up from the swamp. Her senses retuned and she fought the desperate drag of the mud to sit up. Beside her Shawe struggled, with only one functioning arm, to keep Copernicus' face clear of the filth. Diega lunged over to help. She slid her hands under Copernicus' head and he stirred, fighting to open his eyes, but the poison had now spread further and he couldn't manage it. Diega felt as if her heart were ripping apart, a burning pain radiating across her chest. She cringed, unable to stop her distress from surfacing. Shawe cursed beside her. His arm was a mess, the skin sloughing off around the new stab wound, but his expression was still set into sheer unyielding stubbornness. Diega had always hated that look, but now she knew it meant he was going to race death right to the end, no matter what. And it was coming fast.

She grabbed painkillers and some of Eli's slowing and healing serums off her belt and prepared to inject them into Copernicus, but he jolted away as she tried, struggling to say something.

"He doesn't want them," Shawe interpreted. "He needs the pain to keep him going."

"I don't want him to suffer," she said.

"He loves it," Shawe said. "All that serious soldier trutt – deprivation and resilience and other such stupidity. He's always too trutting serious for his own good." Diega thought she saw a flicker of emotion in Shawe's dark green eyes.

"Here, then." She tried to inject the painkiller into the gangster's arm instead, but the needle broke off, unable to puncture his skin. He laughed roughly.

"Don't bother with me, sunshine. We don't have the time." His eyes met hers and she understood what he meant. Her heartbeats hammered faster. They had to find the healing plants right now.

Diega stood, looking for bearings in the swamp, a barren slough that stretched out indefinitely on all sides but one, where a clump of straggly trees led into a forest cloaked in a thick miasma mist. The mud left no trace of prints, and all their navigation equipment was still down – which left them again at the mercy of finding someone to beg for help, except, unlike Rambeldon, this place looked completely deserted. The sky here was even gloomier, overcome by the alien darkness consuming the entire planet. *The X.* Diega glanced toward Caesar, standing several paces away. He was swiping his muddied hands down his shirt in a compulsive frenzy that bordered on panic. It seemed so completely out of character for the usually unshakable Pride King that it struck instant fear in her. She thought he must have been poisoned, or possessed or whatever the trutt else could go wrong. Shawe saw Diega staring and snorted.

"Kitty doesn't like getting dirty."

Caesar's golden eyes snapped to them, and Diega saw humiliation, overshadowed immediately by cold anger. He released a deep rumbling growl and started to shake, his face distorting alarmingly between human-breed and lion.

"What's happening to him?" Diega asked, backing away.

"He's turning," Shawe said, standing up.

"Into what?"

"The Lion. If he loses control over it, it takes over, then the beast comes forward and the man becomes the shadow."

"You had to make fun of him, didn't you!" Diega yelled at Shawe. "Make him stop. We need him to carry Copernicus."

Shawe shook his head, looking around them. He spotted Caesar's blade in Diega's belt and pointed to it. She handed it to him.

"Here, kitty – look at this."

Shawe threw the blade at him and Caesar snatched it out of midair. He turned it over in his mud-caked hands and the touch of it snapped him out of his turn.

"My father gave me this," he murmured. "He was the greatest man who ever lived." Caesar crossed himself three times and kissed the blade.

Shawe gestured for Diega to hand over his weapons and other belongings and when she did, he took a long swig of his flask, "And my father gave me this. He was the biggest drunk who ever lived."

Caesar eyed him with cold contempt. "Perhaps the second," he said. "A man who disrespects his father's name is no man to me."

Shawe's stare hardened and he clenched a fist. Diega stepped in fast before everything unraveled again.

"Maybe you had a father who cared if you lived or died," she said. "I didn't, neither did Copernicus – in fact, his father tried to kill him. Buried him alive. Should he praise his father for that?"

Caesar looked down at her, his expression unwavering. "Whatever he did, he made him the man he is today."

"The man he is today is a dead man if we don't move now." Diega's words threatened to overcome her. "You said you owed him, so prove it."

For a moment Caesar didn't move and Diega feared she'd lost him, but then he stepped closer to Shawe and with a mutual savage reluctance, they locked hands and crouched down. Diega helped maneuver Copernicus into their grasp and they lifted him. Shawe didn't even flinch as Copernicus leaned heavily on his injured arm, and Diega had no choice but to stand in awe of the gangster's strength.

"Which way?" she murmured, more to herself than the others, but Shawe grunted, "The forest."

It made sense to head toward the one place in the swamp that offered shelter, and therefore a greater chance of inhabitants. For once Caesar made no arguments so they started forward, trudging and squelching, making slow progress in the clinging shin-high mud. Diega's muscles burned and cramped. With every step, she searched for solid ground and found none, feeling depleted and lightheaded with hunger and thirst. She grabbed a quick-boost hydration satchel off her belt and downed it, then offered one to the gangsters. Both grunted a refusal, neither wanting to look weak in front of the other. So she drank the second one as well, and felt an immediate boost in her energy. In the sky above the light kept dipping, over and over. Each time Caesar's back twitched and Diega was reminded of what the dragonfly had said – once the land was in darkness, an army of monsters would invade. She forced the fear out of her mind and took the lead, her spare blade clutched in one hand. Shawe started to sing and hum a galley tune about brotherhood and war. He really was completely tone-deaf.

Caesar glared at him until Shawe stopped and said, "Something in my teeth, kitty?"

The Pride King narrowed his eyes in a calculating lion smile. "I see you've forgiven Kane's betrayal?"

Shawe snorted.

"What betrayal?" Diega glanced back at the two gangsters carrying Copernicus. She was sick of the whole trutting story. "He cheated with Copernicus' girlfriend first and Copernicus reacted."

"You both talk way too much," Shawe muttered with annoyance.

Caesar clicked his tongue in the gangster way and said, "One of my girlfriends, too."

Diega shot Shawe a look of disgust. "What's wrong with you? There's not enough women in the city without having to break up other people's relationships?"

"Can I help it if women find me irresistible?" he demanded. "Besides, if K-Ruz and Kane weren't so pathetic in bed, the girls would never have come to me."

Caesar and Diega both made dismissive sounds – having a moment of bonding over finding Shawe ridiculous and foul.

"Seriously – how could you do that to your best friend?" Diega asked him, expecting his usual weak blaming. Instead he took her by complete surprise with a flash of sincerity.

"It's the only regret I have." He glanced up at Copernicus slumped between them. "He already knows."

"Everything happens for a reason," Caesar said.

"Everything happens because of alcohol," Shawe countered.

"Then stop drinking," Diega told him.

"Sure, sunshine. I'll quit right after you quit. How about that?"

He had her there. It was easier said than done – so much easier. She decided to keep her mouth shut.

Finally they breached the first line of trees, thin leafless shapes with rambling branches and twisted trunks covered in warty knots and nodules. The wafting, cloud-like mist became thicker the further in they went, until they could only see shadows through the haze. Birdsong echoed in the quiet – jootoos, whipping whistles and tee tee tees. Outlines of larger bison-like creatures moved through the mist, seeming to be part of it, maybe made of it. The animal activity gave Diega hope there would be people here who would help them, but the further they trekked into the slough without encountering anyone, the more her hope faded. The mud became thicker and deeper, the sky darker, and Copernicus' head sank low, his grip on Shawe's shoulder loosening. Diega watched him, her spirits lagging, sinking into a despair more deadly than the mud. Even Caesar looked like he was struggling. Only Shawe kept pushing strongly, until finally he spoke, his voice bellowing in the silence.

"I hear something."

Caesar lifted his head, his eyes sharpening. "I hear it too."

"To the left," Shawe urged, and they started toward the sound with renewed strength.

They pushed through the consuming mist, but balked as a desperate scream pierced the air. They scrambled for cover behind a clump of gnarled tree trunks. Diega peered out. In a clearing some distance from their hiding place, a green figure that looked like a Vidris Slimer, an algae-blood plant-breed, was struggling and gurgling, trapped in a pond of sinking death mud. A cluster of giant toads had circled the drowning creature, lashing out sticky whip tongues, trying to snag it for their next meal before it sank out of sight. Diega immediately thought of Eli. He would see this creature and run to save it out of the goodness of his heart, but the goodness in hers was negligible. What she saw was someone who might know where the Eti River was – and there was nothing like saving someone's life to induce gratitude. She spoke her thoughts to the others.

"What other trutting choice is there?" Shawe muttered. "You distract them while me and kitty get the Slimer."

The insult furrowed Caesar's forehead and fury glowed in his eyes. Diega elbowed Shawe and gave him a warning look. He shrugged. "Get going, sunshine."

Diega gritted her teeth and slipped out from behind the tree line. She kept low, running up behind the toads. The monsters were swelling, releasing deep, barking croaks while the Vidris continued to scream. When Diega was close enough, she yelled out, "Hey!"

The toads' eyes swiveled toward the sound, and she must have looked like a much better food option than the stringy Slimer because they all started to turn toward her in their plodding way. Diega was already backing up, ready in case they started jumping. As they edged forward, she caught sight of the poison glands beneath their eyes starting to expand. She leaped for cover behind a crooked stump as toxic blood spurted her way. By the sound, the toads were now moving fast. Diega lunged out from her hiding place and took off, running and stumbling through the mud. She drew her blade, preparing to fight for her life, but before she could turn to face the toads, something seized her from behind, sinking three daggers in her and lifting her off the ground. A giant, sucking mouth cavity latched onto her back and she felt a surge of weakness as a massive leech began to drain her. Blackness closed in from all corners of her mind. She couldn't get the blade around, her arm flailing uselessly.

The leech's body suddenly exploded, drenching her in her own hot blood, as Shawe stabbed the creature through.

"You owe me, sunshine," he said into her ear as he dragged her to her feet.

Right behind them the toads were advancing quickly, and more monster leeches were sliding up out of the mud and inching their way forward. Diega's legs failed and Shawe grabbed her by the jacket, hauling her backward toward the tree line, where they'd left Copernicus. Caesar ran parallel to them, wading through the thick mud, carrying the Vidris. It was panicking, grabbing at the Pride King's face with slimy hands. Caesar wore an expression of barely contained revulsion. Behind them a leech lunged forward and latched onto one of the toads and the two groups of animals quickly turned on each other, giving them a chance to widen the gap.

Diega managed to find her feet and fought forward beside the gangsters. A distant buzzing sound reached her ears, and for a horrible moment, she thought the queen's Neridori guards had found their way into Murkmire, but she was even more horrified when she looked over her shoulder and saw a black mass speeding toward them. Long proboscises hung below the thin dangling legs of hugely oversized swamp mosquitos, attracted by the smell of blood.

Shawe shouted a curse.

Diega knew she didn't have the strength to outrun the fast-moving bloodsuckers. Every step through the thick mud took supreme effort. Her steps faltered again. Shawe looked over his shoulder and yelled, "You giving up, princess?"

The words and fierce green of his eyes spurred her on. Every muscle in her legs burned and shook.

At the sound of the mosquitos, the leeches had begun to re-bury themselves in the mud and the toads were leaping frantically to get clear of their path. Diega glanced back to see a hungry mosquito catch up with one slower toad and make it a blood meal, draining it to skin in seconds. Another mosquito reached Caesar and attempted to stab its proboscis into his back. The powerful gangster boss swung around with exposed claws and eviscerated the creature in one swipe, the gurgling Slimer clutching harder around his neck.

When they reached the edge of the forest, the plant-breed slid out of Caesar's arms. It uncovered a burrow in the mud and jumped in, holding it open for them to follow. Caesar and Diega lunged and slid through, with Shawe dragging Copernicus right behind. They crashed down headfirst, falling a short distance into more mud.

Chapter 33
Eli

AQUAIS

SCORPIA (LANORIA)

Open-flame torches, chained to the walls, reached creeping, shadowy fingertips across the uneven stone floor to where Eli lay on his side. Consciousness played at the corners of his mind, returning first in sounds – the rising-falling, wailing screams, the scuttling, scratching and gnashing; then in feeling – the pounding inside his head from where it'd struck the ground, the raw dryness of his throat. He swallowed painfully and lifted a hand to his face. The touch jolted him awake from his half-dream state and he struggled to stand but failed, feeling like the only vertical person in a horizontal universe, carrying all the weight of the worlds on his back. He paused a moment to focus his strength and saw the Morsus Ictus lying beside him. He scrambled for it and snatched it up. Clutching the blade in front of him, Eli looked around, taking in his surroundings. A shiver rippled over his back.

Along the walls of the corridor, blacked-out canvases hung in heavy brass frames tangled in spider webbing. Eli followed the threads up to a low ceiling, a matted mess of intertwining webs, with silks as thick as rope. Eyes gleamed through the gloom. Dust caught in Eli's throat and he coughed, the sound echoing down the long, narrow corridor. A terrible, howling wind suddenly rushed from the darkness. It paused to taunt Eli, pushing him one way and then the other, before shoving him against a wall and sweeping away cackling. Beside his head, arms reached out of a blackened canvas. One tried to wrap around his neck, while the others pinned him to the stone. He fought violently against them, stabbing Ev'r's blade deep into their rot-soft flesh. He ripped free and stumbled into the center of the corridor, his eyes darting from the floor to the ceiling, then behind him into blackness. He held his breath and listened. Faint sounds of a struggle, running footsteps and muted yells, reached his ears. *Ismail ...*

With fear pounding in his chest, Eli started to edge toward the sounds. The stone floor creaked, groaned under his boots and something scuttled overhead. He reached a sharp bend and paused. The architecture made it impossible to see what was lurking ahead before turning. He clenched the hilt of Ev'r's blade and ducked swiftly around the corner. A figure stepped into his path, a two-headed creature with a bleached-white body covered in pus-filled sores. It moaned and lunged for him, razor claws pushing out from slimy fingertips. Eli tried to dodge it, but tripped over and slammed into the ground. It loomed over him, preparing to strike. He scrambled up and leaped around it, fleeing fast, his wings beating and legs moving, possibly faster than they'd ever moved before. He left the staggering miscreation behind him, and took another corner into a wider hallway. Strange and terrifying torture devices hung like art on the walls. He tried not to look at them, running past a metal vault door with screaming and groaning echoing from behind it.

The corridor led into another with rows of crypts fixed to both walls, guarded by statue gargoyles. They watched him pass, their dead stone eyes swiveling to keep him in sight. At the next turn he came to a quick stop, hearing the fighting sounds just ahead. He crawled through the shadows and peered around the corner. A clan of mutant creatures, fused forms of machine and flesh, some slithering, some lumbering, others tapping on many insect legs, had Ismail surrounded and pinned to the floor. The scullion struggled against them, using all his skills with little effect. Ismail snarled and sunk his teeth into one of the mutants' necks, half ripping its head off. The others sought revenge, pounding and kicking him in a frenzy. Eli held the Morsus Ictus in one shaking hand and edged forward, preparing to rush them, but before he could, they stopped. The mutants dragged Ismail to a row of dusty tombs built into the side of the corridor. They hoisted up his struggling form and dumped him into one. From below, dead hands wrapped around the scullion, holding him down, while the mutants slammed the lid and locked it from a place beneath the tomb. Eli could hear Ismail kicking from inside the crypt. The creatures moved away arguing over Ismail's belongings with grating, raucous voices. They'd taken Ev'r's backpack and journal – everything she had owned, except for the Morsus Ictus.

As soon as the sounds of the mutants died down, Eli rushed for the tomb, leaping over the fallen mutant's body. Ismail's knocking had become slower and fainter and finally stopped as Eli reached the crypt. He struggled for a moment to open the lid, but it was firmly sealed. He dropped to his knees and looked beneath it for the unlocking latch. His fingers crept through webs and grime until finally they found what seemed to be a keyhole. He grabbed the lock-pick from his weapon belt and shoved it into the hole, twisting. The mechanism was stubborn with rust and refused to budge. Eli worked at it, holding his breath, his throat dry and torrents of sweat streaming down his face, stinging his eyes. His arm began to cramp.

"Come on!" he exploded after twisting at it for what felt like hours. He shoved the pick further in and felt it click. The lid of the tomb lifted. Eli scrambled to his feet and looked inside.

It was empty.

He leaned further in and rotting claws grabbed him by the neck and yanked him down. He dropped without relief, wings smashing against rock, until a hand shot out from one side and seized him.

Chapter 34
Croy

KULLRA FORNAX

NŸR-CORUM (THE FILTER)

Croy brought her dragger down on the floating jetty.
Halfway to the Tower, she'd had a sudden memory of the
Quartermaine interrogation. She'd heard Kellor talking about
why she'd taken Victoria Kilner's body to the filter ... *I
wanted to take her home ...* Not to Saint Arabel Borough,
where Victoria had lived in the Purple Wing neighborhood,
but *home* to the Filter – *where she was remade.* The laboratory, or traces of it, had to be here – somewhere.

Croy had spoken to the guards at the top of the Filter,
posted there since Victoria was found, and told them she
was continuing her investigation. They'd waved her
through and now she found herself alone on the jetty. The
ten or so on-shift Filter workers had glimpsed her black
cloak and retreated to their shed on the other side of the
facility.

Croy moved along the jetty, stepping lightly on her scarred leg out of habit even though she felt no more pain. She stopped at the end of the structure where Kellor had chained Victoria's body between two anchor poles. For a moment, she saw Victoria still there, with the symbols carved in her flesh. Suddenly her dead eyes flickered open and she reached a shaking hand toward Croy. Then the image vanished, leaving Croy's heart racing.

She fought to hold her composure, scanning the rippling waters all around her. She wasn't sure what she was looking for – a clue? a key? She felt strongly the truth of Shah-Jahan's words, and a part of her mind had already broken down and crumbled from the pain of the implications, but somehow she was able to shut off that part and focus coldly on the search. She had to find something, otherwise Nÿr-Corum and everyone in it would be destroyed. Already the influence of the Arequium Mors was infecting the city. Her thoughts turned to the dead smugglers on the Strip and to the fight she'd witnessed at the Old Docks. She realized now they were both fueled by the Mors, and it was only a matter of time before the whole city erupted into violence.

Croy checked behind her, searching for darting shadows, but the darkness was still and the only noises in the Filter were the slow grinding whirr of machinery and the lapping of the waters. Croy recalled the positioning of Victoria's body, arms outstretched, chained midway down the anchor poles. Why like that, why there? It had to be significant. Croy turned and stepped back, gripping the steel rings on the poles where the chains had been fastened, and leaned out over the water. After a moment of consideration, she leaned back in. She placed her Firestorm and I-Sect down on the edge of the jetty and gripped the rings again. One leg at a time she lowered herself into the water and maneuvered herself down until she was in the exact position Kellor had placed Victoria, with her face parallel with the pier. She heard something beep and a light flashed in the waters beneath her. No fire she knew of could exist under water. Something else was down there. Croy had only been fully submerged in water three times in her life, all in shallow tubs, and the thought of dropping below the surface now was terrifying, but less so than what would happen to the city if they couldn't stop the Mors.

Croy took in a deep breath and released her grasp, sinking down into the cold water. It closed over her head and face, and she fought against the panic to get back to the air, just letting herself fall down, down, toward the blurred flashing lights – until her feet hit something solid. She felt it shift and start sliding, drawing her inward toward a large dark form. It took her into an enclosed chamber and she heard the shudder of doors closing. In a roaring rush, the waters around her began to drain out. She pushed off the bottom and broke the surface, taking in a gasp of air. The water level lowered all the way until her boots clunked down on metal.

Croy looked around a chamber that appeared to be a vault. It was lit not by fire, but by strange, glowing circular glass-like structures. If the Filter had been full to the top with water, as it had been not so long ago, there would be no way a person could swim down to this place in one breath, and Croy could only assume that whoever had built it had a means of breathing underwater – though the idea seemed impossible.

Ahead of her, Croy saw a transparent door. She stepped to it, looking into a room beyond. A light blazed right in front of her face, running down the length of her body. The doors parted from the center and Croy drew her knife and entered.

The room was large and empty, the walls and floor coated in a white, shiny substance Croy had never seen before. She walked further in, dripping water with each step. She stood in the middle of the space, looking around, until she spotted a small flashing light on the ceiling and stared at it. She saw the light reflect off the shrapnel pedant hanging around her neck – and then it flared into a life-size image of John L. Croy was so shocked that she fell over backward and scrambled away. She gasped as the image moved and she could see, behind John L, the same laboratory where she was now – except it wasn't empty, it was full of machines and work desks. John L lifted his head and looked straight at her and Croy swallowed back the emotion rushing up inside her. So many annums had passed since she'd seen anything more than a charcoal sketch of him – and now he stood before her as vividly as if he were alive.

"Saint Croy," John L said and tears sprung to her eyes. He was the one who had made up that nickname after she'd refused as a child to answer to her real name, Barastyna. She used to try to give her belongings away to other kids who she thought needed them more, and he'd call her *the Saint*, not without some bemusement.

John L's gray eyes shifted as he gathered his thoughts. Windscars carved deep ridges in his battle-hardened face. "You're here – it means you know. And I want to say before anything else – that I deserve your hate. We used you. We used all of you, with no regard for your lives, or your suffering. You weren't people to us, you were just data." His voice caught on the last word. She'd never seen him cry, but he looked close to it. "I'm not the person you think I am – there are things and people I could blame for what I've become, for what I've done, but I won't. All I need to say, all I want you to understand is this – you changed me, having you in my life made me *feel* when before I was just frozen. I didn't *want* to care for you, adopting you was just supposed to be a cover, but it just happened. I couldn't stop it." He touched his chest. "You became *my* child, *my* daughter – and I loved … I loved … Perhaps you'll remember me with nothing but hate …" He lowered his eyes, looking suddenly aged and tired. "But

I'm shutting down this program, and corrupting all the files. They'll kill me for it, but I'm not afraid to die. I only wish my death could take away what I did to you ... but nothing can. If anyone can survive this, you will. Never forget – you're a storm. You're —" John L cut his words short as the doors behind him opened and other people started to file in. Croy recognized Ezra Quartermaine and Van Pritchard, and another man she assumed was Rogan Kisslefish from his oversized mouth. They all had some kind of transparent mask over their noses and mouths, with tubes leading to tanks on their backs.

John watched them out of the corner of his eye and spoke very quietly.

"Everything you need is here – just remember what you used to call the third ship I flew on." He looked back to her. He opened his mouth, trying to say something, but couldn't form the words. He reached out and his image faltered and vanished.

"John!" Croy cried out and the word echoed around the empty chamber. She grabbed at a sharp ache in her chest, feeling crushed and suffocated. She gasped, forcing herself to get control, to focus on his words – *everything you need is here – just remember what you used to call the third ship I flew on*. The third Fleetship he'd served on was the *Talouse* – but when she was a child, first leaning to speak, she'd called it ...

"The Tooth," she said aloud.

From beside her feet a bench rose up from the ground with a small box resting on it. The box had light shining from inside it, beaming up in the shape of a book. Croy hesitated, then touched a finger to the light. The image opened like a real parchment book. She started reading the words, many of them not making any sense to her until she found a section on the project brief: to create human–Dray hybrids that could be controlled by Pritchard and the rest of them to block the Arequium Mors. She flicked again through images of experiments, of people they'd used and destroyed. The pictures were gruesome, but she already felt so numb and disconnected that she barely registered the horror until she found a long list of names. All the names were darkened except for a handful that were highlighted in green light. She read over the lit names – *Barastyna Croy, Kellor and Castor Quartermaine, Victoria Kilner, Darius DeCavisi.*

Seeing Darius there sent a wave of shock through her. She touched a finger to her partner's name and the pages flicked again to information about Darius. She skimmed it, feeling lightheaded and nauseous, really taking in only one part of the writing – the bit that spoke about them impregnating his mother with Dray DNA. After he was born, his father became suspicious, so they eliminated both his parents and made it look like a Dray attack in the mines. Their execution was carried out by John L. Tears trickled down her face and part of her wanted to reject it, deny it, ignore it, but she'd come too far to return to ignorance. Instead she flicked back to the list of names and pressed on her own.

She was, as Shah-Jahan had said, the first test subject. Her mother had caught John L stealing her from her bedroom and he had killed her and Croy's father. Their images flashed up and she leaned low over the pictures, crying into them, her tears falling through the light. She'd never seen her parents before, but recognized herself in their features. They were so young, their eyes bright with hope of what was to come.

At the end of the light page she saw the words *first test subject still showing the strongest signs of Dray integration, even compared to the half-breeds. She must never be permitted to leave the city and interact with Drays or they will sense her in their rete.*

All the failed attempts at becoming a Fleetsman suddenly made a lot of sense, but her anger was barely felt in the face of grief. Croy's eyes went back to her parents' images and she stared at them without blinking until a buzzing in her head rushed her back to clarity. She knew what it meant – the Arequium Mors had found her.

She grabbed hold of the white box and lifted it off the bench. At her touch, the light book folded back inside it. She pushed the cube into her kit pack, wrapping it in gauze. She only hoped it would survive the water.

She ran back into the vault chamber where she'd entered, then turned to face the glass doors as they closed. A light image of John L was standing in the laboratory watching her. He held up a hand. She turned away.

The waters started to gush back in around her and Croy gasped, trying to prepare herself to go back under. When the water level was over her head, she heard the vault opening up and the platform slid back out. She didn't know what to do, so she started kicking her legs and scrambling upward through the water as though she were climbing. She managed to fight her way to the top, overshooting the edge of the pier and surfacing beside the jetty almost halfway down. She started to drag herself out, then froze and slid back into the water. The Filter workers were standing on the end of the pier, staring down with entranced eyes. Her Firestorm and I-Sect lay at their feet. With fear driving strength through her body, she used the jetty to propel herself along through the water toward her dragger. When she was close, she climbed up the structure and out, making a run for it. Her ride roared to life with zero reluctance. The workers whipped around toward the sound and started to run at her, but she was in the air before they were even halfway there. She accelerated to full speed and burst out the top of the Filter, where the guards opened fire on her, their eyes also lost to the call of the Arequium Mors. She dodged their attack and sped away. She had all the evidence she needed, but who could she trust to take it to? There was only one person – Darius. She had no

I-Sect to call him, but with the Change of Shift siren blaring through the city, she knew where her partner would be – the Tower.

Chapter 35
Silho

OMAR MONTANYA

MOUNT SIRIA (THE CASTLE SCORN)

The first few steps had hurt the most, but from there her body had gathered strength with every step after. She didn't know the exact science of how long it should take a person to recover from so much blood loss – or if it was even possible to recover without a transfusion – all she knew was she felt sharply focused and strong, maybe even stronger than before, and she didn't question it, she just kept putting one foot in front of the other, until she saw the massive barred door looming up ahead of her. The sight spurred her on, and she ran toward it, her bare feet thudding on the smoothed rocks of the path. She reached the bars and suddenly felt a surge of apprehension. It wasn't a door to keep people out – even the biggest of the gargantuan-breeds could pass between the bars with ease. This door was built to keep something in – something huge beyond imagining.

The image of the firebird dragon, which had appeared on her back after they'd defeated the Skreaf, began to heat up. She didn't know if that was a warning to stay away or an encouragement to enter, but either way there was only one direction she could go. Silho climbed a row of stairs up to the bars and walked through, staring at the massive columns of metal as she passed them. As soon as she entered the cave tunnel beyond, she smelled something – a strange combination of hot metal, smoke and a horse stable. She gripped the Omarian knife tighter by her side and continued on. The further in she walked, the louder the sounds became, the snorting and grunting, the stomping, the rushes of what first sounded like water – and then like what it really was – fire.

Silho reached the end of the tunnel and stepped out with trepidation onto a tall walkway held up on long, precariously balanced rock pillars. The walkway cut through the center of an enormous cavern. Silho looked around and the sight rendered her speechless and amazed. On ledges and in caves all around the walls of the vast lair, firebird dragons sat and lay, ate and squabbled – snorting smoke and sparks and snapping enormous jaws. Dragons had been long extinct on Aquais, but there must have been hundreds of them here. And she only needed one – one she could climb onto and fly up through the center of the castle and out into the open air. It had seemed like a good plan when she had first found the dragons through the walls while looking for an escape route, but now it seemed more like insanity. How was she going to get onto a dragon's back without it incinerating her?

Taking in a deep breath, Silho stepped further out onto the walkway. It was crumbling at the edges, with some parts of the path completely collapsed in, leaving a view down to the lava river – so far below it looked like just the thinnest of red lines. As she walked, Silho kept looking around to see if any of the firebirds' glowing yellow eyes were turning her way, but they didn't seem to even notice her. They all had shimmering green scales just like her bloodline marks, with huge spines on their backs and spikes around their heads. It felt like she was walking in a dream. She was staring so much, and not concentrating on the pathway, that she didn't see the section ahead that fallen away. She stepped right into it and fell through. On impulse she immediately dropped the Omarian knife and grappled at the loose rock, trying to find a handhold to cling to. She managed to grasp the edge, but it fell away and she found herself grasping at air. A hand shot down and seized her wrist and her first thought was *Copernicus*, but another man's face appeared above her.

"Got you." Lecivion said, triumph in the words.

He startled her so much that she automatically blinked into light-form and actually managed to draw some strength from the burning fortress of his body-lights, when before she'd thought it impossible. Surprise registered in his stare. Silho used the strength she'd taken from him to reach up and grab his arm with her other hand and swing her body hard, trying to use her weight to drag him down as well. He had to let her go to stop himself tumbling over the edge, and as he did, she released him too, managing to grab onto the side of one of the pillars beneath the walkway. Lecivion's furious face appeared, looking under at her from where he was lying on the path above. He reached out, trying to get hold of her arm. She tightened her grip on the pillar, but could feel the rock loosening under her fingers. It wasn't going to hold for very long.

"Come here!" Lecivion growled, taking another swipe at her. She could hear the boots of more Omarian soldiers running along the walkway, sending pebbles and rocks scattering down into the abyss below. A crack appeared in the pillar where she clung.

Silho desperately searched around her, looking for something else to grab. There was nothing within reach, except Lecivion's waving hand. Then she spotted something below them – a firebird sitting on a ledge that was jutting out from the cavern wall. It wasn't directly beneath her, but if she managed to kick off from the pillar hard enough, there was a chance she could propel herself across to it as she fell. But it was going to take some serious power, more than she naturally had in her legs. She looked again at Lecivion, who was still stretching out trying to reach her, his burning fingertips brushing against her hair. She swiched to light-form. He sensed it and yelled, "Don't you dare!"

She managed to draw again from his lights before being forced to look away, her eyes searing. She used her enhanced strength to hurl herself backward off the pillar and toward the firebird ledge below. The air rushed around her and her stomach twisted. She thought she wasn't going to make it and started kicking, trying to propel herself further, but she ended up overshooting and landing on the dragon's back. She started to slide down the scorching hot scales, but grasped onto one of the creature's back spines and dragged herself up between two of them to balance. The firebird gave a grunt and Silho was shunted left to right as the dragon stood and turned around to look right at her – its face directly in front of hers. The depth and beauty of its ancient eyes mesmerized her. The dragon sniffed at her, then raised its head, looking longingly toward the sky. As it did, Silho noticed the huge chain and lock around its neck, keeping it prisoner here in the cavern. Sounds drew her attention to above them, where Lecivion and his soldiers were running down steps cut into the side of the cavern, rushing toward her.

"Listen. I want to free you," Silho said to the firebird in Urigin, hoping by some chance it might comprehend. "Will you help me?"

The dragon snorted steam and something about its stare told Silho it understood. It turned its face away from her, as though readying itself, and Silho saw a partially broken spike on its head. She stood up on the creature's back and ran across it to the spike. With some effort, Silho managed to twist it around and break it off completely. Cautiously, she sat on the creature's neck and slid down to stand on the chain beside the lock at the firebird's throat. It felt like standing directly in front of a furnace. Silho crouched down and pushed the spike into the lock. Eli had been teaching her lock-picking. His skill made it look ridiculously easy, but that was far from the case. He'd taught her that success depended on setting up the tool properly before beginning to lever it. She tried to remember exactly what he'd said about the alignment and angle, but it was difficult to think around the pounding of her heart. Lecivion was getting closer and closer. Silho held her breath and twisted the spike; at first nothing happened, so she pressed harder and slightly upward and heard a click. The firebird heard it too, its body jolting. Silho dropped the spike and scrambled back up the dragon's neck. It pulled back against the chain and the open lock fell away. The dragon gave a deep snort that sounded like excitement and moved to the edge. Lecivion, on the stair just above them, saw what was happening.

"Stop!" he commanded. "Oren!"

Silho looked back at him and heard her mother's voice in her head, *Don't be me.*

"I'm not Oren," she shouted, then gripped tightly to the firebird's head spikes and said, "Go!"

The magnificent creature spread its wings and leaped off the edge, soaring upward. Silho heard a thud behind her and glanced around to see that Lecivion had jumped onto the dragon's back and was now climbing toward her, a look of manic determination on his face. She was facing him, so didn't see the top of the cavern approaching fast. The fire-bird struck it, the gap leading out, slightly too narrow for the creature's body. Silho was struck by a boulder and lost her grip as the dragon broke free. She tumbled off its back and fell to a flat roof terrace at the top of the castle. She landed badly and when she moved, felt a sharp pain in her chest – maybe broken ribs.

Silho held an arm across herself and struggled to sit up, glimpsing the turrets and towers of the castle, the lava gushing down its walls and the scorched plains stretching to the volcanic mountains on all sides. A violent wind blew ash and sparks everywhere. Lecivion landed on his feet on the other side of the rooftop and started moving toward her. Silho fought through her pain and stood, facing him. His steps hesitated, then stopped. His mouth twisted into a humorless smile and he said derisively, "What are you going to do, Silho Brabel? What's your plan?"

As he lifted his hand to trap her in light-form, Silho spotted the Solace in his belt and said, trying to delay him, "Wait! You called me Oren back there …"

"Yes," Lecivion said flatly. "Slip of the tongue. You look like her and I don't mean that as a compliment."

"You said she was a Draigar," Silho said to keep him talking. "I want to know what that is."

"It's of no consequence," he replied.

"Are you afraid to talk about her," Silho baited him. "Is it still too painful? I feel sorry for you – to be broken by love like that."

Lecivion snorted, the flames burning in his eyes. "Draigars are a race of people who live in the farnorthern lands of the world Hydria – or at least they did until I killed them all …"

"Why did you kill them?" Silho asked.

"We saved them from the ratha demons and your mother was payment rendered. When she left, I let the rathas back in to finish the job they'd started."

"So it was revenge?" Silho said.

"Her family was very important to her. I can imagine it would have caused significant distress to hear of their fate, especially since all she ever dreamed of was to go home ..." The memory of it made him smile.

"You wiped out an entire world just because some girl didn't want to be with you anymore?" Silho said, unable to keep the revulsion out of her voice.

"Not the whole world – just half of it," Lecivion replied, unaffected by her hate. "The North of Hydria still stands after the four barbarian kings, Apollo of Corinthia, Kleomedes IV of Thesolon, Sphairos of Armen and Sirion of Anacharasis made an unwitting pact with the ratha demon king, Mordan-Grieg, which resulted in the sparing of the North."

It seemed to Silho as though Lecivion was enjoying the sound of his voice as he recounted the history of this world Hydria, which he had all but destroyed. It gave her time to back up to the ledge of the rooftop and cast a quick glance over. There was another flat terrace a short fall below. She couldn't jump it and survive, but she could skid down the slanted wall.

"I wouldn't if I were you," Lecivion said. He raised his hand and Silho leaped up onto the ledge and jumped. She landed on the tilted roof and started skidding and tumbling down to the terrace below. She slammed down onto the rock and staggered up to her feet as Lecivion landed right behind her. She spun around, backing away. His eyes stayed locked onto hers.

A deafening screech ripped through the air and they both ducked low as several gigantic forms swooped across just above them. Silho stared up into the ash-hazy red sky and saw her dragon under attack by several larger firebirds. She felt a horrible pang watching it fight for its life.

"That's the way of nature – survival of the fittest. Beautiful, isn't it," Lecivion said.

"It's horrendous and so are you. Do you ever think if you hadn't been so jealous and possessive, if you'd let Oren visit her home, then maybe she wouldn't have left you?"

Lecivion momentarily froze, but then he recovered and said, "I told you that you hadn't taken anything from your father, but I was mistaken – you've got his big mouth – Englan Chrisholm, diplomat to Hydria … The smartest fool I've ever known. Instead of turning her over, he let her convince him to defy me – why? Because he cared for his baby." Lecivion said the words as though the very idea was pathetic.

The firebirds swooped over them again and Silho saw her dragon breathe fire at the other three, forcing them to back off. Lecivion saw her watching and said, "It's an interesting thing that only the females can spit flames. Just like women and their words."

He was trying to be scathing, but the information triggered a thought in her. Omarians could only breathe fire after they'd completely drained someone's life-force – but if the female dragons could do it all the time – maybe she could as well. It was from the firebird bloodline that all their skills were de- rived. She pictured herself exhaling fire and felt the dragon image on her back heating up and a pressure swelling in her chest. A lightheaded hope swept through her.

"Enough talk," Lecivion growled. "Time for surrender … or pain."

"Pain, then!" Silho shouted.

She lunged forward and expelled a blast of blue fire right into his face and at the same time grabbed the Solace from his belt and slashed out toward his neck. He managed to turn away, but it nicked his neck. Silho spun back to the ledge and jumped up – there was a third terrace below. She jumped off and skidded toward it, clutching Solace and hearing Lecivion crashing down right behind her.

Chapter 36
Diega

MURKMIRE SLOUGH (ETI RIVER)

Diega panted heavily, staring up at the giant blood-sucking needles stabbing through the mud searching for them, but they were too far down to be touched. Gooey algae gunge held the mud walls of the tunnel together. Globules slopped down on their heads like congealed rain. It looked extremely unstable. Beside her, Shawe was supporting Copernicus. His condition had worsened again. His eyes were horribly sunken and his clothing hung off his wasted body. He wasn't moving at all. Diega touched his chest, feeling his ribs stretching the skin. His heart was still beating, but barely.

Dizzy specks of light danced before Diega's eyes. Caesar was staring at her back with a grim expression. She reached behind her and touched the three large stab wounds from the leech's fangs. The skin felt numb.

"She's as white as a Midnight Man," Caesar said to Shawe, talking over her.

"I'm fine," she said, but knew she'd lost too much blood, and with this mud the wounds would be infected in seconds. She'd used all the coagulator and antiseptic off her belt, so she took Copernicus' supply from his and squirted it over her shoulder. There weren't any bandages left in either belt, so Shawe ripped off the tattered remains of his shirt and tied it roughly around the wound. She tried to object, but he shut her down.

"I know you want full access to my body anyway," he told her.

"I can't think of anything in this universe I want less than your body," she returned.

"All lies," Shawe muttered as he fastened the last knot.

At a gurgling sound beside them they turned to see the Vidris Slimer crouching nearby, staring at them with mud-brown eyes, half-hidden under smooth, green hair. His skin was transparent, showing a network of white veins transporting algae around his body.

"Grateful." The Slimer spoke in a gurgled dialect of Urigin. "So grateful."

"Good," Shawe said. "Then take us to the Eti River and whatever the trutt weed we need to cure this guy here." He gestured to Copernicus. "He's been stabbed by an Omarian."

The Slimer scratched his head for a moment then replied, "The Envader Algac is a very strong medicine. It can be used to cure flesh-rotting diseases – maybe also poison-sickness."

"Where is it?" Diega asked. "Where can we find it?"

"The Envader grows at the place where the Morak Flow becomes the Eti River."

"Then take us there now," Caesar commanded. "You owe us life."

"I can't," the Slimer replied. "Not me. It is far, far away."

Diega clenched her fists, the nails biting into her palms, but the Slimer continued before she had time to lose herself, "Me, I cannot take you by myself, but I know someone who will help."

He cupped his hands and sent out a gurgled cry that echoed through the mud tunnel, far into the distance. After a second, the ground beneath them began to tremble, then shake, and they heard a sound like a subterranean train roaring toward them. Diega looked up to see a huge white creature bearing down on them, taking up the whole tunnel. She braced herself for the impact, but the creature came to a sudden stop right in front of them. It lifted a blind worm head and sniffed.

"What is that?" Diega asked the Slimer, staring with caution at the unfortunately phallic-looking creature.

"Caecilian speed worm," the Slimer said.

"That looks exactly like —" Shawe started.

"We know what it looks exactly like," Diega cut over him.

"Of course *you* do. It's not as big as mine, though," Shawe said with a smirk.

Caesar gave a deep sigh of disgust, then he and Shawe hoisted Copernicus into their arms.

"Follow. This way," the Slimer beckoned them. He patted the speed worm on its nose and climbed up onto its head. The gangsters followed him up, with Diega behind them. They copied the Slimer's movements and found themselves lying face-up on the worm's back, its cool, soft skin creating a protective half-cocoon around them. Diega could feel the worm's body gurgling under her.

The Slimer called a *coo-ee* and the speed worm reared back and took off. Diega scrunched her eyes shut and gritted her teeth as the tunnel whirred above them at a sickening speed. Over her lifetime she'd flown at some extreme speeds, but nothing came close to this. She felt like she was going to pass out. Finally the creature came to an abrupt halt and the Slimer sat up, pushing through the tunnel roof, opening a trapdoor for them to see out.

"Look there." He pointed. "Over there is where the Morak meets the Eti. In the border waters you will find the algae you seek. It is the color of mud with blue and pink spots and it is very fast, so you must move quickly."

Diega nodded her thanks and stood up with difficulty on the speed worm's balloon-like body. She scrambled through the trapdoor and the others followed, struggling to maneuver Copernicus out together. The sky above had darkened even more. The trapdoor sealed over below them and they felt a momentary rumble as the worm took off. Then it was gone and they stood alone, staring at the Eti. It was a wide, muddy river, its surface a garden of aquatic flowers, moss and algae. Reeds grew thickly along its banks.

"We need to get closer to the water," Diega said, and two gangsters hoisted Copernicus up, bits of his skin sliding off in their hands. All his teeth and hair had fallen out. He looked nothing like himself and was sinking further as they watched. Out of the three of them, Caesar was the least injured, but he eyed the water with distrust.

"Kitty can't swim, so I'll go find it," Shawe said and started lowering Copernicus.

"No, I'll go, just keep him breathing," Diega said. She couldn't deal with standing there and waiting.

She trudged fast to the river's edge and pushed through the reeds, scanning the murky waters for brown algae, but it was a swamp and everything was trutting brown. Desperation kept both her fatigue and fear at bay and she swam further out, dragging herself through the clogged plant life. Her heart, thudding like strikes of a hammer, skipped suddenly as she spotted a speckled brown plant. It was lolling on the edge of a lily pad, half in and half out of the water. Diega slowed her gasping breaths, forcing herself to calm. She sank low in the water and stalked silently toward it. When she was close enough, she lunged, just managing to grab one end of the algae clot as it tried to escape. It emitted a high-pitched squeal, struggling violently, trying to ooze through her fingers. Diega kept a tight grip on it and started back to the bank.

She made it almost to the water's edge, then a whisper drew her attention back to the river. Something was moving out near the center. It was a ripple in the air, a gliding transparent form. The more Diega stared at it, the more it looked like her little sister. *Impossible*. Diega shook her head, trying to clear her thoughts. The form twirled closer, with mesmerizing movements. Something cold and wet wrapped around Diega's neck. It yanked her forward out of the shallows and into the deep water. She heard Shawe yell as it dragged her beneath the surface, further and further down.

Diega fought as she sank, but she couldn't see anything actually holding her, just felt the grip tightening the more she struggled. Finally she came to a stop, her foot clipping something. She stared down through the murk, and gave a gurgling yell. Her foot had touched the head of a corpse. Lining the bottom of the river were thousands of bloated, half-eaten bodies. Some stared with dead eyes, the hands of others brushed slimy fingers against her. It was an underwater graveyard, a garden of the dead, tied to the bottom of the river, swaying silently in the current, like strands of decaying seaweed.

Diega almost lost her grip on the Envader Algae, but squeezed her hand closed just in time. Tiring fast, she stopped kicking just for a moment to gather her strength. As she did, the grip on her body released. A thought came to her. She cupped her hands around the algae to hide its struggling, then relaxed all her muscles. Immediately she was freed and started to float upward. A mat of lily pads prevented her from breaking through the surface, so she had to kick and use one hand to drag herself up. She gasped in air, but then the cold grasp seized her ankle and hauled her back under. It happened again, then a third and fourth time. Diega gagged, unable to get any air, drowning so close to the surface. Then, through the thrashing of her struggles, she saw a dark form approaching rapidly, until it was right in front of her – a monstrous crocodilian face. The predator, enormous beyond belief, struck, snapping massive jaws an inch from Diega's face. She thought somehow it had missed her, then a creature became visible, trapped in the mouth of the monster crocodile. The natural form of the shape-shifter who had attacked her was a gangling goblin creature. Its arms flailed for a second and then the monster crocodile sank back down into the swamp. Diega burst up into the air, nearby to Shawe, who was scouring the waters for her. He lunged at her.

"I've found it," she gasped and retched as he dragged her back through the reeds. Caesar helped them scramble up the slippery mud bank. She dropped down beside Copernicus and held the squirming algae above his face. He looked a thousand year-cycles old. *Not him, not him ...*

"What do we do with it?" she panted, struggling to catch her breath.

The plant had stopped wriggling and was now hanging limp and silent. Diega loosened her grip slightly. As she did, the algae slipped out onto Copernicus' face, and in an instant spread to form a cocoon all around him. Diega and Shawe fought to drag the sludge out of his mouth and nose but they clogged back up straight away. His body started to convulse and Diega felt choked with terror. She'd grabbed the wrong plant, and it was strangling the last gasps of life out of him.

The air shivered around them, and a blinding square of light flared from nowhere. Forms leaped from the light and landed in the mud all around them. *Omarians.* Caesar reacted first, slashing up with his claws and opening one of the fire-wielders' necks. Boiling blood sprayed over Diega and Shawe and over the algae cocoon trapping Copernicus. Before they could move again, the Omarians caught them all in light-form and started draining their strength.

They fell to their knees, and Diega watched in mute horror as the algae cocoon suddenly shot past the Omarians, right to the river's edge. Before they could blink, it was gone. He was gone. Copernicus Kane. *Gone* ...

Chapter 37

Eli

AQUAIS

SCORPIA (LANORIA)

Ismail dragged Eli up onto a ledge, one hand pressed over his mouth. Eli grabbed for his night-vision specs and shoved them onto his face. He saw Ismail, his eyes shining red. He was pointing downward to the bottom of the well below them. There the most monstrous viper Eli had ever imagined to see lay coiled around itself, sleeping soundly. It was the width of a large mass-mover craft and the height, Eli estimated, of a building. Not a hut, either – more like a tower. This thing could accidently swallow him whole and never feel him going down. Eli had never been afraid of snakes before, he'd always been fascinated by reptiles of all kinds, but he thought he felt a snake phobia now brewing inside him, threatening to manifest into hysterical laughter. The only thing that stopped him was the sight of the viper's diamond pattern. It reminded him of the commander's bloodline marks and brought him to sharp control as he focused on why they were there.

Eli felt Ismail taking the Morsus Ictus out of his grasp and he blinked to access the navigation map through his front-core. Their current location was not far from the x-point of the portal on the map. Eli pointed upward and Ismail nodded. They started to climb the wall, which was slimy with black gunk oozing out of every crack. Their progress was agonizingly slow, but finally they made it to a ledge above, where they found a hole just big enough to squeeze through. The navigation indicated for them to take it. Eli's rational mind rejected the idea, but it was the fastest path to the portal and, in reality, they'd abandoned rationality a long while back. Ismail crawled through first and Eli followed, the pair of them squirming through the suffocatingly small tunnel until Ismail suddenly stopped, slumped down to his stomach, gasping, "She can see me!"

"The snake?" Eli whispered, panic rising to his throat.

"No," Ismail managed through gritted teeth and Eli realized he meant the witch. His panic doubled. He didn't have his electrifier or any of his weapons. His hand found a rock and he grasped onto it, expecting to feel claws against his throat any moment.

"Block her out! Your mind is so strong," he said to Ismail. "Fight her to the end!"

He placed a hand on Ismail's back so he knew he wasn't alone, and pushed thoughts of Ev'r to the front of his mind so that the scullion would see them.

After a few moments, Ismail's shaking lessened and he managed to lift up to his hands and knees. When he spoke his voice was back to military.

"Proceed on objective: obtaining the portal."

He started to move again and Eli followed, relieved Ismail was up and also terrified that anything could be stalking them through the tunnel darkness. He would never have imagined that terror and relief could occur simultaneously, but somehow his brain was managing it. They passed through onto a narrow bridge that led over another well where something foul-smelling scuttled around in the dark. This place reminded him of the walks he used to take with his gran'pa down the Wintress River boardwalk. He used to peer into all the concrete blocks they passed. The blocks had small holes where creatures – frogs and crabs, spiders and other random, leggy things – would hide, except now he felt like an insect trapped down inside the blocks with all the creepy-crawlies hunting him.

They went through another tunnel and came out onto a third ledge. Eli's navigation beeped in his ear – they were almost at the spot.

Ismail nudged him and pointed down. Some distance below them, large wrapped cocoons hung in various places around a net-like lair. Eli saw some of the cocoons were squirming and it gave him a sickening feeling of being shrunken in significance, shunted down the food chain. Beyond the cocoons, a towering pile of treasures had been hoarded on a platform. According to the navigation, the painting was there.

The walls of the well trembled, and a croaking-growling sound echoed from beneath them. Ismail and Eli hunched lower as a set of meaty, multi-jointed arms and legs pushed out from a hole in the wall, dragging through a bulbous sack body. At first Eli thought the creature was an arachnid, but then it stood up on two of its limbs and climbed along the lines of its net lair, carrying the bulk of its weight at the front. Wriggling things seemed to be constantly hatching out of its stretched skin and it used a clawed hand to rake them off and stuff them into its mouth. Black mucus dribbled down its chin. He'd never seen a predator like it, not even in his nightmares. The crimson glow of its eyes fell on the closest co-coon and it scuttled forward and ripped it open. Eli flinched at the piercing scream that exploded into the silence, cut off to a gurgle. The creature fed with a noisy guzzling and crunch-ing of bones.

"I'll draw it away. You retrieve the portal and evacuate," Ismail whispered to Eli.

"No, it's too dangerous. It'll catch you," Eli murmured back. "We'll wait for it to leave again."

"There's no time for that," Ismail insisted. "I can out-move it."

"I'm not leaving here without you," Eli said, looking the scullion in the eye.

Ismail clenched his jaw with frustration. "Just focus on the mission – get the portal and keep running. I'll find you. I can hear your thoughts."

Ismail climbed further up the well to a higher ledge. He glanced down at Eli, who tensed, readying himself, then the scullion stood and Eli's stomach sunk to his toes.

"Hey!" Ismail shouted.

The monster spun around, head first and then body, and its eyes fell like spotlights on Ismail. It opened a mouth with many rows of razor teeth and released a scream that soun-ded like a cyclone blasting through the well. Ismail turned and darted through a hole in the wall. The creature bounded up after him, passing within inches of Eli, who shrank back with his arms over his head. It vanished, and Eli didn't let a second pass. He whirred his wings and flew over the net lair to the platform behind the cocoons. He ran to the treasure stash and climbed into it, flinging handfuls of gold and jewels aside searching for the painting. His hands closed over something wooden and he dragged out a frame. He stared at the picture inside it and his heart leaped – tiny pictures making up a whole – Englan Chrisholm's style. Grasping the frame against him, he ran to the edge of the platform and started to fly off, but then he doubled back. He couldn't leave people trapped in these cocoons. Using a gold-handled blade he found in the stash, he cut open the first squirming cocoon. Unfortunately the creature inside was a monstrous mutant, who instantly tried to strangle him – his act of kindness backfiring in a major way.

A terrible scream from above distracted the mutant – Eli looked up to see the monster had returned and its gleaming red eyes were set on him. He let out a shriek of hysterical laughter and beat his wings frantically, ripping out of the mutant's grasp and crashing over to the ledge on the wall. He scuttled into the first hole he saw. It was extremely cramped and he had to drag himself along, pushing the frame in front of him. He felt the ground shaking and looked back to see the creatures eye-lights beaming in at him. Eli felt sure that something that big couldn't follow him in there, but then he cursed as it started to compact its disjointed body and squeeze itself inside. The small space did, however, drastically reduce its speed and Eli managed to keep ahead of it. Then the tunnel started to widen out, until he could run hunched over and then straighten up, clutching the frame to his chest. The deft creature began to gain as Eli barged through the darkness, smashing through thick webs and stumbling over fallen rocks and hoarded bones. He felt it closing in fast, and a thought came to him – was it better to keep running and get attacked from the back or turn and land the first blow? He skidded to a stop and swung around.

Strangely, the monster had already stopped some way behind him and stood there rocking backward and forward on its haunches as though it wanted to come after him, but something was preventing it. It gave a sudden shriek and tried to go back the way they'd come, but then changed its mind and charged at him instead. Eli gasped, stabbing at it with the gold-handled blade that he'd taken with him, but the monster completely bypassed him and kept going. Eli realized then that it was frightened, and that whatever this creature – the most terrifying creature he'd ever seen – was afraid of was now chasing him too.

He took off after the monster, hearing a sound start up in the air behind them – a frenzied, high-pitched squealing, mixed with a chattering and a whirr of so many wings that it sounded like a stampede of hooves. It echoed everywhere, making it impossible to know where it was coming from. They came to a split in the tunnel where it veered off into two. The monster hesitated and lunged one way, then it released a horrendous, blood-curdling scream. Eli lunged away from it and saw a swarm of glowing bugs with pixie faces, large bulging eyes, sharp fangs and scorpion tails engulfing the creature. Eli had seen pictures of them before. They were Hiltees – piranha pixie-breeds. They reduced the monster to dust in seconds.

Eli didn't wait for them to start on him. He took off sprinting, crashing through the other tunnel, hearing them flying right behind him. He stared at the navigation in front of his eyes and saw the end of the tunnel was coming up fast. He didn't slow, barging out of the tunnel and into a much wider corridor, similar to where he had first landed. Eli spotted a large stone statue standing nearby and, using all his adrenalin-enhanced strength, knocked it over and dragged it across to block the hole he'd come through. Moments later, he heard the Hiltees hit it and start drilling.

"Imp-breed!"

He turned and saw Ismail hunched at the end of the corridor. He snatched up the portal and raced toward the scullion, whose leg was badly ripped up and gushing blood.

"Hiltees. They're coming," Eli gasped.

"Leave me! Get to the elevator!" Ismail shouted.

"No!" He grabbed hold of Ismail and forced the scullion to move. Together they staggered in the direction of the elevator, following the route Diamond had mapped out for them.

Finally they saw the elevator up ahead. The rusted doors were hanging open. Eli could have literally screamed with joy, except that he was terrified it would bring some kind of horrendous mutant smashing up out of the ground to stop them. The gnashing whirr of the Hiltees echoed close behind them. They raced forward and crashed into the elevator. Eli threw open the control panel and connected it to his external computer system. He started typing override codes, reconnecting the elevator to Scorpia's power core. When nothing seemed to be working, a terrible thought occurred to him – maybe an ebomb had already taken out the power core. The swarm of Hiltees appeared at the end of the corridor ahead of them.

"Get us moving, soldier!" Ismail yelled.

Eli's hands flew over the keypad as he hit it with everything he had. He almost passed out with relief when the lights of the elevator flickered on and the doors screeched shut. *Now to get it moving.* The Hiltees hit the elevator hard, rattling it violently as they started to eat their way through. Ismail slammed his boot against a hole as it opened up. He yelled, the ferocious little creatures biting through into his foot. Eli smashed in the last code and the elevator gave a shake and a shudder, then started moving. At first it crawled, then gathered momentum, and soon they were rocketing out of control. Before Eli could even muster a scream, the elevator collided with a ceiling and the doors blasted open.

Chapter 38
Croy

KULLRA FORNAX

NŸR-CORUM (THE TOWER)

The Tower, once a mundane workplace full of scuffed hallways and stuffy air, had become a nightmare of stalking shadows and lurking threat. Croy moved through the corridors as quickly as she could, dreading that the Arequium Mors had followed her and were about to turn the whole damn place against her. She feigned her limp so as to not rouse suspicion and kept her head down, cutting a straight line for the training rooms. Darius often hung out in there before a shift, working out with his teammates and other Controllers who liked to lift weights. She glanced around the training room door, trying to remain unseen – he wasn't there.

Next she checked the mess hall, the dragger maintenance bays and the locker rooms – all without success. Panic started to rise inside her. Her throat felt too tight to breathe. Where was he? She was too afraid to stop to ask anyone, or to go and get a replacement I-Sect, in case it attracted attention. Her drive to find Darius so they could release the evidence and salvage the city was fast being replaced by a desperation just to find him so she knew he was alright. Screw the rest of the city. If something had happened to Darius, she didn't want to go on living.

With every muscle in her body shaking with tension, she headed for the administrative offices. Darry had told her they would be assigned new areas on their next shift, which was now, so perhaps he was there, picking up their orders. She reached the reception area and was walking toward the front desk when a voice spoke in her mind. It was faint and she couldn't decipher the words, but it drew her attention to the corridor behind reception. She knew where that led – VP's office. Going anywhere near him at this time felt like the worst of all terrible ideas, but the voice whispered again and she felt a fearsome tide drawing her in. She thought it must be Darius. What if VP had realized she'd taken the information and had trapped her partner to destroy the evidence?

Croy let her body lead her, ignoring her mind full of John L's words and warnings. Her whole life had been built on and driven by what he'd said, what he'd done – all poison and lies. She moved through the shadows to VP's office door and leaned in close, listening through the keyhole for Darry's voice, but instead of her partner speaking, she heard VP and then Castor Quartermaine – it sounded like he was sobbing.

Croy clutched for her Firestorm, but it was gone. She only had her knife now. She drew it and crouched down, trying to decide what to do – leave them and run, or go in and fight. She had to get to Darius and this would only slow her down or worse. The decision was abruptly taken out of her hands as the door flew open. Croy stood and VP's assistant, who was on his way out, baulked at the sight of her.

"Controller Croy!" he gasped. He was a groveling lick-spittle whose name was Martin or Kevin or something like that – she could never remember. She held the knife behind her back and nodded to him as he informed VP of her presence. Then he moved around her and continued down the hallway, casting back a questioning look.

"Croy," VP's voice called her into the room.

She braced herself and stepped from the shadows into the light. Her eyes mapped out the situation – VP standing, with his other assistant, over Castor kneeling in front of them. Kellor lay slumped in one corner, unconscious, blood trickling from the corner of her mouth. As Croy's gaze swept over the girl she heard the voice again, Kellor's voice, calling for her help. She and the twins were connected by the Dray *rete*, through the implants in their bodies.

Croy's eyes went to VP and she saw him for what he really was – not an intimidating boss, but a soulless psychopath, someone who could run experiments on people with no mercy or remorse, as though they were nothing more than breathing bags of meat. He'd killed John L out of revenge because he'd shut down their experiment and ruined the data. And when Ezra Quartermaine had tried to come clean for whatever reason he had, which Croy suspected could have only been selfishly motivated, VP had tried to kill him as well.

VP must have seen something in her eyes, because his hand hesitated and twitched toward his gun, a Hooster 5. Castor looked over at her, his hands chained behind his back and his face badly bruised, bleeding and tearstained.

"Help her," he whispered, his desperate eyes going to his sister.

"Shut up!" VP's assistant shouted and booted Castor in the chest. The boy crashed over sideways. Croy felt Castor's pain radiating through her own body. Its heat ran into cold fury. She saw her next few steps playing out before her eyes.

"I'm sorry, sir," she said to VP. "I've been given classified information to pass on to you."

VP narrowed his sharp stare, and Croy wondered if he could see through to her intentions.

He nodded to his assistant and said, "Stay here," then gestured to Croy. "Come with me."

They stepped outside the door into the shadows and he said in a lowered voice, "What is it, Croy?"

"They've found something at the bottom of the Filter," she whispered back.

Emotion flickered through VP's eyes, then died out cold.

"What did they find?"

"A facility," she said, watching his face.

He shook his head, playing ignorant extremely well. "What kind of facility?"

"The one where you tortured and killed all those children." She let the truth speak and as VP's eyes stretched wide she stabbed the knife into his chest, shoving it deep into his heart. He gasped, and despite all his wealth, all his power, his purple cloak and his calculating mind, he was dead in seconds – as dead as the fox he wore around his neck with such pride. Croy wrenched out her blade and let him crash to the ground. Then she had a second thought. She grabbed his Hooster and dragged off his purple cloak. She was going for his I-Sect when the door opened and his assistant looked out. His mouth gaped open. He went for his gun and Croy shot him point blank in the face. His head exploded and body dropped. The blast resounded around the corridor and she knew it would bring people running. She lunged into VP's office and dragged Castor up to his feet.

"My sister," he sobbed. "You have to help her. They've hurt her. I couldn't stop them."

Croy picked open the shackles around his wrists.

"Carry her," she said, gesturing to Kellor. "We need to get out of here fast – do you understand?"

Castor managed to compose himself and nodded. He grabbed his sister up and held her close and Croy threw VP's purple cloak over them.

"Keep your head down," she instructed and guided him out the door, stepping over the bodies of VP and the assistant. They made it to end of the corridor and took a right as people were appearing out of the administrative offices and peering around, all looking to each other for what to do next. *Herd animals*, John L had called them. Croy pushed the words and the speaker out of her mind.

She and Castor moved fast, almost clearing the administrative section of the Tower before a voice called out behind them.

"Croy!"

Croy's skin chilled. She glanced over her shoulder but didn't slow. It was Angeline. Croy turned away and stepped up the pace, but Roth's girlfriend ran after them, chasing them until she caught up. She grabbed hold of Croy's arm.

"I'm sorry," Angeline puffed. "I've been trying to find you. I have to tell you something. I didn't know who else to trust." She glanced at Castor, who was wisely keeping his face in the shadows and the purple cloak drawn firmly around them.

"I'm in the middle of an official escort," Croy told her.

"I know. I'm sorry," Angeline repeated. "It's just ..." Tears spilled from her eyes. "Roth was acting strange this morning. I saw him ..." She bit her quivering lip.

"What?" Croy prompted, her heart beating faster.

"I saw him push our neighbor over a railing. I think he ... killed him." Angeline stared at Croy with wide, terrified eyes, half in shock at what she was saying. "And his face ... he didn't look – like him. I was afraid. I hid."

Pain tightened all over Croy's body. The Mors influence was taking hold – and Roth had fallen to it. A moment of grief was all she could spare for the man she thought her heart had broken over.

"Listen to me," Croy said to Angeline. "Something is happening in the city. Get to a ship and get out through the gates. Trust me. Get out while you can." She turned and grabbed hold of Castor's arm, directing him away. She didn't hear Angeline following and didn't look back.

They reached the Tower parking point and Croy scanned it for Darius' dragger, but it wasn't anywhere in sight. There were other places he could have parked, though something inside her was now saying he wasn't there. She didn't know whether to trust that feeling or not, but they couldn't stay at the Tower any longer. The whole city was about to go up.

Croy ran to her dragger with Castor at her heels. She crouched down to access the engine of the ride beside her, boosting the ignition, bringing it to life.

"Fly fast. Stay right behind me," she told the kid. He nodded, climbing on and draping his sister over his knees.

"Stop!" a voice yelled behind them and Croy heard the click of a Lockwood Hand being armed. She knew whose gun of choice that was. She turned to face Knightsbridge and Newton, with Kisslefish standing beside, but apart from them. The trainee's expression was tortured with utter dismay, but Knightsbridge looked smug and Newton as cold as ever.

"I knew you were rotten scum, Croy – 'the Saint', my arse!" Knightsbridge mocked her. "Absconding with prisoners, impersonating a Purple Wing, stealing a dragger. They'll take your badge for this. Get off. Get on your knees."

Before Croy could respond at all, Kisslefish raised a metal bar he'd been holding behind his back and slammed it into Knightsbridge's head. The big Controller roared. Croy leaped off her dragger and rushed him. She grabbed him by the collar and pressed the pressure point in his neck, knocking him out. Newton seized her from behind, lifting her up, and Kisslefish smashed the metal bar over him as well, again and again with raw fury, until he dropped Croy. Newton grabbed the trainee by the throat and headbutted him savagely. Croy kicked Newton's legs out from under him, slamming a hand into his neck as he toppled, cutting his senses. Kisslefish tumbled over on top of him but scrambled up immediately, blood gushing from his nose. He grabbed the metal bar and raised it above his head, trying to smash it down on Newton's face. Croy intercepted and the trainee fought her.

"I hate him," he yelled over and over until the words dissolved into sobs and he sunk to his knees. Croy held his shoulder as he cried, his arms clutched around himself.

"You need to get out of here, kid," Croy told him. "The city is falling."

He looked up at Croy with bloodshot eyes and she saw he believed her without question. He whispered, "Please, wherever you're going, take me too."

Croy started to shake her head, but Kisslefish grabbed her arm and yelled, "Please!" He started sobbing again. "Please – please – please! My father will kill me."

Croy didn't know if Kisslefish knew anything about what his father had done, but she could see he was terrified.

"Get up. We're flying out of here," she said.

Kisslefish uttered a shaky thankyou. He scrambled up and they ran toward Castor, still sitting astride the dragger. He looked Kisslefish over with suspicion and dislike, as Croy jumped onto her own machine and gestured for Kisslefish to get on behind her.

She revved up the engine and felt Kisslefish grab her waist as she released the dragger, soaring into the air beside the tower. In the chaos of her mind the question kept repeating – *Where are you, Darry? WHERE ARE YOU?*

Chapter 39
Eli

SCORPIA (THE GALLERIA MAJORA)

Eli ricocheted across a smooth marble floor, ending up with his legs up a wall and his body twisted painfully around a chunk of metal debris. He extracted himself limb by limb and rolled upright. What was left of the elevator hung charred and fractured in a broken wall behind him; just ahead, Ismail lay sprawled out on his back with the portal painting on top of him. Eli scrambled over to him and dragged the picture off. Ismail gazed around them, his eyes distant for a moment, then they sharpened and he sat up fast, clutching his chest. A look of recognition and fear shadowed the scullion's face and Eli followed his line of sight to the chamber around them where art hung askew on collapsing and broken walls. They'd landed in what was left of the Galleria Majora. It made Eli immediately think of Ev'r. A bomb impacted close by with devastating power. It shook the Galleria, bringing chunks of rock and plaster down on their heads. Another bomb fell straight after, this one more distant. Scorpia was clearly on the brink of complete disaster, but they'd done it – they had the portal, they had the enchant – now they just had to go through. Eli held the painting against his side.

"We can't go through unarmed," he told Ismail. "We'll have to go back to the hangar and restock, then cross over from there."

Ismail looked up and the desolate blankness of his expression sent Eli's nerves spiraling down into the bitter acid of his stomach.

"They're coming," Ismail said, his voice hollow. "Run. We failed the mission and this is where I die. I saw it in the vision, but you can still save Zara. You have to leave me and go."

A light flared from the picture.

"No!" Eli yelled, holding it up as it began to shake.

He flung the painting away from them just as it blazed to full light and Omarian shapes appeared in the portal, many more of them than in the tunnels of Duskmaveth or in Adliden. It looked like half an army was coming. The white light blasted out as the Omarians crashed through the portal. The explosion propelled Eli back and he smashed into a pile of rubble. Pain shot through his back and wings, but he struggled to his feet, holding a brick in his hand, ready to fight. He expected the Omarians' attention to be on him, but none of them were even facing toward him. They were all watching Ismail. He was still kneeling in the same spot. His head was hanging at a strange angle and his shoulders had started convulsing. The tremors spread to the rest of his body and grew violent, flinging him one way and then the other. Vapor poured out of his chest and mouth and formed into the body of the Mocking Witch. Ismail collapsed back onto the ground as the witch muttered a death curse, taking out the first line of Omarians. The others immediately retaliated, but found their skills of small effect against the powerful dark witch. She extinguished their fire blasts even before they threw them and they couldn't use light-form, because she didn't have body-lights – she was already dead.

Eli coughed, the air filling with the reek of smoke and dark magics as the two forces collided again and again. As one line of Omarians fell, another moved up to take its place, battling the relentless zombie witch. Behind her Ismail lay twitching, with fragments of the destroyed portal scattered all around him and the He-Ro at his side where it had slipped from Eli's grasp. Eli ducked low and dashed toward him, but a fireball exploded at his feet, knocking him back again. He groaned and rolled onto his knees. He started to crawl toward the scullion, the witch's screams shaking the Galleria as she laid waste to the Omarians. Gore and hot blood rained down on Eli's head. A severed hand splattered to the ground next to him. He recoiled, but then pounced on it and shoved it into his bag – *the blood antidote for Jude!*

Before Eli could reach Ismail, the scullion's eyes blinked open and locked onto the witch's back. A moment passed, and then Eli saw a flash of reflected light as Ismail ripped out the He-Ro embedded in his chest, then drew the Morsus Ictus and held it over his heart. Eli saw his intention in the grim lines of his face.

"No!" he yelled.

Eli scrambled but he wasn't fast enough – Ismail brought the deadly blade down with brutal force, driving it deep into the zombie heart and wrenching it back out, only to stab again and again until he slumped down – dead.

The Witch gave a terrible scream and fell to her knees. The Omarians started to close in around her, stabbing her and blasting her.

Eli reached Ismail and snatched up the He-Ro from beside him. He ripped Ismail's shirt open wider and held the device over the gushing wounds, triggering the attach code. The machine clamped down, sealing the wounds and embedding deeply into Ismail's chest, once again taking over the heart's function.

"Come on, come back, come back," Eli whispered, shaking Ismail's shoulders. The scullion lay motionless and gray-faced. He'd only been dead for a moment, but perhaps the dark magics had done something to him, or maybe the destroyed zombie heart was poisoning him.

"Ismail!" Eli yelled. He grabbed Ismail's head and bent down, breathing into his mouth, trying to resuscitate him. Something heavy struck Eli from the side, knocking him sideways and sending a burning pain shooting through his chest. He grasped at it and lifted his head, the Galleria seeming to spin around him. The Mocking Witch had dragged herself over to them and was trying to slide her disgusting, rotten body up onto Ismail while the Omarians continued attacking in a circle around her. She threw a curse at the fire-wielders, sending another line crashing. "My love," she gasped, her claw fingers fumbling up toward Ismail's face, "we enter the afterlife together. You will be forever mine."

Eli felt so furious and violated on Ismail's behalf that he wanted to projectile vomit right into her maggot-ridden face, but instead he jumped up and landed a kick into her side. She rolled off Ismail with a screech.

"He's not your love!" Eli yelled at her. "And he's not going anywhere with you!"

She rose up with a terrible scream. As she flew at Eli, he grabbed a metal rod at his feet and shoved it into her wide open mouth, shunting her back. At the same time the re-gathered Omarians hit again. They circled her, pressing in close, striking and slashing and stabbing with so much manic rage that she just couldn't regenerate fast enough. Finally she screamed her last curse and exploded like a blood bomb, taking the majority of the Omarians out with her. Eli threw himself over Ismail, trying to shield him from the fallout. When he struggled up Ismail had started to stir, his eyelids twitching.

"Ismail! It's alright," Eli said. "Open your eyes."

Ismail blinked and looked up at him.

"She's gone," Eli told him. The last few Omarians writhed on the ground around them.

Ismail stared at Eli in utter disbelief, out of military mode and now talking as the man. "I can't hear her anymore – at all. She's not in my head ... I don't understand ... In the vision I died here ..."

"You changed the future," Eli said.

"I ..." Ismail shook his head, wordless, and Eli helped him sit up. Ismail lifted the hem of his pants and saw the shackle was gone – vanished. He was free of her – and alive. While Ismail stared in shock, Eli rapidly scooped up all the fragments of the painting he could see. Part of him was thinking maybe there was some way to fix it, while the other part already knew that it was impossible.

"We have to move," he said, "while they're still regrouping."

Ismail nodded and struggled to his feet, leaning on Eli's shoulder for support. They limped away through a smashed wall and out into the main entrance of the Galleria.

Half the great stained-glass roof had come down and the walls had collapsed in, blocking the exits. The ground continued to tremble with bomb blasts. Eli felt a breeze on his face and looked up. There was a rift in one of the walls that they could climb through, but there was no way to get up there except by flying. Eli buzzed his wings and tried to drag Ismail up with him, but it was no use, the scullion was far too heavy. Eli sank back down and Ismail rasped, "Go first."

"I'm not leaving —"

"— without me. I know," Ismail cut him off. "You're one stubborn imp-breed."

"Snack-size," Eli said. "That's what Ev'r calls me."

Ismail snorted and the shadow of a smile played at the corners of his mouth – the first suggestion of happiness he'd shown. It made him look like a different person, as though a thousand hard year-cycles had lifted from his face.

"You don't make any sense to me even though I can see your thoughts," he said to Eli. "But whatever happens from here … I'm in your debt." He gritted his teeth and with a horrible cracking sound self-broke his shoulder blades, and two black bat wings ripped out from the skin. Ismail stretched them and flapped up to the rift. Eli flew after him, leaving behind the dying Omarians, the broken portal, and any hope of saving the others. *Copernicus … Diega … Silho …*

Chapter 40
Copernicus

PRATERIUS

MURKMIRE SLOUGH (ETI RIVER)

He was buried, crushed beneath a ton of earth, with chains biting into his wrists. He couldn't turn his head and each gasp only clogged his mouth and nose with more mud. Panic paralyzed him. He couldn't breathe. He couldn't move. There was no escape.

A hand punched through the dirt and grabbed him by the face, wrenching him up out of his grave. Fingers cleared his mouth and he gasped, blinking up at Christy Shawe.

"Mate, you're a sorry trutting sight," Christy laughed.

Copernicus' eyes snapped open and he gasped in a mouthful of water. It tasted rusty like blood. He spat it back out immediately, his senses telling him he was underwater and enclosed on all sides by a spongy matter. He grabbed a handful of the slimy substance and ripped. It tore easily enough and seemed to shrink around him as he fought his way out into

422

the open water. A massive blur of body-heat rushed in at him and he kicked backward to avoid the impact. The body of a huge reptilian creature brushed past him and, with a moment's thought, he seized onto it, grabbing the spikes of its back. It sliced through the water, dragging him upward.

As they neared the surface light, Copernicus felt an intense flare of heat. He immediately recognized the vibration patterns, *Shawe, Diega, K-Ruz*, and there were others as well – *Omarians*. Even before he broke the surface, Copernicus was ready for what he would see. As the crocodile lunged out of the water, Copernicus threw himself onto the gigantic reptilian's back. He ran along the length of its body and onto its head. It snapped up at him, propelling him high into the air. As he fell, he caught fragments of the scene on the bank below – the rainbow flare of Diega's skin, Shawe's savage grin, the flash of Caesar's eyes and the Omarian firebird bloodline mark. While still airborne, Copernicus grabbed for his blade, but his hand came up empty, his belt gone. He landed in the middle of the fight with no weapon, so he sank his fangs into the first Omarian within his grasp. The warrior collapsed and the others attacked, dropping their control over Caesar and Shawe – a fatal error.

Shawe struck first, landing a devastating blow to one Omarian's head. Caesar's claws dispatched another two with frightening speed. Copernicus heard the drone of light-form vision trying to lock onto him and he thought *not this time*. He knew their strengths and was ready for them. He murmured an Illusionist enchant and vanished from sight. He moved fast, rolling behind Diega and grabbing the blades from her belt. He threw them, taking out another three. He spoke a second enchant, and changed his and the others' appearance to Omarian, sending their attackers into deep confusion. They turned on each other, their defenses broken. Caesar and Shawe didn't need a written invitation, annihilating the fire-wielders until only one remained.

The lone Omarian panicked and snatched a small painting out of his jacket. He cried out the words, "Behind the red star smiles the darkness – Omar Montanya!"

Copernicus smashed him to the ground, seizing the portal as it started to open, light blasting into the darkness around them.

"Grab on!" he shouted, extending his hand to the others. Diega moved first, Caesar moved faster and Shawe lunged last – hitting him like a mass-mover at the last second before they were all dragged through the portal.

Chapter 41

Croy

KULLRA FORNAX

NŸR-CORUM (SAINT MARIREAD BOROUGH)

Croy circled over her house, scoping it out for trouble, but the gridway running alongside her neighborhood was all but empty. She gestured to Castor and they both swooped down to park at the side of the house. Croy's hands were trembling, so much emotion crashing through her that she felt ready to explode. The only thought keeping her from breaking down was finding her partner. The only way she knew, without having to go and steal an I-Sect, was for Shah-Jahan to call him through the *rete*. She didn't completely understand how it worked, but she understood enough to feel the connection between her, the twins and the Dray, like a web or a net binding them together. If Darius was half-Dray, as the files she'd found indicated, he'd be able to hear it. He wouldn't understand it, but maybe she could send him a message through the Dray captain. The truth behind Darius' uncanny ability of knowing exactly where she was at any given time suddenly became clear. She'd always thought it was partner intuition, but it was the Dray connection they shared.

She edged through the front door of her house. Shah-Jahan was still sitting in the same chair. His skin had paled even more, trickles of blood still running down his neck from the puncture wounds of the head cage. He raised his dark eyes to Croy and she froze, seeing herself reflected back and behind her – Darius. She turned to face her partner. He held the aim of his Predator 6 on Shah-Jahan, not dropping it an inch as Kisslefish and Castor, carrying Kellor, barged in on her heels. Castor saw Shah-Jahan and had an immediate reaction. He ran to him and fell down at his feet, cradling his sister and crying. Kisslefish just stared and said, "Whoa."

Darius never took his eyes off Croy's and she saw so many emotions running through him, the strongest of them betrayal. It cut deeply inside her. He didn't understand yet.

"I went to the Tower to look for you," she said. "I lost my I-Sect."

"And I came here looking for you," he replied, his voice burning ice.

"Darry – listen to me – let me tell you —"

"Tell me what?" he shouted. "I was worried about you! I came here and found this – thing!" He stabbed his gun toward Shah-Jahan. "You know what they did to my —" the words choked him "— to my parents."

His eyes went to Shah-Jahan and Croy could see Darius was going to shoot him. He'd lost his control.

"No!" She put herself in between them. "You don't understand!"

"What's not to understand?" Darius said. "Everything you say is a lie! Do I know you at all? You're all I have! I love you!" He pointed the Predator to his own head. "Him or me!"

"Darry," Croy whispered. She started shaking.

"Him or me? Choose! Now!" His finger tested the trigger.

Croy saw only one way to save both Darius and Shah-Jahan. She grabbed VP's gun out of her jacket, put it to her head and fired.

Chapter 42

Eli

AQUAIS

SCORPIA (THE GRAVEYARD)

Eli ran into the hangar, colliding with Penman. The little 0318 was beside himself, beeping frantically. He grabbed onto Eli with every tentacle he had and dragged him toward Jude and SevenM. Diamond and Flintlock were standing beside the stretcher, trying to help the Ar Antarian, but the lines of poison had crept over his face and he was convulsing with brain trauma. There was no time left. Eli ripped the severed Omarian hand out of his bag and plunged a needle into it to extract some blood.

"Too slow!" Ismail said, limping to them. "Here," he grabbed the hand off Eli and threw it to Flintlock, saying, "Crush it. Over the wound!"

Flintlock's eyes went to Eli for confirmation and he nodded, ripping away the bandages over Jude's injury.

The Corámorán squeezed the severed limb in one huge fist, completely pulverizing it. Gore poured down over the gaping stab wound. Eli was so panicked that he didn't even register the foulness of the task – he just wanted Jude to stop thrashing, to open his eyes, to be okay …

For a moment nothing changed and Eli couldn't breathe around the terror that they hadn't been quick enough, or that it wasn't enough blood to work – but then Jude slumped down, still.

The wound started fizzing and bubbling and the healing came rapidly, almost instantaneously. The blood dried up and the flesh and skin closed over. The poison lines retreated, fading to nothing. Eli grabbed an oxygen mask off the bench and held it over Jude's mouth and nose and the Ar Antarian started to blink. SevenM struggled up onto his legs as Jude opened his vivid blue eyes. Eli found himself too numb with shock to cry. He just stood and stared at him, afraid to move in case he was dreaming.

Jude sat up, his eyes going to Eli. He started to say something, but stopped abruptly. Instead he jumped off the stretcher and grabbed Eli into a crushing hug, his metal arms wrapped tightly around Eli's wings. Penman had swooped SevenM up in the air with joy.

Eli gasped out, not realizing he'd been holding his breath the whole time and then he started laughing and couldn't stop as tears rolled down his face.

"You're naked," he said to Jude. "This would be so awkward if I wasn't so happy to see you!"

Jude laughed, thumping him on the back. Eli felt someone else hugging him as well and had a strange moment of thinking it was Ismail, but then he felt Diamond's hands pickpocketing him.

Jude stepped back and wrapped a sheet around himself, while Eli turned to the others. He felt sluggish with fatigue, as though he was emerging from a dream. He spotted Luther and Moses lying on another stretcher in the shadows and ran over to them. Luther's eyes flickered open weakly as Eli crouched down beside them, patting Moses' coat and feeling the wolf breathing.

"How do you feel?" Eli asked the Midnight Man.

He gestured *okay* and even attempted a toothy smile. It made Eli remember what he'd seen in Ezra Quartermaine's laboratory – the spectral-breed experiments, the pain and death. He wasn't sure Luther had been part of it, but he felt the pieces fitted.

"Luther ..." Eli paused, searching for the words he wanted to say to this man who had been willing to throw down his life to save him – on more than one occasion. "You know how I was lecturing you about what to do to seem normal?"

Luther gave a nod.

"Forget everything I said. Just be yourself ... You don't need to change at all. I like you exactly how you are."

Luther stared at Eli with his unblinking snake eyes, then he opened his mouth and spoke with one of those deep, mellow voices that make women all breathless. "Thank you."

"You can talk!" Eli said. "I can't believe you can talk. Why haven't you been talking?"

Luther gestured, *I prefer not to ...*

"Okay," Eli said, smiling at him. "Whatever you prefer ..."

Eli felt Jude's hand on his shoulder and turned to face his friend. He already knew what Jude's first question would be and was dreading it.

"Silho?" Jude's blazing blue eyes cut straight to Eli's heart. "Diega?"

Eli rose slowly, his whole body feeling weak. His eyes lifted to Ismail, standing behind them, and the scullion gave a nod of support. "We tried everything to get a portal – *everything* ..." His hand rummaged in his pocket and drew out the fragments of canvas he'd gathered up. "Destroyed," he whispered and Jude's eyes clouded with pain.

A bomb blast trembled the hangar, clanking bottles together and overturning equipment on the benches. Jude took one of the pieces of painting and held it up. "They look like the pictures on Silho's neck and back."

The words made something click in Eli's mind. He had been thinking the same thing when he'd seen the painting in Adliden – *it looks like Silho's skin* – but at the time he'd been too distracted to focus on what that might mean. He recalled reading that only male Omarians could paint the portals ...

"Because females *are* portals," Eli finished his thoughts aloud, and all the others looked at him.

Another missile struck a nearby building and they heard the roar and felt the quake as it imploded and crashed to the ground.

"Get under cover!" Eli said. He bolted over to Nelly's enclosure and opened the door. She jumped out at him, terrified and furious and overjoyed to see him. He gave her a quick kiss, and she burrowed into his pocket as he ran to where the others were hiding beneath one of his bolted-down workbenches. He slid under it, the hangar lights flickering and dimming. Flintlock was too big to fit under the bench, so she had to half-sprawl with her legs sticking out. Eli's mind went into overdrive and he spoke rapidly.

"With the painted portals, you need the picture and you need the access enchant. Maybe it's the same with Silho, we need to find out the words to access her."

"How?" Jude demanded.

"I don't have the faintest, but —"

A piece of paper, with one line of writing, dangled in front of his face and he read the words in his mind – *In my mother's house are many mansions – Silho Brabel*. It was the paper Silho had found at Englan Chrisholm's place. Eli remembered the commander had given it to him to run tests before everything fell apart.

"I may have borrowed this from your pocket while we were in the desert," Diamond said sheepishly. "It's definitely an enchant."

"This is it!" Eli said, taking the paper. He couldn't believe it. They'd gone into every nightmare hole in the entire city searching for a portal, and the answer had been with them all along. He just hoped it wasn't too late. He looked up at Jude and saw hope in his friend's face.

A third bomb shook the entire hangar, exploding some of the lights. Diamond gripped Eli's arm.

"Should I just say the words?" he asked the group and Ismail said, "Do it! Otherwise there won't be any city left to bring them back to."

Jude nodded in agreement. "Read it out," he said.

Eli gulped and held up the paper.

Chapter 43
Diega

OMAR MONTANYA

THE SCORCHLANDS (DRAGONSDEN)

A tidal wave of brutal heat smashed over them, driving Diega to her knees, her hands shielding her face. Through her fingers she glimpsed an ocean of glowing orange and black molten lava surging all around them. Someone grasped her shoulder and wrenched her backward. Diega sprawled out, putting her hands down, the surface searing her skin. She scrambled up, only then realizing the full horror of their situation. They had landed on a sinking piece of volcanic rock in the middle of a lava river, and she had been crouching precariously close to the edge. The thought sent the blood rushing through her. She coughed, squinting through the sulfur- and ash-choked air. Beside her Copernicus still gripped her arm, his eyes streaming from the intensity of the heat, sweat pouring down his bare chest. A pillar of black steam billowed up suddenly beside their floating rock, followed immediately by a roaring lava geyser. It shot up into the air, raining sparks down on their heads. They got onto Caesar's skin and he cursed, hitting at them and unbalancing the rock. Shawe, standing at the front, managed to steady them. He was looking around, his face impassive, as though they were in any bar in Greenway and not on a boat ride through hell.

"When you three ladies have finished crying and jigging about," he said, "we'll get off this rock."

His eyes went to Diega. The sparks were burning into her as well, but she refused to show pain in front of him. He just smiled as though he knew it.

They passed under a burned-out husk of a tree and Shawe grabbed for a branch. He cracked it off and shoved it down hard into the lava. It worked as a rudder, propelling them sideways, where they smashed into the side of the river. They all saw the opportunity and made a leap for it, landing the jump, but barely. Once they were off, the rock bobbed away, staying afloat for several seconds before upending and sinking out of sight. Shawe turned to Copernicus with an outstretched hand.

"You riding a trutting crocodile out of that river. Absolutely bloody priceless, mate. Saving your trutting skin was worth it just for that sight."

Copernicus grasped his hand and Shawe slapped him on the other arm, and that was as emotional as things were going to get between them. Diega, on the other hand, felt like she'd just jumped off a cliff. Copernicus was here. He was alive. She wanted to grab hold of him, but held back. He turned to look at her, and his eyes said everything that he couldn't.

She held up his weapon belt and he lifted his arms, letting her clip it back in place. With their eyes locked, she felt as though the world had gone back to rights, at least for this one moment in time.

"What happened?" she asked him. "We didn't think the algae had worked."

"Wasn't the algae," Christy spoke up. "It was the fire-breather's blood."

He turned his back and rolled his shoulder to show where he'd been wounded, both now completely healed.

"As soon as the blood hit me, I felt them closing over."

"I saw it happen," Caesar confirmed. "And I saw blood splatter the algae."

"Lucky for you," Shawe said to Copernicus.

"There's no such thing as luck," Caesar said, regarding Copernicus with his dark-rimmed eyes. "The Great God saw you save my son. It's said a man who saves a child's life will come before God's eyes and be forever in his sight. He repaid you – life for life."

"What a load of trutt!" Shawe said. "He'd be fertilizing flowers if we hadn't carried him halfway across the universe – you and me, not God."

"The Great God worked through us," Caesar said.

"I worked for myself," Christy insisted. "Always have, always will."

"Each time I believe that I cannot possibly think less of you, you open your mouth and it happens again," the Pride King growled.

"Suck it," Christy said, grabbing his own crotch.

"Enough," Copernicus intervened. "We're on the Omarians' planet. They have Silho here somewhere."

Diega cast her eyes across the barren rock plain behind them. It stretched all the way into the distance to the surrounding volcanic mountains, all spewing a constant blazing stream of lava. Everything was black and scorched, even the orange sun. Diega realized, with a jolt, that the darkness was here as well – she could feel it – the Indemeus X, spreading like a heavy sickness creeping over the land. She looked up into the sky and gasped as her Ohini Fen powers rushed back to her. This was a new planet with daylight stars, the source of her Fen skills. Their glowing forms were concealed from her behind thick layers of smog and ash, but they were still there and they filled her with strength. She grabbed her broken blade out of her weapon belt and morphed it back together. The relief was almost overwhelming. She felt as if her hands had been untied.

The three men were surveying their surroundings.

"It's this way," Caesar said, tasting the air. "I can hear voices ..."

"They must be in your head, then, because my hearing is just as good as yours as I can't hear anything," Shawe said.

Caesar looked him up and down. "You're profoundly deluded if you think your senses are anywhere close to mine."

"Profoundly – that's a big word for you, kitty," Shawe mocked him.

"I usually try and keep things simple for you," Caesar returned.

"I said *enough*," Copernicus repeated.

"I'll say when it's enough," Caesar growled.

"No, *I* will say when it's enough!" Shawe bellowed.

Diega shook her head – men and their trutting egos. She sidestepped them and walked out across to the edge of the black rock plateau ahead of them. In the far distance, the ragged silhouette of a castle loomed high into the burned sky. Lava was bubbling up from the turrets of the castle and pouring down the sides of the monstrous structure. Diega glanced back at the men, still arguing. They could stay here. She'd go and get Silho herself.

She started climbing down a crumbling black rock slope to another open plain below them. Soon the sound of voices was replaced by bootsteps as the men appeared behind her. Caesar and Shawe were pathetic enough to be trying to outwalk each other. Copernicus' normally smooth stride was still slightly dragging. Though his body had recovered, there was no doubting he'd taken a hit. Diega spotted a skeleton laid out on the rocks not far from where they walked. The dimensions and shape of the bones she'd only ever seen in museums.

"Dragon?" she murmured.

"Diega! Fall left!" Copernicus suddenly shouted. She threw herself sideways and rolled as a blast of volcanic fire burst up from the ground right where she'd been standing. She scrambled back up, then felt the ground tremble, fall still, then tremble again.

"Footsteps," Copernicus said, reading the vibration. "Something huge, moving fast in our direction."

"Keep going to the castle," Caesar said, turning toward the sound. "I'll hold it back."

"If kitty's staying then so am I," Shawe put in. "I'm not having him making me look gutless."

They both drew their blades – two enemies, standing side by side – two of the most powerful men of Scorpia, and two complete idiots. There wasn't time for final words. She and Copernicus just took off.

It was almost impossible to run in such extreme heat, but they attempted it, and as they closed in on the castle, Copernicus said, "Primary plan for entry, I'll use an enchant to disguise us as Omarian soldiers. Back-up plan – vanishing enchant, you morphing their weapons and then brute force."

"Understood," Diega replied, feeling back in her element.

But when they reached the narrow bridge stretching to the castle gates, they found it completely unguarded. They ran the entire way up and into an entrance hall without seeing a single soul. Diega thought either the Omarians never had intruders here, or she and Copernicus were about to get ambushed. She hoped they would find some relief from the crippling heat inside the veils of shadow shrouding the castle, but if anything it was worse, as though they'd stepped inside a giant oven. The walls were too hot even to touch.

A distant bestial scream sent a spike of fear through her. She turned to Copernicus, who had his eyes closed, sending his senses out around him.

"Can you see her?" Diega asked him.

He shook his head and Diega hoped it only meant he was weakened and not the other option.

Their eyes met.

"Split up. If you find her first, take her and get out," Copernicus ordered.

"Same," she said.

He didn't agree – just turned and vanished down one corridor, while Diega took another.

Chapter 44
Diega

OMAR MONTANYA

MOUNT SIRIA (THE CASTLE SCORN)

Diega ran, keeping to the shadows. An immense thirst dragged at her, and her lungs ached, but she pushed herself on, winding through a maze of black-rock corridors and deserted rooms. Finally she reached a hallway that seemed more brightly lit. Her skin prickled with nerves. She smelled a sharp metallic scent and immediately recognized it. A doorway appeared up ahead. She slowed her steps, moving with caution until she was beside the door. With her blade in one hand, she peered around into the room and saw red on the floor, dripping from a table with leg stirrups and smeared across the bars of a cage built back into one rock wall. Equipment had been shunted away from the table and there were drag marks leading across the floor to a meaty lump. Steeling herself, Diega stepped into the room and walked over to it, nudging it with her foot. Then she recognized it as a placenta. The blood drag lines continued past it to a large metal cask that looked like a bin with a chute going into the wall.

"*Fsx*," Diega cursed under her breath. She didn't want to open the lid. She didn't want to see Silho in there. It was not so long ago that she'd wanted Brabel dead – she would have even killed her herself – but now all she wanted was to find her alive.

Diega forced herself to move to the bin and throw back the heavy lid. On a stash of crumpled papers and towels that were blocking the chute hole, the body of a woman lay pressed up against one of the walls. She had no pulse and her abdomen was cut open wide. She'd been given a rough caesarean and then been left to bleed out. By her bloodline marks she was human-breed, cat-blood. The tear tracks had dried on her face.

Diega grabbed a towel to cover the girl's head and recoiled as she uncovered a tiny baby boy, lying so still like a little doll, his skin pale gray and streaked with blood and birth matter. An unexpected grief hit her and she reached down and picked up the cold bundle. She held his little face against her cheek and rubbed his back.

"No, no, no," she whispered. "No ..."

Part of her realized it was crazy hugging a dead baby when she needed to be moving on as quickly as she could – but part of her couldn't let him go. Tears welled in her eyes and she found herself crying aloud for the first time since the United Regiment guardians informed her parents that Ariana had been one of Englan Chrisholm's victims. This universe was so sick and twisted – she was tired of it.

The baby shivered against her and she pulled away, staring down at the tiny infant lying in her arms. His eyelids flickered. He was alive.

A force struck Diega from behind, slamming her against the bin. All her strength drained from her and the baby slipped from her grasp, back onto the towels beside his dead mother. Diega clung to the side of the bin, fighting to keep upright, but the drag was too intense and she fell straight onto her back, smashing her head on the rock floor. She stared at the ceiling with dizzy sparks buzzing around her and heard footsteps approaching.

A man came to stand over her. He leaned down and she saw firebird dragon bloodline marks and orange-black eyes with long, thin pupils. A red *Tehron*, similar to Silho's, glowed from his eyes, and she remembered his face as one of the Omarians who had attacked them at Sirenseron.

She swore at him in Fenlen, *"Kitcher."*

The man squatted down and ran a hand over her body, touching everywhere, though it felt more like a medical examination than assault.

"Yes, you'll do," he murmured.

Diega fought against his light-form vision, trying to break out from his influence, but he was far too strong. The man turned sharply at movement behind them and Diega saw a group of other Omarian soldiers dragging Shawe into the room.

"Imperator Hycinion – we found this one near Dragonsden," one of the Omarians said.

Shawe spotted Diega and yelled out, "Get off her or I'll break your trutting neck!"

He tried to fight, but even Shawe's enormous strength was reduced to nothing. The Omarians started kicking him with their pointed shoes, hard enough to kill.

"No!" The Imperator stopped them. "Lock him up. Let him watch."

The soldiers hauled Shawe to the cage in the corner and threw him inside. Fire from their hands welded the doors locked. Once their light-form influence was lifted, Shawe leaped up and grabbed the bars; the metal burned his skin with a hissing sound, but he didn't let go.

The Imperator grabbed Diega up and dumped her onto the operating table. She felt the dead mother's blood seeping through her clothes. He gestured to the other soldiers and they came forward to assist. They took her weapon belt and chucked it onto the ground, then strapped her down and hooked her up to the abandoned machines, stabbing needles into her arms and injecting burning liquids. They worked silently until one of the soldiers took a sudden step back from the table.

"It's happening – we've run out of time!" he yelled. "He'll take us all!"

"Silence!" The Prince's orders are to continue working!" the Imperator commanded. His soldier kept yelling, so he threw a fireball back and incinerated him, without so much as a blink.

Diega shivered. They started to rip her clothes away and she shut her eyes, going somewhere else in her mind – *if you're not here, it doesn't hurt*. She sensed she was going to die on this table, and could only think it was what she deserved.

A roar shook the air, and the Imperator paused. He looked over his shoulder and listened. Then his eyes widened. He abruptly broke off what he was doing to Diega and said to the others, "To the roof – now!"

He ran out the door, the others following. Their draining influence lifted off Diega, but she stayed lying where she was – too drug-weakened to move and too soul-dead to care.

"Hey! Wake up!" Shawe shook the bars of the cage. "Morph me out"

"I can't," she said, the chemicals slurring her words.

"You can! I saw you have your skill back!"

"I don't want to live anymore," Diega whispered.

"What!" the gangster spat. "What the trutt do you mean, you don't want to live anymore? We just crossed half a trutting planet, and now you're giving up?"

Diega let her heavy eyelids blink closed and she murmured, "She was right there. I let her die – for a bracelet – a piece of metal ..."

"What are you talking about? Who died?" Shawe demanded.

"Ariana." She hadn't said her sister's name aloud in so long. It hurt.

"Who the trutt is Ariana?" Shawe said.

Tears trickled out of the corners of Diega's eyes. "Sister."

"Your sister? Wasn't she taken by the witches?"

"I saw them take her," Diega said, and felt a rush of relief at finally confessing the truth. "And I didn't do anything to help her."

The gangster gave a harsh laugh. "What do you think you could have done? If you'd tried to get her back alone, the witches would have killed you. If you'd run for help, they would have vanished anyway. Either way, there was nothing for it."

These were the words she'd longed to hear for so very long, but she found they did nothing to lift her now.

"I was jealous," she continued, whispering her final confession. "My parents loved her and they didn't care about me. I heard my mother saying once she wished they'd never had me." The words ripped open old scars, sending fresh pain coursing through her.

"So blame them!" Shawe said, his fury rising. "What the trutt were they doing saying things like that? It's straight unluck you were born to them – you were just a kid. You didn't deserve that!"

His words stirred a flicker of anger in her. It was true. She hadn't been unlovable. She had been just a normal little girl, trying to find acceptance, craving love – and they'd treated all her efforts like an embarrassment. Diega remembered the many nights she'd sat in her room, sent there for some minor misbehavior or another. She'd hugged herself and cried, hoping she would hear her mother's footsteps on the stairs coming to see her, to talk to her, to tell her it was alright. She never came – not once. But Ariana had, every time. She'd snuck in food, a book, a toy, a comforting smile – always – and Diega had let her die ...

"I just let her go." Diega felt immense pain in her chest and let her mind drift into darkness to escape from it.

"Okay, answer one question." She heard Shawe's voice from a distance, calling her back. "Did you know she was going to get hurt or killed?"

It was a question she'd never asked herself, but in all honesty ... "No, I never thought that."

"You didn't know. If you had, would you have helped her?"

"Yes." Diega answered without hesitation.

"Then, conversation over – problem solved. Morph these bars – we need to go!" Shawe said.

Diega didn't move. None of this mattered. Nothing would bring her sister back.

She could hear Shawe breathing heavily, waiting for her. Suddenly he said, "Listen, when I was a kid, my brother was a baby. Our mother was useless as tits on a bull, and our father didn't give two stuffs on the best of days, so I was lumped with him. How well do you think a nine-year-old kid like me is going to do watching a baby? I just wanted to hang around with my boys, not wipe his arse and trutting bottle feed and figure out why the hell he was crying all the time. The number of times he could have got killed ... Once he set the house on fire; another time he locked himself in a box; once he climbed up on a high wall and jumped; once he stole a transflyer and crashed it; once I even sold him to a scullion for half a pint and then he ended up in the river. What I'm saying is, my brother means everything to me – you saw what I was willing to do to rescue him – and still he could have died a thousand times when we were growing up. Because I was a kid, too – and I didn't think! Are you hearing me, sunshine? You were a kid! You can't blame yourself! It wasn't your fault!"

"But your brother's still alive," Diega said numbly. "You saved him."

"Okay. How about this – my father liked my brother more as well. I know how it feels to never once be good enough or do anything right – to be knocked around and put down all the time. Growing up all I ever heard was *you're stupid, you're useless, you're weak, you're a girl, you're an embarrassment, you're not my son* ... And when the United Regiment shot him up, I could have run out and dragged him to cover, but I didn't, because I honestly wanted him dead. And I don't feel a scrap of guilt."

Diega turned her head to look at him – she saw sadness deep in his eyes, but his *Tehron* shone out of him like a sky full of green stars.

"I don't care at all," he repeated. "You look forward – you don't look back. Do you understand? Diega – you never look back!" He shouted the last words and shook the bars.

A thin cry rose from the bin and Shawe's eyes widened.

"What is that?"

The sound drilled into Diega's mind.

"The baby!" she said. Instantly, she morphed the bars of the cage and Shawe burst out. He ran to her, but she gestured to the bin.

"No – get the baby first!"

She ripped out the tubing in her arms and stomach as Shawe lifted the squirming infant out of the bin. His weak cry rose to a shriek.

"No, no, kid, kid, listen – no crying, shhh, shut it – seriously ..." Shawe tried to rock the baby, patting at it awkwardly.

Diega sat up and slid off the table, hitting the ground hard. Her face and legs were numb. She dragged herself to her weapon belt as Shawe put the squealing newborn against his chest and started singing a soft Galley tune. The tiny boy quieted, closing a little hand around one of Shawe's fingers. The gangster's skin looked so scarred and worn in comparison.

Diega grabbed the narc-gone off her belt and sprayed it into her face, canceling the effects of the drugs in her system. She stood and clipped the belt around her, then Shawe handed her the baby. He had the Omarian bloodline marks of the firebird dragon.

"Something's going down," the gangster said, nodding to the door.

"Then let's go," Diega replied, using a towel to bind the baby to her chest. The feeling of wanting to give up lingered faintly, whispering in her ears, weakening her limbs, but she forced herself to move. She could feel the baby's heart beating against hers. If she gave up now, he would die with her, and that was unacceptable. That thought kept her moving – one step at a time.

Shawe went to the door and paused beside it. He peered out, checking one way and then the other, then gestured to Diega. She followed him out of the room and into a long corridor. It felt distinctly wrong to be heading into battle with a baby in her hands instead of an electrifier, but there wasn't much she could do about that. The Omarians had taken her blade, the only weapon she'd had left.

"Do you have a spare blade?" she asked Shawe as they jogged toward the end of the hall.

He reached down and snatched something out of his ankle holster, handing it back to her. She turned the rusty-looking relic over in one hand, keeping the other on the baby's back.

"What am I going to do with this?" she asked. "Give someone tetanus?"

Shawe snorted. "Shows how much you know! That blade is ancient Serpian and has more bite to it than anything you've ever held in your hand. If your boss saw it, he'd probably faint on the spot – it's that prime."

"Sure," Diega muttered.

The heat ahead of them intensified, rippling the air, and Diega's steps hesitated.

"I can't," she said, holding up her hand to shield her face, unable to even lift her eyes.

"Harden up, princess!" Shawe barked. "Follow me and keep moving!"

She gritted her teeth and pressed forward behind him, his bulk providing some cover. They ran all the way to where the corridor widened out into an open cavern. The path led them to a bridge crossing over the top of a lava river that ran through the middle of the castle. As they moved across it, lava spat up at them and Diega tried to shield the baby's head.

Just as they reached the other side, Shawe stopped suddenly. A narrow path had been cut into the black rock ahead of them. It looked barely big enough for the gangster to fit through.

"Brace. It's about to get a whole lot hotter," Shawe said.

"That's not possible," Diega replied – she already felt so close to fainting.

"Just keep moving. You don't want me carrying you again, do you?" he said.

Diega clamped her teeth together and started chanting in her mind *keep moving, keep moving, keep moving …*

Shawe pressed into the hole. His hand brushed against the rock and sizzled on contact. He cursed and pulled his arms in close, trying to keep from touching again.

"The baby. He can't take this," Diega gasped, unable to breathe in the scorching heat.

Shawe glanced back. "He's napping!" he grunted. "He's Omarian."

Diega hunched down to check the baby and saw Shawe was right. The infant was sleeping soundly, his little mouth making quick drinking movements.

"He must be hungry," she murmured.

"Let's just keep him alive for now, then worry about food once we get off this rock," Shawe said. "Heads up – there's a step here." He started to move upward, but then stopped. "Get ahead of me!" he ordered, dragging Diega and the baby past him up the stairs.

"Why? Do you want to use me as a shield?" Diega muttered.

Shawe shushed her and gestured behind them to where a shadow was stalking over the wall. Shawe gripped his blade ready.

"It's me, you gadfly." They heard Caesar's voice and then he stepped around the corner. He had a bleeding wound in his chest and burns on his neck.

Shawe snorted. "Trust you to show up when all the work is done."

Caesar gave him a cold stare and said, "Sounds like it's just beginning." He pointed up the stairs.

"Yeah and look who sensed it first – me," Shawe gloated.

"Really?" Caesar narrowed his eyes in a feline smile.

Diega caught movement behind them and whipped around. Copernicus was standing on the stairs just above them, beside a doorway cut through the rock. He gestured for them to follow and started running upward. Diega immediately headed after him, hearing Caesar say behind her,

"But don't sweat it, Shawe, you're still second."

"At least I'm not third," Shawe grunted, his boots thudding on the steps.

"I was further away," Caesar insisted.

"You have all the excuses in the world, don't you, kitty?"

Diega sighed, blocking their arguing out and concentrating on keeping her legs moving in the heat. The steps seemed to go on forever, winding them high up and through the heart of the castle, until Diega heard the shouts and blasts of fire that Shawe and the others had picked up on. The stairs flattened out into a tunnel with a circle of light at the end.

Copernicus slowed his pace and, keeping as close to the wall as possible without touching it, edged down toward the light. He stopped just inside the shade and Diega pressed in beside him. They peered out to a flat rooftop where the Omarian Prince, Lecivion, and a group of his soldiers had Silho cornered. She stood on a ledge wearing a tattered, bloodstained dress, clutching the Solace and breathing blue fire on any Omarian who tried to get close enough to lock her into light-form. She was driving them back, the heat of her flames too much for even the fire wielders to take. Above them, giant shadows circled in the burned sky. Lecivion suddenly lunged in and grabbed Silho. She tried to stab him with her blade, but he put his hand up, trapping her in light-form. He dragged her off the ledge and threw her to the ground.

Instantly, Copernicus sprang forward, out of the tunnel and into a sprint. Shawe and Caesar barged past Diega, as she tried to follow, and bolted after him. She cursed and saw Copernicus casting an Illusionist enchant, creating many copies of himself and the gangsters to distract the Omarians from focusing their attacks.

Diega started to run out, but heard the baby make a small sound and hesitated. She sensed movement behind her and sidestepped just as an Omarian soldier tried to stab her with the bone blade coming out of his wrist. She felt it brush against her side and spun around, slashing downward with the blade Shawe had given her. Immediately she realized the blade was no ordinary metal – it made her movement much faster and the blow much harder – slicing through the Omarian's bone as though it was barely air. He yelled and tried to trap her in light-form but she stabbed the blade into his chest and her entire arm broke through it with the enhanced force of the weapon. He dropped down dead and she stared in shock at the rusted blade in her blood-covered hand before a shout seized her attention. She gripped the baby and turned.

The real Copernicus had grabbed Lecivion by the shoulder, trying to drag him away from Silho, but the Omarian prince threw fire at him, forcing him back. Lecivion caught Copernicus in his light-form, draining him fast. Silho was struggling up off the ground, trying to help him, as the other Omarians rushed in at her. Multiple images of Shawe were intercepting them, while the real Shawe smashed them back one after another. Everything was happening too fast.

Caesar struck Lecivion from the side, tackling him before he could finish Copernicus. The two men rolled across the roof, grappling for a moment before Lecivion caught him. He tried to drain him, but Caesar yelled and Diega saw his body stretch bigger and change – exploding out into the form of a huge lion. The great beast released a roar and threw the Omarian prince off him, sending him flying across the rooftop. Diega saw Silho and Copernicus stagger to each other and fall into each other's arms.

The light from the red sun suddenly dipped low, casting them into an unnatural twilight and Diega felt a strange crushing sensation all over her body. The remaining Omarian soldiers immediately stopped fighting, looking around with terror twisting their faces.

"Look! They're here!" one of the soldiers screamed, pointing over the edge of the roof and down to the plains surrounding the castle. The others hesitated, then broke ranks to look.

Diega did the same, holding the baby close and moving to the ledge to peer over. On the plains below, the air was hissing and distorting like disturbed holograms, and figures were materializing – monstrous creatures, towering shadows wearing dead faces as masks. Diega heard the dragonfly Tickleback's voice in her mind. *The first signs of the apocalypse are a darkening of the light that only outsiders can see. After this – the Mors come.*

She watched as hordes of Omarian soldiers ran out from the Castle gates far below. They attacked the Mors, trapping the first line of them in light-form and draining them in seconds. The Mors didn't even put up a fight. For a moment Diega had the thought that maybe they weren't as bad as they looked, but then she sensed a buzzing in the air and the Omarian soldiers all turned on each other while the Mors watched on.

Lecivion, who was standing on the ledge on the other side of the terrace, saw his army decimate itself. He screamed in fury, shouting orders to his men still on the rooftop to go down there and attack, but Diega could see by the looks on their faces that he'd lost them. The Lion-Caesar roared, pacing the rooftop, but no one was even looking at him now that a much larger threat had arrived. The soldiers started backing away, preparing to flee, and Lecivion sent a fireball at them, incinerating all those it hit. Diega pressed back against the ledge; even from that distance the heat was unbearable. She turned her face away and caught sight of the Mors below starting to move out among the dead Omarian soldiers. It looked as though they were cutting off their faces.

"Diega!" Copernicus crashed in beside her, Silho and Shawe behind him. Diega nodded at Silho. There wasn't any time for any more of a reunion. The castle had started to shake.

"What the hell?" Shawe said, staring around them.

"This world is ending," Diega said. "We have to get out of here now!"

"You don't say! Anyone have any ideas? Because I have trutt-all at this point in time," Shawe replied.

"The *Ory-5*!" the commander said. "Diega, do you still have it?"

"I have it!" she said, feeling a jolt of excitement. She dropped her blade to the ground and grabbed at her sock, digging the coin out of the secret pocket.

She held it up and Copernicus said, "Morph it, now!"

She called the word *Xpel* and threw the coin into the air. It stretched, morphing back into the transflyer. Seeing it spread out and re-form in front of them gave her a surge of hope that they were actually going to get out of this alive. A massive shadow fell over them and they felt a wild rush of wind, so strong it pinned them to the ground, as a gigantic firebird dragon landed on the rooftop, crushing the *Ory* flat with one foot. Diega and the others stared up at the astonishing creature with shining dark green scales and a long row of spikes stretching from its neck all the way down its tail.

Lecivion stepped out from the side of the firebird's leg.

"You didn't think I'd just let you leave again," he said, his voice hard and emotionless, eyes locked onto Silho.

Diega glanced over at her. "Again?"

"He's crazy. He thinks I'm my mother," Silho said, gripping the Solace, and staring back at Lecivion with loathing.

"You're not going anywhere," he replied.

Shawe gave a derisive snort and Copernicus said darkly, "I'll assure you she is, and you can try to stop us and get left behind to die with your planet, or you can give us a portal and we'll take you with us."

The shaking of the castle had stepped up. It was now quaking so much that they were struggling to stay standing and Diega thought she felt it starting to sink.

Lecivion gave a cold bark of laughter. "You must think I'm extremely stupid. I'll give you a portal so that you can take me with you? I've been to over four thousand realms in our universe and I haven't as yet needed any help." He set his burning stare back on Silho. "Now, Oren, come here ... or else."

He spoke a word in Omarian to his dragon and it leaned down, its massive face looming over them, burning breath escaping through its teeth, each of them bigger than Diega's whole body. She held the baby tightly against her.

"What now?" Shawe grunted.

"Over," Copernicus uttered and Diega understood immediately: they were going over the ledge. Copernicus could walk up flat surfaces and walls, and he could also run down them. He tried to grasp Shawe's arm, but the gangster, who hadn't yet worked out what "over" meant, pulled away.

"*Over*," Diega said to him through gritted teeth, moving her eyes to indicate the ledge. Shawe cursed, finally getting it. He linked up with Copernicus on one side and Diega on the other. Copernicus held Silho around the waist.

"You've got five seconds to decide," Lecivion called out.

The four of them started preparing to leap up and over.

"What about K-Ruz?" Shawe muttered. They could still see the lion roaming on the other side of the rooftop.

"He's on his own," Copernicus whispered back. "We can't do anything for him in that state."

"No. I trutting hate the gadfly, but it can't be said that we ran away holding hands and left him to rot."

"Who will know?" Diega demanded.

"I will!" Shawe said.

He broke away from the group, running toward Caesar. The firebird tried to stomp him, but he swerved just in time. Diega felt her heart skip a beat.

While the beast and Lecivion were momentarily distracted, Copernicus tightened his grip on Silho and dragged Diega and the baby close. He jumped up onto the ledge and straight over. He started to run down the outer wall of the pitching castle, with Diega and Silho clutching onto his back, their legs dangling beneath them.

With Lecivion above them and the Arequium Mors below, there seemed no way for them to now escape this dying land. Diega just hoped that Copernicus had a plan. She heard a screech and looked up to see the firebird, with Lecivion riding on its back, preparing to drop down after them. Another dragon scream sounded nearby and Diega caught sight of a smaller firebird speeding their way, and, at that point, she felt it wasn't a matter of *if* they were going to get killed, it was only a matter of *who* would do it.

In the time it took her to abandon all hope, the smaller, faster dragon had reached them, but instead of snapping them up or burning them alive, it just brushed past them. Copernicus seized onto its back, dragging himself and Silho and Diega up to its spikes. Diega was lying awkwardly half across him, on her side, trying not to crush the baby. Copernicus wrapped one arm around a spike, then helped her and Silho to also find a grip. Diega clutched the long spine as hard as she could, the wind rushing past them, a hundred times the speed it had when they'd been riding the Neridori. The dragon raced around the black castle with the bigger firebird and Lecivion in pursuit. The turrets and towers had started to collapse and their dragon swerved suddenly to avoid an avalanche of rock. It brought them up and around to the side opposite where they had started from.

"Shawe!" Diega heard Copernicus yell out and blinked through watering eyes to see the gangster having what looked like a fist fight with the lion. He avoided a swipe from Caesar's claws and punched him in the face, knocking him over onto his side.

"Shawe – jump!" Copernicus yelled out again as the dragon swooped down toward the rooftop where he stood.

Shawe saw his opportunity. With his massive strength, he heaved up the knocked-out lion and threw him over his shoulder. He ran toward the edge and, as the dragon hurtled past, he took a flying leap. Copernicus tried to grab him, but missed, Shawe ricocheting off the firebird's neck and spinning in the air. Diega gasped, seeing him falling. There was a blur of golden fur as the lion suddenly regained consciousness and managed to sink its claws into the dragon's side with Shawe hanging onto his back. Caesar snarled, his mane blowing wildly in the wind as Shawe climbed him and managed to get a handhold on a spike near to Diega. He turned to give her a cocky grin, but they were all shunted savagely as Lecivion and his dragon rammed into their firebird. Diega lost her grip and almost fell. Shawe grabbed her with his legs and helped her scramble back up. He pushed her and the baby between two of the spikes and she straddled the dragon holding on with her legs as well as her arms. She could see the baby had started to cry again, but the roar of the wind drowned out his small voice. Diega heard a droning sound and suddenly felt all the strength leave her as Lecivion caught her, Copernicus, Shawe and Caesar in light-form, his skill powerful enough to drain them all at once. She could feel herself losing her grip and couldn't do anything about it.

"Watch everyone you love die!" she heard Lecivion's voice roar from where he sped beside them on his dragon.

"Stop!" Silho screamed back at him. She held up a hand, trying to use her light-form skills on him.

He just laughed and said, "I told you, Oren, you'd regret betraying me."

"And I told you. I'm – not – Oren," Silho replied and her voice roared louder than his. Diega saw her stand up on the dragon's back and completely let go of her grip, somehow staying there. She lifted both hands toward Lecivion and Diega saw, through the thin fabric of Silho's dress, the dragon on her back starting to glow green. It burned brighter as their struggle intensified. She heard Lecivion scream out, "You're not strong enough!"

"Wrong again!" Silho yelled back.

Diega felt her strength return to her as Lecivion filtered all his power into holding Silho off. She heard him gasp, saw his eyes widen in shock and then he exploded into ash, as she drained all of his lifeforce into her hands, and breathed it out as a huge blast of fire. His ashes blew away in the wind and the two dragons separated paths. As their firebird sped them over the plains, far above the Arequium Mors, Silho collapsed and Copernicus caught her with one hand, dragging her close to stop her from falling. After a moment she recovered and lifted her head. Diega saw the burns around her face rapidly healing. Their eyes met and Diega mouthed, "Nicely done." It was the first encouragement she'd ever given her and it came easily. She'd saved them all.

Diega heard Shawe grunt in pain from behind her and looked back to see the lion had sunk his claws into Shawe's leg and was trying to drag itself up on him as the firebird flew faster, over more plains and mountains. From this height and at this speed it felt as though nothing would ever be able to catch them.

All of a sudden the firebird was losing altitude, dropping from the sky even though it seemed to be still flying straight, as though the air itself was being sucked downward. They were freefalling. Diega realized the whole world was sinking just like the castle and they were being dragged downward into the realm of the Indemeus X.

She could see Copernicus thinking fast, but what could he do? Her mind turned to the baby strapped to her chest. She and the others had all had the chance to live, but he'd just been born. It wasn't fair. Bitter anger burned in her chest – there was no good force in the universe watching out for them or anyone else. They were completely alone. Maybe it was better that it was all ending now.

She heard Silho gasp and looked up, expecting to see her fear, but Silho's eyes were blazing with a white light that burned brighter and brighter until it consumed them all.

Chapter 45

Eli

AQUAIS

SCORPIA (THE GRAVEYARD)

No sooner had he whispered the words *This is not working* than it began to work. There came a sound like fabric ripping and a flare of light with a heat blast so fierce it made Eli feel like his face was melting off. Flintlock seized the bolted-down bench they were hiding under and wrenched it up, tipping it over in front of them. The group sheltered behind it as fire exploded out into midair, rushing forward and then dragging back with a ferocity that almost swept Diamond away. Jude just managed to grab her and they all huddled against each other, clinging to the bench until the pressure lessened. Eli peered over the top of their shelter to see a form appear in the light – it almost looked like … but couldn't possibly be …

"A dragon!" Jude shouted beside him, confirming his eyes weren't playing tricks on him.

"It's them!" Eli yelled, spotting the commander sitting on the creature's back.

He leaped up and went to run, but Ismail grabbed him back and slammed him to the ground. A blackness had opened all around the dragon and was trying to swallow it whole. It screeched and beat its gigantic wings, trying to escape.

"We have to do something!" Eli yelled.

"Drag it free!" Diamond cried out, pointing to a length of chain close by that Eli used to hoist engines. Flintlock grabbed hold and threw the chain with impressive accuracy, closing a loop around the dragon's tail. She heaved back with her enormous strength, but it wasn't enough to counter the force that was dragging them down. Jude grabbed the chain to help her. Ismail rubbed his hands together, creating zaps of electricity, then held them up, magnetically drawing the chain toward them. Luther flared as well, using Cos magics to move the earth, shifting the dragon inch by inch away from the void. They worked together, their combined strength finally dragging it clear. A cyclonic rush of smoke-choked air that for a moment took the shape of a man with outstretched arms and no eyes battered the dragon violently, before the white light cut off and the eyeless form was dragged backward into the earth. The void closed and the exhausted dragon slumped down into the crater in the hangar floor.

Eli and the others raced for the edge. Jude jumped down first, SevenM and Penman beside him. He caught Diega as she rolled off the dragon's back. Her legs buckled and she struggled for a moment to stand, but then found her feet, clutching something against her chest. Next Christy Shawe hit down, wrestling with a huge lion. Beside him the commander and Silho climbed to the ground. Eli literally didn't know what to do first – he ran in circles for a few moments and then launched himself at his friends, screaming with joy. The commander caught him just as Diamond rushed over with a hose to spray the dragon, trying to revive it. The creature started to drink slowly. Diamond flew down to its head, putting the hose directly into its mouth, while Flintlock jumped in to help Shawe contain the struggling lion. Shawe looked like Flintlock's paler, less masculine cousin.

Diega grabbed hold of the bundle strapped to her chest and lifted out a tiny baby. Eli stared in shock, but Diamond squealed, "It's a baby!" She dropped the hose and flew over, trying to take it.

Diega whipped the baby away, demanding, "Who are you?"

"Hi, I'm Diamond and I love babies," the imp-breed girl said rapidly, making it sound like a group therapy confession. "He's severely dehydrated, he needs immediate care."

"Trust me, she's brilliant," Eli reassured Diega, who gave a reluctant nod. Diamond helped her climb out of the crater and they took the baby over to the stretchers so Diamond could check it.

Eli turned his attention to Silho, who appeared to be the most weakened out of all of them. The commander was holding her up, with Jude on the other side of her. She was covered in dried blood and her eyes looked extremely pale. Eli noticed Ismail standing back in the shadows of one wall, staring at Silho.

"Silho!" Eli hugged her, then rushed to explain, "You're a portal. The writing on the paper from your father's house was the access enchant."

She processed this information for a moment, then looked up at Copernicus, her eyes misting over. He wrapped his arms around her and held her tightly against him. Jude took a step back.

Another massive bomb blast shook the hangar, bringing dirt down on their heads. Everyone ducked as another hit and another straight after.

"We have to change kitty back," Shawe yelled above the noise, "so he can call off his cats!"

Eli was confused for a second, then noticed that the struggling lion was casting the shadow of a man across the wall behind him. *Caesar ...*

"Once he's turned, nothing can change him back except time," the commander said.

"I know something." Diega called out from the benches. She ran over and jumped down beside the lion. With Shawe and Flintlock holding him down, she grabbed an object from Caesar's belt, which had tightened around one of the beast's legs. It was a blade.

Diega spoke beside the lion's ear, "My father gave me this. He was the wisest man I ever knew."

The great lion roared, blinked, then comprehension flooded his golden eyes and he morphed back to a naked man. Shawe threw him a towel from one of Eli's workbenches.

An ebomb struck nearby and the lights and open holoscreens of Eli's computer system wavered under the shock. Eli's internal security held, but it was fast overloading.

"Quick, speak to the city before the system crashes," Eli said to Caesar, who blinked in confusion, but then rapidly regained his senses.

Eli flew up out of the crater and hacked into the city-wide projection system. He focused the camera on Caesar, from the waist up, and a hologram opened beside him – the image that everyone in Scorpia would be seeing.

"Okay – go," Eli said.

Caesar swallowed, composing himself, then spoke, "Crook'd Town Pride, your boss is returned. Cease bombing – immediately!"

Another explosion trembled the hangar, another immediately followed, with a third on its back. They were falling like rain.

"The Androts," Copernicus said.

"He's not going to be able to control them," Shawe said.

Jude spoke up. "But I can." He walked in front of the camera beside Caesar. Cleared his throat and took over.

"City of Scorpia, I am Isaiah U, your rightful king. I am Ar Antarian – and I am machine-breed." He paused to show the numbers on his neck. "My father was Miron U, my brother was Kry 939993, and I am claiming my right to the throne. Under my rule, there will be equality in this city. Those of you who wish to live by gangster law may do so, and those who wish to live under my law may do so also. The city will be divided proportionately. Androts, all machine-breeds, you will be free to live as you wish – as citizens – as equals." He glanced at Caesar. "The Gangster King, Caesar K-Ruz, has agreed to open all the Androt prison camps and release everyone."

Caesar's eyes darkened, but he had no choice but to nod in agreement. If he refused now the Androt bombs would continue and destroy them all.

Jude finished his speech and they waited. And what they heard was silence – stillness.

Chapter 46
Diega

SCORPIA (THE GREENWAY BREAKWALL)

The star glowed, a lowlight inside the meridian sphere. Diega had formed the new constellation by hand, using white fire and the old Fen magics, and now it was ready to be freed into the sky. Named for her sister, it would be a window from the afterworld through which Ariana could look down on those she loved still on Aquais. That was the Fen belief.

Diega kneeled down beside the meridian sphere and opened a second, smaller box she'd taken from Eli's hangar. She lifted out Ariana's bracelet and dropped it into the sphere, where it hung suspended in the center of the star. Diega whispered the words and the meridian morphed away. Ariana's star shot upward through the sky and took its place in the shimmering legion above.

Diega closed her eyes and let the starslight shimmer along her bloodline marks. She'd spent many weeks going over and

463

through her conversation with Shawe and had come to a resolution in her mind. Ariana's death had not been her fault, and though the guilt still remained, she had to try to let it go. This was the start. She whispered a final goodbye to her sister.

Diega stood up and looked out over the city from the Greenway breakwall. It had seemed like an appropriate place to come for the release. Baby Alejan snuggled closer to her in his sling, a little thumb in his mouth. She stroked a hand over his silky hair. Never in her life had she imagined herself mothering anything. She'd never even wanted children, but this little boy had, in one cry, crashed down all her defenses.

Diega had thought at first that Silho would take him, since he was of her own race, but Silho had been struggling to recover both physically and mentally, barely even able to care for herself, let alone a baby who needed constant attention. Eli had begged Diega to adopt him herself, and said he would help raise him, but she'd thrown the idea aside – her lifestyle was too busy and dangerous and she felt as though she knew nothing about caring for a child. It wasn't for lack of feeling; it was because she wanted to do what would be best for him.

She'd taken him to the recently set up facility near the center of the city that was taking in all the war orphans. She'd stood in the corridor of the building, looking into a room packed full of kids eating their dinner on rows of benches. The people running it were clearly flat out. Maybe they were good people, maybe they weren't – there was no way to know. But one thing was for sure – there were way too many children and way too few carers. Diega had a vision of the baby crying in the dark of night – reaching shaky arms up for someone who would never come – and she'd left the place still holding him. Shawe had been standing outside. He'd been going with her to see Copernicus, and was waiting impatiently as always.

Feeling overwhelmed, she'd spoken the truth to him. "I don't know what to do. I don't want to leave him here."

Shawe echoed Eli's words: "So, keep him."

"You really think I'm mother material?" she said incredulously.

He looked her up and down and demanded, "Why not? Nothing wrong with you."

Coming from Shawe, it was high praise and it was exactly what she desperately wanted to hear – though hadn't admitted it to herself. Eli only ever saw the best in her, but Shawe knew the worst and still thought she could care for the child. She could have literally kissed him. Instead she looked down at the baby, allowing herself to really look into his eyes. He wasn't hers, he wasn't Fen, but she already loved him.

"Alejan," she whispered, naming him.

"Alien?" Shawe repeated, loud and rough, missing all the nuance and beauty of the name.

"Alejan!" Diega repeated. "It means *angel* in my language."

"Angel? Alien? For trutt's sake, give the boy a proper name! Call him Rob or Liam or Michael or Conan or Neal, even ..."

"His name is Alejan," Diega insisted.

"Okay, why don't you just tie a sign around his neck that says *punch me now*. He's never going to be able to get the girls with a name like Alien."

"Somehow you managed it with a name like Christy! Isn't that a girl's name?" Diega shot back.

Shawe's chest puffed out and he said, "There isn't a single name in this city tougher than Christy! In fact – call him Christy Shawe Junior! That's it, I don't care – I'm calling him Christy Junior, no matter what you call him."

He'd stomped away, and she hadn't seen him since.

Diega looked out over the city. It had been massively damaged, almost half its buildings gone, whole levels flattened and crashed down on one other. But in the last few weeks, the rebuilding had begun. An entire quarter of the city had gone to the gangsters to rule as they pleased. The other three quarters of the people had voted to have Jude as their king, and he'd already proven a skillful leader. He'd re-established a military presence, and brought all the necessary amenities back online. He'd converted the palace into a place of refuge and learning and opened Sirenseron's gardens to all, breaking down the lofty barriers that had separated his father, and all the Ar Antarian kings before him, from the people. Caesar had remained true to his word and freed the Androts and machine-breeds, and Jude had granted them all citizenship and equal standing. And even though the prejudice and anger remained, it was a step forward. It was hope when before there had been none.

Diega looked up into the dark sky and felt her heart sinking. She could see the planets Bandos and Eumaios glowing large above the city, but Praterius had completely vanished as though it never was. Dragged down by the Indemeus X, as Tickleback had said, into a nightmare in-between place of neither life nor death. Diega's mind paused on images of the dragonfly and beetle girl, on Sesame and the drones, the Vidris Slimer, and sadness weighed her down. She clutched Alejan tightly against her.

Eli had set up all kinds of monitoring devices to warn if they were being targeted by the X. As Tickleback had said, only outsiders to a planet could see the telltale darkness, but so far it appeared Aquais wasn't under threat – although they really still had no idea who they were dealing with, or how to stop him. The influence of the Mors still niggled at Diega's mind and no one spoke the truth they all felt – they were living on borrowed time.

The trackers had been given a new Headquarters and Copernicus had made some comments about maybe even expanding the team. Since returning to Scorpia, Diega's feelings for Copernicus had shifted. When she saw him and Silho together now, it still bothered her, but it didn't hurt anymore, and she could only assume it was because she was trying to change herself.

She sensed movement behind her and turned to see Christy Shawe appear from the shadows.

"Your boss asked me to check on you, said you'd turned off your com," he said, walking toward her.

"Yes – five seconds to myself is way too much to ask for," Diega snapped.

Christy snorted. "You know what he's like – has to control everything or his underpants get all in a bunch."

That made her smile. Nobody talked down to Copernicus like Shawe did.

The gangster leaned in close to Alejan's face and said, "Hello, Christy Junior. Hurry up and grow already so we can get away from your mother here and get up to no good – hit the bars, the pubs, and a few other places I'll teach you about later."

Diega turned Alejan away with a mix of annoyance and strange warmth. No one else had yet referred to her as Alejan's mother. She looked up at Shawe and saw a powerful man with fiery green eyes, who never stopped, never gave in, never gave up – and he was looking right at her. She felt a strong surge of desire.

This was going to be a problem.

Chapter 47

Eli

AQUAIS

SCORPIA (LIBERTYTOWN)

Inspiration had struck while he was sitting on the toilet at the new Tracker Headquarters. It was such a strike of clarity that he had to jump and run to his computer despite his current indisposition. Without a second's pause, he'd typed in his new theory and equations, based around the blood antidote for the fireblood poison of the Omarians. He calculated it again twice, and three times after that, with the same conclusion. This was it. This was the formula to change Ev'r back.

He'd been so beside himself with excitement that he'd run out to Ismail, standing on the balcony of the new Tracker Headquarters, and tried to tell him – but only ended up babbling something about pink and purple balloons, tripping over his pants, and faceplanting. At that exact moment Smudge K-Ruz had turned up out of the blue to see him.

Suffice it to say she hadn't returned any of his calls – but he wasn't giving up. Unfortunately, Diamond seemed to be applying the same principle to him. She hung around like a bad smell, peppered him with fly-by kisses, wrote him novel-length love letters and sprinkled glitter on his head every-where he went. It was exceptionally difficult to look manly with glitter in his hair. But perhaps the most disturbing part of it was he was starting to really enjoy her company. She was, by an immeasurable leap, the most brilliant person he had ever met, but never seemed to have a bad word to say about anyone or anything. She understood him when he spoke, not just about tech and inventing, but about life, growing up in Ufftown and being a half-breed. They connected on so many levels, yet Eli still didn't feel that spark of attraction. He'd always believed love should be like getting struck by light-ning, not slow growth like mold. But maybe he'd been wrong. Maybe this was actually the best way – to start off as friends and go from there. He didn't know, but one thing was sure – he'd well and truly sailed into the Port of Confusion as far as what he wanted from a partner was concerned.

Now he stood in the transflyer bays above Headquarters, loading in the dart-vials for a mega-drop over Golmaria. He jolted as Diamond's face popped up from behind a bench.

"You're thinking about me, aren't you?" she said.

Ismail, loading the transflyer beside Eli, started and clutched at his chest. Since Eli had removed the zombie heart and transplanted an internal robotic heart in its place, he'd grown even stronger, his biceps like boulders. Clearly he'd gotten Eli's share of muscle as well as his own.

"No!" Eli said.

"That's a yes!" Diamond squealed, bouncing up and down.

Ismail shook his head, looking confused and slightly disturbed. "Can you please bed that girl already," he muttered to Eli.

"I'm a little busy at the moment," Eli said, bright red splotches breaking across his face. He really hadn't had a whole lot of experience in the bedding of girls department – a few acutely embarrassing moments along the way, and then a long stretch of involuntary celibacy. Ismail read his thoughts, then looked as though he sincerely wished he hadn't. Nelly gave a deep sigh of disgust from inside Eli's pocket. She still hadn't completely forgiven him for leaving her with Diamond and Mr Nimbles, but they were getting there.

The doors to the top-floor craft bay slid open and the commander, Silho and Diega, with baby Alejan, stepped in. Both Silho and Copernicus were finally starting to recover their strength – they'd been hit hard, both physically and psychologically, but Eli knew they were helping each other through it. They'd even moved in together. Eli had wondered how the commander, who was a lot more rigid than most with routines and order, would cope with having to share space, but he hadn't heard them arguing yet. Inevitably it would happen – but at the moment the only loud sounds coming from their apartment were the type that sent Eli scuttling away denying that he'd heard anything, even though he'd heard everything, or at least enough to know he shouldn't be interrupting.

Silho came to him now and looked over the dart-vials. "I think you've found it this time," she said with an encouraging smile. The Solace, her mother's blade, was hanging from her belt.

"I think so too," he replied, smiling back.

Ismail said nothing. Eli knew he still didn't believe that the transformation could happen, but Eli's endless positivity had worn him down into at least participating. The more days that passed, the more time he spent as himself and less as the soldier. His military skills were becoming more a part of him as a whole, rather than a completely different persona that blocked out his emotions. Ismail had some scars that would never heal, but the scullion was making amazing progress all things considered. He still wasn't a big sharer by any stretch of the imagination, but he had started to talk a little bit more about his past.

The scullion nodded to Silho and kept loading. Eli knew Silho wanted to get closer to him, that she felt a sense of family bond with him, and had been ecstatic to see him alive, but Ismail always kept his distance. He had decided not to tell Silho that her carer Hammersmith had, in return for drugs, sold her out to the Omarians, implanting their tracking device into her back. Nothing good could come from it – only more pain for Silho. So he and Eli kept it to themselves, though Eli knew the guilt was eating at Ismail.

"All stocked?" Copernicus asked.

"Locked and loaded, boss, and ready to fly," Eli told him.

The others had all said they would come with him for support – all of them except Jude. Eli felt a pang in his chest.

"I'll just call ..." Eli hesitated. "Well, I was just going to call Jude and let him know we're going."

Copernicus' face tightened and he moved away to inspect the craft. The commander really hadn't appreciated all Jude's attempts, after everyone had been reunited, to win Silho over. He'd made a lot of accusations against the commander, and even Eli felt as though Jude had majorly crossed the line. Even so, he was torn between feeling for Jude's desperation to be with the girl he loved and the pain it had caused the commander. Silho had made it clear all the way though, she was staying with Copernicus – end of story. Her loyalty to him had never wavered. It made it easier to forgive Jude – for him anyway. Eli didn't think the commander would ever forgive him.

Silho moved over to join Copernicus and Eli dialed the palace. The call went straight through to Jude's desk, where he was sitting with SevenM and Penman behind him.

"I just wanted to let you know we're flying out to Golmaria now," Eli told him.

"Good luck, and be careful," Jude said.

"Thanks. See you when we get back."

Jude gave his warm smile, but Eli saw sadness in his eyes, longing. He ended the transmission and the picture fuzzed out. Eli pushed the heaviness off his chest and turned to the others, saying, "Okay – all aboard. Not you, Diamond – I see you there!" He pointed to her trying to sneak inside the newly completed *Ory-6*. Slowly he was becoming an expert on Diamond's covert shadow-stepping.

"Rats' tails," the imp-breed girl cursed, and Mr Nimbles hissed at him.

"Soldiers only. No civilians. Go and visit Flintlock," he told them. The Corámorán was now living with a group of other gargantuan-breeds who had been excluded from their clans for a variety of reasons, and by all reports she was doing fine, gradually learning to be her own boss. The type of mental conditioning that she'd been subjected to didn't change overnight, but she was fighting.

As for their marriage, it had taken Eli a while, but he'd finally convinced her that she didn't need to stay married to him, that she should be free to chose who she wanted to be with, instead of being forced. It was funny, though: once their relationship had been officially annulled, he'd actually missed calling her 'his wife'. It'd had a nice ring to it, but the truth was they weren't in love with each other. Mutual admiration, close friendship – but not love. And so Eli's search continued.

* * * * *

They reached Golmaria just on sunrise. Even bathed in the golden beauty of the new day, it still looked gloomy and haunted. Silho and Copernicus immediately picked up on the position of the Ravien. They were still under the ground, but now they'd shifted to the bore holes on the other side of the city. Diega, with Alejan in his baby capsule beside her, positioned the craft over the deep wells.

"Okay, dropping the darts," Eli said, tension making his arms feel rigid.

He flicked the switch, and they watched as pallet after pallet of the vials dropped down into the ground. The Ravien started crawling out. Eli held his breath, biting his lip as the monsters started convulsing, shivering, dropping ... and changing ... without changing back.

Eli heard Ismail inhale sharply.

"It's working," the commander said. "Take us down."

Diega sailed the *Ory-6* down to the desert in front of the bore holes. Everywhere along the entrance of the city naked people were sitting up, looking dazed and confused.

Ismail burst out of the craft even before it had fully touched down and Eli followed. As Ismail set off running, Eli adjusted his scanner to Ev'r's previous physical form, allowing for a margin of weight loss or gain, and scanned the masses of transformed people. His machine started beeping and Eli raced, following the navigation to the match's location. He lowered his scanner and looked ahead of him to a group of the changed. At first he couldn't see her, but then he spotted a person looking up at him through a fringe of white blonde hair – those eyes – that smile ...

"Snack-size," Ev'r mouthed.

Eli ran to her, skidding down in front of her and throwing his arms around her.

A moment later, he heard the sound of running boots and felt Ev'r's body jolt. He pulled away and saw her eyes were focused behind him, where Ismail stood watching them.

"All a dream," she murmured, disappointment crushing her low to the ground.

"No," Eli said. "Ev'r, listen. The Mocking Witch brought him back to life with her own heart – but now she's dead – he's free and you're free. It's really him."

Ev'r's eyes bore into Eli. He could see she couldn't believe what he was saying; she couldn't even fathom it. He thought she might actually start punching him.

Ismail came and crouched down beside her. "Zara, it's me," he said. And then it looked like she was going to punch him instead.

Eli maneuvered himself out from between them and stood up, backing away. He watched Ismail showing her his scars, sharing the memories that only they would have, convincing her, until she grabbed hold of him with so much ferocity it looked like they were going to rip each other apart. Their happiness beyond measure brightened every corner of this forgotten city.

No tears came to Eli's eyes – not this time. After all the fear, all the pain, all the suffering and death – this was a moment of pure joy that he would never forget for as long as he lived.

He backed further away, letting them have the space to themselves. He turned to find Silho and the commander standing some distance behind him. He walked to them, and the commander gave him a nod.

"You did it. You resuscitated the world's most dangerous woman." His voice was heavy with misgiving.

"The second most dangerous woman," Silho corrected him.

"My mistake," he said, a faint smile curving his lips.

She gave Eli a hug, then the three of them headed back toward where Diega waited in the *Ory-6*. They passed many groups of recovering people, who were starting to speak with each other.

"I think we're going to need a bigger craft," Eli said.

Copernicus took his com and dialed in to the new military base. "Santana," he said, "we have a situation. We're going to need a mass-mover. The largest one you have."

Suddenly the ground began to quake and a roar blasted the air, intensifying until it was deafening. Eli blocked his ears, looking to the commander for instruction. Copernicus had his eyes focused on one of the bore holes ahead of them. Eli saw a realization surface in his expression.

"Back!" Copernicus shouted, gesturing to him and Silho to run. Eli clutched Nelly in his pocket as the three of them took off toward cover. The quaking rocked the ground and with a crash, a massive craft, of a design Eli had never seen before, rammed up out of the bore hole and skidded along the sand, finally coming to rest a short distance from where Eli and the others stood. On a front panel of the craft, Eli spotted some words written in ancient-Urigin: *Scorpian Manticore*. Silho and Copernicus drew their weapons and aimed them at the craft as a platform began to lower from its base.

"Identify yourselves!" the commander demanded as silhouettes appeared on the gangplank.

A male voice called back, "Controllers DeCavisi and Croy ... and Shah-Jahan RaAhura."

Acknowledgments

To the people who own my heart – my husband, George and my sons, Josef and Daniel.

All my love to my wonderful family – Berto, Emma and Charlotte, Dad and especially Mum, my best friend and always the first reader of everything I write.

With deep gratitude to my incredible agent, Sophie Hamley, again and always.

My heartfelt thanks to everyone at Momentum Books, most especially Joel Naoum and Mark Harding for their ongoing support and creative brilliance, as well as my continually amazing editor Sarah JH Fletcher.

To all my wonderful friends and family for their encouragement and love, with an especially huge thanks to Dan Hanks, Claire Byrnes and Karla Johnston, and to the whole crew of incredible Momentum writers.

Infinite gratitude to all the artists who inspire my work with their writing, art and performance. Most especially Clayton Watson and Jaime Jasso.

And finally much love always to the readers who have stepped into my world and given back so much support and reassurance. This book came to be because of you.

www.ingramcontent.com/pod-product-compliance
Lightning Source LLC
Chambersburg PA
CBHW030925020726
47498CB00001B/114